DISCARDED

Southborough Library
Southborough, MA
01772

The Children of the Company

TOR BOOKS BY KAGE BAKER

The Anvil of the World
The Graveyard Game
The Life of the World to Come
The Children of the Company

Southborough Library
Southborough, MA
01772

The Children
of the Company

KAGE BAKER

A TOM DOHERTY ASSOCIATES BOOK
NEW YORK

This is a work of fiction. All the characters and events portrayed
in this novel are either fictitious or are used fictitiously.

THE CHILDREN OF THE COMPANY

Copyright © 2005 by Kage Baker

All rights reserved, including the right to reproduce this book,
or portions thereof, in any form.

Portions of this novel were first published, in earlier versions,
under the following titles in the magazines listed:

"Son Observe the Time," *Asimov's,* May 1999
"The Fourth Branch," *Amazing,* June 1999
"The Queen in the Hill," *Realms of Fantasy,* December 1999
"Black Smoker," *Asimov's,* January 2000
"The Young Master," *Asimov's,* July 2000
"The Applesauce Monster," *Asimov's,* December 2001

This book is printed on acid-free paper.

Edited by David G. Hartwell

A Tor Book
Published by Tom Doherty Associates, LLC
175 Fifth Avenue
New York, NY 10010

www.tor.com

Tor® is a registered trademark of Tom Doherty Associates, LLC.

Library of Congress Cataloging-in-Publication Data

Baker, Kage.
The children of The Company / Kage Baker.—1st ed.
    p. cm.
"A Tom Doherty Associates book."
ISBN 0-765-31455-X (acid-free paper)
EAN 978-0-765-31455-0
1. Dr. Zeus Incorporated (Imaginary organization)—Fiction. 2. Immortalism—Fiction. I. Title.

PS3552.A4313C48 2005
813'.54—dc22

2005041829

First Edition: November 2005

Printed in the United States of America

0 9 8 7 6 5 4 3 2 1

This one is dedicated to . . .
Garrett, Patrick, Megan, Skye, Anya, Adelia, Jesse, Thomas, Katie

May you, who are so much brighter and better than we were,
learn from history and find a way to save the world.

ONE
1863

MAN OF SHADOWS

The man has an air of authority. Dignity, too. Gravity, integrity, and all you'd want to see in the face of a judge. He is a consummate actor.

His name (at least, the name he has used for the last couple of millennia) is Labienus. He is a Facilitator General for Dr. Zeus Incorporated, and the Executive Section Head for the Northwestern American Continent. This means he has a great deal of power, more than a cyborg is generally granted. If his mortal masters had any inkling of how much power he actually has, they'd be terrified.

But Labienus's mortal masters are in their offices in the twenty-fourth century, safe in some urban hive. Labienus, at this moment, sits in his Company HQ office in 1863, and it is as far from the urban world as he can manage. The view from his window is trackless wilderness.

The local Native Americans have long since learned this is no place to visit for any reason whatsoever, and no prospector will ever manage to straggle this far into the mountains. Were one to do so, however, and were he to climb painfully up the side of a particular towering peak, and were he to look at a particular cliff wall when the light was striking it in a particular way . . . he'd be astounded to find himself looking into a paneled and carpeted room, where a smooth-faced man would smile out at him before pressing a button to trigger an avalanche to sweep him away like a mosquito.

And the man is smiling now, and humming a sprightly little tune to himself as he scans the file of a low-ranking drone he has just damned. As head of Black Security, it is occasionally his duty to consign his fellow immortals to the nearest they can come to eternal fires. He doesn't mind the work. He likes cutting away unnecessary things.

He orders a disk generated of the material he's just scanned, and a moment later it pops obediently out of a slot in his desk. He takes it and crosses the room to a seldom-used cabinet, where he unlocks and opens a file drawer. At the very back, beyond the slots headed BUDGET REPORTS 1700–1850 and GENETIC SURVEY FOR YUKON REGION, is a small file case he'd labeled in a moment of whimsy. It reads simply DOOMED.

Labienus pulls it out and glances through it. There are a few disks in there, and several paper files. He drops the disk inside, but as he does so the foremost of the paper files spills forward, opens.

An image stares out at him. It is not a human face, as human is counted in 1863, but it might have passed for human sixty thousand years earlier. Prognathous, big and wide, with immense broad cheekbones, nose like a boulder fallen from the cliff of the sharply receding brow, massive jaw. Hair and beard are neutral, the dun color of winter hills where no snow has fallen, and the hair begins far back and is worn long. The eyes are pale, almost colorless. For all its inhuman quality, the face is intelligent and calm.

Labienus finds his smile freezing, and averts his eyes. With a grimace of self-contempt he makes himself look again, stare down the face. It's only a picture, after all! Still, after a moment he prefers to gaze out the window at the big trees, remembering when he first saw Budu.

One day it might be known as Jericho, but at that time it had no name, no walls, no surrounding desert thick with potsherds. It hadn't much more than a few reed huts and they sat low on the low earth, no raised mound, at the edge of a lake. It was a green place. There was a lot of rain. When there was a cloudless night, the stars were not in patterns you or I would recognize. Uncounted generations yet before it would occur to anyone that marks poked in clay with a cut reed might serve to freeze a moment in time, or make a hero immortal.

Life prospered in this low place. There was so much food, of all kinds, that it was easy to have a baby every year and feed them all. What it was not easy to do was to find room for them all, crowding around the fire.

The father was a fist, the mother was a vast belly with a pair of sloe-eyed

babies at gourdlike breasts. A boy might be edged away from the fire, especially if he was one of many boys and there was no special reason to value
him. A boy might be pushed from the breast, for no reason that he could see
except that there were too many children, and if he was too small to be of use
yet he might wander off at times unnoticed.

So a boy might escape, occasionally, to the high places where there was
plenty of room. He might look down on the huts crowding the low place, and
his resentment might in time find expression. He might make songs about
the ugliness of the cookfire smoke hanging in the clean air, or the stink of
crowded bodies, or the unfairness of life. He would do very well on his own,
if he was a resourceful and self-reliant little boy, feeding himself from the
abundance all around him.

He might tell himself stories, too, as he lay in the tall grass watching the
clouds cross the sky: how the clouds and the stars were people, and he was
their child, not the child of the dirty people in their low village. His mother
was not that smoke-wrinkled fat creature in the hut; she was a glorious goddess of towering cloud, with high domed breasts yielding pure snowmelt. And
his father . . . perhaps his father was the darkness between the stars, since
that was bigger than the stars themselves. Perhaps the boy was a star himself,
accidentally fallen to Earth, and didn't belong in that muddy village at all. Perhaps one day the other stars would notice he was lost and come find him.

There might have come a day when he had been beaten by an older
brother, and run crying up to the high place, and sat there alone on the height
looking down on the village, hating them all. But the wild places loved him,
the big rocks and the cedars and the grasses loved him, and so . . . they might
have listened to him when he fervently wished that something very bad
would happen to the wicked dirty people down there. Perhaps they told him
he had the power to bring punishment down from the sky.

And perhaps something very bad had happened after all . . .

He might have watched, too astonished to be frightened, as the tattooed
strangers crept up on the far escarpment across the valley and peered down
at his village, where the tiny people went to and fro like ants. And maybe like
ants the strangers had come swarming down, screaming, and speared his
people and set fire to their huts.

Then the boy might have felt terror, watching the flames, then he might
have trembled where he crouched in the long grass like a rabbit. But there

might have risen also a sense of wonder in his heart, an awe that was nearly joy. *He* had made this happen!

Being very little, he might not have understood what occurred next. Gods might have come, tremendous beings with animal bodies and the upper torsos of giants, galloping down into the low place, swinging flint axes. And if the gods made death and death and more death, so that the strangers who had invaded his village were slaughtered in their turn, the boy assumed they too had come down from the sky at his call.

Eventually there would have been only a few ants crawling feebly here and there, and smoke rising and big birds beginning to circle, and perhaps then the boy would have been bewildered to see the centaurs break apart and become giants walking on two legs, leading great bridling stamping beasts. Perhaps he held his breath as the biggest of the giants turned his flat head slowly and stared up at the hills, and seemed to see the boy in his hiding place.

Perhaps then the giant had walked up the long slope, never taking his pale eyes from the boy, unhurried, swinging his flint axe in one bloody hand as he came. But the boy would not have been afraid; and when Budu towered over him at last, and held out his red hand, the boy would have taken it eagerly.

He would have ridden in the crook of the Enforcer's arm after that, far above the smoke and the pitiful ant-bodies and the crying survivors, and how happy he would have been! And if he was loaded into a magical hut later, that shone like the sun and the moon and rose into the air toward the stars, if it took him to join his true brothers and sisters, it would have been no more than the boy expected.

Perhaps all this was nothing more than a story the boy made up, or an imperfectly remembered dream.

But from that day afterward, he was the child of the gods, and claimed his birthright.

It was good to be the son of a god, though he was perfectly aware he was exploiting the mortal monkeys' ridiculous superstitions. It was better still to be a new life form with all mortal weakness burned away, a *cyborg*, brilliant and immortal, heir to the technology of the future! And to be a Facilitator was best of all.

The Company sent mere Preservers scurrying through the mortal world after plants, after animals, after mortals' genetic material, even after their clumsy clay pots. Preservers were like mice gleaning grain from an endless harvest, drones programmed with obsession for their own petty little disciplines.

Enforcers, the pale-eyed giants who rescued him, had no job but to patrol endlessly and descend like avenging demons upon mortals who made war on one another, so that the peaceful tribes would prevail and civilization would dawn at last. The Enforcers were too short-sighted to see that the very civilization they fought for would render them obsolete, too rigidly focused on their conception of righteousness to pay attention to any other work.

But a Facilitator manipulated mortal destinies to the Company's advantage. A Facilitator shaped the raw stuff of history! Facilitators were able to adapt, to improvise, to see all sides of a question and understand every one, and that was power. Labienus set aside the name he had been given in the Company school and took the name *Atrahasis*. It meant "Great Wise One."

Being the Great Wise One had kept him amused for a while, even as he began to suspect that the mortal masters who had reached back through the past to create him were no better than their pathetic ancestors upon whom he looked down. Impossible to resist dropping the odd technological artifact here and there, knowing how doggedly future archaeologists would label spark plugs or Phillips head screws as "ritual objects of unknown purpose." Atrahasis had even touched up a few cave paintings, daubing flying saucers amid the bison and wooly mammoths.

This was the gloriously fluid time before history began, when there were nearly infinite possibilities. Nothing yet recorded, except in the pattern of stones tossed to a cultivated field's edge, in the layers of ash and scrapers left in a cave, in the crumbling brick foundations of unnamed settlements. This was the perfect time—if one was an immortal creature, immeasurably wiser than one's flawed mortal creators—to lay one's own foundations for power among the mortal masses.

Not that he ever desired to rule them.

There was water, and mud, and there were reeds.

That was all. No cities, no arts, no industry. In short, no civilization.

The mortals hadn't cared; they'd been happy enough, living in little clutches of reed huts that were too amorphous even for villages. They'd been well nourished, too, hunting for ducks, fishing, gathering roots and wild grains.

Young Atrahasis hadn't cared, either. It was all one to him if the monkeys never came down out of the trees, let alone built themselves nations. He much preferred the social life at Old World One, in the company of his fellow junior executive immortals.

And, while it was true that there were only so many times one could attend a fancy-dress ball in the costume of a god before it just wasn't amusing anymore, there was still the sex, and the unending delicious gossip. There was the ongoing challenge of how to falsify his monthly reports to his superiors, so that his utter lack of productivity was disguised.

Best of all were the times he got out on his own in his personal aircraft, soaring above the marshy world. It was fun, swooping over the reed huts and watching the little mortals scream and point at him. And when he flew by moonlight, over the wide land and the glittering water, under the white stars: oh, then he truly felt like the son of heaven.

But the day had come when he had been called into the office of Executive Facilitator Nergal, and kept sweating in the antechamber a full two hours before being called in at last and told, with exquisite understatement, that Dr. Zeus had a special place for slackers and liars, not a very nice place really, and would young Atrahasis care to do a bit of work for a change? Such as, perhaps, organizing the mortals in his assigned region into a useful, civilized society?

He didn't have to be told twice.

Shaking with anger and fear, he had flown out above the land between the two rivers. The first mortals to encounter him did not fare well, especially after they shot arrows into his glider.

But mortals certainly came to fear him, in time, and so they obeyed him. He bid them call him Enlil.

There was water and mud, which must be separated, even as the Lord gathered the waters under heaven together unto one place and let the dry land appear. Atrahasis ordered the mud raised into arable fields, the water drained away into canals. The weary little mortals leaned on their shovels and looked around at this flat, arid-seeming place, where the old easy life would no longer be possible.

They asked the cruel young god whether they might not rest now; and in response he gave them oxen and plows, and barley to sow. Atrahasis made them farmers. By day they toiled for him in the fields; by night they filed back in long rows to the long reed houses where he stabled them, and slept guarded by his security technicals. Any who tried to escape were punished spectacularly.

But after a few generations they had come to accept this, for Atrahasis explained their cosmos to the mortals. The gods, it seemed, had grown tired of drudge work, and so they had created mortal mankind to do it for them. Mortals had no other purpose in life but this labor. Mortals who worked diligently at draining the marshes, or planting the fields, would be rewarded in this life by being granted a little dry land and a house, and perhaps a day of leisure once a week.

The afterlife, unfortunately, was a dark and horrible place of twittering ghosts, so suicide had better not be thought of. But if a mortal worked hard all his life, and begot many children who worked just as hard as he did—why, it was just possible that mortal might be granted a slightly less gloomy corner of the underworld for his own, and might even sup of the crusts and dregs from the gods' own table.

And they believed him! The darker and more unpleasant Atrahasis made their world, the more desperately the little mortals clung to what he told them, the more obedient they became. It helped, of course, that he could back up his words with all manner of stage effects to awe them.

It helped also that he could kill them with impunity; for he had discovered that as long as he could meet an annual production quota of barley for the Company's mills, and present statistics showing an overall increasing birth rate among his mortal charges, Dr. Zeus was fairly disinterested in the occasional sacrifice.

And when the rivers rose one season and drowned three-fourths of his mortals, Atrahasis waited out the catastrophe on high ground, watching with a peculiar thrill as bloated corpses were swept past his feet.

He told the survivors it had been their own fault, for not loving him enough.

His security techs wearied of playing overseers after a century or so. Atrahasis therefore had them sort through the mortal population for those who
were most servile; these he raised up, and gave them titles, and a little power
over their fellow mortals. He noted, with amusement, that they were far more
zealous in their oppressive duties than his techs had been.

Some two or three showed greater than average intelligence; these he
made bureaucrats, and set them to tallying the crops that went into the Company warehouses as offerings to the gods. When he got around to bestowing
on them the divine gift of making counting-marks with reeds on clay tablets,
he was more than a little annoyed to learn that they'd already figured it out
for themselves.

By now Atrahasis had redeemed himself in the eyes of Executive Facilitator
Nergal. No slacker he! His city was a perfect geometry of green and golden
squares, yielding abundant barley, yielding melons and pomegranates, chickpeas and dates, grapes and cucumbers, and fine flocks of sheep and goats. His
mortals bred in such numbers that it was hardly worthwhile to pursue those
who escaped. Besides, the escapees invariably settled down and started little
farms of their own, so indoctrinated they were.

His own personal ziggurat of sun-fired brick arose, like an incongruous
mountain, the house of the great god Enlil. He told the mortals that it must
stand high above the smoke and stench of the city. The overseers sang the
praises of the gods, and cracked their whips with gusto as the patient laborers
raised terrace upon terrace.

There remained only to design a palace to sit atop it, and have his tech staff
install all that was necessary to make life gracious. So Atrahasis moved out of
his field shelter at last, into his grand house with its penthouse view, advanced sanitation, and doors of imported cedarwood.

And Atrahasis saw that this was good.

Then he celebrated by throwing a party for himself, and invited all those
members of his commencement class who were still on speaking terms with
him. They came and drank his excellent barley beer, and dined on his roast
kid and hot bread, his melons and pomegranates, his chickpeas and dates.
They praised him, lounged with him on his fine furniture, looked down
with him on the Euphrates and the shining canals. By night they sang with

him under the eternal stars. And he was pleased that he had impressed them all.

But the stale gossip of Old World One seemed a bit tedious now, and none of his former classmates were quite as sparklingly witty as he remembered them. After the second day, he found himself wishing they'd leave.

Atrahasis became bored.

His city was practically running itself nowadays. Ships plied the two rivers and brought trade goods for him. Uncomplaining mortals loaded his granaries with wheat and barley, to be shipped to distant Company warehouses in Eurobase One and Terra Australis. The mortals had craftsmen now, gold workers and scribes, carpenters and potters, weavers, charioteers. Atrahasis received commendations from his superiors. A job well done! Preserver drones were sent in to work among the mortals, collecting their works of art, noting down the stories of their heroes. Atrahasis, who found Preservers the dullest people in the world, did not invite them to stay with him.

Instead, he dined alone behind a curtain in his high temple, and issued memos to his staff, who conveyed his will to the mortals far below. He ordered new gliders from the Company field catalogs, and soared alone over night fields. He kept up a desultory correspondence with some few of his old classmates.

He toyed with the idea of wiping the whole project out and starting over again, but he couldn't think of a way to make the rivers rise sufficiently. There was always fire and brimstone . . .

Though of course the Company would notice something like that.

So Atrahasis continued to go through the motions, ordering the construction of libraries, gardens, and canals. When word came of some manner of political disturbance far off to the south, he daydreamed wistfully a little while about watching armies advance, looking down from his high place on bloody slaughter. Then, regretfully, he gave orders for the building of a defensive wall.

It was a splendid wall. So wide across its top, two chariots could race abreast; so high, no slung stones could reach those chariots. And well made, too; no trash or rubble infilling its center, but only solid fired brick. The inner walls were faced with glazed tile depicting the glory of the Great God Enlil. The mortals were proud of it.

Atrahasis was pleased, himself; it had earned him a commendation from the new Executive Facilitator Shamash, who had replaced Nergal, who had been transferred to another region. Not one dark and unpleasant enough to suit Atrahasis, but that couldn't be helped.

He was gazing out upon his wall, musing on the possibility of regime change, when he first spotted the far-off cloud of dust.

When his charioteers came racing back with their reports, when his over-seers sounded the alarm, when it finally sank in on Atrahasis that an army *was* actually advancing on his sacred city—his first reaction was incredulous outrage.

"He calls himself *who*?" he demanded. Below him, in the audience pit, his high priest trembled.

"Enna-aru, o great god," he said, addressing Atrahasis's shadow on the opposite wall, that being the only part of his lord he was permitted to see. "And he calls himself a . . ." He strained to remember the unfamiliar word. "A king. And he says he has come to cast down the oppressor of the people. What are we to do, o great god?"

"Gather in the people behind the wall, and shut the gates," said Atrahasis, stalking back and forth in front of his fire. "Let the young men gather stones for their slings, and mount my high wall. Come back when you have seen to these things."

"Immediately, o great god," said his high priest, and ran like a rat down the dark tunnel through the temple.

Atrahasis went at once to his credenza.

He paused before it, struggling to get a grip on his emotions. Why send a message? He was pretty certain the Company wouldn't dispatch any En-forcers to come barreling in and slaughter the invaders for him. Their patrols had been few and far between in the recent centuries . . .

Should he ask for advice? More security techs? But that would make him seem weak.

At last he transmitted: LOCAL PETTY TYRANT HAMMERING AT MY GATES. FOOTAGE OUGHT TO MAKE EXCITING VIEWING AT THE NEXT SOLSTICE BALL. SHADES OF D. W. GRIFFITH!

"Sir?" Security Technical Vidya saluted. "Orders, sir?"

Atrahasis composed his features into a suitable mask of superior amuse-ment and turned. "Oh, we needn't mobilize your boys for a few hours yet. Let the monkeys slug it out in front of the walls! Just stand ready to defend this place, if any of them break through. If he's a super-duperpower and takes the whole ant heap, we'll evacuate by air."

"And the mortals, sir?"

Atrahasis shrugged elaborately. "The herds need to be thinned now and again. Who am I to stand in the way of progress? Just make certain our air transport is fueled up. I could do with a change of scene after all these cen-turies, couldn't you?"

He took his evening meal of roast lamb, lentils, and wine in his high garden that night, looking out across the plain. Atrahasis felt rather proud of himself that he did not quail at the sight of all those campfires, stretching away through the black night, under a heavy and thunderous sky. After all, a gleaming sky chariot waited patiently in its hangar, down on the fifth terrace, in case he should need to be airlifted out.

All the same, he did not think he'd give the order to evacuate until the fighting reached the temple complex. He could imagine it breaking around his ziggurat like a red tide. The screams, the smoke, the pitiful crying, the foolish little figures dragging themselves like ants . . . the curious *chop* a flint axe made, breaking a skull . . . it was with a pang of disappointment that he realized they were in the Bronze Age now, and he might never hear the music of a flint edge again.

He breakfasted in the garden, too, on goat cheese, figs, and fresh bread, frowning at the hundred columns of smoke that rose against the rising sun. Only cook-fires? When were they going to charge?

The sun was so high he had ordered a parasol erected over his chair by the time something finally happened. Fanning himself irritably, he peered out at his wall. There, the mortals were running to and fro at last, pointing, readying their caches of slingstones. Action!

But . . .

Nothing happened.

Atrahasis waited half an hour, his impatience mounting. What the hell was going on? The mortals were leaning down, apparently paying intense attention to some drama playing out before the city gates.

"Get on with it!" he muttered under his breath, and had a sip of wine. Then he choked, spraying wine across his linen; for the ponderous gates of his city were opening, and a cheer rose along his magnificent wall.

He was pacing like a lion in his audience chamber when the high priest entered the pit, sobbing for breath.

"O great god—" he began, looking up at Atrahasis's shadow.

"What has happened?" Atrahasis demanded, looking down on the back of his head.

"Great god, you are betrayed—may they sleep with scorpions, may vultures gouge out their living eyes—oh, the wickedness—o great god, have mercy on your poor servant who—"

"On pain of death," said Atrahasis, with wonderful calm, "instantly tell me what has happened."

"O great god, your people are seduced," said the high priest miserably. "Enna-aru the king spoke before your gate. His voice was like music, great god; his voice was like a lover persuading his beloved to lie back.

"He did not threaten force, nor did he rage. Enna-aru the king spoke words like lilies, words like honey in the comb. His words went softly into the ears of your people.

"And Enna-aru the king is fair to look upon, like a bridegroom coming to his bride, o great god; and your people are faithless."

"What exactly did Enna-aru the king say?" asked Atrahasis. He was cold with shock, but he could feel a really remarkable rage gathering itself together.

"O great god, he persuaded your people that he comes in peace, to free them from bondage," said the high priest. "He told them the gods are cruel and false. Please don't punish me.

"Enna-aru the king told them he comes as a father to care for them, not as a master to trample upon their heads. Please don't punish me.

"He told them he will cast you down and open your storehouses to the people, that each may help himself thereunto. Please don't punish me."

"He did, did he?" Atrahasis stared down at the high priest's head. The man had a bald spot, which he had never noticed before. It made a tempting target. Oh, for a good old-fashioned flint axe . . .

"Go forth," he said. "Go to Enna-aru the king, who comes in triumph through my city. Tell him great Enlil will speak with him."

Atrahasis changed his garment, put on his finest ornaments, and stationed security techs in strategic places as he waited for his visitor. He could follow the mortal's progress through the streets by the cheering, by the baying of bronze trumpets. He ground his teeth. Punishment, such punishment he was going to mete out on the fickle monkeys . . . it would make the great flood pale in comparison, and the Company be damned. Fire and brimstone? Yes, what about a rain of flaming death? *That* would give the little bastards a story to hand on to their descendants . . . those who survived to have any.

He was waiting by his altar fire when he heard the voices come echoing up the tunnel. The high priest's was querulous, panicky.

"Stop! You must remove your sandals! No man may enter the presence of Almighty Enlil shod!"

"Enlil must learn to bear with this, and more." The voice that replied sounded . . . untroubled. Amused. Atrahasis scowled. He stepped before the fire, throwing his biggest, blackest shadow on the wall.

Two men emerged from the tunnel into the pit: his high priest, and a stranger. They were followed by three more men, soldiers armed with spears. The high priest immediately prostrated himself, craning his head back to address Atrahasis's shadow.

"O great god, Enna-aru the king has—"

"He's not over there, priest," said Enna-aru the king, for it was he. He turned and stared up at Atrahasis, looking straight at him.

Atrahasis blinked. He had never seen such a mortal.

Enna-aru had a face like his own—shrewd, cold, strong, handsome. He was well muscled, unlike the little doughballs over whom Atrahasis ruled. He wore fine garments, not the armor of war, but there was something martial in his bearing.

The high priest turned involuntarily, glimpsed Atrahasis and then threw himself down, wailing in terror. Enna-aru considered the wall of the pit. He backed up a few paces, took a running leap, and vaulted to the edge, where he caught hold and pulled himself up. Not even breathing hard, he rose to his feet and looked Atrahasis in the eye. The two men were the same height.

"You see?" said Enna-aru, and his voice, his voice was . . . powerful, somehow. "This is a false god. He is only a man, like me."

Permission to fire, sir? transmitted Security Technical Vidya. Atrahasis blinked again, the dreamlike moment shattered, and his brain engaged once more.

No! I will handle this. Stand by.

"I have chosen to *appear* as a man like you," he told Enna-aru, with his most intimidating smile. "Rash mortal, why have you looked upon me? Do you not know that you will surely die?"

"No, actually, I don't know that," said Enna-aru, with a beautiful sneer. "Though it's probable you have assassins concealed in here, waiting to get a shot off at me. You hidden ones, consider my archers in the pit below! If I am murdered, the great god Enlil will be stuck full of arrows. Therefore do not do this thing; for I have come to speak with the great god."

Atrahasis took a deep breath. Had his heart just skipped a beat?

"It pleases me to speak with you, mortal king," he said. "And so I will not annihilate you until after we have spoken. Come, we will drink wine in my garden."

He had his finest vintage brought, in his wine service of gold chased with silver. The mortal man regarded them critically; looked at the couch carved of cedarwood, with its purple cushions trimmed in scarlet. And Enna-aru the king said:

"This is all as I expected it would be. You sit up here gorging yourself on the best of everything, don't you? And down there in your city, they gnaw the crusts you throw them."

"They only eat at all because I created the fields, and taught them how to grow barley," said Atrahasis. He realized he sounded defensive, and made an effort to calm himself.

"Oh, please," said Enna-aru the king. "I know better. Shall I tell you how I know?"

"If you like," Atrahasis replied. Enna-aru leaned forward, took one of his cups, and poured wine.

"My land is eight days' journey north of this place. It sits fair on the river, wide black fields, well watered; beyond are highlands good for grazing sheep. Long ago an escaped slave came there, with his wife and child.

"This slave had formerly lived in a city ruled over by a cruel and capricious god. The people there obeyed their lord in all things—they were afraid to do otherwise—but when a flood came and drowned them in their hundreds, that god stood by and smiled, and would not lift a finger to help them.

"The slave was one of those who survived the flood. He saw the god walking through the desolation, smiling at the bloated corpses of the dead, and saw that the god had mud on his sandals and on his robe where it trailed on the earth. He knew, then, that the god was only a man, only an evil man.

"Therefore he took his wife and child, and they fled by night. When they came to the good land, they settled, and the man made himself lord and master of wide acres. He had many children. In time, other slaves escaped and came to work for him. He was a good master to them. He fed them, he gave them land, but he never bid them worship him.

"And he passed down through his sons, and his sons' sons, and all their children through the generations, the wisdom he had learned, which was: those who demand worship are frauds."

And Enna-aru the king raised his eyes that were so like Atrahasis's own, and winked. Atrahasis opened his mouth to speak, but no words came out. Composedly the king went on:

"That slave was my ancestor, O great god Enlil. The god he fled from was, I strongly suspect, your ancestor. And all my life, and all the lives of my forefathers, have been spent in preparation for this day, when I would walk into your city and tell your people the truth about you. Now it is done. Let us drink to the future."

He lifted his cup and drank.

Atrahasis sat staring at him, wondering why his rage had died utterly into white ash. He felt like laughing.

"You're wrong about one thing, you know," he said. "That wasn't my ancestor walking in the mud. That was me. I really am an immortal."

Southborough Library
Southborough, MA
01772

Enna-aru the king yawned. He reached across to Atrahasis and pulled a golden coin from his ear, and held it up.

"I can do magic, too, you see? One of my court magicians showed me that trick. I suspect you have many more."

The laughter came—Atrahasis couldn't stop it, didn't want to. He looked at Enna-aru and raised his own cup in salute.

"Great king, you are a man after my own heart. Dear, dear, what shall I do now that I am deposed?"

"Live off your own sweat for a change," said Enna-aru the king.

"And if I oppose you?"

"I have an army in your city," the king pointed out. "Your people loathe you so much they were dancing as we came in. I don't think you want me to ask them what I ought to do with you. Your priests have seen you insulted; they depend on you for their livelihoods, so they might stand by you, but they know the truth about you now. You don't stand much of a chance, I'm afraid."

Atrahasis was delighted. "What's a poor little false god to do, then?"

"Become a man," said Enna-aru. "You know how to run this city, you understand its infrastructure. Rule it as my viceroy! It needn't be an embarrassment for you, either; almost no one alive has ever seen you, so they won't know you're their former god. I can tell them you're my brother. But if you abuse your power again, I will have you killed."

"Oooh." Atrahasis pretended to shiver. "How kind of you to spare my dignity. And what do you want in return?"

"The good of the people," said Enna-aru gravely. "You must love them. Treat them as your children, not as beasts of burden."

"Children, eh?" Atrahasis said. "But children are a dangerous proposition for a god, you know. Shall I tell you how the world was made?

"Tiamat the Mother and Apsu the Father begot between them elder gods, who proceeded to spawn generations of godlets. And what did these little monsters do, but rebel against their ancient parents? And, when the old couple determined to destroy their vicious brood, what did the ungrateful children do but fight back?

"The Father was killed; the Mother was killed, and a bright young thing named Marduk split her body into a dozen pieces and used it to create the rotting, stinking world in which we walk. There is no love in Heaven, my mortal friend. Why then should it be any different on Earth? And therefore why should I hold my subjects as sons?"

"Because those stories are lies," said Enna-aru the king.

"Are they? Are there then no gods?"

"Possibly," said Enna-aru. "Possibly there *are* shining beings of infinite power and wisdom. But you are only a petty tyrant, and will soon be a dead one if you do not agree to my demands."

"Which makes you no less a petty tyrant, doesn't it?" said Atrahasis.

"Perhaps," said Enna-aru the king. "But I never claimed to be otherwise. And my people love me, o false god, because I am a good father to them. Soon, your people will love me, too. I am their servant, you see, rather than the other way around; it is my business to see that they have what they need to live. When they are threatened, it is my duty to protect them. And so must you."

"I hear and obey, great king," said Atrahasis, and made a mock bow. "How much of this pious claptrap do you actually believe, by the way?"

"None," said Enna-aru the king. "But I intend to make it true."

The army was quartered in Atrahasis's city, and they did not plunder, and hardly raped at all. Enna-aru the king quartered himself in Atrahasis's own temple, with his men-at-arms standing guard. Atrahasis gave him the guest bedroom and showed him where the clean towels were. Security Technical Vidya and his team stood down, and stood down, and wondered thereat.

Sir, how are we going to resolve the situation?

Leave that to me! Atrahasis waved away the transmission as though it were a gnat whining in his ear. He sipped his kefir and watched, fondly, as Enna-aru the king methodically peeled figs. The mortal even ate with elegance. What an uncanny resemblance to himself! *I'm merely toying with him. He amuses me. When I grow bored with him, he'll die.*

If you say so, sir.

And it occurred to Atrahasis to wonder what his double looked like with a bloody spear in his hands; and he was disconcerted to note how much the image excited him. He cleared his throat.

"It occurs to me," Atrahasis told the king, "that it would be best for my people if this power shift takes place quickly. You said something last night about presenting me as your brother. I think the people would believe that; there is a certain resemblance between us, have you noticed?"

"I had, yes," said Enna-aru. "Useful, isn't it?"

"Of course, I'll probably have to have my priests executed," said Atrahasis lightly. Enna-aru the king set down his cup, and gave him a long hard stare.

"Probably necessary," he conceded at last. "They have grown fat off the fear of the people. And they are the most likely to plot against us. But you will kill them swiftly; no torture. They have only done your will, after all."

"Then it is done," said Atrahasis, and transmitted an order to Security Technical Vidya. "And so we are brothers! Let us send forth messengers to proclaim it in the streets; and then, later, let us appear and make a show of brotherhood. Shall we go hunting together? I have a private preserve outside the city. The wild bull and the gazelle roam there untroubled; and I have two swift chariots and the finest charioteers."

"I wouldn't have thought you were a hunting man," said Enna-aru the king. "Though you seem to enjoy killing."

"I kill only to cull my herds," said Atrahasis swiftly. "You will see how green the park is, how fine and strong the beasts are. I have preserved them from indiscriminate slaughter by common men. Is this not also the work of a lord?"

So when Security Technical Vidya and his subordinates had washed the blood from their hands, they hitched swift horses to a pair of chariots, and sent them out with drivers to await the pleasure of the king.

And first went soldiers bearing the heads of the executed priests, that the people might see them and rejoice, which they did. And next went messengers crying aloud the news that Enna-aru the king had appointed his brother to be lord over them, and the people rejoiced about that, too. Finally Enna-aru the king and his new brother were driven forth in their chariots, in lordly progress through the streets. Atrahasis marveled at the grace and strength of the king, poised swaying in the jolting chariot. And Atrahasis caused Security Technicals to toss trinkets of gold, and the ornaments of the priests, to the cheering multitudes.

———

The Preserve of Enlil lay two miles from the city, fenced with high palings and wire specially hooked up to deliver a blast of Enlil's wrath to would-be poachers. Was there a faint whiff of charred flesh on the air, as the chariots bore Atrahasis with Enna-aru the king to that place? But no corpses in view, at least.

Security Technical Rulon opened the gate, bowing low, and admitted them. They rode in and Atrahasis watched for the king's reaction.

"Is this not fair, o king?" he demanded. "Look! A green paradise. You will see no scars here from plow or mattock, no ditches to stink, no trees hacked for firewood. No mortal intrusion at all. And see the wild cattle, there at the watering place? The water they drink is pure, untainted by anything men might do. They have never been hunted. Have I not done well, to set this place apart?"

"It is a beautiful park," agreed Enna-aru.

"I have not been such a bad lord, you know," said Atrahasis. "I have kept my distance from my subjects, but you will never hear that I was unfair. I never favored any man over another, even when they tried to buy my favor with offerings of gold. I never debauched their wives or daughters, either—" He saw Security Technical Rulon turn a shocked face to him, and caught the fleeting transmission: *What are you trying to prove to this monkey?*

Atrahasis flushed with humiliation that became rage. *What the hell do you know about strategy, you oaf? Mind your own business!*

He drew a spear from its case and struck his charioteer on the shoulder. "Drive! Let us hunt the wild bulls!"

So they rode forth into his acreage. Atrahasis seized the reins from his charioteer and drove with reckless speed, splashing through the streams, scattering the herds where they drank. He wheeled among the frightened and disoriented cattle, singling out the biggest bull at last. Enna-aru the king followed warily. The bull galloped off some distance, and they pursued; but when he turned at bay, pawing the ground, then Atrahasis vaulted out on the chariot-tongue. There he clung a moment, before leaping to balance upright on the back of the left-hand horse in his team. From that high vantage he sent his black spear down, with such force it pierced straight through the bull's broad neck and into its immense heart.

It dropped without a moan. Atrahasis sprang down beside it, wrenching out his spear. The blood ran and smoked on the earth. It pleased him nearly as much as though it were mortal blood. *Why haven't I done this before?* He looked up, eager to see if Enna-aru had been watching. The king, indeed, watched with narrowed eyes.

"You have excellent skill in the hunt," was all he said.

"Butcher my bull, and build a fire," said Atrahasis to his charioteer, with some asperity. "My brother king and I would feast."

They killed twice more that day. Atrahasis took down another bull, this time leaping from the chariot onto the bull's very back, felling it with a stroke that drove through and penetrated its lungs. Enna-aru the king cornered his own bull, circling and turning in the chariot, until the baffled animal charged and got a spear through the eye into its brain. Atrahasis thought that he might have been watching himself in a mirror, so shapely was Enna-aru, so powerful.

"Is this not fine sport, my brother?" he asked as they washed in the stream.

"You have succeeded in impressing me," said the king. "Very male, all this, isn't it? I daresay not one of the laborers who till your fields would be brave enough to leap on a bull's back. Nor light-footed enough, after a lifetime of following the plow. Still, I have seen acrobats do as much."

Atrahasis was silent a moment.

"How wise you are, mortal man," he said at last.

He watched the king as they rode slowly back through the city, followed by surly Security Technicals bearing massive sides of beef. At one point Enna-aru bid the chariots halt in the street, and got down and called for an axe; with it he cut the beef into pieces, and handed them out to the crowd. They blessed him and cried that he was their lord, they called on him to live a thousand years, they prostrated themselves and kissed his feet.

And though Enna-aru smiled broadly, and was genial as a favorite uncle before them all, Atrahasis noted that his eyes remained a little distant.

"Such generosity, o king!" he said slyly, when they had ridden on. "Truly my people love you."

"That was showmanship," said Enna-aru. "And they don't love me; they don't know me. But they love a handout now and then, and the promise that things will be a little better. If you had understood that fairly basic fact, I might not have marched into your city uncontested."

"Ah! So my fault was simply ruling by the *wrong kind* of showmanship?" said Atrahasis.

"No," said Enna-aru the king. "Your fault was that you never gave a thought to what your people wanted."

They dined once again on the terrace. A cool wind brought the smell of the river, the sound of frogs, the murmuring of rushes in the twilight. A round moon rose slowly out of the purple east, looking as though it had been painted on the horizon.

"See how she lifts free of the earth?" said Atrahasis. "Red with smoke and dust at first, and then yellow; but the higher she ascends, the purer her light becomes, and she outshines even the stars. You and I have lifted free of the mud ourselves, o king. You shine upon those peasants down there; but who are your own people?

"The idiots in the street sang their love for you; but their love meant nothing to you. I saw that. Your eyes are clear, you have no fond illusions, you know the world for the shameful place it is, you know the *truth*. You are a unique mortal.

"What is it you desire, o king?"

Enna-aru looked at him curiously.

"A better world," he said. "Full of better men."

Atrahasis looked up at the first stars.

"I am going to give you a gift," he said.

Atrahasis carried the frame out himself, set it up in the garden as Enna-aru watched, uncomprehending. He tested the fabric, the pads, the taut straps; and when all was ready he lifted it onto his shoulders and stepped out to the edge of the terrace.

"Now," he said, "o king, you will see how close a man may come to being a god."

He leaned into the night and swept down, down, until he caught the thermal rising over the massed cook-fires of the city. Up he floated then, turning as he soared, circling, and the white moonlight glittered on the distant river and on the irrigation channels, but shone full and steady on his high terrace and the tiny figure of Enna-aru. The king stood motionless, face turned up to him; he did not cower or tremble, as a mortal might have done. In his steady regard Atrahasis flew high, and higher, up where the stars hung like lamps in the blue night; and Atrahasis had never been so happy in his life.

At last he drifted down, mothlike, and landed with a light foot beside Enna-aru.

"Magicians and acrobats you have seen, o king; but never the like of this," he said triumphantly.

"Never," admitted Enna-aru the king. He stepped close and examined the glider, peering intently at its tight-stitched fabric.

"It will bear two," said Atrahasis, edging over within the frame. "Will you dare to fly, mortal man?"

Without replying, Enna-aru stepped in under the frame. He worked out the harness buckles for himself, and drew them tight; took firm hold of the frame, and stepped toward the edge.

He never cried out once, not during the initial plunge, not in the moment when they lifted on the thermal like a blown leaf. Atrahasis looked into his face and saw that it was shining.

When he returned to his chamber that night, there was a figure standing just within, obscured by shadows.

"You had better check your credenza," said Security Technical Vidya.

"What are you talking about?" said Atrahasis, but he crossed to the cabinet and switched it on.

"They want to know what the hell is going on," said Vidya. Atrahasis saw the long green line of transmission and recoiled, but all he said was: "Forty messages. Well, that's certainly some kind of record. Wouldn't you think they'd have learned to trust me by now?"

"I don't think it's a matter of trust," said Vidya. "I think it's a matter of Executive Facilitator Shamash having a bright young protégé in need of a posting. I think it's a matter of looking for any excuse to boot you out on your ass. Sir."

"Really," said Atrahasis.

"Yes. Really. Sir."

"I am obliged to you for the warning, Security Technical," said Atrahasis, kicking off his sandals. "You may go."

Vidya did not move. "I have been given certain orders, sir. You have twenty-four hours to bring the situation under control, and then I am to act. Permission to speak freely, sir?"

"Granted."

"Do I have to point out the obvious? This mission is in jeopardy. A Company operation yielding millions in annual profits may be lost. The city you built is occupied by a hostile force. We will *fail* here, sir."

"I think you're wrong," said Atrahasis. "Consider the progress of recorded history. Perhaps it's my time to step down. The age of priests comes to an end, doesn't it? And civilization takes the next step upward, to an age of kings. Isn't that what the Company wanted? Wasn't that the point of all this? Somebody has to write *Gilgamesh*, after all."

He lit the lamp. In the blaze of gold that filled the room, he saw the contempt—and, infinitely more galling, the pity—in Vidya's face.

"What is wrong with you?" said Vidya, without raising his voice. "You, of all people, are infatuated with a mortal. You are attempting to win his approval. A stinking little monkey has defied you in front of the other mortals, and you fawn on him and call him brother. What's next? Will you drink from one cup together? Will you offer to comb the lice from his hair?"

He mixed the cup himself, in the gray hour before the sun rose. He carried it out to the garden and sat, watching the stars fade. White mist moved a while above the river, was thick over the river fields. The first laborers emerged from their huts and drove the teams of oxen down, into that mist, vanishing from sight as they would vanish in the abyss of time. Living ghosts. Their grandfathers were forgotten; their grandchildren would not remember them. Only this moment existed for them and it was all sweat, all stink, all grinding poverty.

And so it has always been. And so it will always be.

Enna-aru the king emerged from the temple, gilded by the rising sun. Atrahasis looked at him and smiled. He lifted the cup.

"Drink with me, brother. To a better world, and better men."

"I will," said Enna-aru, and took the cup and drank. He passed it back to Atrahasis, who paused a moment and then drank down what was left.

He set down the cup and felt the biomechanicals swarming from under his tongue, massing in his bloodstream to neutralize what had been in the cup. He flushed, felt the prickle of sweat under his armpits, felt the twinge in his lymph nodes; only psychosomatic reaction. After a moment he breathed more easily. The heat and nausea faded steadily.

Enna-aru the king sat tranquil, cutting open a pomegranate with his curved dagger. The red drops fell like blood. He set aside half and broke the other open, revealing the rubies set in yellow membrane.

"Pomegranate seeds?" he said, offering it to Atrahasis.

"No, thank you," Atrahasis replied.

By noon the king was feverish. Atrahasis watched the flush grow in his cheeks, watched his eyes take on a certain glassiness as he studied the maps of the city canals and the grain warehouses.

By twilight the king was sweating and faint, and the blotches had begun to come up under his skin. Atrahasis led him to the couch of purple cushions, with soothing and solicitous words, and had sherbet fetched for him.

By midnight the king was raving, with brief periods of clarity wherein he struggled for understanding. Atrahasis sat beside him, wiping the sweat from his brow. The king's guard crowded in the corridor, watched from the doorway.

"If he dies, we will kill you," said their chief, in an almost conversational tone. The king jerked and shuddered at the sound; Atrahasis rose in fury, but by the time he had turned and approached the mortal, there was nothing in his face but meek sorrow.

"Speak softly, if you love him," he whispered. "He has the fever, but why should he die? Enna-aru is not like other men."

The mortal looked past him uncertainly, into the golden circle of lamplight where the king lay marked with black sores. "You have poisoned him," he said, but without conviction.

"Fool. Those are the marks of fever, and you know it," said Atrahasis. "What man commands disease? The gods alone send it, to punish whom they will. But the gods have no power over Enna-aru the king, surely. He will live."

"He is not like other men," admitted the chief. "Yes, surely he will live."

He left quietly. Atrahasis returned to the bedside of the king, and sat. Enna-aru opened his eyes, the glaring eyes of a hawk, lucid and suspicious.

"This is not punishment," he said thickly. "Nothing but fever."

"Merely a touch of fever," Atrahasis agreed, and put a wet sponge to his cracked lips. "Undoubtedly the result of traveling. The fever will break. What shall we do when you're well again? Shall we take our wings and ride the night wind, my brother? How cool it will be, up among the white stars."

Before dawn the king was lucid for an hour, though he had gone blind; but he summoned his generals and his bodyguards, and turned his face to their voices as though he could see them. He gave orders that there was to be no rioting, no slaughter. There was still command, even in the hoarse ruin his voice had become; they backed out of his presence and went down to maintain good order in the streets.

Just as the sun rose, Enna-aru stopped breathing. Atrahasis sat patiently waiting for him to resume, but he never did.

He was still sitting, staring at the king, when Security Technical Vidya came in an hour later. Vidya looked at Enna-aru, and smiled.

"Good work, sir. That'll impress them. Shall we display the body, sir?"

Atrahasis said nothing for a long moment.

"I wonder if this is what I would look like," he said at last.

Vidya cleared his throat.

"What are your orders, sir?"

Atrahasis did not look up. "Tell the people to pray for the king. Tell his generals to obey him."

"So . . . you don't want this announced right away," said Vidya.

"No. And send for his chief bodyguard."

The mortal came swiftly, and bid his lieutenants wait in the corridor. He stopped, aghast, at the sight of Enna-aru the king.

"You see how it is," said Atrahasis quietly. "Had he any heirs?"

"No," said the mortal. "He was only a young man! How could he die?"

Atrahasis said nothing. The mortal lifted his eyes to the window, looked out, at the city with its shops and warehouses, at the green and yellow fields stretching to the river. He looked sidelong at Atrahasis.

"You are thinking this is a rich place," said Atrahasis. "You are wondering who will rule here now. And it has just occurred to you that *you* might be king."

The mortal blinked, opened his mouth to deny it—then went pale.

"How did you hear my thoughts?"

Atrahasis smiled. He rose, standing his tallest, and put every cheap trick of theater he knew into his reply.

"Did you think we gods were really so easily defeated, mortal man?"

The mortal backed away a pace, staring. Then he threw himself to the ground, in terrified self-abasement.

"Great Enlil, forgive us! Do not punish us! We were misled!"

"How loyal you are to your king," said Atrahasis bitterly. "How faithful to his ideals. I could crush your skull now with my foot; I could grind your brain into the tiles. Never have I so ardently desired to do a thing, mortal. But I will tell you how you will preserve your little life."

"Spare me!"

"Shut up. You will go forth to the people, and say the king has been wounded by treachery. Not mine; kill one of your underlings, and hold his head up before the multitudes, and tell them thus have you done to the traitor, in the name of Enna-aru the king.

"Then, mortal, you shall be king in this place. And you shall declare that Enna-aru has been taken up among the stars to heal his wound, and dwells now with the gods. You will rule and grow as rich as one man may be, but you will see to it that we gods receive our portion in all things.

"Vidya will be your high priest, and he will instruct you in the desires of the gods, and will serve you; but only so long as you obey the will of the gods. Disobey, and our vengeance will be cruel and subtle. You will lament in ashes a thousand years on the floor of the house of the dead."

"I hear you," said the mortal, weeping. "I obey you." He crawled forward in an attempt to kiss Atrahasis's feet, and Atrahasis stepped back in horror.

"Never touch me, mortal," he said. "Go now."

The mortal rose and fled into the corridor. A moment later Atrahasis heard a strangled cry as his will was done, and an innocent was stabbed and beheaded.

———

Evening came, and Atrahasis heard the massed prayer rising from the city be-low, with the fumes of burnt offerings. He lit incense in his own quarters. Now and then he went to look at Enna-aru the king.

The moon rose, and he dined alone on his terrace, though he ordered and set aside a portion for Enna-aru. He heard the clash of arms and the ex-change of passwords as the army kept civil order through the night. He car-ried the untouched plate in and set it by Enna-aru's bed.

Dawn came grayly, and once more the mortals led oxen down through the mists to the fields. Atrahasis, watching, wondered why they were not at home praying for the king. He went in and lit more incense. He ordered a morning meal for two, and set half aside.

Another evening, and another, and the city remained calm and well ordered. Goods were bought and sold. Enna-aru's soldiers settled into their quarters and made friends, romanced girls, found favorite beer shops. On the floor by Enna-aru's bed, full plates were laid out in a line, in progressive degrees of spoilage.

The prayers for the king fell off a very little, in their volume and intensity.

On the evening of the sixth day, Atrahasis looked down at the tranquil city, and hated it.

He called to him Vidya, and said: "Do you suppose we could get away with bombing the damned place to the ground?"

Vidya, after a pause, said: "You've lost it, haven't you?"

"Go fuck yourself," said Atrahasis.

He went into the chamber where Enna-aru lay, blue as lapis lazuli, and quoted:

"For whom have I labored, boatman?
For whom have I lost the blood of my heart?
I have not gained any advantage to myself;
Only the serpent has gained the advantage."

No golden voice to answer now. There was silence.

But not stillness; something moved on Enna-aru's face.

Atrahasis leaned close, and saw the maggot fall from the king's arched nostril.

He stiffened, overwhelmed with revulsion. Then he turned on his heel and left the room.

"Have that carcass dragged out and burned," he told Vidya in a light and carefree voice. "And send a transmission to Old World One; mission accomplished. Peaceful (apparent) transfer of power, civilization continues without a hitch, no loss to the stockholders. I'm on my way to Egypt for a well-deserved holiday. They can forward my next posting there."

"Yes, sir," said Vidya. "I'll have your air transport powered up, sir."

"No; I've had enough of flying," said Atrahasis.

He wrapped himself in a cloak, and went down through the tunnels and out of the city by secret ways, and glided away through the night like a serpent.

But he had gone back to his duties at last. What else was there for an immortal to do, besides plot for power and sound out prospective allies?

He had first come down the Nile on a reed boat, in a time before there were any pyramids at Giza. Nothing then more remarkable in that landscape than a great outcropping of rock that resembled a lion's head, which likeness successive generations of mortals had increased by chiseling out eyes and a muzzle. Graffiti was scrawled across its lower surfaces now. Not yet the Sphinx, it stared gloomily across the land that wasn't yet Egypt. Atrahasis—not yet Labienus—sympathized with it.

He had liked the delta country once. The river was wide and clear, the air was purity itself. Dawn wind came across the green murmuring reeds and when the young sun rose above them it really might have been a god, such was its brilliance and clean heat. No smoke in the sky; light sharp as a diamond.

Then the mortals had come. For a while the crocodiles and floods had kept their numbers down, but they had multiplied at last, and spoiled it all. At this point in time it was only the smoke of their cook-fires that muddied the face of the sun, and this was bad enough. In the time to come the very dust of their mummified dead would rise like a pall, the gases of their sewage, the chemical fumes of their cities. All this fresh young world lost to ancient bricks, blackened corpses.

Atrahasis put it firmly out of his mind, as the river bore him to the city of white walls. It had been built to rule both Upper and Lower Kingdoms. Two dynasties had come and gone and the third was prosperous, expansive, so the damned place was sprawling now. Shading his eyes, he could see the necropolis on its ridge. The world's first pyramid was no more than a foundation yet. Mortals swarmed over it like insects, setting the little limestone blocks.

He sighed and glanced down from his high seat to the water, where a ridged back paced his boat, drifting unobtrusively near. Poor old crocodile. There had been a time when Atrahasis might have given an order and had a clumsy slave tossed overboard like a crust of bread, and before the river gods converged on him the slave would have screamed his thanks at being so honored. One couldn't get away with that nowadays. Too much history was being recorded.

When his boatman docked and bowed him ashore, Atrahasis walked through the streets and the mortals fell back before him, gaping at the splendid lord in his finery, marveling at the tall spearmen who went before and followed him. They wondered at the mortal slaves who bore the carved chest that was splendidly covered in beaten gold, inlaid with turquoise and lapis. They thought surely he must be an ambassador bringing gifts to the king.

But he did not go to the palace. Atrahasis went swiftly to the house of Imhotep, the high priest, he who was the king's chief minister, he who had designed and was overseeing the construction of the latest thing in monuments to royal glory.

The mortal onlookers nodded to each other knowingly. No surprise that this regal-looking stranger was calling on Imhotep first. Imhotep might claim he was merely a man, but everyone knew better. He had miraculous healing powers, he knew the name of every star in the sky and their secret paths, and his ability to work spectacularly showy magic was famous. Of course he must entertain gods from time to time! Before Atrahasis had stepped through the courtyard gate, word was spreading that Imhotep had another divine visitor.

To Atrahasis's annoyance, he was not at once admitted to the august presence of the high priest of Ptah.

"He is bathing, my lord," stammered the mortal woman. She clapped her hands and servants ran to her side. "A chair for the great lord, a basin for his feet! Will you have beer, my lord? Will you be pleased to wait in the garden, where the air is cool? I will fetch—"

"Tell him the priest of Zeus would speak with him," Atrahasis snapped.

There was a beat while the mortals present wondered who Zeus might be, before a servant said: "Our lord will not permit us to disturb his bath—" The woman turned and waved him to silence.

"I will tell him," she said, and hurried away. Atrahasis waited, enduring in stiff-lipped silence as well-meaning mortals brought a chair for him, seated him, drew off his sandals and washed his feet. He still hated to be touched by the creatures.

He focused his attention on the interior of the mansion and heard the splashing, the raucous whistling of—of all things—the Grand March from Verdi's *Aida,* interrupted by the mortal woman's urgent murmur. There was a response, more splashing, and then the whistling resumed. Atrahasis tracked it through the mansion as it came nearer to him, and at last the high priest Imhotep stepped out into the garden.

Imhotep was a stockily built man with black button eyes, smiling in wry apology as he approached Atrahasis. He had a generic olive-skinned Mediterranean appearance, and might have disappeared into any crowd anywhere with perfect invisibility, so ordinary was his face, so easily could he pass for human.

His hastily donned linen kilt was damp, and he was still toweling his shaven head dry as he came.

"Sorry, friend," he said in Cinema Standard. "I was at the construction site all day and got pretty stinky. You want a beer?"

"Please," said Atrahasis, as a servant dried his feet. Imhotep asked the servant to bring a pitcher of beer and two cups. He ducked his head and hurried away.

Imhotep gave his ears a last dig with the towel and hung it around his neck. He thrust out a hand to Atrahasis.

"Facilitator Grade One Imhotep, how's it going and to what do I owe the honor?"

"Executive Facilitator Atrahasis," he replied, shaking Imhotep's hand gingerly. "The god Zeus has sent you a gift, divine son of Ptah. I'm here to brief you on its use."

Imhotep grimaced. "Don't call me that where the servants can hear, okay? Not in their language, anyhow."

Atrahasis was amused. "Don't you want them to respect you?"

"They respect me just fine as a mortal man, which is what I've worked really hard to convince them I happen to be, so let's not scare them, all right?" Imhotep sagged onto a garden bench. He regarded the carved chest, still being held on its poles by the mortal slaves; cocked his eye at the honor guard of security techs in loincloths. "That must be one hell of a present. What is it, another capacitor?"

"I don't believe your project budget could support one," Atrahasis replied delicately. "And it's hardly necessary for the second phase of your mission here."

"Second phase, huh?" Imhotep rubbed his chin. "Okay." In the language of the country, he addressed the mortal bearers. "Boys, you want to set that thing down?"

The slaves glanced nervously at Atrahasis, who nodded. They lowered their burden and straightened up in obvious relief. At that moment the servant brought the beer, and only after he had offered them their cups and retreated to a respectful distance was the conversation able to proceed.

"What second phase?" Imhotep asked. "I've got Zoser and his court in the palm of my hand, with stage illusions galore. The step-pyramid's on schedule. I'm dealing out miraculous cures and promoting good hygiene. Wasn't that the point of this junket?"

"As far as it's gone, yes," Atrahasis said, sniffing his beer and setting it aside. "But now you need to know more."

"I see."

"The chest is not to be opened until you have it in your private chambers. You will find inside it certain equipment, and a number of scrolls."

"Scrolls? What do I need books for?"

"Think of them as stage-dressing. They're to impress your initiates."

"What initiates?" said Imhotep, reaching for his beer. He turned the cup in his hands uneasily. "I thought the whole deal with me becoming a god didn't happen until way later in history."

"Of course. This is another matter entirely. You're to start a, to put it in the mortals' parlance, a 'Hermetic Brotherhood.' The most secret of secret societies. You'll feed them snippets of philosophy and arcane gibberish as revelations from the gods. Flashy conjuring tricks to impress them. Hints of real science, with demonstrable results. The equipment in the chest is for that purpose."

"Don't tell me there are still Rosicrucians in the twenty-fourth century, and they're paying the Company to do this?" Imhotep sighed.

"Not at all. You're simply laying the groundwork for certain others to build on at a later date," Atrahasis told him. "The real challenge will be convincing your little king that the whole affair is his idea."

Imhotep looked unhappy.

"Okay," he said. "I can do that. No problem." He drained his beer in one gulp and reached for the pitcher. "More?"

"Not for me, thank you." Atrahasis turned in his chair and surveyed the garden. "Quite a comfortable posting you have here. It must nearly make up for the air pollution and the crowds of mortals."

"It's great," said Imhotep earnestly. "And the pollution's no worse than anywhere else. You try living in the same cave with the rest of your tribe through a six-month winter—now, that's pollution!"

"Undoubtedly," said Atrahasis. "Still, one can't help wish the wretched things would grasp the basic principles of birth control." He transmitted the rest of his thought subvocally: *Or that the old Enforcers had been allowed to continue their useful work.*

Imhotep gulped down a second beer even more quickly than the first.

Hey, times change. I hear most of them are adapting real well to the new jobs.

Atrahasis considered him coolly. *You don't find what was done to them shameful? How professional of you. I'd have thought you could summon a little outrage on their behalf. You were one of Budu's recruits, weren't you? Just as I was.*

That's right.

Yet you never spoke out on behalf of our immortal father, when the orders came.

Imhotep narrowed his eyes. *What's it to you? I went to him and we talked, if you must know. Sure, he had his reservations about closing down the old operation. But he was smart enough to see that times were changing, and he's changed with them. Not like that dumb ass Marco.*

Marco was rash, I have to admit.

He was a loose cannon! He'd grab any excuse to slaughter mortals. Budu's smart, and he's got self-control, and he's going to be just fine. It's not like there aren't going to be plenty of wars to keep him busy.

How true.

At this moment they were interrupted. A tiny brown naked mortal came marching into the garden, fists clenched, scowling in furious determination, heading for the street. Imhotep spotted him and jumped up.

"Excuse me a minute. Benny, come back here!"

Atrahasis turned, staring in disbelief, as Imhotep ran after the mortal in-fant and caught it. A conversation took place in the ancient tongue that would be translated approximately as follows:

"Whoa! Where do you think you're going? Remember what Daddy said about chariots?"

"No potty go."

"Oh. Benny, you have to go potty like a big boy now."

"No potty go!"

Imhotep looked around. "Okay, okay. Come on. Big boy on the tree like Daddy showed you, all right?"

"Big boy."

Atrahasis averted his gaze as Imhotep led the infant to a fig tree in the cor-ner, where it urinated. The mortal woman came running from the house, call-ing for the child, and Imhotep turned and waved to her.

"I caught him, honey, it's all right."

"How did you get the door open?" she demanded of the baby. It just glared up at her. "My lord husband, I put the latch on!"

"He's a magician," said Imhotep, grinning in embarrassment. "Like me."

"Horses might have killed you under their hooves," she admonished the baby, gathering it into her arms. "Crocodiles might have eaten you!" She glanced over at Atrahasis and crimsoned in a blush. "Ten thousand apologies, my lord!"

"It's all right," said Imhotep. He put his arms around her and kissed her. "I'll be in soon. Send Aye and Pepi and a couple of the others out, okay? And unlock my study. I want that chest taken inside and set against the far wall."

"Will our guest stay for dinner?"

"I don't think so," Imhotep said.

"No potty go," the baby informed them.

"We'll see about that, kiddo," Imhotep told him sternly, and the mortal woman bore the protesting child away to the house. He returned to the stone bench to find Atrahasis regarding him in scandalized disgust.

"We adopted," explained Imhotep, looking a little shamefaced.

"No wonder you don't mind the pollution," Atrahasis said at last. "You're actually living in intimacy with them!"

"It's part of my job," said Imhotep. "She was a gift from the king. What was I supposed to do? You know the procedure on this kind of mission. And anyway, since when is sex with them against the rules?"

"True enough," Atrahasis said, but mentally he crossed Imhotep off his list of possible allies.

"I know she'll die one of these days," Imhotep went on defensively. "The kid will die, too, maybe fifty years down the line, but in the meanwhile he'll have had a good life and . . . well, they all die, don't they? And I'll be somewhere else by then anyway. I've been through this before. I can handle it. The Company doesn't care, as long as I get the job done, right?"

"Whatever it takes," Atrahasis agreed.

He didn't stay to dinner.

Imhotep might be besotted with mortals, but he had indeed gotten the job done. In founding an occult society that promised secret knowledge and earthly power to its members, he had forged the first link in a long chain that would ultimately terminate in that remarkable cabal of scientists and investors calling itself Dr. Zeus Incorporated.

Not quite in keeping with the high moral purpose expressed in the Company's mission statement. However, Atrahasis had learned—long before he became Labienus—that the mortal masters were the first to jettison their principles, when it was necessary to get something they wanted.

VICTOR THE POISONER

From time to time, Labienus has considered compiling a book of wisdom of his own, perhaps an immortals' version of *The Prince* or *The Art of War*.

He has never done so. For one thing, when one is immortal, there is no point in passing on wisdom to the next generation lest it be forgotten, for it cannot be forgotten. Nor would it do, after all, to empower up-and-coming young rivals by letting them in on one's secrets.

And Labienus has no bright subordinate in training, in any case, no youthful immortal he can impress or mentor.

So his desire has never progressed beyond a list of maxims. The first one is, *It is not enough to tend one's own garden. One must assiduously sow weeds in one's neighbor's garden, and encourage snails there.*

He unlocks a drawer now, and draws forth another paper file. It is bulky, it is clumsy, but hard copy has certain advantages to a conspirator. And there is something so satisfying, really, in holding in one's hands the tangible damnation of one's enemies.

The file is labeled simply HOMO UMBRATILIS.

Labienus opens it. The first thing to greet his eye is an image, a straightforward Company identification shot of another Executive Facilitator. His designation is Aegeus, and he looks as benign as the chairman of some philanthropic foundation.

His expression makes Labienus's lip curl in distaste. *Hypocrite,* he thinks. Their rivalry is an old one.

They were assigned to the same mission once, in the dead ages past when he had been Atrahasis. The job was above and beyond the usual level of Company need-to-know obscurity. They had been sent with troops to an island in the Pacific and told to kill all the mortals they found there. Long before their transport had touched down, Atrahasis had discovered that his partner was no higher in rank than he was, and moreover that Aegeus was pompous, self-important, and crude.

Atrahasis had entertained himself awhile subtly insulting Aegeus with exquisite courtesy. When they finally reached their destination, Aegeus had let him do most of the killing; and this proved to be a complicated affair, for the mortals turned out to be neither the Neanderthal brutes he had expected nor even their cave-painting cousins. And they were rather better at defending themselves than Atrahasis had been advised. Given the hazardous nature of the job, he expected a plum posting as a reward.

So it had annoyed him a great deal when he later learned that Aegeus, rather than he himself, had been appointed the new sector head for Southern Europe.

Labienus has never forgotten the slight.

Both men have built private empires within the Company. Both have made plans to seize power, on that distant day in 2355 when the Company is expected to fall, and both have taken certain drastic and occasionally bloody steps to guarantee supremacy then. Only their methods have differed.

Aegeus has gone for show, for extravagance, flaunting his power base. He has committed tremendous resources to long-range plans. In doing so, he has presented his enemies with an immense target. The question, therefore, is simply one of strategy: which arrow to use, and when, for the most satisfying result?

Labienus tilts his head on one side, considering Aegeus's image. Smiling at last, he takes a fine silver pen from his desk and dips it in an inkwell of Bavarian crystal. He sketches a beard and curling mustache on Aegeus's face. Aegeus has his lips closed in the picture, sadly, so Labienus is unable to black out one of his teeth; but he settles for drawing little horns on Aegeus's head, and adding a pair of vampire fangs over his lower lip. He sets the picture aside, chuckling as he reflects that a petty impulse, properly directed, can do one a world of good.

So, with a light heart, he considers the other Company portraits in the file.

Two immortals. One is a drone, a Literature Preservationist designated

Lewis. The other is an Executive Class Facilitator whose promising career has been oddly derailed. He is designated Victor. Lewis smiles from his portrait. Victor does not.

Lewis is fair-haired, handsome, clean-shaven. There is determination in his features. There is an earnestness that verges on absurdity. There is no doubt he is plucky. Also thrifty, brave, clean, and reverent. *Fool,* thinks Labienus.

Victor has white skin, red hair. His neat beard is sharply pointed, his mustaches even more so. His green eyes are as unreadable in their expression as a cat's. He has posed stiffly, formally. He looks reserved. Unapproachable. Labienus smiles at his picture, almost with real affection.

Hitching his chair closer to the desk, he turns his attention to the documents. Some appear to be transcripts of testimony. He has compiled them over long years, with terrific patience. A lucky find; a careful decryption of private journal entries; an interview with an ancient mortal that had cost him nothing more than a bottle of good wine and a sympathetic-seeming ear.

The topmost stack looks fabulously old, vellum inscribed in brown ink, uncials decorated here and there with flowers and strange tiny marginalia. It is written in a mixture of sixth-century Gaelic and Latin.

The edges crumble as Labienus reads.

When my name was Eogan, I lived in the community at Malinmhor, having gladly embraced my vows for the peace of our Lord Jesus Christ, and I thought I had the best of the bargain. No heavier tool to lift than a pen cut from the quill of a gray goose, and the beauty of the red and green and yellow and black inks was a pleasure for my eyes, and how smooth were the sheets of fine white calfskin waiting for me! And how sweet to refresh myself with the Gospel that I copied, there in the little scriptorium, when I could still believe in it!

What a world of grace fell away from me when that pagan man came among us, three weeks before Beltane in the five hundred and seventh year since Christ's birth.

But no blame to him, poor man; God knows he had the worst of it. The truth is the trouble started well beforehand, and I knew nothing of it, happy and alone as I worked. So blinded with the beauty I made by day, that I never noticed the frightened faces when I joined my brothers and sisters for supper in the refectory of evenings.

And we didn't speak aloud much—it was a monastery, after all—nor would I have believed in the trouble, had anyone explained it to me. If our community lay in the shadow of the high bare hill Dun Govaun, what harm in that? No rational Christian had anything to fear from a mound of dead stone. If pagans had feared the place in the past, if they'd told stories of babies carried off or folk seduced by small demons—well, they were pagans, weren't they? At the mercy of darkness, as we brothers and sisters in Christ were not. Though I remember being awakened by the screams of a brother in his nightmares, I do remember that much now; but it signified nothing to me at the time.

When the pagan came, it was neither by day nor night but in the long hour between when the light had not faded, and when we neither fasted nor fed but sat at table with our meal not yet begun, and our brother the Cook had just brought out the oat-kettle, and Liath our Abbess was neither silent nor speaking, for she had just drawn in her breath to lead the grace. The pagans believe such in-between moments make doorways into the next world, you know.

In that unlucky moment the door opened indeed and our brother the Porter led in a young man in very fine clothes, which were perhaps too large for him.

"This is the guest Christ has sent us, who comes requiring meat and shelter for the night," said the Porter, and he withdrew to his duty. The man stood surveying us all with a pleasant face; and from the dust on his rich garments it was plain he'd traveled far, and from the harp he bore, slung in its case on his back, plain his profession of *fili*, of chronicler after the manner of the heathens. I thought he looked too young to have learned so much lore as those people are required to know.

"A blessing on this table," he said, and our Abbess corrected him:

"*Christ's* blessing on this table, and all here."

"Oh, by all means," he replied mildly, and smiled at the Abbess.

He dined, then, with us, and revealed that his name was Lewis, that he was indeed a pagan well trained in his craft of relating the old histories, and had come to offer us a bargain: he would give us all he carried in his head, the wonder-tales and songs of the old pagan heroes, in return for food and lodging. Our Abbess looked across at me with the eye of a cat after a mouse, for both she and I collected these tales avidly (though we did not believe them at all).

So the bargain was made, with the understanding that the pagan should observe no pagan rites whilst among us, especially on the old feast day that was three weeks off, but attend Mass daily instead. To which Lewis agreed, readily, without anger. After dining he was shown the bath-house, and then the guest-house, and he took his leave of us for the evening with the urbane manners of a king's son, which we thought he must be.

When it grew light next day he met me in the scriptorium, for the purpose of fulfilling his end of the agreement, and settled himself on a stone seat. He took his harp from its case, and frowned to himself as he tuned it. I will record here that Lewis was small-boned, high-browed, with fine clean-shaven features and fair hair, though it did not curl. His eyes were just the color of the sky in that twilight time in which he had come.

When he had tuned the strings to his satisfaction, he said to me: "Brother Eogan, tell me first what tales you have collected thus far, from other travelers, so I waste no time in repeating them. Have you *The Cattle-raid of Cooley*?"

"Yes, in good truth, we have."

"Have you *The Destruction of Da Derga's Hostel*?"

"Yes, in good truth, we have."

"Would you mind awfully if we switched to Latin for this?" he inquired in that tongue. "It'll go quicker."

"Fair enough," I replied in the same language, and we conversed in Latin after that.

"What about the Finn MacCool stories? Any of those?"

"Well, we did get a couple of songs about him from an old man who stayed here last winter," I told him, noting that my red ink had sat too long and giving it a shake to mix it. "I don't think his memory was very reliable, though."

"Ah! Well, I've got the complete cycle. Sounds like a good place to begin, wouldn't you say?" He grinned and fished a horn plectrum from the pouch at his belt.

"Let's hear it," I replied, and poised my pen over the lovely white page. Dear God, how I've missed writing, just the physical act of moving the pen, making the ink flow!

He had hours and hours of material on the Fenians, tales I'd never heard before as well as the two stories the old man had given us (and as I'd suspected, the poor creature had garbled them badly). I myself was born Christian, and since my parents were zealous converts, they'd always frowned on their children listening to the old pagan stories. I knew all about Patrick and Moses and Noah, but I could never hear about Cuchulainn or Deirdre until I became a monk. Ironic, isn't it?

Lewis recounted the whole cycle to me, all about Finn growing up in the forest because evil King Goll had killed his father, so the boy was raised in secret by a pair of druid women, who conjured a wolf-spirit to be his protector. Spellbinding! Lewis was a good storyteller, too. He had a mobile, expressive face, elegant gestures, and a nice light baritone. My pen swept across the page.

We didn't even take a break until I got a paralyzing fit of writer's cramp, just after the part where Finn calls his father's ghost from the Land of the Blessed, and the old chief gives him advice. I got up and walked back and forth in the narrow stone room, swinging my arms, while Lewis took the opportunity to pour himself a cup of watered mead from the pitcher we'd brought.

He sipped and held the cup out to the light. "My goodness, who's your Beekeeper? That's great!"

"A former pagan," I admitted. "Nobody else quite gets the formula right, I must confess. You see, that's part of the Abbess's plan here—there's so much that's worth preserving in Eire, so much wisdom, such traditions, so much great literature! If only it wasn't *pagan*, you see. Not that I expect you to agree with me on that point, of course, and no offense intended—"

"No, no." Lewis waved his hand. "Quite all right. I understand perfectly—"

"But these stories, for example. It's absolutely criminal that the druids didn't bother to write any of them down. You must realize that in another generation or two they'll be completely forgotten, don't you? And, though we won't be the poorer for losing our false gods, it really would be too bad to lose Finn."

"My thoughts exactly." Lewis nodded. "That's one of the reasons I'm here, to tell you the truth. I can see the writing on the wall, and my profession doesn't really encourage me to write on it myself—so to speak— *but . . .*" He set down his harp and leaned forward. "I have rather a daring proposition for you."

I stopped pacing. "It's nothing sinful, I trust."

"Not at all, at least not by your standards. Look, it's simply this: I'm a bit more than a simple bard. I have some religious credentials as well, in my religion I mean. I was trained for certain rituals I'll never be able to perform nowadays, with so few of us left."

"But you're a young man," I said doubtfully. "I thought most of the *vates* had died off years ago."

"I'm older than I look." Was he evading my gaze, there, for just a second? "In any case: I'm quite resigned to the druids being dead as last year's mutton, but it kills the heart in me to know their more, ah, arcane knowledge will be lost. The sciences. The sacred rites, the ceremonies and all that. Now, I couldn't ever tell you Christians certain things, being sworn to secrecy, but if you happened to overhear me talking to myself—say if we happened to be sitting in the same room at the time—and you happened to write down what you heard, well, it wouldn't be a sin for you, would it?"

"I'm not so sure about that." I sat to consider it. "Preserving heathen history and legends is one thing. Preserving a false faith . . . I seem to remember the Blessed Patrick stating quite clearly that druid books ought to be burned, not preserved."

He sighed and had another sip of mead. "I know what you're thinking: what if this is some pagan plot to keep the Old Religion going? I'll tell you what you can do: once you've made my *Codex Druidae*, you can bury it in a lead casket ten feet below the floor of this room. I'll swear any oath you like that it'll remain there, undisturbed, unseen for a thousand years and more."

"It's a strange request . . ." I tugged at my beard. "Still, I know how I'd feel in your position. Couldn't we finish this cycle of stories about Finn MacCool first?"

"Naturally." He brightened up, setting down his mead and reaching for the harp. "How's your cramp? Feel up to some white-knuckle iambic pentameter? I was just about to come to the part where Finn's woman is stolen by demons of darkness . . ."

"Finn married?" I grabbed up my pen.

"Not exactly. It was like this . . ."

So we went on like that, he and I, and the hours lengthened into days. From sunrise until midday we'd work on the stories of Finn, or the tale of Conchobar's quest for the Four Blind Boys, or other fascinating material, with me copying fast in simple brown ink, leaving margins and capitals to be elaborated on and illuminated later. If the weather was fair we'd move outdoors, where the light was better and Lewis wouldn't have to keep retuning his strings. Sometimes the Abbess would come to us, unable to restrain her desire, and read over my shoulder or listen with her eyes closed, to hear about Fergus and the Seal-Woman. But in the afternoons, when she had gone, we'd go inside and work on the *Codex Druidae,* the forbidden book. The actual text took no more than a week or so to rough in. I planned to spend more time on the illumination.

I must say, any reservations I had melted away once I actually heard the so-called sacred knowledge of my ancestors. No wonder they'd kept it secret! Most of it was utter nonsense. I remember one absurd formula for producing children out of nature, by combining tiny bits of the parents' flesh in a glass dish. Some of their astronomy was fairly good, at least. They knew, like Pythagoras, that the Earth was a sphere, but they had this notion that the Earth revolves around the Sun! In fact, they thought—but it's just too stupid to waste the ink in telling over again. I confess I was laughing as I took most of it down. No wonder Lewis had abandoned the priestly caste to be a bard.

And in any case, he was a kindly young man, and I couldn't imagine him shutting unfortunate criminals into wicker cages and burning them alive. Not that he wouldn't have been strong enough; one time he took his turn at serving the evening meal, though as a guest he needn't have, and I saw him hoist the great fish-cauldron on his shoulder and bear it from the kitchen as though it weighed nothing. I watched him mend a set of beads for one of the sisters one evening at table, prizing and closing the bronze links with powerful clever fingers. And his speech was graceful and witty, making us laugh so, it was as if Christ Himself were there telling jokes.

This happy time lasted until Beltane Eve. On that afternoon, Lewis and I were sitting out of doors, and white thorn blossoms were dropping on the calfskin from the bush above me, so I kept having to brush them away as I took down Lewis's account of the Daughter of the King Under the Waves. Suddenly he stopped. A second later the birds, who had been singing delightfully, stopped, too. "Liath is coming," Lewis announced, raising one eyebrow, "and something's wrong—"

When she came into view I saw he was right, for her face was dark with unhappiness. She wasted no time, but came straight to Lewis, and in blunt

Gaelic addressed him: "Pagan man, have you any knowledge of the ways of the *sidhe*?"

His mouth hung open a second in surprise. "I have," he said.

"Good, for we have need of it. Brother Crimthann has been stolen away from us by the *sidhe* of Dun Govaun, and must be rescued."

If Finn and all his host had suddenly leaped alive from my page, I could not have been more bewildered. Fairy folk? Fairy folk kidnapping one of *us*? But the *sidhe* were mere heathen fables, they didn't exist! And I saw that Lewis was no less amazed, though courteously he asked her to explain.

It seemed that Brother Crimthann, who was one of the younger members of our community, had been troubled lately with bad dreams. In his dreams, the *sidhe* came into the cell where he slept, as easily as if they walked through smoke, and bore him away with them to their palace under Dun Govaun. There he suffered torments of fleshly temptation, but by morning woke in his cell again with no sign of the ordeal of his dreams: not even the guilty emission of a young man so tempted. He had sworn that the *sidhe* were not beautiful, either, but pale and small and silent.

At this I saw Lewis start forward, like a hound catching a scent. "Now that is a strange thing, truly," he told the Abbess.

"Strange, but not so strange as this: Brother Crimthann did not come to prayers this morning, nor later, nor was he to be found in his cell. But Brother Aidan's hut adjoins his, and Brother Aidan swears that in the third hour of the night the moon shone into his cell, bright enough to flood between the stone chinks; and as you are a pagan and learned in these things I need not tell you that there was no moon last night." The Abbess looked at him grimly. "Now, this is a pagan matter. The Blessed Patrick gave us prayers against the *sidhe,* but I never read anywhere that fairy women carried him away from his holy bed. Can you go to them, then, and win our brother back with that fine pagan talk of yours? Bring him alive out of Dun Govaun, and Christ will bless you for it, druid though you are."

"I will," said Lewis, "and gladly, good Mother. Only tell me where to find Dun Govaun, and I'll go there straight."

"Brother Eogan knows," she told him, and gave me a Look of Order. "Eogan, show him the way."

"This is really marvelous," Lewis said as we pushed our way through the heather. "Tell me, Eogan, have you ever noticed this sort of thing going on before? Strange lights in the sky, unusual marking in the fields, cattle inexplicably slaughtered in grotesque ways? Any nocturnal goings-on in your cell?"

"Certainly not," I replied stiffly. "I sleep soundly at night, at least since I stopped having to shave my tonsure. I daresay Brother Crimthann will, too, when he's past thirty and not quite so easily tempted by the flesh."

"Cheer up! Baldness looks good on some men. You think that's all it is, then, with Brother Crimthann? He's been sneaking out at night to visit a girl?" Lewis leapt nimbly up on a rock and peered ahead, shading his eyes with his hand. "Ah. That must be the famous Dun Govaun."

"That's it." I regarded it sourly. "The supposed hall of the fairies. Absolutely ridiculous! It's a completely smooth and solid hill. Not even a rabbit hole on it anywhere. As for Brother Crimthann, he's simply run away, if you ask me. That's the trouble with these boys who get all inflamed by the idea of monastic life before they've had a chance to see what sleeping with a woman's like." I bent to untangle a branch of gorse from the leg of my trews. "Chastity seems like such a wonderful idea until the first time someone actually tempts them, and then they go all to pieces. Hysteria, night sweats, and Satan everywhere they look."

"Not one of the better innovations of Christianity, if you'll pardon my saying so," Lewis remarked as we hurried on. "But let's climb Dun Govaun. I'm eager to see if anything's up there. There are, er . . . certain stories amongst my people, of creatures like the ones Brother Crimthann described. We've never been able to verify anything, of course. So what do you think the place is? Not a natural hill, at any rate."

"Nothing more than the burial mound of some heathen king," I said dismissively; but I glanced upward, for by then we had come to the base of the great hill, and I felt my opinion curdle in my heart. Perhaps a *giant* heathen king.

"There's a place in Britain—" began Lewis, and then he stopped still in his tracks. He seemed to be listening intently to something. His face lit up. He began to laugh.

"Well, I'll be damned," he said, in rather poor taste under the circumstances, I thought. "They're here, Eogan! There are actually living things inside this hill."

"How do you know?" I was unable to see what should amuse him so.

"Let's say it's druidical wisdom," he replied, chuckling, and began to pace rapidly along the side of the hill. "Yes—there should be a concealed opening, and I'll bet it's just about here—"

"What in Christ's name are you babbling about?" I demanded, running after him until he suddenly vanished before my astounded eyes. I froze, staring at empty grass and windy sky. To my horror his bright voice went right on.

"Here it is, no doubt about it. Eogan? What's the matter? Oh." His head appeared in midair, a vision no less terrifying. He must have seen how frightened I was, for in a soothing voice he said: "This is only a conjurer's trick, man. There's magic in your Bible, isn't there? Moses and Aaron working spells against the Pharaoh's magicians? And this is less than that, believe me."

"But—" I said, and that was when I felt my faith first shifting under me. All this while, I had believed that Christ's coming had scoured sorcery out of the world, as the sunrise dispels darkness. Though the old stories might be good to tell and listen to, and the days of the heroes sentimentally longed after, no such wonders existed any more, if indeed they ever had.

Yet my logic had been flawed, hadn't it? For the old prophets did work magic, Christ Himself had done so, and where in Scripture did it say that we lived in an orderly and rational world?

Lewis extended a disembodied hand, in a gesture meant to calm me. "Come around here, and I'll show you."

Christ forgive me, I went to see. As I approached, the rest of him appeared whole and sound, and I saw the wavering stripes of shadow he was pointing out so proudly. They were like the blurs that used to dance before my eyes when I'd worked too late by one candle. "Now, watch this," he told me, and closed his eyes. I heard a humming sound and a snap. The mouth of a cave yawned before us, black dark and deep. I made the Sign of the Cross against all evil.

"What did you do?"

"I just—broke the spell. In a manner of speaking. I'll bet Brother Crimthann's in there." Lewis's smile faded as he considered the thing he'd revealed to me. "Good Lord, a real abduction. What should we do now, do you suppose?"

"You—you said you'd rescue him!" I sputtered.

"I did, didn't I?" He looked unhappy. "You wait here, then. I'll be back as soon as I can." To my astonishment, he turned without the least hesitation and proceeded down into the darkness, and I realized he had no weapon with him larger than a penknife. I watched his back dwindling into the shadows a moment before I ran after him, calling on the power of Christ to shield me.

"Oh—" He half turned as I caught hold of his cloak. "That's all right, you don't have to come. Really, you'll be safer out there. I can see in the dark, had I mentioned that?"

"No," I replied, groping after him. There were strange smells in that darkness, but I didn't want to be thought a coward; and wasn't the power of Christ greater than anything that might be down there? It must be, mustn't it? "I'll bear you company."

"Well, that's thoughtful of you. Be careful, Eogan; the passageway's getting narrower, and there's some kind of threshold we're about to cross. Here. Step up with me now—"

Then it was as though lightning had come down from Heaven into that black place, and I was struck and thrown like a spark from a smith's anvil.

Hours and hours later I heard Lewis saying, "Well, that was certainly stupid."

I sat up painfully, feeling as though I'd been beaten. We lay in half-darkness, in an angle of corridor lined by panes of milk-white glass that glowed softly. Behind us, set into the floor, was a simple metal grating.

"Eogan," said Lewis, and he sounded almost embarrassed. "Eogan, there are people coming for us, and I'm afraid I have a problem."

"What is that?" How groggy I sounded.

"I seem to be paralyzed."

I grimaced. "Your neck's broken, then. I'm sorry, man."

"No, it can't break, but—" He paused a moment and then spoke rapidly. "Eogan, I'd like to make a confession. Will you hear it? Will you be my *anmchara*?"

"But you're a pagan!"

"I'll convert. Will you? If I ask you in Christ's name?" His voice was desperate.

And of course I must say yes, and so I was bound to his secret. I leaned close in the darkness to hear Lewis, as he drew a deep breath and confessed.

"You see . . . I'm afraid I'm rather more of a pagan than you thought. In fact, I'm not strictly what you'd call a human being."

"What are you, then?" I sat back to stare at him. He was certainly sweating like a mortal man, but we had entered a world where the *sidhe* existed after all, so what else might be true?

"The word *cyborg* won't mean anything to you. You'd call me a homuncu-lus, I suppose, grown from a mortal infant but changed by, er, alchemy. The masters who created me live nearly two thousand years in the future, Eogan. I work for them here in the past, finding things they want and hiding them in places that won't be disturbed until they're needed. I've been functioning for four centuries now." He swallowed hard and seemed to get his panic under control. "They made me immortal and indestructible; at least they thought so. They know everything—well, not quite everything, or I wouldn't be lying here now, would I? I can't die! Can I?"

"I don't know what on Earth you're talking about," I told him, trying even now to hold tight to my orderly rational world. "But I've seen men fall and lose movement down one side of themselves, or lose the power of speech. I think that's happened to you, Lewis. I'm sorry."

"It *is* something like that, actually," Lewis babbled. "When we stepped on that grid, it damaged me. Only my head is working. I don't know how long my emergency backup systems will run before shutting down, too. I can't seem to reset myself. Will you swear to me to fulfill a duty? As my confessor, Eogan!"

"Of course," I assured him. As his *anmchara* I had that obligation, what-ever nonsense he spouted as he lay dying.

"Go back now," Lewis begged me. "Go back and seal the *Codex Druidae* in lead, and bury it ten feet below the floor of your scriptorium. You'll find the lead casket with my things in the guest-house."

"Why is this so important?" I asked, trying to be rational.

"Because it'll be worth an awful lot of money to the Neo-Wiccans when it's dug up in 2350," he replied.

I had not the slightest idea what he meant by that at all, nor was I ever to get him to explain further, for his eyes went wide suddenly and he gasped. "God Apollo! Look at that."

This last was not a timely prayer but a reaction to the creatures that were suddenly there with us in that dark hall, things like horrible children. Small, with skins pale as ashes, and tiny weak faces set low on big heads. They were naked, save for goggles of black glass worn over eyes that were perhaps as weak as the rest of them. No genitals at all. I wanted to yell with revulsion at the sight of them; but a voice like the devil spoke within my ear, wheedling, coaxing, imploring.

Please, it begged me, *please! Rise and bring the changeling with you. Pleeease go with us. We're going somewhere nice. You'll want to come.* And, though I detested the little voice before and after I heard it, while it twittered away at me I could no more deny it than a call of nature. I prayed to my sunlit Christ to deny them power over me. Still I obeyed them, got to my feet and picked up Lewis. His head hung down like a broken doll's, and I was certain I'd killed him; but as I moved to follow the pale children, I heard him murmuring inexplicably: *"Mass hysteria,* was it? *Faked photographs,* was it?" in tones of indignation.

Down the long hall we went, and it was dark and warm, reeking with strange animal smells. We came to a door, neatly made. The pale children bid me put my shoulder against it and push my way in. I shoved through into a tiny stone chamber, lit by white glass beyond the door ("Watch out! Careful of my head," fretted Lewis as it nearly knocked on the jamb). Then we were in and the door had swung shut after us, and I saw that there was no handle on the inside, and the silky voices had stopped, and I felt like a fool in a trap, which I was.

Behind me I heard a hiss of indrawn breath.

"Guests," mused a voice in Latin. "How fortunate I am."

"Eogan, turn around," said Lewis in tones of distinct alarm.

I whirled about expecting a dragon, at least, but saw instead a pale child in chains, sitting against the wall.

No, not a child. A thin wispy beard trailed from his chin, and on his big head were wisps of hair. His gender was evident, if small as a baby's. He had a bitter thin mouth, and wide green eyes that were fixed on us with an expression of malevolent amusement.

"Slave," he told me, "bring the mechanism here. I'd like a look at him."

"Slave yourself," I replied, though I'd felt the strongest compulsion to do as he'd bid me. I retreated to the opposite side of the room and set Lewis down. He was staring, as if fascinated, at the prisoner.

"What on Earth are you?" he inquired.

"And what are you?" mocked the other. "But, you see, I know the answer to that question. We know all about you and you know nothing about us. You passed through the disruption field, clearly."

"Was that what it was?" Lewis's head lolled sideways. "Eogan, hold me up so I can see him." I obliged, while the prisoner giggled at us.

"Yes, and it works well, apparently! Mother will be so happy. My uncles will learn a lot from you, when they open up that ticking head of yours. Enough to improve our defenses, next time." The creature smiled nastily.

"What are you?" I demanded, sifting through my memory for tales I'd heard from other children. "Are you a *luporchan?*"

That sent him into gales of shrill laughter. "Of course I am! Of course I am, slave, and what's more I'm a Prince among *luporchans.* Son of the Queen. Though I'm a bad Prince and in royal disfavor, as you can see." He rattled his chains at us.

"Oh, shut up," Lewis snapped at him. "You're some kind of half-human hybrid, aren't you? And that poor boy from the monastery was being brought here to make more like you, wasn't he?"

"Was Mother feeling lustful again?" The Prince shook his head. "Another hairy baby, I suppose, and perhaps he'll be as disobedient as me. That's the price we pay, though, isn't it?"

"Is it?" Lewis licked his lips. "Listen, if they're going to dismantle me, will you at least tell me what you people are?"

"What *we* are?" The Prince frowned. Then he leaned forward in his chains, looking sly. "I'll tell you a story, *fili.* No harp to accompany me? Too bad. You'll just have to make up the music in your head as we go along.

"This is 'The Tale of the Three Branches.'

"In the Beginning, the great World-Tree bore three branches, and from each branch came a son. The eldest son was wide and strong, practical and brave, but not very imaginative. The second son was tall and graceful, creative and gifted, but prone to silliness and instability."

"I wonder if you're describing Neanderthals and Cro-Magnons?" speculated Lewis.

"Is that what they call themselves? The third son was small and weak and unfortunately something of an idiot, but he had one talent: he could invent clever things. *He* wasn't clever himself, you understand, in fact he could barely speak or think, but he had an affinity for patterns and systems. And from these three sons of these three branches came the three races of man.

"And the children of the two older sons were able to reason and speak with each other, and they interbred: and these powerful and clever ones made war on the kin of the youngest son, to take by force the ingenious things they made.

"It was difficult for ideas to penetrate the heads of the kin, but this much got through to them: they must at all costs defend themselves against the big people, and hide from them somehow. And so this was what the stupid things focused on, with the dedication of ants, to the exclusion of all else, for all eternity, while their big cousins invented civilization and trade and art.

"But the more they stayed in their hiding places the stupider and weaker they became, as generations passed, and it became pitifully easy for the big people to find them, and raid them, and rape their queens. Then a remarkable thing happened! Half-breed children were born in the dark warrens of the kin who were bigger, and cleverer, and braver than the others. And they became the leaders because it occurred to them they *could* lead. So the kin prospered, and found better places to hide, and made more ingenious devices for protecting themselves. And this way, for a while, they had the advantage in the long, long game of hide and seek.

"Sadly, this advantage was lost." The Prince glared at Lewis. "It seems that at the other end of time the big people found a way to create a new race, unnatural and immortal, clockwork and flesh mingled, a disgusting alteration of humanity. Of course they made them a slave race—"

"Oh, we are not either," Lewis said testily.

"—And they reached back through time to plant these vile mechanisms in every civilization, to act as their agents, their spies, their thieves. Need I mention that one of their objectives was to find *us*, and help themselves to our useful inventions?"

"No, that's certainly not true," Lewis objected. "They don't even believe you exist! If they had, they'd have warned me about you. But I was always told you people were a late-twentieth-century hoax."

What that meant I couldn't fathom, but this much was becoming clear to me: Lewis's crazy story must be true, somehow. His enemies knew what he was, and how to harm him. These people were the incubi, the demons the holy saints warned us about. But where in Scripture would I find Lewis, amongst what peoples of the earth?

"Not a slave race, eh?" retorted the Prince. "You know what they think you need to know, nothing more! And I'm sure my marvelous moron uncles will learn things from your disassembled carcass that will give us the mechanical advantage once again."

Lewis gave a disdainful laugh. "So your own people can forge stronger chains for you? Why are you a prisoner, by the bye?"

"Politics!" snarled the Prince. "I had my own plan for furthering our kin. Why not creep out to the big women as they sleep? Why shouldn't they bear and raise our half-breeds? Why shouldn't we live in the sunlight like you? But Mother wouldn't hear of it, and I wouldn't stop, and so here I am."

"How sad for you. Well, this has all been very interesting, but I think I'll leave now," Lewis told him airily. I looked at him, astonished at his nerve. "I have no intention of letting anyone take me apart, thank you very much. Shall we go, Eogan?"

"How?" The Prince gave an incredulous grin. "Have you noticed there's no handle on the inside of this door?"

Lewis ignored him. "Eogan, unpin my cloak. Take out the brooch." I did as he asked and held it in my hand, a well-wrought thing of silver and enamel with a fine long pin.

"Now, bend me a hook from that."

"What can you hope to accomplish?" the Prince demanded. "There's no lock you can pick, either!"

"Slide the hook under the door and pull it inward," Lewis said, and I obeyed him. The Prince started up in his chains, staring in horror as the simplicity of the solution occurred to him.

"Those *idiots*—! But you, my fine machine, you're broken now. You think this big oaf can repair you? You're helpless and they'll come after you, my uncles will, no matter where you hide. They'll hunt you down! If it takes them years, they'll still get you back, and then—"

"Not at all. You see, when my primary system failed my emergency backup system began broadcasting a distress signal," Lewis taunted him. "My masters are already on their way to rescue me. Pull open the door, Eogan."

"Ha! What you have failed to realize is that this whole mound is shielded with lead," shrieked the Prince triumphantly. "Your signal hasn't reached anyone!"

Lewis's grin faltered for just a second, but he turned it into a sneer of defiance. "Well—as soon as I'm clear of this mound, my signal will be heard. And then my masters will come after *you*. See how you like—"

"If you've finished threatening each other," I said, being the only man in the room who could actually move, "the hallway's clear." I looked out into the stinking half-lit way.

"Then I'm off, short circuit or no short circuit," Lewis crowed. Bracing the open door with my body, I got hold of him by one arm and dragged him out with me.

"I'll raise the alarm," cried the Prince, but as the door swung slowly shut on its counterweight I heard him subside and mutter: "On the other hand, would anyone thank me in the least? Why *bother*?"

I took Lewis's other arm to hoist him up; but he got a distracted look in his eyes.

"Listen," he said. "Do you hear it? Someone's weeping."

I listened. "I can't hear anything."

"There's another mortal," Lewis told me. "Brother Crimthann! We've still got to rescue him." Which shamed me, because my earnest desire was to run from there without looking back, Christian as I was and him no more than a pagan, or perhaps less.

But I pulled him with me deeper into the hill and we found another door ten paces on. Even I could hear the weeping then. When we pushed the door open Brother Crimthann screamed, and cowered back in his chains.

"Hush! It's you we've come for, man," I told him. He mastered his terror enough to be silent, pressing his lips together as tears ran down his face. He smelled of shameful things. I left Lewis in the doorway and knelt beside Crimthann, turning his manacles this way and that to look for a keyhole, a seam, anything that I might force to open them. Nothing there! The rings were smooth and featureless, neither iron nor bronze. I pulled so that Crimthann flinched and whimpered, but they held fast.

"I can't break his bonds," I told Lewis. He groaned.

"Let me see them," he said, so I pulled him in and wedged the door with my foot painfully. He studied the manacles a moment as I strained to hold him up, and Crimthann blinked back his tears in confusion.

"I was afraid of this," said Lewis. "I can disable them, but it'll drain my backup system. Can't be helped. Listen, Eogan. This may well finish me. Don't leave my body here! If you can carry it out, my Company will be able to locate me, and they'll come. Now, take my hand and set it on that panel, there, above his head."

I looked up at the little square of blinking lights, bright unnatural colors. "Do you mean this will kill you?" I asked, appalled.

"Oh, no, we don't die. I'm sure they can repair me. But the surge will probably erase—I wonder if it'll erase my *mind*?" I saw his pupils go wide as the possibilities sank in. "My—what if all my memories are gone?"

"Then Christ have mercy on you," I replied, for even then I still believed. I lifted his hand, as he bid me, and laid it against the panel. He sighed once. I felt a stinging shock go through Lewis's body, then, and he made a terrible sound. The panel hissed and spat like a demon unmasked, but the manacles fell away from Crimthann's wrists.

Crimthann needed no urging; he fell forward and crawled at once for the door. Lewis's eyes were blank and blind now, I thought he must surely be dead; but I kept faith and bore him with me out of that cell. We ran for our lives through the tunnel, Crimthann and I, and when I saw the black grate set in the floor I sprang across it with the Salmon-Leap of the old heroes I so admired. No lightning struck me as I hurtled free of the dangerous place. Falling fair, I kept running with Lewis, and did not stop until we came out into clean air.

I fell and rolled on the cold hillside and it was gray dawn, the sun not yet risen on Beltane morning, with the clouds in the east all underlit red. Behind me, Brother Crimthann staggered out and fell on his face, to lie shivering and sobbing.

I rose on my knees at once and turned Lewis over.

"?enogeraseiromemymllafitahW," he babbled, blinking rapidly, and his spine arched back until I thought it would surely snap. Then he went limp again. He opened his eyes and looked around.

"Well," he whispered, "lucky me. Even my backup system has a backup." He paused for a moment, as if listening to himself. "Oh. Not for long, though. It's just transmitting my location. My organics seem to be shutting down—" Panicked, he raised his eyes to my face. "Remember, Eogan! The *Codex Druidae*, you must bury it under the floor. And you won't tell what I confessed to you, about what I am— Oh, no, is this it? Is this what happens to you?"

There was only one thing I could do for him. "What kind of child were you created from?" I asked him. "Had it ever received Christ's grace?"

"What?" He stared at me, bewildered. "No! I was abandoned in the temple at Aquae Sulis." He gave a hysterical giggle. "Some Roman matron's holiday indiscretion, I've no doubt, left behind at the spa, a little unwanted souvenir . . ."

"You won't die," I told him confidently. I swept my hands through the grass that was pearled with the dew of Beltane morning, and I washed that high fine brow of his with it. "I baptize you in the name of the Father, and of the Son, and of the Holy Ghost. Amen."

I think I expected a vision of Christ then, or a blare of heavenly trumpets at least. Nothing of the kind happened. Lewis endured the sacrament patiently, and smiled a small polite smile.

"Why, how nice. You've given me a soul." His smile widened in ironical amusement. "Now I'll live forever, won't I?"

But the color was going out of his face, and then it left his eyes, and they closed and he was no more than a waxen doll on the hillside. I rose to my feet and looked full into the rising sun. All the birds were singing.

And even then I had not lost my faith. I carried Lewis down from Dun Govaun, with Brother Crimthann silent beside me. We returned to the community and the Abbess was moved to tears, that the brave pagan had given his life to rescue our brother. Yet everyone agreed the story had a happy ending: for hadn't Lewis accepted Christ's grace and gained an immortal soul? And his body was laid on a bier in our little church, and we celebrated a grand funeral Mass for him. That night I kept the dead watch for my friend, alone with the tall candles around his body and my sorrow and exhaustion.

At some hour in the night I opened my eyes and they were there, the two strangers. One was a knave in oil-stained clothes. The other wore the fine garments of a gentleman. They were standing at the bier and the knave had his hand on Lewis's face, prizing open one eye with his dirty thumb. I leaped to my feet.

The gentleman turned coolly to face me. "I suppose you're the one we have to thank." He gave a brief bow. "My name is Aegeus. We've come to collect our friend here."

"Can you make him live again?" I asked.

"That's what we're determining now." He nodded at the knave, who had pulled open Lewis's mouth and was examining his teeth. I didn't like to see him handled so disrespectfully. "What do you think, Barry?"

"Maybe." The knave gave Lewis's hair a casual tousle. "Most of the organs have died. He'll be in a regeneration vat for a few years, but he might be all right."

"What about his memories?" I demanded.

"Probably wiped out." The knave yawned. "Maybe retrievable. We won't be able to tell for a while."

This so broke the heart in me that I knelt down, with tears brimming in my eyes. The one who called himself Aegeus paced close and stood over me.

"But let's talk about you, my friend. You've seen a lot more than you ought to have seen. What are we going to do about you, eh?" I looked up at him sharply. He was smiling a hard smile.

"I took a vow," I told him in indignation. "To bury that damned silly book and keep silent about what he had to tell me. I don't break vows." It was true, then.

"The silence of the confessional, eh?" His face became much friendlier. "Perhaps we can do business, after all. A mortal who knows enough to keep his mouth shut can benefit from being our friend, you see. What do you want in life, anyway? Land? Cattle? Or, wait, you're a monk. Something pretty for your church, here?" He waved a hand and looked around.

"Only heal him." I nodded at Lewis. "Only save his mind, if you can." I thought of all the stories of enchantment Lewis knew, all the remarkable people he must have known, the things he must have seen: Rome in its decline, perhaps the Blessed Patrick, perhaps even the old heroes when they breathed mortal air and hunted the red deer.

"Of course we'll make every effort. He's a highly valued operative, after all," Aegeus told me. "Now, look. You do as he told you, and keep your vow of silence, and you'll be a fortunate man. I'll see you again soon. Let's go now, Barry."

"Right," replied the knave, and pulled Lewis from the bier and threw him over his shoulder like so much merchandise. They walked toward the door.

"But his body," I cried. "It'll be gone! What will I tell the others?"

Aegeus stopped and turned, tapping his upper lip thoughtfully with one finger. He grinned. "Ah. You can tell them a miracle occurred. The Holy Angels came and carried him off bodily to heaven! This is an ignorant age. They ought to believe that."

I only stared at them, too shocked to reply; and he waved cheerily, and they walked out into the darkness. I think it was then that my faith died in me utterly.

Yet in the end I told his lie, for I could think of nothing else, and my brothers and sisters rejoiced, and the story spread, so poor Lewis became vener-

ated as a local saint. But I knew the truth for what it was. And, as I thought
over the whole story—what the Prince had said, what Lewis had revealed of
himself—nowhere in it could I find any trace of Christ's power, or His mercy,
or His love. My God was irrelevant to those pale folk hiding in their mound,
and to that knave in his oil-stained clothes.

And for all that we had a celebrated saint and a miracle to call our own, the
peace of our community had been broken. There was never any molestation
after that, mind: the night after Lewis's body was taken away, there was a violent thunderstorm and brilliant lights playing about on Dun Govaun. Perhaps the kin had fled to some new hiding place, or perhaps Lewis's Company
had avenged his injury.

But Brother Crimthann tried to hang himself one night. He was caught
and survived, yet our Abbess had to watch him continually as she would
watch a child, for he would weep and rage at the smallest thing.

My life was no joy to me, either. I kept faith with Lewis, I found the lead
casket and buried the *Codex Druidae* where he'd bid me, deep down under the
stones of the scriptorium floor. For all I know, it lies there still. Indeed, I have
assurance it must.

I found his harp, too, and kept it safe, though it broke my heart to see it and
remember his voice. I thought perhaps the two strangers might come back to
claim it. The more I thought about this, though, the more I began to dread the
idea. One night I took the harp and what little I owned, and, breaking my
vows, I fled the community to lose myself in a distant land.

It was for nothing, anyway. On the third night of my exile, I woke in the
heather to find Aegeus crouching beside me.

"This'll never do, you know," he told me sternly. "You're supposed to stay
where we can keep an eye on you."

"I buried your book!" I sat up. "I told your lies. Leave me in peace, can't you?"

"Can't do that, I'm afraid." He shook his head. "You're a security risk.
Look, we're not so bad. You'll have to come with me now, but you'll be all
right. You'll work for us and live a long, happy life."

So I went with him in the strange ship, and I learned more of the way the
world is run—no Christ there running it, either—and I was given lands and
livestock and a fine house. All I must do to earn my wealth is keep silent and
open my door, certain nights, to certain strangers who come and depart in

haste, after meals and a change of clothes and horses. Sometimes they leave packages, which other strangers come and collect later.

They seldom answer my questions, and never my inquiries about Lewis; so I fear that they failed to save him, though in most other respects they seem as powerful as gods. I have seen many things that men would think were miracles. I am supplied with every comfort a man might want for his flesh. My masters seem to think it will make me happy.

But I have not been happy since: until this last Samhain night, when I lay in my too-comfortable bed with banked coals warming the room, very unlike the hard pallet on chilly stone in the place where I was blessed.

I heard my name called, there in the darkness. I sat up and saw Lewis, just as he had been, brightly lit as though he stood in sunlight. He looked puzzled.

"Am I having a dream?" he wanted to know.

"No; it must be me dreaming, because you're dead," I told him.

"Dead?" He looked appalled. His jaw hung slack a moment before the memory seemed to come back to him. "Good Lord, what am I doing here then?"

"Well, I—I'd supposed you'd come back to offer me spiritual comfort," I ventured.

He shook his head dubiously.

"Sorry, old fellow, I haven't a clue. Unless—perhaps they've succeeded in reactivating me." His eyes lit up and he rubbed his hands together. "Not that that explains how I got here, but I'm not complaining."

"But you're not really here," I pointed out.

"Of course I am! Look." He made a grab for a pitcher that sat on the table, but his hand passed straight through it. He overbalanced slightly and righted himself.

"Damn! How embarrassing." He frowned. "Well—I suppose the possibility exists that I'm actually floating in a regeneration vat at a Company repair facility, and I'm coming to you now by means of some sort of electromagnetic projection."

"What on Earth does that mean?" I rubbed my eyes wearily.

"I don't know how I'd explain it to you. Actually I don't know if it's even possible," he added. "No, I think I'm the one having the dream, and you're the illusion. That must be it. I'm in a nice warm vat somewhere, with all my organics being regenerated, and my brain's come back online and I'm having a rather peculiar dream. Still . . . you don't look well, Eogan."

"I've lost my faith."

"Gosh, I'm sorry to hear it." He looked sympathetic. He seemed to be searching in his mind for something nice to say, and then an expression of incredulous delight crossed his face. "Great Caesar's ghost! You don't suppose that baptism business actually worked, do you? You don't suppose this is my *soul* talking to you now?" He took a few swaggering steps back and forth.

"I wish I could believe that, Lewis." I leaned my head in my hand.

"I suppose I don't believe it, either. But how can we know for sure? Wouldn't you like to believe that your God would let me into your Christian Heaven? Assuming I died, of course?"

"More than anything, Lewis. If there is such a place, you'll be there. But I don't know," I replied, anguish coiling in me like a snake. "I used to know."

"Oh, who knows anything? If you're simply the result of my nutritive solution being a bit rich, then I'll wake up when the Company decants me and go on about my business of making money for them, forever and ever and ever. And if I'm nothing more than your dream—maybe sent to you because your Christ wanted to cheer you up a little—then you'll wake up in the morning, and go on with your mortal life until it's over. Let's be happy, Eogan. Your life's too short, and mine's too long, to mourn. Do something that gives you joy."

"What?" I demanded. "What, in God's name, can I do?"

"Well . . ." He waved his hand. "You used to enjoy writing, didn't you?"

That was when the stranger, arriving late and pounding on my door, woke me to a black room and unrelieved night.

But then I dared this thing, to write down what I'd seen, and my heart hasn't been so light in ages. Lewis was right: this is real joy to me, the dance of my goose quill across the bare page. Perhaps it would violate nobody's trust to begin it again, the copying down of knowledge? I'm not fit for the Gospels any more, but I remember so many of the hero-tales Lewis told me. The community at Malinmhor has only the one copy we made. I could set them down again.

I will, I'll uncover the harp and watch as the sunlight moves across the fine wood and glints on the strings. I'll imagine Lewis sitting there talking to me, sipping the heather-honey mead, or singing as the birds chatter in the soft air beyond the stone windowsill. We'll set Finn galloping with his band of heroes, and Cuchulainn will perform terrible wonders, and it will all flow out of my pen like gold. God have mercy on me, a miserable sinner; what other grace can I hope for?

Labienus shakes his head, looking pained. It is with some relief that he turns to the next transcript, for though it is of paper no less crumbling and ancient, it is printed in a straightforward and easily readable font, written in simple Cinema Standard. Is it a diary entry? A private confession? Some immortals write compulsively, out of a need to put distressingly eternal lives in perspective. Labienus considers it a weakness. He tsk-tsks at Victor's portrait before reading . . .

The man was floating in blue space, motionless, and his gentle expression suggested that he was enjoying the pleasantest of dreams.

"This is the one I mentioned the other day," said Aegeus in a low voice. "He's been in here for a full decade. It's taken that long to regenerate him."

"Poor devil," I murmured, scanning him and recoiling at what I perceived; nearly every major organ had had to be regrown. "Does it really take that long to replace an immortal heart?"

"As a matter of fact, no," replied Aegeus, watching my expression. "There was extensive damage to his biomechanicals as well, you see. To all intents and purposes, this man died."

If he was anticipating incredulous horror on my face, his expectations were rewarded. "But that can't happen," I cried. "The biomechanicals are impervious, aren't they? What about his brain?"

"Victor." Aegeus was smiling as he stepped closer to me, but there was no warmth in his eyes. His voice dropped still lower. "You're a Facilitator. We're in a class of our own, you and I. There are certain half-truths told to the others, surely you've come to suspect that! Not lies. Truth Dilute, if you will. If we didn't present the facts in the most advantageous way now and then, the common rank and file would grow unduly alarmed, to say nothing of those idiots in the twenty-fourth century who *think* they're running the Company. All they have to see are the valuables we collect for them, here at our end of time. As long as their shareholders get results, they don't really care how we obtain them.

"Now, what you need to know about this poor fellow is: we've never before seen injuries of the kind he sustained. We don't know what the accident has done to his brain. What happened was a fluke, a singular occurrence. Why, then, upset the hardworking field operatives by letting it be known that they aren't one hundred percent indestructible, when they're all of ninety-nine point nine? The chances of anything of the sort ever happening again are positively astronomical."

"I'm exceedingly glad to hear that, sir," I replied, resolving to withhold my questions.

"And you may be sure the Company has used this unfortunate opportunity to learn, that we may prevent such damage happening in later models," Aegeus continued, turning to look again at the man. "He was a good operative; doubtless he'd be gratified to know that his misfortune gave us invaluable information. Indeed, with any luck you'll be able to tell him so."

"I, sir?" Was this to be my first assignment? I straightened my spine and attempted to look shrewd and perceptive.

"You," Aegeus said, and my keen looks were wasted on him, for he kept his eyes on the dead man. "He's scheduled to be decanted and revived in three days' time. You're to act as his handler, Victor. His guide. His psychopomp, if you will." He smiled at his joke. "Ease his transition back to immortal life." He turned and fixed me with a direct stare. "Find out how much he remembers about his accident."

Ah. That was the agenda. I nodded, intent on showing him I was a fellow of few words.

In his vat before us the man slept on, with his new heart and his brain that might—or might not—have a half-thousand years of memories within its convolutions.

In my opinion, one of the hallmarks of a true Facilitator is the ability to absorb unpleasant realities while remaining focused on the job at hand. I believe I was rather better at this when I was nineteen; I was not, as yet, aware that there *were* any unpleasant realities for us immortals.

And so I was able to watch with a certain detachment, three days later, as the dead man was dredged out of his vat in a creel of copper mesh and deposited on a steel table, where technicians intubated him and drew the oxygenated fluid from his lungs. I watched him coughing, jerking to life, shiv-

ering and vulnerable, not really conscious yet. He groped blindly as they
hosed the last of the fluid off him—I had enough of a sense of empathy to
hope that they were using warmed water, at least—and then lay quiet under
the rush of air, as the technicians moved in to perform the necessary diagnostic procedures.

I extended a scan myself: he seemed fully functional, as immortal as any of
us once again. The technicians finished with him, lifted him onto a stretcher
and threw a blanket over him.

He was taken to the infirmary dormitory, to a private room, and there I
waited next day for his return to consciousness. I amused myself by studying
his features and speculating on his mortal origins.

My biological inheritance is Saxon and Danish, as my skin and hair bear
witness; he had more of the look of a fair Celt about him, and something of a
Roman as well, in his even and precise features. We were both men of slight
stature, but whereas I am fairly solidly made, he had a swimmer's build. His
body bore no mark of whatever accident had precipitated ten years in a regeneration vat.

I confess that I yielded to the temptation to lift one of his eyelids, ostensibly
to determine what color his eyes were but in truth to see if I could prod him
awake. He slept on. I threw myself back into my chair with a sigh of ennui.

Callous young brute, wasn't I? And so easily bored. Most of my classmates
had already departed Eurobase One, flown off to exciting missions in the
field in places like Byzantium or Spain or Cathay. Of course, they were mere
Preservers: a Facilitator requires more subtle and detailed education. No
grubbing after rare plants or animals for *him*! His job is to sway ministers and
kings, and thereby arrange mortal political affairs to the Company's advantage. He must, therefore, learn from masters. That was why I was still cooling
my heels here, watching the neophyte class toddle through its immortality
process and listening to Aegeus pontificate.

Not that it seemed like pontification then. At the time I hung on his every
word, and, to an even greater degree, on his meaningful silences. The true
significance of silence is another thing one fails to appreciate at the age of
nineteen.

I was examining my thin little beard and wondering if I ought to comb my
mustaches or curl them when I glanced over the top of the mirror and saw
that the man had opened his eyes. Hastily I slid the mirror into my belt

pouch, but the man didn't seem to notice. He was staring at the ceiling in a vacant kind of way. Gradually he began to look around him, to take in the frame of his bed and the wall fresco.

"God Apollo," he whispered to himself.

"H'em!" I enunciated.

He sat bolt upright—nothing wrong with the fellow's reflexes—and saw me at last. "Good—is it good morning? I'm afraid my chronometer seems to be offline," he said.

"I shouldn't be surprised if it were," I said, hugely amused at the joke. "How do you feel?"

"Fresh as a daisy, thanks," he replied. His eyes tracked around the room. "I'm in a repair facility. Aren't I?"

"Eurobase One, in point of fact," I informed him.

"Ah! Of course," he said with some satisfaction, but as he followed the thought further his face grew blank. He was trying to run a self-diagnostic. The results must have been inconclusive, for he turned to me in panic.

"What happened? Something's wrong with my memory. *How long have I been here?*"

At last I was able to let him in on the joke. "Ten years," I told him, grinning, but when the shock registered on his face I felt like the wretched little worm I was. "Sir," I added.

"May I ask who you are?" he said, rather quietly under the circumstances.

"Facilitator Grade Two Victor, sir, at your service." I bowed, trying to do it with military precision. "I've been assigned to help you through your period of readjustment. Do you remember your name?"

After a long moment, he spoke with some care: "To the best of my recollection, I'm Literature Preservation Specialist Grade Three Lewis."

I nodded encouragingly. "You were on duty in Ireland. Do you have any memories of being there?"

He knotted his fingers together. "I remember the village. No, it was a monastery! That was it. I was working with the Christians there."

"Very good," I told him. "Your mission was to plant a copy of the *Codex Druidae* there for future retrieval. You were to bury it in a lead casket. Have you any idea whether you succeeded?"

"Lead," he muttered, wincing. He put up his hands and massaged his hollow temples. "It was shielded in lead. That was the trouble . . ."

"Was there any failure in the casket seal?" I pressed.

"No. I don't know. I couldn't—" He opened his mouth but the words wouldn't come. After a futile moment he made an eloquent gesture, suggestive of releasing a bird from between his hands. "No use. It's gone."

"Do you remember what happened to you?" I ventured to inquire.

"No." He lifted his eyes to mine, pleading. "Do *you* know what happened?"

"No," I told him truthfully. "Only that you were so badly damaged it's taken the Company this long to repair you. You don't suppose the Christians discovered you were a cyborg? Superstitious peasants and all that, jabbing pitchforks into your circuitry?"

"No!" He shook his head decisively. "I remember that much. They weren't a bad lot of mortals. I was quite fond of them."

I nodded, thinking that he was probably right. It would take a lot more than an angry mob to do what had been done to Literature Preservation Specialist Grade Three Lewis.

I let him rest while I hooked him up and ran a diagnostic on his conscious processes. A Literature drone! That was the strangest part of the mystery, to my way of thinking. He wasn't a Facilitator; he wasn't even an Anthropologist, and they were famous for throwing themselves into harm's way with mortals. Just some little Preserver chasing around after old manuscripts. How on earth had he managed to find himself in that much danger?

"There's storage space I can't access," I informed Lewis. "You may have memories in there, or you may have so much oatmeal. In any case, blocked or destroyed, we can't get at them just at the present time. Cheer up! If you feel up to it tomorrow, I'll take you to Level Three for some cautious exercise."

"Thank you," he said absently, staring up at the fresco again, as though the story of his lost time might be written there. "Victor," he added, giving me a brief courteous smile.

I went in search of Aegeus to make my report. To my astonishment, I located his signal in that sector of the compound reserved for the mortal servants.

My astonishment increased when, on emerging from the mountain, I found him seated in the mortal children's play garden, watching a pair of the little monkeys with evident amusement.

"Look at this, Victor." He chuckled, waving me closer. "Look. The boy's hopeless, but the girl's quite a charmer. As they go, of course."

I followed his gaze and was, quite frankly, appalled at what I saw. They couldn't have been more than five or six, but had evidently sustained some sort of abuse in their brief lives to date. Had they been rescued from a cellar? Their ghastly pallor, their emaciated appearance, their attenuated limbs in proportion to their swollen bellies and domed heads, all bespoke neglect. What had the poor things done to deserve such treatment?

The boy could never be made right. He had retreated from the sun to a nest of shade under a bush, and sat there rocking to and fro, silent, keeping his hands clapped tight over his eyes. Probable mental retardation, too—severe alopecia with only the barest traces of clumps of hair on his pale scalp.

The girl showed more promise, was even pretty in a terrible sort of way. Her hair was fine as floss and stood up like flames all over her head. She had picked a double handful of poppies and was playing some inexplicable game with them, sweeping them back and forth, crooning to herself in a thin voice. She might be mad; she might simply be a child absorbed in play. She had great pale blind-looking eyes, enormous eyes in her tiny weak face.

No, this was no abuse; some sort of chromosomal damage. Sad, but it happened amongst mortals. I couldn't fathom what these two imps of misfortune were doing at a Dr. Zeus base, however.

"Their names are Fallon and Maeve. I wanted you to see them, Victor," Aegeus told me.

Wanted me to see them? "Who rescued them?" I inquired, trying to keep the horror out of my voice. Aegeus turned to regard me.

"No one rescued them, my boy. They've spent their whole lives here, at Eurobase." He watched me closely to see what my reaction would be. Under the circumstances, frank honesty seemed advisable.

"Sir, I confess myself to be utterly baffled," I said, sitting down abruptly. My movement drew the little girl's attention—apparently she wasn't blind—and she came wafting toward us, waving her poppies our way. I found myself drawing back, hating the thought of her touching me, and felt prompt shame. "These are genetic defectives! Certainly not fit for the immortality process. They're useless even as servants. What are they doing here?"

"Genetic defectives," Aegeus repeated thoughtfully. "Yes, you'd think so, on first glance. And if I told you that they are, in fact, very far from being defective? That they represent a new and improved strain of *what they are*?"

"You'd confuse me even further."

"Good lad! You're learning never to lie to a superior. You've earned another morsel of knowledge reserved for Facilitators alone, Victor. Observe little Fallon. You're not seeing him at his best today—he doesn't care for the outdoors much—so I dare say you'd be rather surprised to see his playroom.

"Fallon has all manner of wonderful toys there. There's a clockwork galley full of tiny manikins who actually make its oars move. There's an orange tree in a pot, in whose branches blossoms burst forth, wither, and are replaced by fruit, which is small and green and then expands, only to wither and be replaced by buds once more—and all worked by a device so subtle it's beyond my comprehension. There's a camera obscura, though it seems to work in reverse somehow.

"Fallon doesn't play with his marvelous toys, you understand. He doesn't quite comprehend *play*. He made them."

"I see, sir," I said, thinking I did. "What might be called an idiot savant."

"Not at all." Aegeus held out his hands to Maeve, who had come to the edge of the grass and stopped there, pacing back and forth in her slow dance, trailing her flowers and watching him out of the corner of her eye. What a smile now lit her face, as she accepted his invitation and stepped forward, crossing some magic line that had forbidden her to venture onto the pavement until bid. The poppies fell, forgotten; she took Aegeus's hands in both her own and pressed her mouth into his palms, one kiss and then another kiss.

"Pretty Maeve shows such promise, I'm sure she'll be a great lady some day," Aegeus told her. "Shan't she? With so many fine clothes, and a garden full of flowers, and lovers and lovers to pick them for her. Maeve is so wise and good. Though she doesn't make clever toys like Fallon, does she?"

The tiny creature's expression changed at that. Her upper lip drew back from her teeth—they were barely visible, the faintest dots of pearl in her colorless mouth. I realized she was looking disdainful. Then she spoke, and I nearly jumped out of my skin.

"Fallon makes toys for *me*," she told us, in a voice like a silver flute.

"Does he indeed, my treasure?" said Aegeus.

"He does. I tell him, and he makes them. He will do anything if I tell him."

"You see how it is, Victor?" Aegeus patted her cheek fondly. "The little girl gives the orders, the little boy obeys them. If she took it into her sweet head to order him to fly, why, he would! He'd devise some brilliantly simple mechanism neither you nor I might have thought of in a thousand years, perfect and immortal creatures though we are. Isn't that so, pretty Maeve?"

But she'd lost interest in what he'd been saying; she was staring away enraptured at the pattern of sunlight and leaf shadows on the garden wall. Aegeus let go of her hands and she drifted away from us, lifting the hem of her gown as she went, her slow dance resumed. She found her way to the wall and danced for the shadows a while, and then fell to running her fingertips over the stones, tracing their pattern under the pattern of light and shadow.

"These aren't human children, are they?" I stated.

"Oddly enough, they are," Aegeus told me, watching Maeve. "Rather more human than you or I, my young friend, given what we are. Not a kind of human one sees often, however, in spite of the fact that they've always existed. Certainly not *Homo sapiens sapiens*. These creatures are on the order of hybrids, actually. I believe the designation that's been decided on is *Homo sapiens umbratilis*."

Man of the shadows? I'd have been fascinated, were I not so repelled.

"We got the genetic material in Ireland," Aegeus explained. "Ten years ago. A distress call came in from a disabled operative, in a place called Malinmhor. We went in to pick him up for repair, and what a mess we found!"

"Lewis?"

Aegeus nodded. "So badly wrecked he'd been unable to help himself. The local monks had had to rescue him, for heaven's sake. The burning question of the hour, of course, was: who on earth could have done such damage to one of *us*?

"We made it our business to find out pretty damned quickly, as you can imagine. It seemed the holy monks weren't the only mortals who had a community at Malinmhor! There were creatures living in a warren nearby. Some sort of fantastically inbred mortal family, as near as we could tell. Quite subhuman, stunted physically and emotionally. Their brains were so far from normal that ordinary solutions to problems were quite beyond them, but they'd developed a remarkably sophisticated technology to compensate.

"And they knew about us." Aegeus smiled. "At least, they had created a disrupter field to protect themselves against cyborgs. Lewis blundered into it when he ventured inside their hill with one of the monks. Bad luck for him, but not necessarily for us."

"I see, sir," I exclaimed. "He led us to an exploitable resource!"

"Precisely," said Aegeus, smiling. "You've got an Executive's grasp of the situation, I'm pleased to observe. Waste nothing! Though of course we had to wipe them out. No one damages Company property, even a lowly Preserver, with impunity. But we helped ourselves to their genetic material first, and then we set a grand breeding experiment in motion."

A grossly illegal one, but it certainly wasn't my place to say so. We Facilitators are frequently obliged to weigh the greater good against mere regulations, or so it had been explained to me.

"The first pair we got died, poor little things. I think we very nearly have the mix right now. *Sapiens* enough to communicate with—Maeve at least— and *umbratilis* enough to provide us with certain opportunities. And what's that proverb—? 'Keep your friends close, but your enemies closer'? Look at this, Victor, look what she can do."

Aegeus pointed at the girl, who had turned to the boy and fixed him with an imperious stare. Though he could not have seen her—he had his hands still pressed to his eyes—he turned in her direction like a blind worm. Slowly, clumsily, he got to his feet and came to her side, groping with his hands out before him, keeping his eyes tight shut and his head turned from the sun. He looked like a new-hatched bird, with his pinched face and sealed eyelids.

Impatient with his slow advance, she seized his hand and yanked him closer. He stumbled forward and bumped his head against the wall. She paid that no notice, but pressed his fingertips to the stones, trying to make him feel the pattern as she had done. No use; he opened his virtually toothless mouth and wailed, and I was startled to hear the quite human-sounding crying of a hurt child.

"Oh, dear, he's bumped his little head. Let him alone, now, Maeve, beauty," said Aegeus. He went to them and picked up the boy, who curled into his shoulder to hide his face. Something about his movement was horribly like a grub burying itself in earth. "Poor Fallon. He needs to go back inside. Come along, pretty girl."

Maeve had been staring blankly at us, but as soon as Aegeus extended his hand she took it, smiling. He walked away, leading her and carrying the boy, for all the world like a loving father and his two children. I followed after a moment, thoroughly unnerved.

"You've taken this very well, young Victor," Aegeus told me. "No less than I'd have expected of you, however. You understand that this is all highly classified?"

"Of course, sir."

"Of course. Now, having said that—" Aegeus gave me a shrewd look over Fallon's bowed head. "Just how much does the unfortunate Lewis remember about his accident?"

"Almost nothing, sir," I replied.

"Very good," said Aegeus. "*Very* good."

I need hardly say that I was tremendously flattered at being made party to such secrets, though I had bad dreams that night, and for many others, wherein dreadful pale children came and stood beside my bed. Aegeus must be grooming me for some powerful inner cabal, surely! I decided to curl my mustaches after all, when they grew in sufficiently.

"Good morning, Lewis." I announced myself after peering around the frame of the door to be certain he was awake. He was indeed; he'd pushed back a tray of half-finished breakfast and was staring fixedly at an access code pla-quette. I could see the flashing green letters reflecting in his eyes as he inte-grated at high speed. "Catching up on current events, are you? I trust you slept well?"

"Yes, thank you." Lewis shut off the flow of codes and looked up at me. "Victor. No problem with new memories! I don't suppose you've been able to learn anything?"

Nothing I had any intention of telling him about. I smiled apologetically and held out the clothes. "What about a bit of fresh air and exercise?"

"That's a splendid idea," he said with genuine enthusiasm, and climbed out of bed and dressed himself without further prompting from me. Wasn't he game? Just the sort of mild-mannered chap to obey all Company directives. A good fellow, but nothing more than a Preserver, after all.

"I wonder if it might be possible to interview the rescue team that brought me in?" he inquired as we made our way up to Level Three.

"Not a bad idea," I conceded. "Of course, it's been ten years; I should think it might take a while to track them all down. Now, we'll start you on the Cletes Reflexive at primary speed, if you feel up to it."

"By all means," he said as we stepped out of the lift, so readily I wondered if he remembered what the Cletes Reflexive was.

The testing ground wouldn't give him any clue, if he'd forgotten. It looked like a pleasant formal garden laid out within an immense greenhouse, with flowers and statuary, fountains and paths. It was barricaded with iron bars to a height of fifteen feet all around, and locked securely; but nearly every year some foolish mortal servant trespassed, to his brief regret.

I pressed my palm to the via plate and the gate swung open. Lewis and I stepped in upon the square of white paving where the Reflexive began. "You're quite comfortable with this, old fellow?" I questioned. To my eyes he looked rather nervous, but he grinned and flexed his arms.

"Can't wait! Set 'em up."

So I reached into the top of the hollow post that rose from the pavement, and set the speed at primary. There was a click and the faintest humming noise, quite inaudible I suppose to a mortal. Lewis cleared his throat.

"Let's see, shall I give my memory a test, too? Something from Homer, I think." Lewis stepped out into the gravel pathway and proceeded along it warily as he recited:

" 'Ogygia is an island lying far out at sea, where the daughter of Atlas dwells—' " He sprang aside neatly as a spear came hurtling up through the gravel, sure impalement for anyone with duller senses. He paced on. " '—crafty Calypso, a fair-haired, powerful goddess. Her no one visits, neither god—' " He ducked, avoiding the discus-bearing bronze that spun on its base to strike at him. " '—nor mortal man; but hapless me some heavenly power brought to her hearth, and all alone—' " He leaped from the path and balanced along a row of iron spear-points set beside the way, swift and sure from point to point, a painful walk but the only alternative to treading on the mines concealed on that section of the path. " '—for Zeus with a gleaming bolt smote my swift ship—' " Springing nimbly down he threw himself flat on the path, narrowly avoiding the steel dart a frowning god spat at him. " '—and wrecked it in the middle of the wine-dark sea!' "

He crawled the next few meters, for golden flowers on either side of the path tilted their trumpet-throats and sent jets of acid arching clean across. As he crawled, he continued indefatigably: " 'There all the rest of my good comrades perished, but I myself caught in my arms the keel of my curved ship—' " He scrambled to his feet as soon as it was safe, and dodged the stone post that came bashing across the path. " '—and drifted for nine days.' "

An espaliered tree let fall a little crimson fruit, which rolled down the embankment to fall at his feet. He snatched it up and flung it from him, reciting: " 'Upon the tenth, in the dark night—' " There was a bright flash and detonation from the far end of the greenhouse. " '—gods brought me to the island of Ogygia, where dwells Calypso—' " He paused at the edge of the pretty meandering stream, just long enough to crouch and spring into the air, some ten feet above the inviting stepping-stones. From the shadowy water beneath them great eels darted up in frustration, following Lewis with their dead eyes.

He landed safely on the opposite bank and went on: " '—the fair-haired, powerful goddess. Receiving me, she loved and cherished me—' " He began to sprint now, past the inviting bench that would have tipped him backward into a pit. " 'And often said that she would make me an immortal—' " Whirling automata rose from the lilies beside the path, armored figures bearing razor-edged scythes, and the last ten meters of his journey were an intricate dance at tremendous speed through their zone of hazard. " '—young forever!' " Unshredded, he somersaulted through the air and landed beside me again.

"Not bad," I told him, comparing his time to the optimum score. "Care to try it again on intermediate?"

He improved time on the second round, giving me some of the *Elder Edda*, and went on to advanced with a bit of second-rate stuff by Ausonius.

"Though frankly Ausonius is rather second-rate at his best," Lewis admitted, crashing to the pavement as he completed the third round. "Nice enough fellow, as I remember, but the muses kept their distance."

"You remember Ausonius?" I inquired, unlocking the gate.

"Yes! Quite clearly. Beautiful estate in Gaul. He quite knew how to entertain a guest, even if he couldn't write an original line to save his life." Lewis followed me out and I led him down the hall to the sauna. "I remember Ausonius, I remember everything. *Except what happened in Ireland.* Didn't the Company send in investigators? In ten years I'd have thought they'd have found out something, talked to people at least. I remember monks and nuns they might have interviewed—"

His questions were certainly good ones, just what I'd have been asking myself if by some unthinkable chance I were in his position. A distraction was in order . . . I watched his face sidelong as we passed the door to the gymnasium baths and kept going.

"Excuse me, but wasn't that the door we wanted?" He pointed back along the hall, slight panic in his eyes. Was this another hole in his memory? I grinned and threw open the door to the executive baths.

"Well, old man, if you like—but I thought you'd enjoy a bit of rarefied atmosphere, after what you've been through." I strutted into the deluxe bathing accommodations reserved for Facilitators and their guests. Lewis stepped across the threshold after me and stared.

"I don't remember this," he said, taking in the bathing grotto with its elaborate mosaics in porphyry, in gold and semiprecious stones. The attendant mortals hurried forward to disrobe us—I suppose they got rather bored in there all day, with so few of us to wait on—and in short order we were being steamed, splashed, and scrubbed with fragrant oils. For some little while there was no conversation other than groans of pleasure. I couldn't imagine a drone got an experience like this very often, and Lewis certainly seemed to be enjoying it to the fullest.

Though he did look over at me during our third soak in perfumed waters, when the servants had temporarily retired for fresh towels, and murmured: "Please understand that I don't want to complain, but—is this really appropriate? Having mortals wait on us this way?"

"They're enjoying it!" I scoffed. "Can you imagine what they'd be doing if they weren't working here? Starving, most likely. Scratching out a living on miserable little stony farms and dying young."

"I suppose so," Lewis agreed reluctantly. "But, you know, it never used to be the policy—we're their servants, really, not the other way around."

"Exactly, and we work a good deal harder for them than they do for us," I explained to him, as though he weren't my senior by a good four centuries. But I outranked him, you see, and I thought that gave me insights that might never have occurred to one of his class. Yet I was merely parroting Aegeus as I went on: "After all, our lives are dedicated to preserving the best of their world for them, all their art and literature, and occasionally even their wretched mortal selves. Don't we deserve a little luxury?"

"This is rather a lot of luxury," Lewis observed, as the fresh scrubbing team came on duty: a pair of mortal girls, identical twins, looking flushed and lovely in exceedingly brief cotton tunics. Aegeus had personally selected them for the sauna, and I couldn't resist a smirk as Lewis's eyes widened at the effect.

"I think, on the whole, that this old place has seen some distinct improvements during Aegeus's administration," I said judiciously, looking up one brief tunic as my maiden came to swathe me in a towel and lead me to the massage table. "Worked wonders, hasn't he? Took a great rambling old training compound, and transformed it with grace notes for all the senses."

But Lewis wasn't listening, had actually engaged his girl in conversation, *in her own language.*

"You don't mind this work, child?" he wanted to know!

"I know nothing but happiness, my lord," she replied in the hushed tones the mortals were encouraged to use. But she dimpled at him, and I had the jealous fancy that Lewis got the pleasanter and more thorough massage that afternoon. There was just possibly a bit of edge to my voice when I inquired, as we went on after we'd been dressed: "Does any of this seem to have helped your memory?"

"Not much, I'm afraid." Lewis looked apologetic. "I've been in awe. This is all quite a contrast to what I remember of Ireland."

"Well, you were out in the freezing peat bogs, among monks," I pointed out. "Living in cells like flint beehives! No wonder this place—" But he had stopped, staring at me, or through me, with a haunted expression.

"Beehives, yes," he muttered. "Hives. Termite mounds. Oh, what was it? The brothers in their hives and the . . . damn, damn, damn. *Something* almost in my mind. I can't get it clear."

"That's bound to be a good sign," I said encouragingly, making a mental note to go straight to Aegeus. "Perhaps your access channels are attempting to reroute."

I changed the subject and saw him to his room, where I left him, promising to return next day for a stroll around the perimeter of the grounds.

Aegeus's private rooms were what one would expect of the brilliant and sophisticated administrator that he was, magnificently furnished. Clearly, becoming an administrator was the goal to be striven for.

Mere field personnel seldom acquired enough personal possessions to adorn a private retreat, and even if they did, they were generally on the move so much it was scarcely worth getting them out of storage. Might I have a classic bronze like that one day, or that fine Samian ware at just such a table, with its carved griffin-legs? To say nothing of that wardrobe!

"Sir." I inclined in the informal bow that was appropriate for the occasion.

"Victor." He waved me in, looking up from his desk. "Sit, please, sit. Tell me how the poor Literature drone is coming along. Any sign of his memory coming back?"

"I'm afraid something seems to be surfacing," I answered.

"Really? What a shame." Aegeus reached for his penknife and began to cut a new quill thoughtfully, slicing away at the shaft with sharp, precise strokes. "Something to do with the programming the Literature operatives get, I suppose. His brain won't stop trying to tell the story . . . and sooner or later he'll access the file where we locked it away."

I felt a slight chill at this, but tried to sound every inch the competent underling as I said with assurance: "I'll simply see to it that he never manages, sir."

Aegeus kept his eyes on the pen he was cutting.

"Will you? Good lad. You'll find what you need in here." He gestured with his knife at a tiny box next to his inkwell, a lovely thing, a miniature chest banded with silver and semiprecious stones. I reached forward and lifted its lid. There was nothing inside but a sealed phial of opaque glass. Drawing it out, I said: "And this would be . . . ?"

Aegeus frowned at his pen. "Something to wipe his memory again, of course. Derived from Theobromos, if you must know! You'll administer it at the first sign of trouble. He may resist; you'll do whatever's necessary."

I sat there speechless a moment. Aegeus lifted his eyes to mine.

"You have qualms? Natural enough. It must seem perilously close to what the mortal monkeys do to one another."

He was correct, though I'd never have said so much aloud, and there was still more: I had been taught, always, that our immortal brains are perfect and inviolable. The mortal *soul* is an illusion, but our eternal consciousness is surely its nearest approximation. That the Company would force one of us to give up some part of himself . . . The horror must have been evident in my face. Aegeus leaned forward and spoke in a low voice.

"Now, young man, we'll see what you're made of. You've been shown something classified, and you understand its importance to the Company. You've had ample opportunity to observe what a comparative nonentity is Literature Preservation Specialist Lewis. You've been given a task, an unpleasant one certainly, but undeniably necessary, and well within your abilities. So much depends on what you do next, young Victor."

He waved his pen in a general sort of way at the splendid room wherein we sat. "A future like mine, in rooms like these, isn't that what you'd like? It's certainly what the Company has had in mind for you, ever since that bright day when your aptitude testing indicated you were Executive material. I can't think for a minute you've any intention of throwing away that future. You weren't given immortal life to spend it down there wading in muck amongst the mortals. That's for talentless little Preserver drones—who'll never miss a memory they'd only find disturbing, after all."

"I shall manage the matter to your satisfaction, sir," I assured Aegeus. He smiled.

"See that you do," he told me.

"I thought we'd go more easily today," I informed Lewis next morning. "Just the stroll around the grounds, and then another session in the baths, eh?"

"Yes, thanks." Lewis accepted the fine cloak I'd brought for him—even in summer, the Cévennes can be chilly—and followed me down the hall with alacrity. "I woke up this morning and realized I'd been dreaming of sunlight, and that was when it occurred to me I haven't seen it in ten years! It feels positively unnatural. Do I look pale?"

"Not at all," I said tactfully. We climbed the staircase to the exterior portal and I activated the panel. A moment later we stepped out onto the mountainside, to a wide view of heath and stony ranges. Lewis's face brightened at once. He drew in a deep breath of air. "You're a nature enthusiast, I gather?" I said.

"Not particularly," he admitted. "But even the middle of nowhere has a certain savor, when you've been out of commission as long as I have. Look at this! Rabbit tracks. Birds. Smoke at fifteen kilometers—that's a village of mortals, isn't it? It's, let's see, it's early summer—they're haymaking down there, can you smell it? And there are cattle pastured over there, somewhere, and I can smell apple orchards. Chestnut trees. Ah!" He rubbed his hands together and started forward, his cloak trailing after him through the brush. I followed dubiously.

"We ought to go no farther than the perimeter," I said. "I thought we'd walk along the edge to the gate and go back in through the quadrangle. There are some really exquisite pleasure gardens concealed back here—"

"Oh, by all means." Lewis stopped and allowed me to take the lead. "I'd love to see a fountain again. Never in my life imagined I could be so hungry for sheer sensation! Do you suppose we can arrange to go out tonight? What on earth will the stars look like to me now?"

"Do things really seem so different?" I asked, eyeing him as he strode along beside me. He looked different in the sunlight, certainly. His pale features had lit up with warmth and color, his eyes shone.

"Yes, absolutely," he told me. "It must be the near-death experience. You wouldn't have any idea how long it'll be before I'm given another posting, would you?"

"The Company will want to be sure you've fully recovered," I told him, rather peevishly, because we had just come to the pavilion gate and he was failing to react to the grand spectacle of the pleasure gardens. But he was only a drone, after all, wasn't he? "I should think you'd be in no hurry to go back down there. Not when you've got the run of all this."

I waved an arm at the expanse of perfect lawn, the fragrant stepped terraces of flowers arranged in subtle gradations of height and shade, white through cream pink through deepest rose, the trees artfully clipped and trained to render each one the flawless expression of an artist's conception of a tree. And Lewis was old enough to remember the classical world, and so surely he could appreciate the statuary that rose in graceful postures here and there! Extravagant passion in tones of snow, masterworks by Praxiteles that had never known defacement by mortal vandals, having been bought new from the master himself and shipped straight here to this garden *from his studio*. Really, what drab mortal place could compare?

Lewis hastened into the garden after me then, and made a point of exclaiming over everything I showed him. But why on Earth should I have tried to impress him? Why should I have any regard for the opinions of a miserable little scuttler after scrolls and codices? Did I need further proof he was beneath my concern, when the poor fool was eager to go down amongst the monkeys again and resume his work? Bargaining with savages for their inky and imperfect knowledge!

As Lewis was widening his eyes in polite appreciation of a particularly fine group representing the Three Graces honoring some dictator or other, I had a sudden inspiration.

"Of course, this is nothing, compared with the library," I remarked casually.

"Splendid collection," Lewis agreed. "I remember it well."

"Ah, but not the New Wing, I don't think," I told him slyly. "There have been some improvements in recent years. You'll remember the old electronic stuff, I dare say. Aegeus has made a few interesting acquisitions for us. Would you care for a look at the originals of Aristotle's *Treatises*?"

Yes! Now I'd got his attention. Lewis turned around to stare at me in such haste he nearly tottered on his long cloak.

"The originals?" he gasped. "You're never talking about the books Theophrastus left to Neleus? The ones Faustus sold to pay his gambling debts?"

"The very same," I told him smugly. "The complete set, I need hardly add. They were in wretched shape, of course, but we've had them restored—perhaps you'd like to give us your opinion of the job we've done?"

"I should say I would," Lewis cried, and nearly raced me the whole way to the library.

I was gratified to watch his astonishment, confronted with Aegeus's work. The library that Lewis remembered was a rather chilly place, dull banks of electronic storage with a few plain work terminals and interface consoles. Not a cozy room, or one that invited lingering.

Ah, but Aegeus's new wing opened out of the old like a blossom out of a dry gray stem. Through paneled doors one stepped into the beautifully climate-controlled chamber beyond, jewel-toned, richly carpeted and indirectly lit, hung with tapestries that Aegeus had had specially commissioned by masters, celebrating the literary glory of the classical world. There were plenty of inviting little nooks, well cushioned, in which one might curl up with a scroll some Preserver like Lewis had snatched from the conflagration of time. There were graceful Roman bronzes depicting the Nine Muses ranged along the wall of terminals and consoles, where one could pull information out of the depths of the sea-blue screens like a supplicant coaxing an oracle to speak.

But it was the wide glass case along the eastern wall that was the glory. Safely displayed there were the treasured texts, works known to mortal scholars only by paraphrase, but possessed by us in their entirety! The complete poems of Archilochus and of Sappho, all one hundred twenty-three plays of Sophocles (mortals had been able to keep only seven!), Theophrastus's *General History of Science* and—the very jewel in the crown—the complete works of Aristotle himself, the lost manuscripts that had passed through so many tragicomical adventures before disappearing from mortal ken forever in a cheap little shop in first-century Rome.

Lewis stood staring, taking in the beauty, the elegance, the rarity. Inexorably he was drawn to the cabinet at last, as though it were exerting a magnetic force. There he pressed his palms against the glass and looked down at what was, after all, just so much brittle old paper.

"Oh," he said quietly. Good gods, I thought to myself, is the man crying?

A mortal servant had risen to his feet, and came close now with an inquiring look. I turned and crooked a finger at him.

"Fetch up a siphon and some of the thirty-year-old single malt, if you please. Or—no! Let's have wine for the occasion. I think a bottle of Falernian would be appropriate, don't you? Or perhaps Valpolicella?" But Lewis wasn't listening to me. "Bring both," I told the servant, who bowed and sped away in silence.

I am afraid I was swaggering, as I joined him at the cabinet and entered the code to unlock it. "Shall we see what the old boy had to say?" I suggested.

"Oh, but they're nearly a thousand years old," Lewis gasped, actually wiping away a tear. "We shouldn't, really—"

"Nonsense. They've been stabilized long since. Here we go!" I drew out one of the nasty old things and unrolled it on the reading table for his perusal, under the soft light of a shaded lamp. He bent over it like some priest over an altar, biting his knuckles.

"Rather a nice prize, wouldn't you say?" I said smugly. "This was Hieron's work—have you met him? Very good man in your line, handles the Mediterranean acquisitions."

"Oh, how I wish I'd been stationed down there," Lewis moaned, finally giving in to irresistible impulse and reaching out to touch the scroll. "Look at this. Aristotle's observations on Egyptian technology!" He began to read avidly, and I realized I'd lost my audience again. I sank back onto one of the couches to wait impatiently until the mortal returned bearing our wine.

I sampled both carafes and decided on the Valpolicella. At my nod, the servant filled our cups. Lewis was too immersed in the scroll to notice. He chuckled suddenly and read aloud, in the original Greek:

"'This art of flight is said to have been present in Egypt from the time of

Horus, and I am assured that the priests conceal detailed charts for travel between the stars, which the kings of the former time steered between as mere men followed the course of the river; though none now have understanding of the sacred texts.'" Lewis looked up, grinning, and noticed the servant standing there offering him a cup of wine. In fact, the mortal had been rather craning his head to read over Lewis's shoulder. When he noticed this, what should Lewis do but step aside with a gesture of invitation!

"Please, it's hilarious," he said, smiling. "Do you read Greek?"

"Oh, yes, my lord," the mortal replied, hastening to peer at the scroll.

"Then you'll appreciate the joke. Though you've probably seen it a dozen times!" Lewis looked wistful. "I can't tell you how much I envy you, working here. I'd just start at one end of the case and read my way through."

The mortal looked up a little nervously. "Well—I would, my lord, if I were allowed to open the case."

Lewis's jaw dropped. "You mean you can't?"

"Of course he can't," I told Lewis crossly, sipping my wine. "None of the mortals have clearance to handle anything this valuable. They're *mortals*, after all. Left to themselves, they ruin anything they touch. Isn't that so?" I demanded of the servant. He lowered his eyes and murmured:

"Unfortunately so, my lord."

Lewis stood there speechless a moment before he drew himself up and set his chin. "But Aristotle himself was a mortal," he told the servant! "I think you can be trusted to read this text a little while, don't you, without tearing it or chewing on it?"

"I would never do such a thing, my lord," the servant assured him. "I was trained in library science."

"Well then." Lewis pulled out a chair for him. "Please, sit and read."

I'm not certain who was more shocked, the servant or myself; but after a frozen moment the mortal hastened to obey, as Lewis took his wine and carried it to the cushions next to mine. His eyes were angry.

I must protest against this policy, he transmitted in silence. *Why shouldn't they be allowed to read their own books? Aren't we preserving these things for THEM, after all?*

Old fellow, you must understand, I replied as casually as I could. *He's a good enough creature—and one of ours, of course—but you've been down among them yourself. You know the villainy of which they're capable. Destructive little Bar-*

*bary apes for the most part, and human intelligence only makes them worse. How
many libraries have you seen burned in your time?*

But the mortals built the libraries, too, argued Lewis, sipping his wine. I was at
least pleased to note that he stopped and inhaled the bouquet before taking another, more appreciative sip. *It takes thousands of them to create an archive of human wisdom; only one to set a torch to it. Wouldn't you have to say, then, that the
work of the librarians is more typical of mortal behavior than the work of the arsonist?*

I really didn't know what to say. This was absolutely the last sort of talk I'd
expect to hear coming from someone who'd nearly been murdered by the little brutes.

Well, you've known more of them than I have, I conceded. *Doubtless you've
some insight I lack. I wouldn't want to leave even that one alone with the scroll,
though. What do you want to bet he'd slip out of here and run down the mountain
with it, if there were no alarms? He knows it's valuable. He'd sell it in a second if he
had the chance.*

Lewis shook his head impatiently. *You don't understand. We all know why
they're driven to thievery. But I can tell you from experience that mortals love their
literature. When I was in Ireland, Eogan—*

"Eogan," Lewis cried aloud. "That was his name! That was the monk I was
working with—and the abbess sent us out to the hollow hill, after the fair
folk. I thought it was all absurd, I had no idea—" He turned to me. "I'm accessing the blocked files now. We'll have to find Eogan, if he's still alive. He
was there with me, we went into the hill and actually found them—and—he
got me out afterward, when they . . ." He fell silent. Cold sweat broke out on
his brow. The glass vial was in my hand, unseen.

"Perhaps you'd better not—" I began, when all hell broke loose, and from
a completely unexpected quarter.

A section of wall to my left began to move. Seeing it out of the corner of
my eye, I thought it was a draft moving the tapestry at first; then I realized
that the tapestry wasn't there any more, or at least that part of it wasn't. A
rather titillating depiction of Sappho and her companions had vanished in a
pattern of light, and the edges all around it curled up. For a moment one
could glimpse the plaster of the wall behind, illuminated by the same pattern
of light, as though the wall were outdoors and slanting beams of sunlight
were playing through leaf-shadows on it. There came a rumbling like far-off
thunder.

Then the plaster had gone, and one saw the stone and mortar underneath. Then it all dissolved, like mist, and two small figures came walking through. The girl strode confidently, the boy groped hesitantly after, though his great blank eyes were open now. They were both naked.

To be precise, this was the actual moment when pandemonium erupted. Lewis leaped to his feet. The girl looked down, noticed that she was naked, and screamed shrilly. The mortal servant caught up the volume of Aristotle, and ran for the cabinet with it. Only after he'd thrust it inside and shut the cabinet did he take to his heels in the direction of the door, nearly bowling over Aegeus, who was entering in some haste.

"My dress," Maeve shrieked. "My pretty dress! You stupid, *stupid* Fallon!"

She flew at the boy and began to beat him with her tiny fists. He dropped the exceedingly odd device he had been carrying and cringed, putting up his hands to protect his head.

"Not supposed to make my dress go away," Maeve wept. "Just the wall! You bad boy, bad boy!"

"Now, now," exhorted Aegeus, bearing down on them. "Naughty Maeve! Look, you've drawn blood on poor Fallon. Stop this at once." He caught her hands. "It's bad to go out of your room without asking. You've been told and told! It's bad to hurt Fallon, too. You know he was only trying to make you happy."

"But he lost my pretty dress," wailed the child.

"Silly girl, we'll get you another," Aegeus assured her. "Twice as nice and ten times as pretty, shall we? Sweet little Maeve." He lifted her in his arms.

She sniffled and nodded, subsiding, and Aegeus now had leisure to notice Lewis.

Lewis hadn't made a sound, but had backed up as far as he could go and was flattened against the cabinets, as though Aristotle and Theophrastus would somehow protect him. He couldn't take his horrified eyes off the children. Aegeus considered him coldly. The hair stood on the back of my neck as though I were a mortal creature, I couldn't have told you why. But—

"Oh, dear," was all Aegeus said.

Lewis lifted his gaze to Aegeus. He no longer looked frightened. There was wrath in his face, and bleak understanding. He said, very quietly: "What have you done?"

"Poor Lewis," said Aegeus. "You've remembered a great deal too much, haven't you? And now you'll have bad dreams again, when we've worked so hard to make them go away." He sighed heavily and looked at me. "Victor, Lewis has had a nasty shock. Fix him a drink."

No need to tell me twice. I poured out another cup of Valpolicella, dispensing the vial's contents into it with a gesture so clumsily concealed Lewis had surely noticed, had he been able to pay attention to anything but the two horrible children and their protector. I brought the cup to him. Not even looking at it, he raised it to his lips and gulped the wine down.

He didn't bother to scan first. Why should he? He was among his own people, wasn't he? Safe on a Company base, not amongst savages.

He set down the cup and looked across at Aegeus again, saying in tones of accusation—unbelievable nerve, to *Aegeus!*—"They're hybrids, aren't they? This is forbidden!"

Aegeus didn't bother to reply, but the coldness in his face set and froze. Lewis looked down at the boy curled into himself on the floor, at the girl who had forgotten her anger and was staring, fascinated, at the Roman bronzes. She pointed imperiously.

"Fallon," she ordered, "make them dance for me."

Opening his eyes, wide and liquid as a rabbit's, the boy got painfully to his hands and knees.

"Poor things," Lewis gasped. "They don't know what you—"

Then he stiffened and turned to me, terrible question in his eyes. I braced myself, expecting an assault; but he staggered forward and fell, and lay like something discarded on the fine deep carpet.

"Pity," said Aegeus. "Now we've got it all to do again, I suppose."

"I thought—" I stared down at Lewis, who was neither moving nor, so far as I could tell, breathing. "I thought we were simply going to block his memory again."

"To be sure. He's got to be deactivated first, you see?" Aegeus turned Maeve's face to his own. "Leave the old statues alone, dear."

"Yes, sir," I found myself saying. "What will happen to him now?"

"Oh, back to the tank, for further erasure." Aegeus stepped forward and looked down at Lewis's sprawled body critically. "I wonder how much we'll have to obliterate this time. I must take greater care my little monkeys stay in

their cage, in future." He said this teasingly to Maeve, who dimpled. "Pretty
Maeve, can you make Fallon build you something to take away bad dreams?
This poor fellow has such bad dreams. You'd like to help him, wouldn't you?"

"No," she said impishly. "I want a new dress." Aegeus laughed at that and
she laughed, too, like the tiniest silver bell. The boy was still crawling toward
the Roman bronzes, staring up at them with his enormous black eyes.

Labienus turns the page. The next section is a transcript of an interview, one
of his own private intelligence forays. What a wreck the old mortal had been,
knotted with age, what an old mud-colored thing with his white hair and his
network of wrinkles! Unsettlingly like a chimpanzee. He'd had all his wits
about him, at least.

I will tell you about Maeve.

Me, you wouldn't be interested in, for there is nothing extraordinary about
my life. My mother had been shamed, was about to drown herself in the
Loire when one of the immortal lords spotted her and offered her his protec-
tion. This was just before Justinian became emperor of Byzantium, I think, in
the time the mortal men reckoned the sixth century after the birth of Christ.

But my mother's savior was about the usual business of the immortals who
work for their Company, which is to walk among mortals and preserve fine and
rare things that would otherwise be destroyed by them. The lords and ladies do
this, as I understand, because there will come a day in the distant future when
men will need the things they have wasted. In that hour the Company will be
able to open its strongholds and come to mankind's rescue, showering down
its harvest of their treasures. Who could find fault with such benign masters?
Especially as their mercy does not extend to things alone; they save people, too.

Anyway, the mortal girl came with the lord to this mountain, to this ancient stronghold that the immortals call Eurobase One: and some weeks later
she died giving birth to me, for she was not strong.

I was strong, but I was not perfect as a child must be perfect to be given
eternal life. They were very kind to me anyway, the immortal lords and ladies.
I've never lacked anything, never gone hungry a day in my life! I was lucky

that I could live with them, and not with the ignorant savages in the mortal world down the mountain.

And they gave some thought to my future, too: I was apprenticed to old Claude, who was an artist, a genius, master of gardens without peer. The lords and ladies themselves said it was a thousand pities he couldn't be made immortal, but mortal and aging he was. So I was given to him, to climb the high ladders and prune where he directed, and to kneel for hours on the cold earth, planting out hyacinth bulbs where he pointed with his stick. He taught me his art. I was very grateful.

But I don't know where Maeve came from.

I was sixteen when I saw her first, the little creature with the hair like moonlight. She had got into the pergola somehow, though the gate was locked, and she had tugged her feeble brother after her. They were in there making a mess of the pomegranates, pulling them from the espaliers, bowling them around and breaking them open, scattering the red beads without even tasting them. It was their tiny crazy laughter that called us.

Old Claude was so angry with them, he lost all sense; he was especially proud of those trees. He advanced on them howling curses, waving his stick. The children stopped, staring at him, but they did not run as sensible children would. The boy cowered and sank down, hiding his face, covering his big blind-looking eyes. The girl remained on her feet. She looked at Claude with no fear at all, though his stick was whistling in the air and his eyes were starting out of his head in wrath.

He kept coming, and when I saw that she would not move I ran to put myself between them. I crouched over her and Claude's stick came whistling down on my back. That only made him more angry, and he beat me with all the strength of his old arm. I didn't mind; I have a strong back. I said, "Master, the little girl is mad! She didn't know it was wrong."

I was mistaken to think this would make him stop belaboring me, because he got in three more good blows before we heard one of the lords laughing.

"Stop! Stop, if you please, worthy Master Claude," he called, striding down the walk toward us.

It was the lord Aegeus, still chuckling as he surveyed the ruin all about us, the broken branches, broken fruit. The child ran to him and buried her face in his cloak, and he swept her up in his arms, where she looked at us disdainfully.

I knelt at once, but Claude remained on his feet. He took liberties; the lords and ladies allowed it because he was an artist. His back was stiff with his anger. His jowls were flushed red with it. He clasped his shaking hands on the knob of his stick and stared at Lord Aegeus in silence, so that the lord had to speak first.

"Worthy master, my apologies," said the lord, smiling. He knit his brows at the little girl, pretending to be stern with her. He said, "Naughty Maeve! Look what you've done now. Did *you* spoil this pretty garden?"

And she said, "Oh, no!" though her tiny hands were pink with the juice, and that was the only color to her skin anywhere. She looked like a ghost, she was so white.

Claude made a sharp noise in his throat. I looked over at the little boy, who was still trembling where he lay.

The lord said, "You didn't? Who was it, then?" And she pointed her finger at the boy and said, "It was Fallon!"

The lord looked as though he wanted to laugh afresh, but he bit his lips and then he said: "Now, you know that's not true. Poor Fallon doesn't do things unless you tell him to do them. You're the one always getting into mischief, little fairy! I want you to apologize to our dear Master Claude for all this mess."

She dimpled and said, "No!" and Claude shouted: "Most divine Lord, never in seventy-five years of faithful service have I seen such wanton vandalism!" and Lord Aegeus looked at him rather coldly as he said: "Sadly true, Master, for everyone knows the young people of today have no respect for their elders. I can assure you that this child will not misbehave here again, however. Calm yourself! Your boy will clean everything up." And his gaze turned to me and he said, "Rise, boy. And, please, accept my thanks for moving so quickly! My poor cherubs would have broken like eggshell if your master had landed a blow."

I rose awkwardly and ducked my head in acknowledgment of the lord's thanks. I wondered, how could they be his children? The lords and ladies do not beget their own kind, I knew that. They take mortal children and give them immortal life, if the children are sufficiently perfect. But the girl and boy did not look like any mortal children I had ever seen. They were so little and pale, and their eyes were so big.

Anyway Lord Aegeus carried them away, and I cleaned up the mess they'd made.

I saw her sometimes now and then, over the next few years. Sometimes the boy would be with her, though less and less as time went on. There were rumors that he was a genius of some kind, but he never looked well.

She grew up very quickly, and not in the way of being tall, if you know what I mean; she looked like a woman within a few years, with high little breasts filling out the bodice of her gown. She would wade through the beds of annuals picking big bunches of flowers, which drove Claude to distraction, but now that he was aware she was a special favorite of Lord Aegeus he knew better than to complain.

Maybe it was keeping his anger to himself that did for him at last, because he had a stroke when I was twenty. After that I was Head Gardener, and won the title of Master when I devised the three-level topiary walk for the north slope.

The lords and ladies were enchanted with it. They love beautiful things, and they respect artists. Master Simeon by the age of twenty-two! I had all I could ask for in life.

And then I was given more.

When I was summoned to Lord Aegeus's study, I thought he had some request to make relative to my art, maybe for a new kind of rose or rare fruit. They like such things, the lords and ladies. Lord Aegeus was seated by the fire in his study, and across from him in another chair sat his assistant, the lord Victor. Lord Victor was young as immortals go, not really much older than me, and he looked younger already.

Well, they waved me to a third chair. I sat hesitantly, and another mortal stepped forward and poured wine for me, the same wine the lords themselves were drinking. I thought to myself, *This is what it is to be an artist!* and I bowed respectfully over my cup and said, "Thank you, divine Lord."

Lord Aegeus said, "Quite welcome," with a wave of dismissal. He was staring at me in an assessing kind of way, and so was the other lord. I kept a humble silence, as Claude had kept his insolent silences, and it worked: Lord Aegeus cleared his throat and said at last, "Well! You've certainly grown into a sturdy fellow since that day in the pergola. You were only Master Claude's boy then. And you're the master yourself now, are you not? What's your name?"

I told him it was Simeon and he laughed out loud, and the Lord Victor smiled thinly. Lord Aegeus said:

"Simeon! That's appropriate, I must say! Up in the treetops all the time, and as hairy as a monkey, too! But come, don't take offense. All your tests show you're a supremely healthy young simian, and quite a bright one at that."

I murmured my thanks for the compliment. Lord Aegeus said, "Quite," and had a sip of his wine. Then he said, "You've had a few sexual encounters, but you don't seem to have formed any long-term relationships. In light of that, we would like to make you a proposition."

I didn't know what to think. He burst out laughing at the look on my face and Lord Victor turned red.

"No, no!" said Lord Aegeus. "It's only this, good Master Simeon: my dearest Maeve must have a mate, and we've chosen you for the honor."

I just said "Oh," feeling as though I had been struck over the head. He went on: "It should have been Fallon, but he passed away, poor creature. Pity. Still, we learned a lot from him; and dear Maeve is wonderfully vigorous. We have great hopes of her. Now, you needn't be nervous! She may look like a child, but I can personally attest that you won't have to teach her a thing." He grinned broadly and Lord Victor stared down at the floor.

I had a gulp of wine and nerved myself to ask him, "But—if she's your favorite, divine Lord—won't you mind?"

"Mind? Good heavens, no. She's a charming girl, but she is a mortal, as you are. She certainly can't bear *me* children. I'll admit I'll miss our golden afternoons, but the plain fact is, she ought to be bred while she's in her prime." He said the last leaning forward, holding my gaze in a matter-of-fact way.

I said, "I didn't think she was mortal, exactly," and he said: "All too mortal, I regret to say. And human enough for you. But we need very much to see if we can produce something more human still, and so—wedding bells for Maeve."

For a moment nobody said anything, and then Lord Victor cleared his throat.

He said to me, "Does this offend you?"

And I said, "Oh, no, divine Lord," and Lord Aegeus said, "Of course he isn't offended, good sensible solid fellow that he is. Besides, you're rather a romantic choice, I think. You were her knight-errant, once upon a time in the pergola. Yes, throwing yourself between my baby darling and the wrath of Claude. Oh, that's good, *wrath of Claude*!" Lord Aegeus turned laughing to the other lord, who didn't seem to think much of the joke.

I was thinking about Maeve with her tiny perfect face, with her moonlight hair, with her big liquid eyes and silvery laugh. I thought about the bodice of her gown. I told myself that it really would be a great honor to be awarded such a wife. I said, "But will she love me?" and the Lord Aegeus assured me, "She can be quite affectionate, my friend. You'll treat her well, of course—she has never been treated otherwise—and really she doesn't require much. Flattery, presents, a sense of romance. In addition to the obvious physical attentions," and he almost leered as he said it. That was a disconcerting thing, seeing a divine lord with such an expression. They look so wise and noble as a rule.

But I agreed to take Maeve, because I did think she was the most beautiful woman I'd ever seen. I think I'd have agreed even if I'd known about what followed, to be certain my sperm count and motility were all that was desired. They were painful and embarrassing tests, but I told myself it was no worse a thing than careful cross-pollination in an orchard or a greenhouse. And what rose or apple blossom was so fair as Maeve?

But she didn't love me.

She was in a furious sulk the day of our wedding. Still she was lovely; her pouting lips were sensual. Lord Aegeus gave her to me in the pergola, to make it the more romantic, as he said. He had her gowned all in white like a bride, and—to give her a sense of ceremony—placed my hand in hers. He even broke open a pomegranate and presented it to me to feed her, and at first she spat out the bright seeds without even tasting them, fierce; but he spoke to her sternly and she obeyed at last, and crunched them sullenly. They crimsoned her tiny mouth, made her more desirable still.

So it was done, and Lord Aegeus placed his hands on our two heads and said, "Be fruitful and multiply, my children!" Then he gave us a bottle of wine, a good vintage from the lords' and ladies' own cellars, and left me to manage the rest of it.

I took her to my suite in the servants' quarters, hoping she would be impressed with how important her new husband was: but she thought nothing of my rooms, or my bromeliads, or my drafting table, or any of my things. All she would say was, "Hairy beast!" and flounce away from me. She made a game of it, answering "Hairy beast" to anything I said to her: Would you like to bathe, wife? *Hairy beast!* Shall I light a fire, wife? *Hairy beast!* Shall I play the lute for you, wife? *Hairy beast!*

But I still had the bottle of good wine, so I went into my kitchen and prepared a wedding supper: partridges in a sauce of shallots and cream, with fresh bread and white grapes. I set it out, poured the wine and seated myself; she came at once and clambered up into the chair opposite, trailing her bridal finery. Without a word she fell to, reaching into the dish and taking a whole partridge to eat with her hands.

Even in that she was graceful, tearing daintily with her little sharp teeth. I didn't get much of the food, watching her spellbound as I did. You wouldn't believe a girl could have such terrible manners and be so enchanting. She smeared partridge grease on the wine cup when she drank, sucked the bones loudly, greedily tore the soft center from the loaf, even blew her tiny nose in her napkin; but it was all beauty and refinement in my eyes. Beautiful people can do such things, and still be loved.

I drank more of the wine than she did, and it made me bold. When the partridges were all gone and Maeve was idly rolling grapes around on the table, I said: "What about that bath now, wife?"

And she mocked me, she said, "What about that ba-ath now, wife? I don't want to bathe with you. You're ugly and hairy and old."

I told her I wasn't so old, that I was much younger than Lord Aegeus, and she stared with a blank face; then she shrugged so beautifully and said, "But you *look* old." Her gaze wandered to the partridge bones in the dish and fixed on them, suddenly intense. Without looking up at me she said: "Make the bones come alive again!"

I told her I couldn't, and she said: "Yes you can. Just make them stand up in the dish and sing! Fallon could make them do that. Why can't you?"

I told her I wasn't as clever as Fallon. She raised scornful eyes to me.

"Can you make me a new gown without cutting any cloth?"

I told her no, and she said: "Fallon could! Can you make that stick in the fire grow green leaves again?"

I told her I couldn't, and she said: "Fallon could. He could make anything I told him to make, he was so clever. So why should I play with you, stupid thing?"

I set aside my winecup and I said, "Because Fallon is dead, and you're my wife."

She chewed her lower lip and sighed. She said: "My poor Fallon. I was supposed to be Queen in the Hill. He would have done everything for me. We'd have had lots of babies, and they'd have done everything for me, too. Everybody would have brought me presents and played with me." Tears welled in her eyes, perfect as diamonds.

I reached out a hand to stroke her shoulder and she did not draw away. I said, "Don't cry. I saw Fallon. He could never have made babies with you, wife. He was too sick."

"He could!" she insisted. "Fallon wasn't sick. He was just what I wanted him to be. Don't you remember?"

I said, "Remember what?" and she got a sly look in her eyes.

"Ha! You don't have the Memory. Big people don't remember things how they were, but we do. We remember everything from the beginning of the world. Fallon did, and I do, but you can't. Big people think they're so clever, but they're not. We have always been more clever than you."

I said, "Who? You and Fallon?" and she shook her head and said, "Our kin," as though I was just too stupid to waste time on. I said, "We'll make a new family," and she said, "I won't play with you. You don't have the Memory, and you can't make the bones stand up and sing!"

Forgive the plainness, but there was one bone at that table standing up and singing, and I got to my feet and said to her: "Lord Aegeus couldn't do those things either, but you've played with him. We're married, and you'll play with me now."

She stuck her lip out in anger. I wanted to bite it. She said, "He gave me nice presents."

I said, "So will I. Have you ever seen blossom and apples on one bough? I can make those. I can make a rose as bright as your hair, without a single thorn. I can make a pleasure garden all the divine lords and ladies would want for themselves, but it will be yours alone. I can make marvels in the earth, nobody else has the skill to make such places! Even Lord Aegeus. You see?"

I don't know if she saw, crazy as she was, but she didn't fight when I picked her up and carried her away to the bath.

And that was strange, because when we were out of our clothes she was so like a baby I lost all desire. I could have washed her and toweled her as chastely as though I were caring for a child, then, but it seemed our nakedness had the opposite effect on Maeve. She had been capricious snow and ice; now she was a little licking tongue of fire. She laughed and laughed and scrambled all over me in the warm water. I couldn't hold back from her, no man could have, mortal or immortal.

And, I ask you: was it wrong? When she was my wife, and the divine lords and ladies themselves had ordered us to love?

Anyway she liked me very well after that, and let me take her to my bed, and I slept with her in my arms half afraid I'd roll over and crush her, so little she was, a feather, a flame, a snowflake. My wife.

Have you ever been in love like that? I don't think people were meant to live that way forever. How could they? They'd never get any work done. And how can you pay attention to anything but the beloved?

Maeve was a late sleeper, too. Though she walked fearless in sunlight, as dead Fallon had been unable to do, she much preferred the night for wakefulness and play: so of course I kept her favorite hours, though no Master Gardener should do that.

I had duties, and I ignored them. The divine lords and ladies (and, see, this is another example of their generosity) were gracious enough to overlook this fault. They even sent gifts to my quarters, rare wines, fine foods, jewels and gowns for my darling. She accepted the presents and was happy.

My hedges went untrimmed, the annuals went to seed and weeds grew between the stones in the garden paths, but no bolt fell from heaven. Indeed, the botanist lord himself took time from his rare specimens to go out and oversee the work that had to be done before winter set in, bringing in all the potted citrus to the solarium, spreading out straw with his own noble hands!

When she and I weren't making love, or eating, or sleeping, I sat at my drafting table and plotted out the most beautiful garden in the world for Maeve. She loved to climb up beside me and watch, as I worked out the proportions or rendered proposed views in colored chalk. I explained that it was a bower of night, to be at its best in the darkness, like my pretty wife.

She was impatient that it went so slowly. Fallon, I was assured, could have drawn up such plans in an hour, and had the garden miraculously in place before nightfall of one day! That much was surely her fantasy. Fallon may have been a genius, but I know my own work; and no garden is made that way.

Once I asked Maeve where she and Fallon had come from, and she gave me that look as though I were really too stupid to be troubled with and said: "We were stolen."

But I never learned more about it, because she wouldn't say who had stolen the children, or from whom. Perhaps she didn't know.

When she would get bored with watching me she would want to do something else again, so we would, and I thought to myself that even dead Fallon couldn't have worked his miracles if he'd had to stop and do what I was doing every couple of hours. And it seemed to me a fine thing that I should have Maeve's bed and he should have his grave. He may have been a genius, but every time I had ever seen him he had been curling away from the sunlight like a blind worm. My little queen deserved a man, I thought. She'd have a much better life with me!

And, as anybody might have expected the way we were going at it, Maeve had lost her appetite for breakfast before the snows fell. By the time the first bitter storm came down on the Cévennes, there was no possible doubt she was carrying my child.

Now she had no desire for anything but presents, and she was so querulous I had a hard time of it bringing them quickly enough. Her favorite gifts were clothes; Lord Aegeus was kind enough to see that his tailoring staff came to us weekly for measurements and fittings. Warm robes in rich brocade, nightgowns of silk for Maeve's weary swollen body, slippers lined with fleece. When she ordered it I would set aside my work and brush her hair for hours, marveling at the glitter it had, like snow on a bright day. She would close her eyes and croon to herself in pleasure.

Once again I was caring for a child, who had to be coaxed to eat and to take the medicines the divine ones prescribed, who had to be comforted and sung to and held. I told her stories, I told her about how I'd begin her garden as soon as the snows were gone and what rare flowers I'd plant there. This was not conversation, you understand; she wasn't interested in talking; but I thought she liked the sound of my voice.

There was an early thaw that year, and word came from the lords and ladies that I ought to tend to my duties again. I protested that I must stay by my wife, for she needed constant care. By way of answer Lord Aegeus himself came and spoke softly to my little darling as I prepared our supper, and brought a sparkle to her dull eyes. He did me the honor of dining with us; and in the course of our meal suggested that Maeve ought to be moved to the infirmary, as her condition was becoming precarious. There would be nurses to wait on her, and I would be freed to prepare the gardens for spring.

I looked doubtfully at Maeve; but she babbled happily with the lord, more than she would ever deign to speak with me. I saw she wanted to go. So I agreed.

The only thing I could do then was work, desperately, and how I loved my work for the peace it gave me. Can you understand? There was so much to do after the winter, but it wasn't enough. I paced out the area for the wonder I was going to make, Maeve's night-garden, and cut the terraces myself, and laid the forms for the concrete retaining walls and the stairs and balustrades. I spoke at length with the Botanist lord and we prepared seedlings, slips, and shoots. There were fine big hedges and trees in pots, which could be moved on rollers to the locations I wanted and set in place, to shade my darling's pleasaunce as though they'd grown there thirty years. The lord was impressed when he saw my designs.

But Maeve was not impressed, when I would come to the infirmary in the evenings to tell her what I'd been doing. Sometimes she seemed barely to remember me. Sometimes she was impatient and disdainful. Sometimes the lord Aegeus was with her, chatting intimately when I'd come in, and he'd scold her when she was rude to me.

All the while our son kicked in her womb.

So in the morning I couldn't rise early enough, and the lawns had never been so perfectly in trim, and Maeve's own exquisite garden took form and all the immortal lords and ladies came out of the mountain to wonder at it. They took me aside and told me how proud of me they were. They told me I was going to far surpass old Claude. They gave me commissions for designs, pot gardens for their private suites. I devised a way to build a running stream and ferny grotto in a sitting room for the lord Marcus. I devised an arbor of roses black as ink, approached along a walk framed by black irises and black velvet pansies, for the lady Ereshkigal. I devised an apple with the savor of Black Elysium liqueur for the lord Nathan. Immortals have eclectic tastes. But I had their respect, and that was a great consolation to me.

I was hard at work when our little boy was born. Lord Aegeus was with her.

It was the lord Victor who came to me with the news. I was setting the framework of the arbor in place, down on my hands and knees packing in the earth with a maul, when I looked up and saw him there.

He was a cold-looking young man, Lord Victor; so when I saw that coldness laid aside and real compassion in his eyes, I knew something terrible had happened. I scrambled to my feet.

He said, "Master Simeon, Maeve is delivered of a son."

And I said, "Has she died?"

He shook his head. I said, "What is it, then?" and he cleared his throat before he answered me. When he spoke it was with such delicacy, and such chill, and such anger I was almost more concerned for his discomfort than my own. He said: "I have been delegated to inform you that you have the Company's profound thanks for your contribution to their breeding program. A hybrid was successfully delivered this afternoon and, although he does not have the desired characteristics, his survival proves that the program still has a fifty-three point three percent chance of producing its objective. Do you know what that means, mortal man?"

I stammered, "No, my lord."

He said it meant I was divorced now.

I dropped the maul where I stood. I don't think I said anything. He closed his eyes before he went on to say: "The girl will be assigned to another mortal male. They'll try her again, to see what another genetic mix might produce. You're a clever fellow, you must have seen that the Company had plans for Maeve! And you will be rewarded for your efforts, at least: bigger and finer rooms for you, and your operating budget will be tripled."

I said, "May I see the boy?" and he said, simply, "You don't want to see the boy."

It wasn't until years later that I knew what Lord Victor meant.

I found my boy by chance, in the warren of residential rooms attached to the infirmary. It doesn't matter what I was doing there.

I looked in through a door and saw the youth who might have been dead Fallon, except that what clumps of hair he had were the color of mine. He had his mushroom-white hands pressed over his eyes and was rocking himself to and fro on his bed, thumping his big head against the wall. But all across that wall, and on the floor and even in corners of the ceiling, were scrawled equations of such complexity I was dumbfounded, though my grasp of engineering mathematics is better than most mortals'.

Do you know what it is to be cuckolded by a dead man, when he is no more than a film of ashes in his sunless grave? I know.

And it wasn't the first time I felt like a cuckold.

When Maeve had recovered sufficiently from the birth, they gave her to a mortal I barely knew, who worked in their kitchens. He got her with child but did not treat her well, so the immortals took her from him even sooner than they had taken her from me. The child was another boy.

She was passed then to the lady Belisaria's mortal valet, and had another son; and then to the mortal who cleaned the pipes in the baths and reflecting pools, and produced yet another son. I lost track of her bridals after that.

Which is not to say I never saw her. I did glimpse her, now and again, wandering in the gardens to pick flowers or fruit. It was seldom, though, because she was seldom in any condition to walk far. And as the years went on Maeve's tiny perfect face became somehow a parody of itself, the features too sharp, the sweet mouth twisted.

But I finished her garden.

It far surpassed my topiary walk. The lord and ladies said so. How clever of me to make a moon-garden, all white and scented flowers and silvery herbage, best enjoyed under the stars! The scale was a little inconvenient for the immortals, as all the stone seats were set low and the stair risers, too; but the neophyte classes, the children being transformed into immortals, found the place and made it their own. They played there in the long summer evenings. The dark trees echoed back their laughter. I had wanted children to laugh in that garden, but they were not my children.

Still, it was good that the place was used and loved. There was a moment, after I had planted the last narcissus bulb and opened the valve for the fountains, when I wanted to spray it all with Greek fire and destroy it in its completed perfection; but, really, that would have been a very stupid and ungrateful thing to do. If there is one thing the lords and ladies despise, it is wanton destruction, and surely I was better than the mortal men of the villages below us.

So I maintained it, and kept it beautiful. I was kneeling there one day when the lord Victor came and sat on the steps beside me, watching awhile. I was pruning the miniature roses. This must be done as carefully as paring a baby's fingernails, for they are not hardy bushes.

After a time he said, "How are you feeling these days, Master Simeon?"

I told him I was very well, and thanked him for asking.

He was silent, staring at the little bushes. At last he said, "I'm leaving this mountain soon. I'm going off to do some field work at last."

I said, "Are you, my lord?" and he made an affirmative sound. He stared out over the lawns, not seeming to see them. His hand went up to stroke his mustaches. He said, "It's a miserable posting, really. I'm being sent out to chase around after Totila. The Ostrogoth fellow, you know. He's all set to crush Rome again, and the Company needs someone on the spot to protect certain of its interests. I've been accessing data all week. Aegeus thinks I'm out of my mind."

I didn't know what to say, so I just made sympathetic noises, and anyway I could tell that he was only speaking to me as a mortal man speaks to his dog. He went on: "He's right; it's not a good way to begin a career. Not for an Executive Class operative. I'll be wading into the mortal muck with the Preservers! If Aegeus knew I'd requested it, he'd really be horrified.

"But I'm having a, what would you mortals call it? A crisis of faith, perhaps. Not a good thing, when one has a career to consider. I'd really rather not question my beliefs, but the longer I stay here in the midst of all this"— he waved a hand at the pleasure gardens all around us—"the harder it becomes. I think I need to go down into the mortal places and watch *real* cruelty, real stupidity, real vanity. Perhaps then I can look at Aegeus with some sense of perspective. Or at least learn to appreciate his point of view . . ."

His gaze drifted back to me. He sighed, supposing maybe that I had no idea what he was talking about. He said, "Do you know the myth of Jesus, Master Simeon?"

I told him, of course I did. We are all taught about the dark superstitions that the mortals slave under, down there in their villages. Lord Victor said, "Do you suppose the Christ left Heaven for Earth to save mortal souls? Or is it possible he left because God's behavior disgusted him?"

I said it might be so.

He was silent a long time after that. At last he got to his feet, and his shadow fell across the work I was doing. He said, very quietly, "Master

Simeon, I do beg your pardon." I squinted up at him where he loomed dark against the sun and I just nodded, for I couldn't think how to answer him. Then I looked down at my roses again, and I saw his shadow move away from me.

I heard he went down into the mortal world not long after.

Maeve was passed from mortal to mortal, and bore them all nothing but sons, which would have made her a very desirable wife indeed down in the mortal places where women were slaves, as I understood; but it did not seem to be what the immortals wanted from her. This even though some of the boys were quite presentable, kitten-faced children who could converse rationally and walk in the sunlight. Like their mother, they saw no particular virtue in courtesy or other social graces, and like her they were petted and spoiled by the lords and ladies who raised them. Most of them were little geniuses. They were not given eternal life, however.

And then, miraculously, Maeve bore a daughter to the mortal Wamba, who worked as a masseur in the Executive Gymnasium. What a celebration there was! Wamba was given new rooms and all the finery he could wear, and as a further favor he asked if he might divorce Maeve and marry one of the bath attendants, whom he had loved for some time. This was granted to him.

I don't know if Maeve cared. She basked for a while in the glory of having produced a daughter, and really a very pretty one. I saw the little girl when they were parading her around. She was not so pale as her mother. Her skin was like rose petals and her hair like white gold, but she had the same great wide eyes and delicate face.

Yet Maeve, it seems, grew jealous of all the attention paid to her daughter. They caught her pinching the baby when she thought she was alone with it. The infant was taken away, to be raised by Lady Maire, and Maeve found herself in real disgrace for the first time in her life.

Lord Aegeus had no time for her now. All his attentions were focused on little Amelie, the daughter. It was decided that Maeve had performed her duties admirably, and would henceforth be allowed to rest. They allotted her a single room adjacent to the infirmary. She would be given no new husbands, as her health had begun to suffer from constant breeding.

So I asked if I might have her back.

The lords and ladies bestowed her on me gladly enough, commending me for my sense of responsibility, but warned me that marital relations were best not resumed. They didn't need to say so much. Maeve had become a small wizened thing by this time, collapsed and sagging like an old woman, though she can't have been thirty yet. Her skin had begun to mar, also, with thick white blotches of scar tissue. The lords and ladies told me it was from too much exposure to sunlight.

But I couldn't leave her indoors by herself, so I swathed her in a hooded cloak and carried her about with me, and set her in the shade as I worked.

She talked constantly. Mostly it was bitter complaints about the way no one ever brought her presents any more, and how unfair life was. Sometimes she would wander in her mind, and hold long conversations with Fallon. I don't think she recognized me even when her mind was clear. I wasn't angry about this. There had been so many, after all, and maybe time and memory weren't the same for her kind as they were for me. Whatever her kind might be.

I wondered if this was how the immortal ones regard my own race. Are we so brief and small and foolish in their eyes?

Anyway, she didn't last long.

I had taken the midday meal with her, spooned soup into her toothless mouth and napkined her little chin, nodding my agreement to her stream of complaints that never stopped, even while she was eating. Then I carried her to the shade of one of the vast trees I had had transplanted for her, for we were in her own garden that day. I set her down where she could see me, and went to arrange the new bedding plants around the fountain.

I heard her talking to Fallon again, and was grateful, because it meant I wouldn't have to keep nodding to show I was paying attention. After a while I noticed she had grown silent, and I turned. She looked as though she had gone to sleep.

I buried her in the narcissus bed, and then I went to tell Lord Aegeus. Perhaps I should have told him first, but she was already beginning to crumble in on herself; and I was afraid he might have some further use for her poor body.

I found Lord Aegeus in Lady Maire's quarters. They each had hold of one of little Amelie's hands and were pacing carefully beside her as she toddled along, chatting together over her head like happy parents. He actually looked blank for a moment when I told him my news.

But then he was instantly sympathetic, clapping me on the shoulder and commending me for my careful attention to dear old Maeve, telling me how grateful he was I'd made her last days comfortable. He swung the baby up in his arms and held out her dimpled hand to me. He said, "You must thank your uncle Simeon, Amelie. He was a good friend to your biological mamma." And the child patted my cheek and smiled at me with an intelligence that was, maybe, just a bit more human than Maeve's.

Lady Maire exclaimed, "Isn't the sweet thing clever!" And Lord Aegeus kissed Amelie between her wide eyes and agreed that she was the cleverest, most precious little girl in the whole world. I don't think he noticed when I left.

I planted a rosebush to mark the grave. It wasn't one of the elegant ones the lords and ladies so love. It was a wild rose with a single-petaled flower. It bears many thorns, it is half bramble; but the perfume of its white roses is intense, though they bloom in an hour and the petals scarcely last a day.

Labienus sets the documents to one side. He contemplates Victor's picture a while, and presently he begins to grin. So many expressions can be read into that expressionless face, those blank eyes; is he mournful? Resigned? Bored? Labienus is irresistibly reminded of the drawings of Edward Gorey, of all those stiffly miserable Victorian figures trapped in their airless world.

"Disaffected," he says aloud. "Disillusioned. Disinclined. Poor Victor. Aegeus is a pompous ass, isn't he? I wonder whether you'd like a change of masters?"

Yes. Victor must be turned. It shouldn't be difficult.

LOST BOYS

Labienus glances up at a red file folder, secure in its locked glass case with other Red Level Deniability documents. This particular document is the record of an experiment. Certain twenty-fourth-century mortals would be horrified to know any evidence of their work was in Labienus's possession, let alone that their project had been co-opted by him. He smiles wryly, remembering Project *Adonai.*

On impulse, he orders the case to unlock itself, and he pulls the folder down. But another file pops out with it, tumbles down, fluttering open as it comes. Labienus seizes it in midair, but it has opened.

He frowns at the picture he sees, and the memory that rises by association. The shot is of a black man with a lean face, fine features, bright hard gaze like a young hawk's gaze. Labienus remembers the child the man had been. His mouth twists, as though he tasted bitterness.

He has no protégé of his own, no bright second-in-command . . .

He can see the woman in his mind's eye, immortal, blue-eyed and blonde, but without any of the chilly grace he likes in an immortal woman. Unacceptably disorganized for an Executive. Untidy, credulous, earthy, *sentimental.* Just the thought brings her voice back into his ears, gossiping on and on . . .

I was sweeping down my front steps when I first saw him, or rather when he saw me. It's not as though I swept every day! I mean, we had servants like all other respectable households were supposed to; but if you've ever lived in

Amsterdam for any long time, or at least in that year 1702, you'll know how hard it is to get the damn servants to actually serve. My God, so touchy! I mean, look at that wet nurse of Rembrandt's, practically sued him for palimony and I know for a fact their relationship was the most innocent you can imagine.

Where was I?

On the steps, sweeping, because Margarite had retired to her bed with the vapors over something, God knows what, probably because Eliphal had been muttering again about the way mortals cook, which I wished he wouldn't do because she's very clean really for a mortal, and as for using too much butter, we were in *Amsterdam* for Christ's sake, not a health spa, and where was she going to get hold of polyunsaturated fats?

See, this is just the sort of domestic calamity our mortal masters failed to foresee when they founded Dr. Zeus Incorporated, though you'd think being up there in the twenty-fourth century would give them a clue. But that Temporal Concordance of theirs only tells them about big things like wars and disasters to be avoided, I guess; they have to rely on us, their faithful immortal cyborgs, to manage the little details of business for them here in the past. I know they're all scientific geniuses, to have come up with time travel the way they did, but I can't help thinking they must be a bit lazy.

So anyway I told Margarite, there there dear, you just take the afternoon off, and that was how I came to be out on my front stoop with the broom, in my old black dress with my hair bound up in a dishcloth, which is not really the way an Executive Facilitator wishes to be seen by a prospective Junior Trainee, but there you are.

"I am shocked," observed a little voice, "to behold the beautiful and celebrated Facilitator Van Drouten engaged in drudgery better left to mortals."

I looked down with my mouth open and there he was, standing beside the Herengracht in a pose as arrogant as a captain of the Watch, plumed hat doffed but held on his hip in a lordly sort of way. All along the canal other women were leaning over their stoops to look, because you see a lot of unusual stuff along the canal but not often a teeny-tiny black kid with the poise and self-assurance of a burgomaster.

"Hello, Van Drouten," said Kalugin, who was standing beside him looking sheepish. Kalugin's an old friend, a big man but one of those gentle melancholy Russians, and why the Company made him a sea captain I can't guess.

He's the last person to scream orders at people. "I'm afraid we've caught you at rather a bad time."

"Oh! No," I said, when I had got over my surprise. "Minor household crisis, that's all. Goodness, you must be Latif!"

"Charmed, madam," the child said, and he bowed like—well, like a captain of the Watch, and a sober one at that. "And may I say how much I've been looking forward to the prospect of learning Field Command from one of the unquestioned experts?"

I had to giggle at that, I mean there I was looking at my least executive, but he stiffened perceptibly and I thought: whoops. Dignity was clearly important to him. But, you know, it is to most children.

"Very kind of you to say so, with me such a mess," I said, descending the steps. "And welcome to Eurobase Five. Shall we go inside? I can offer you gentlemen cake and wine, if you've time for a snack, Kalugin?"

"Unfortunately, no," he apologized, taking off his tall fur hat as he ducked through the low kitchen door, which was the one we ordinarily used, and not the grand main entrance.

"Not even for a cup of *chocolate*?" I coaxed. He looked as though he could use a little Theobromos.

"Theobromos on duty?" Latif inquired, looking up at us. "Isn't that prohibited, indulging in Theobromos before nineteen hundred hours?"

Of course it is, technically, but the young operatives who aren't allowed Theobromos yet have such puritanical attitudes . . . almost as bad as the mortal masters, on whom it has no effect at all! Our masters were horrified when they discovered that chocolate gets us pleasantly stoned, because they thought they'd designed us to be proof against intoxicants. They even tried to forbid it to us, but must have realized they'd have a revolt on their hands if they did, and settled for strictly regulating our use of the stuff. Or trying to, anyway.

"I really can't stay. My ship won't wait," Kalugin told me, with real regret. "But I have some deliveries—besides young Latif, here—a moment, if you please—"

As he shrugged awkwardly out of his fur coat he transmitted, *And here's the young Executive himself, and good luck with him!*

Oh, dear, is he a brat? He seems like such a polite little boy, I responded, as Latif inspected the Chinese plates ranged along the passage wall.

Polite? Certainly! Even when one doesn't quite meet his particular standards. Kalugin unstrapped the dispatch pouches he'd brought with him. *He graciously agreed to overlook at least four flagrant violations of Company protocols he detected on my ship.*

"Here we are—diamonds for Eliphal, I believe, they've been rather uncomfortable—and these are the credenza components Diego ordered." Kalugin presented them to me with a slight bow. "Have you anything to go?"

"Not at the moment, thank you." I accepted the pouches.

"Then I must attend to duty." Kalugin put his coat back on. "The young gentleman's luggage will arrive within the hour. Latif, best of luck in your new posting—Van Drouten, I'm desolated to rush but you know how things are—perhaps we can dine at a later date. Have you still got that mortal who works such wonders with herring?"

"Yes, which was why I was sweeping, but I'll tell you next time—" I said, following him as he sidled into the street and put on his tall hat. My goodness, I thought, he *was* in a hurry!

"Now, that's interesting," said Latif thoughtfully, and Kalugin stopped dead.

"What is, young sir?" he asked, and not as though he wanted to.

"I must have missed something. Or am I mistaken in my interpretation of Directive Four-Oh-Eight-A regarding acknowledgment of delivery of all Class One shipments? I thought the Executive Facilitator of a Company HQ signed for all packets above a certain value."

"Um—" said Kalugin, looking like a trapped bear, but I knew what the problem was now. Latif had been training under Executive Facilitator Labienus, who is a martinet. Not the best influence for a child, even if Labienus is a big cheese. I've never cared for him, personally.

"Except in cases where delivery occurs no fewer than six but no more than twelve times within a calendar year," I told Latif. "And then it's at my discretion whether I sign or not."

"Yes," Kalugin agreed, throwing me a grateful look. "Well. I'll just be going, shall I?"

"Marine Operations Specialist Kalugin," Latif executed another perfect bow. "*Dos vedanya!*"

"The pleasure was all mine, I assure you," Kalugin called over his shoulder, and was gone down the Herengracht like a shot. Beside me, Latif cleared his throat.

"Insofar as my arrival seems to have been unexpected," he said with beautiful delicacy, "I would be happy to report to my quarters until a more convenient time for my briefing."

"No, no," I told him. "We can chat as I work. So, you've been studying with Labienus at Mackenzie Base?"

"Yes, madam, for the last eighteen months." He fell into step beside me as I took the deliveries and climbed up into the house.

"Well, that's nice. He's a very efficient administrator, Labienus. Very military, isn't he? Of course, personal styles vary widely," I said, and Latif snorted.

"I've learned that much already. During my first semester I studied under Houbert."

"Ah. I've heard he's . . . a little creative." It was the politest word I could think of.

"Yes, madam, I would say that's one way to describe him," Latif replied. "In any case, this will be my first experience at a Company HQ actually within a mortal urban community, observing field command and interaction with mortals in a situation where cover identities are used."

I nodded, and told him: "Sounds scary, doesn't it? But, really, you know, it's not that difficult. Especially here in Amsterdam. This is a very civilized town." I lifted my skirts to clear the last step, which is just a little higher than the others, and really I've been meaning to get that fixed, but somehow I never get around to it.

"It's even a boring town, nowadays. I wish you'd been stationed here back in the fifties! I could have taken you around for a sitting with Rembrandt—the Company bought so many of his canvases!—or maybe a chat with Spinoza. We used to buy a lot of his lenses, though of course he had no idea he was grinding them for credenza parts, but he never minded special orders and I used to love to get him talking . . ."

We had been making our way down the narrow passage, with Latif obliged to stay a bit behind because my skirts were so wide, but when my hoops caught that damn little hall table as they always do he was agile enough to grab the Ming vase before it leaped to its untimely death.

"Nice catch!" I congratulated him, knocking on Eliphal's door. He just stood there gasping with the vase clutched in his arms as Eliphal opened the door and stood peering down at us.

"What?"

114 Kage Baker

"See?" I waved the packet at him. "Diamonds."

"Oh, great!" He took them and looked over his spectacles at Latif. "Who's that?"

"Eliphal, this is Latif, who's going to be studying with me. He's an Executive Trainee, you know that experimental program where they're sending some neophytes into the field for early hands-on acclimatization?" I explained. "He'll be playing—gee, I guess I can tell people you're my page, would you like to tag along after me when I go shopping and hold my fan and stuff like that? And, Latif, this is Cultural Anthropologist Grade Two Eliphal; he's playing a diamond-cutter who rents a room from me. I was just telling him about Spinoza, Eliphal."

"Well, what a little fellow to get such a big assignment," said Eliphal, leaning down to him like a kindly uncle. "And how old are you, Latif?"

"Five, sir," said Latif coolly, putting down the vase and bowing. "I recently read your dissertation on Manasse ben Israel, and may I say how impressed I was with your insights into the influences at work during his formative years?"

"Uh—thank you." Eliphal straightened up, blinking.

"You're quite welcome."

"Come on, sweetie, let's deliver these. Dinner's at five, Eliphal. So, let's go on upstairs and you can meet Lievens, not the painter of course though he's our Art Conservationist, he's supposedly a cabinetmaker I'm renting to like Eliphal, and so is Diego our Tech, and Johan and Lisette—they're our Botanist and Literature Specialists—they're playing my son and daughter and help me run my business, and then we've got the mortal servants—you've worked with mortals before?—well, ours are very nice though a bit temperamental, Margarite and Joost, childless couple, they've got Code Yellow security clearance," I informed Latif as we climbed up to the next floor.

"I see," Latif answered. "Which would mean they actually share residential quarters with us?"

"Yes, in fact their room is next to yours. They don't snore or anything, though," I added, turning to see if Latif was looking upset. Sometimes young operatives are afraid of mortals, until they get used to them. I think it's because of the indoctrination we all get when we're being processed for immortality, in the base schools. But, you know, it takes hardly any time before you learn that they're all just people and not so bad really, and I think half of what you learn in school you just sort of have to take with a grain of salt, do you know what I'm saying?

Anyway if Latif was bothered by the idea of living next to mortals he hid it well, because he just shrugged his little shoulders and said: "How nice. And I understand your cover identity is as a widowed dealer in East Indian commodities?"

"Oh, yes, smell!" I exhorted him, pausing on the landing. I took a good deep sniff myself. "Ahh. Pepper, cloves, cardamom, and nutmeg just now. The whole top floor is warehouse space, you see, and actually I don't just *pose* as a spice merchant, we really do business here. I think I'd have made a great businesswoman if I'd stayed mortal, I really enjoy all those guilders on the account sheet and the exotic bales coming from the ships. It defrays operating costs like you wouldn't believe. There's my first word of advice as a field commander, okay? Always find ways to augment your operating budget, if you want to rise high in the Company ranks."

"Very good, madam, I'll remember that," Latif was saying, as Johan's door banged open and he came running out in a panic.

"Van Drouten! Van Drouten, what do I do? Kackerlackje's having a seizure!" And he held up the miserable little dog who was having a seizure all right, and I knew why, too, the damned thing had been eating paint again, and if I've told Johan once I've told him a dozen times: if he can't watch a pet every minute of the day he shouldn't have one, I think it should be a general rule that cyborgs shouldn't keep pets anyway because they always die after all and it hurts nearly as badly as when a mortal you're fond of dies.

Anyway I told him, "Take him out in the back and make him vomit! And I'll see if I've got any bicarbonate, all right? You know, if you'd kept an eye on him like I told you—" but Johan had gone clattering down the stairs out of earshot. I sighed and turned to Latif.

"I think that mutt is trying to commit suicide. Here's another piece of advice: Never let your subordinates keep pets, but if you must, make sure you've got a Zoologist stationed with you who knows how to physic a dog, or you'll wind up doing it."

"I'll remember that, too," said Latif, looking appalled.

———

The mortal with his trunk came after that, so I helped Latif get it up to his room. He insisted on squaring everything away before we went back downstairs, and I had to hide a smile at how finicky-neat he was, all his clothes pressed just so and severely grown-up in their cut. He even had a miniature grooming kit in a leather case! Silver-backed brushes and all; he only lacked a razor. Small wonder he looked askance at the toys I'd set out on his bed.

"Sorry about those," I told him. "I wasn't expecting somebody quite so, um, mature."

"It was a charming thought," he said courteously, giving one of his hats a last brush before setting it on a shelf. "And, after all, it does go with the character I'm portraying. I suppose I'll need to observe mortal children to see how they behave, won't I? Certainly all the rest of you seem to be doing a splendid job blending in with the mortal populace."

"Oh, it's easy, really," I assured him. "Easiest part of the job. What's hard is coordinating the actual running of the station."

"I can't wait to observe," he replied, laying out his monogrammed (!!) towel beside the washbasin. "What shall we start with? Duty rosters? Security protocols? Access code transfers? Logistics?"

Was there a little boy in there at all? The machine part was up and running, trust Labienus to see to that; but we work best as whole people, you know, same as the mortals.

"Logistics," I replied. "Want to come watch me get dinner for nine people on the table when the cook's sick?"

I made *erwtensoep* because we already had the peas soaking and it's easy. Latif perched on the edge of the table and stared as I chopped leeks and onions, and after a while ventured to say: "I think I'm getting this, now. This really is total immersion simulation, isn't it? You, uh, really and truly do have to *live* the mortal experience, don't you?"

"Not like a nice Company HQ with everything just so, is it?" I smiled at him. "No military command post with precise rules. I know Labienus, he's such a cyborg! Probably gave you that impression of absolute order, but the truth is that working for the Company is much more like this, like—like—"

"Chaos?" said Latif, and hastened to add: "Except that this is actually order artfully disguised as chaos, of course. Isn't it?"

"Sometimes," I told him, pulling out the potato basket. "See, you have to be so flexible. Like today, when Margarite isn't feeling well. And suppose I drew up a strict duty roster and I was all settled down to transmit reports at my credenza according to rules and regulations, like I was just last week, and Magdalena, that's the mortal girl from next door, dropped in to show off her new baby?"

"That's the Anthropologist's department, I would think," said Latif hopefully.

"Eliphal? Not likely, sweetie. And then, see, while I was sitting there pouring Magdalena and me nice little glasses of gin, there was a pounding on the door and who was it but some poor Facilitator who'd been riding day and night from the Polish front with a dispatch case of classified material from the king of Sweden he absolutely had to have scanned and transmitted *right then* so he could get it back before anybody'd noticed it was gone? And he had to be fed and given a fresh horse, I might add.

"Fortunately at that point dear baby woke up, wanted to be fed, so Magdalena retired to the next room while I apologized and ran the Facilitator back to Diego's room where the document scanner is, left him there to figure out where everything was, it was all so rush-rush I didn't even catch his name, and ran back to bring Magdalena her gin and sit down with her.

"We'd each had time for a sip, and Magdalena was just beginning to tell me about what Susanna over in the Jodenbreestrat told her about the play she saw—and down the stairs came Lievens in a panic to hiss in my ear because he'd run out of stabilizer for the lost Purcell score he was getting ready to seal up in one of his cabinets so it could be rediscovered in 2217 AD, and he had to have more *right then* because the cabinet was scheduled to be shipped to Scotland in three days. So I had to apologize to Magdalena and ask her to hold that thought, run back to Diego's room and ask the Facilitator to let me edge by him while I transmitted an emergency request to Eurobase One for a drum of stabilizer to be sent by express flight so it could arrive in time.

"Then I had to edge back past the Facilitator and my hoops knocked off his papers where he had them stacked, poor man, and I had to apologize and help him pick them up before I could run back and sit down with Magdalena, and she'd just got to the juicy part of this play—will you hand me that paring knife, dear? Thanks—when there's another knocking on the door.

"*So,* I apologized again, profusely, to Magdalena but fortunately baby needed a change at this point, so she busied herself with that while I went see who was at the door, and it was Hayashi from Edobase, standing there on the doorstep in full Japanese costume feeling terribly conspicuous. Apparently there'd been an accident with his trunk! And he wanted to know if I could get him a change of clothes and a spare field kit before his ship put out again?

"So I hurried him back through the house and thank God Magdalena didn't look up from baby's mess or she'd have seen a samurai complete with sword tiptoeing past the doorway! And the only person in the house who had spare clothes Hayashi's size was Eliphal, who was just coming down the stairs on his way out the door to one of those minyan things, but they ran like mad back upstairs and I ran back in to Magdalena, and I needed another gin by this time, I can tell you.

"We'd just leaned down for the first sip when there was Margarite in the doorway; it seemed she'd only just noticed we were out of cooking oil and she was three-quarters ready with the *vleeskroketten* she was making for dinner, and wanted to know what she should do?

"Well, of course, what she wanted was for me to go out and buy a jar of oil, but I wasn't having any of that, I just tossed her a guilder and said, go down to Hobbema's on the dam, and she sulked away looking martyred but—"

"Why do you allow insubordination in a mortal?" Latif inquired with a slight frown.

"Because she prepares fish beautifully, and she's married to Joost, and Joost really is a treasure," I explained. "He's smart, he keeps his mouth shut, and he knows the best places to buy good horses in a hurry without paying a fortune. Sometimes you just have to put up with certain things in mortals, you know? So anyway, I turned back to Magdalena, who had just got to the part of the play where the pirate chief is about to ravish his sister all unknowing, when the front door opened and in came Lisette, all in high spirits because she'd just closed a deal for an unknown early Defoe manuscript.

"In fact she was waving it as she came running in, and went leaping into Diego's room to scan it and collided with the Facilitator, and both their sets of priceless documents went flying everywhere and you never heard such screams!

"So then, Magdalena quite understandably got the impression that my daughter was being assaulted by a Swedish cavalry officer, and—I'm not frightening you, am I, dear?"

"No! No, not at all!" said Latif, though his eyes were wide and staring.

"Well, the point is, you see how things can get?" I waved the paring knife. "It's hard keeping up the appearance of an ordinary mortal family without alarming the neighbors."

"I suppose so."

"You'll have days like that, too, when you're a full-fledged Executive Facilitator, mark my words." I dumped the last of the potatoes into the soup kettle. "We all do."

"I bet Suleyman doesn't," said Latif.

"Who? Suleyman? North African Section Head Suleyman? Oh, he's a lovely man! You know him?"

"He recruited me," said Latif.

"He was here on business one time— Recruited you? Really? Where?" I dug around in a drawer, wondering what Margarite had done with all the long spoons.

"From a slave ship," said Latif in an offhanded sort of way, and I looked up at him all ready to cry out *You poor baby,* because he was after all such a very small boy sitting there in my kitchen, and how much tinier had he been when Suleyman had rescued him from such a horrible place—but I could tell from the look in his eyes that the last thing he wanted me to do would be to exclaim over him.

At least now I knew why he wanted to grow up so fast. So I just said, "Well, we all get off to a bad start in life, or the Company wouldn't be able to snatch us away from the mortals, I guess. It was plague took my whole family but me; there I was, all alone with corpses when the nice immortal lady found me and recruited me for Dr. Zeus." I located the spoon at last and turned to stir the soup. "So, you know Suleyman. He's one of the best, I must say, but he has days when everything goes wrong, too. You just ask him, if you ever run into him again."

"Oh, I will," Latif informed me. "I'm going to be his second-in-command, when I've graduated."

"Really?" I exclaimed. "How nice! You've already been informed of your assignment?"

"No," he replied imperturbably, "But it's going to happen. I'll make it happen."

Well, I didn't know what to say at that, because, you know—we don't make things happen. Oh, we can request assignments, and if we've got the right programming and it suits the Company's purpose, our requests might be granted once in a while—but it's the Company tells us what to do and not the other way around. So I just stirred the soup, and the little boy sat and watched me.

"But enough about me," he said, in that outrageously grown-up voice he affected. "Tell me about yourself. Now that I'm getting some idea of what's involved in running an HQ, I'm more than ever impressed by your command abilities! Tell me, how do you like to relax?"

"Well—you know—like anybody does, I guess," I waved my free hand. "Going out, going to the theater, dining, conversation with the mortals."

"You find mortal conversation relaxing?" Latif raised his eyebrows.

"Sometimes." I looked darkly upward in the direction of Margarite's room. "When they're not sulking."

At this point Johan appeared in the doorway again, tears in his eyes, holding out his damn little dog like an offering. Kackerlackje was stiff as a board, lying on his side and foaming at the mouth.

"Van Drouten—the seizures stopped but now he's doing this—"

"And after all, immortal conversation can be just as irritating," I explained to Latif, tossing down the spoon and wiping my hands on my apron.

The mutt didn't die; he never did. Within a few days he was up and yapping as loudly as ever, and even seemed to remember a little of his paper-training, as opposed to his usual forgetfulness on the subject. What a joy to have in the house, huh?

But as it happened, we didn't have to put up with his presence for much longer, because about a week later I got the notification that Johan was being transferred to Brussels. So I gave him a nice farewell dinner party and we saw him off with his suitcase and animal carrier, and Margarite was so happy the dog was going with him she was in a good mood for a week.

And Latif appeared to be fitting in pretty well, which was nice. He followed me everywhere, observing just as he was supposed to. He seemed to have figured out that commenting out loud on their shortcomings made people uncomfortable, and kept his thoughts to himself now. He asked the other operatives intelligent questions about their particular specialties and made a point of sitting with each of them for at least one day, watching as they went about their various businesses, especially Eliphal.

He had no difficulty with the mortals, either. In fact he went out of his way to make friends with Joost, who was charmed by him, and took him along on his horse-trading rounds. It's always a good idea to have a mortal with you when you're in one of their cities for the first time, I think, anyway. It helps you see it through their eyes.

When we went out shopping, Latif obligingly carried my basket and fan, and put up with all my mortal neighbors who came crowding to stare at him with the excuse that they had some really spicy gossip for me. And I can't think he minded being told what an adorable little fellow he was, or having sugar rolls pressed into his free hand, though the cheek-pinching bothered him, but it would bother anybody. People don't remember very well what it's like to be children.

Actually I guess Latif didn't remember much either, as sophisticated as he was. No, that can't be quite true: there was a day when we were out on the Dam and he stared, fascinated, at a black mortal, a slave or servant probably, who was following behind his master. What a mortal he was, too! Gorgeous, with these long legs in thigh-high boots and his full white shirt with its lace collar open at the throat, skin like polished ebony, striding along in good-humored arrogance, chatting with his master about the pistols they were on their way to buy.

He saw Latif staring at him and grinned hugely, such perfect white teeth, and winked. Latif caught his breath, I swear; and all the way home he was walking with the mortal's long-legged stride, practicing that grace.

But that was about the only time I saw him being a little boy, which worried me. The rest of the time he was stone-cold serious and grimly determined to become the perfect operative. I've had trainee Facilitators in their twenties who weren't as dedicated to learning their jobs. But then, Latif was special, wasn't he? Or he'd still have been in the junior class at a Company training base somewhere, with other children his age.

He watched closely as I dealt with the everyday business of running the station: feeding operatives who dropped in at any hour of the day or night, seeing to it they were issued whatever field supplies they needed, and ordering anything we didn't actually have on hand at the station. There was the station budget to fight with, frantically thinking of ways to stretch it until the next fiscal quarter! There were couriers to greet, pouches to be signed for or sent on their way, dispatches to be transmitted; there were shipments to be received and sent of so many humdrum things that would become priceless over time.

Who needed all those copies of the new London *Daily Courant* or the *Moskovskya Viedomosti*? What about all those Watteau and Rigaud paintings, who on Earth would want such sickly candy-box things? And the Pachelbel scores that the composer just happened to misplace, or those jottings by Hakuseki, would wealthy collectors really pay small fortunes for those in the future? It always amazes me, the garbage that time turns into gold; but, you know, that's how the Company makes its money. If it keeps herring on my table (and makes me immortal, too!) who am I to raise an eyebrow?

And Latif learned quickly, he really was a brilliant little boy, and grasped very well the importance of interfacing with the mortal community, building relationships within it that we could use to the Company's advantage and re-inforcing the illusion that we were a perfectly (well, reasonably) normal mortal Amsterdam family. It helped, too, that I didn't have to keep stopping his lessons to sweep or peel onions.

Yes! Margarite's good mood didn't last past the week of Kackerlackje's de-parture, but she didn't lapse into the usual pattern of headaches and diarrhea that made her unable to cope with daily routine. She went into a frenzy of ac-tivity instead. The house was as spotless as it's ever been, meals were ready on time, and suddenly there was an airy, digestible quality to her cooking that made me realize that maybe it had been just a little heavy before.

Though when Eliphal stopped on the stairs to pay her a gallant compli-ment about the latest batch of *vleeskroketten,* she still glared at him. What was going on in her head? No use to ask Joost; when I brought up the sub-ject he just shrugged and held out his hands, gesturing *How should I know?* Then he swung Latif up on his shoulders and they went out to watch ships being unloaded.

Summer ended, and the canals were pretty with drifting yellow leaves for a week or two before the cold set in. I had to order a new wardrobe for Latif, because he'd outgrown the furred jacket he'd brought from Mackenzie Base, so quickly was he beginning to shoot up. He was going to be tall and impos-ing, and I was glad for him. I don't think he'd felt an Executive Facilitator should be short and undignified. He prowled around the house for a couple of weeks wrapped in knitted shawls until his new coat arrived.

He was bundled up like that the morning I rose early and came down to find him sitting at my credenza, with his little fingers pattering away at the keyboard rapid-fire-speed.

"Good morning!" he greeted me pleasantly, glancing up. "I woke up early and I couldn't go back to sleep, so I just thought I'd check your mail for you."

"Oh," I said, yawning. "Did I have any?"

"Yes." He indicated a stack of printouts as he closed and shut down the credenza. "The usual things. Answers to queries, priority orders, directives. I've sorted them for you in order of importance. I hope I wasn't presuming?"

"No, no, you need to learn this stuff, after all," I replied, sitting down beside him and flipping through the printouts. He really had prioritized them, too; I was quite impressed. "This is great! Gosh, you're a quick study, Latif."

"I'm glad you think so," he replied graciously. "And actually, I was wondering: in view of the rapid progress I'm making, do you suppose it's time I was fast-tracked?"

"Fast-tracked?" I looked up from the printouts to stare at him.

"Accelerated," he explained. "My educational schedule revised to send me on to Eurobase One ahead of the originally estimated date. What do you think? Would you be receptive to the idea?"

"Oh, I don't know, sweetie," I told him dubiously. "Shouldn't you have some childhood? I mean, look at you! You've still got your baby teeth, and you're out in the field already. Don't you think you've been fast-tracked enough as it is?"

He watched me intently as I answered him, and I was half afraid he'd get angry; but he just nodded and made a dismissive gesture.

"You're right, of course," he said at once. "I'll bow to your judgment. I'm undoubtedly not as proficient at this yet as I think I am."

And I was so impressed by the gracious way he took my refusal that I hastened to reassure him about what a little genius he was.

Well, I was right about his being a genius.

Snow fell one morning, and all the muck froze so that the view from the parlor window was just like a postcard, and the houses across the canal were all frosted with white. Really it was perfect weather for curling up beside the window with a nice cup of hot chocolate, but we'd run out; everyone had been craving Theobromos desperately lately, for some reason. It was too early in the day to get blitzed anyhow, and I had work to do.

I admired the snowy scene for a few minutes before settling down at my credenza to check my incoming dispatches, sipping my coffee meditatively. I liked this time of the morning, before the rest of the household was awake, when I usually had some peace and quiet.

The first blast in my little symphony of horror was a communication from Verpoorten in the Brussels office complaining about Johan. Not Johan exactly; Verpoorten said he was an able enough Botanist, though I'd been a little mistaken about what his specialties were when I recommended him for transfer to their gardens project, and right there warning bells began to ring in my head. I hadn't recommended him! He'd been requested, hadn't he? But I read on, appalled.

It seemed that Kackerlackje was making himself just as inconvenient at Brussels HQ as he had in my house, and Verpoorten was a lot less inclined to cope with him. He had had to give Johan an ultimatum, apparently. The dog had to go. Johan had acquiesced in tears, but only on the condition that dear little Kackerlackje be sent back to me, since Johan knew I loved him as much as he did and moreover had always looked after his precarious health like a loving mother.

Boy, there aren't words to describe my consternation. Some Executive Facilitators I know would just give the damn dog all the paint he could eat and then send him diving tied to a rock, but I'm nice, you know? I was so upset I put the communication aside without sending a reply and went into my fiscal file. I'd buy something, that would take my mind off my troubles! Time to order new components for the document scanner, yes, Diego had reminded me about that only yesterday, and Lievens wanted another shipment of red oak for cabinets.

What a surprise I got when my credenza informed me I had insufficient funds for the transaction . . .

Thinking of course that there must be some mistake, I checked my budget balance, and then I got a real surprise.

This has happened to you, right? So you know that after the first frantic denial a sort of icy numbness sets in and you settle down to go over the books with a fine-toothed comb, determined to find the mistake. That's what I was doing when the knock came on the door.

Too much to expect that Margarite would answer it, of course. God forbid she should actually do her job or anything like that. As the knock was repeated a little more loudly I rose to get it, scanning irritably for where in the house Margarite had got to. There was her heartbeat, coming from her bedroom, and some other sounds as well . . . oh, dear, was she throwing up? No wonder she hadn't lit the fires or started breakfast yet. I'd have to do, it, of course—

My annoyance at this fled right out of my mind when I opened the door and beheld my two visitors.

Quite an elegant-looking lady and gentleman, as much as you could see of them for the furred coats in which they were bundled up. They were both immortals, too.

"Executive Facilitator Van Drouten, I presume?" inquired the gentleman. "May we have a moment of your time?"

So of course I invited them in off the stoop, and settled them in the parlor while I excused myself a moment and ran off to grab Lisette, who was just coming downstairs, and asked her to go see what the matter was with Margarite, and see if Joost couldn't be prevailed upon to light the fires so we wouldn't all freeze? Then I found a bottle of gin and three glasses and brought them out to my guests.

They were even more elegant out of their coats, quite exotic-looking, too, for all that they were dressed in perfect up-to-the-minute Continental fashions. The man had been Incan or Aztec or one of those originally; he had the copper skin and the gloomy sneering dignity. The lady had white skin, green eyes, hair like a raven's wing, a real stunner if she hadn't had such a disagreeable look on her face. So had the man, actually. But they both smiled politely as I poured them gin and asked how I could help them.

"You're too kind," the man said, hooding his eyes. "May I introduce myself? I am Security Technical Sixteen Turtle and this is my associate, Botanist Smythe. We're presently stationed at New World One."

"My gosh, what a long way to come," I exclaimed, offering them both their gin. They accepted the glasses but did not drink.

"Oh, we arrived by air transport," Sixteen Turtle said, turning the stem of his glass between his fingers. "We don't expect to be away long." And then he transmitted subvocally: *It's my hope we can resolve this issue quickly, to our mutual satisfaction.*

I didn't know what to make of this, because usually the only time we need to speak to each other subvocally is when we don't want the mortals to hear us speaking out loud, and there were no mortals within earshot. But I gamely transmitted: *Gee, I hope so, too.*

"Amsterdam is truly lovely at this time of year," Smythe told me graciously, though she was looking daggers at me. *May I begin by assuring you that we feel competition is a good thing, generally?*

That's nice, I transmitted back, and out loud I said: "How nice to hear someone say so! Usually all people ever want to see are tulips, tulips, tulips, you know, and of course they don't bloom at this time of year . . ."

"Yes, I was aware of that," Smythe replied, and I remembered she was a Botanist and felt silly.

Competition, transmitted Sixteen Turtle, *can actually stimulate business. And in a global market, there are certainly enough potential customers for everyone.*

What, for tulips? I responded. *My God, don't invest in bulbs! Don't you know what happened last time? The bottom fell out of the market and—* But from their offended expressions I could tell I was off the mark somehow.

Could you come to the point, please? I transmitted, just as Lisette came running back downstairs.

"Van Drouten? I don't think Margarite should get up today—" she blurted, and then noticed I had guests who were glaring at me strangely. "And I'll— just tell you about it later, okay?"

"Please do," I snapped, "and you might suggest to Joost that he deal with her in the meantime."

"He's not here," Lisette informed me, wringing her hands. "He, uh, apparently took Latif out to build a snowman."

"Mortal servants!" Sixteen Turtle shook his head, sounding tolerantly amused. "We have similar troubles with ours."

"At least yours don't sneak out to build snowmen, not in South America," I grumbled, and Lisette took that opportunity to vanish discreetly.

"Oh, we have snow in the mountains," Smythe assured me. *Though not in the plantations of Theobroma cacao. And that, madam, brings us to the point.*

Really?

Yes. Sixteen Turtle lifted his gin and held it under that aristocratic nose of his to inhale the bouquet. *We're quite prepared to tolerate the existence of a rival operation. It's not as though we haven't got an adequate market on the Pacific Rim already, and to be frank, we can't see our operation expanding any further.* He lowered the glass and fixed me with a cold dead stare. *What we're not prepared to tolerate, however, is gross mismanagement to the extent that the Company is alerted, not only to the existence of your operation, but ours as well.*

At least now I knew why we weren't talking out loud.

"Funny, you know, but I just can't imagine snow that close to the equator," I said cheerily, but now I was looking daggers right back at them. *You're black marketeers, aren't you? And you deal in Theobromos!*

Did you think you were the only one to have conceived of this idea? demanded Smythe, but Sixteen Turtle was realizing I really hadn't known what was going on. He lifted his head, peering up our staircase and inhaling deeply, and I did, too, and suddenly singled out the fragrance that had been driving us all subliminally crazy lately, masked as it was by nutmeg and cloves: Theobromos.

My shock was enough to get through to Smythe, too, and she and Sixteen Turtle looked horrified. They'd just as good as confessed to an Executive Facilitator that they ran a Theobromos racket, and moreover brought her attention to one being run out of her own HQ! Not that I think there's anything wrong with the black market, mind you, since Dr. Zeus never stocks enough Theobromos in the Company bases. But it is against Company regulations, and any operative caught at it faces disciplinary measures.

Sixteen Turtle recovered himself first. He smiled broadly and put his fingertips together.

"Ah, but I can certainly imagine your beautiful country ablaze with tulips," he said. *Dear me, I can't imagine this will reflect favorably on your record,* he transmitted. *One of the operatives under your command dealing in contraband Theobromos? And not very well, I might add.*

How not very well? I demanded. *You thought it was my operation, didn't you? You may as well tell me all the details. Has somebody been using my codes to buy the stuff?*

Would it be in our best interests to tell you? Smythe replied, looking as though cocoa butter wouldn't melt in her mouth.

Yes, it would, I told her grimly.

She and Sixteen Turtle looked at each other before he transmitted.

Well, madam, it appears that someone with much audacity but little expertise has recently purchased a great deal of a certain commodity in your name, apparently with the intent of cornering the European black market on that commodity. Nothing to distress anyone in that; as I believe I pointed out, the global market can bear more than one player in this game. However, the player in question has offered the commodity at such absurdly low prices that he or she is certain to arouse suspicion. Moreover, by our calculations, your culprit can't possibly turn a profit! And such practices are not only likely to ruin the individual dealer, they're bad for business generally. This was why we felt obliged to warn you, for your own good—

I remembered my nonexistent budget balance.

I see, I transmitted. I didn't, yet, though. Just at that moment another transmission crackled through the ether, slightly distorted by snow and panic, and unfortunately on a wide enough band so my visitors heard it, too:

Van Drouten! Very angry mortal looking for you! I'm trying to head him off, but—

It was Kalugin, sounding as though he were running along through the frozen streets.

That was exactly what he was doing, too, because a moment later there was a commotion on the front stoop and we could hear Kalugin saying: "Sir, I implore you! Whatever your grievances against the man, the City Watch will look dimly on stabbing him in this good lady's parlor—"

"Excuse me, won't you?" I said, leaping up to answer the pounding on my door. When I opened it I beheld Kalugin, or rather his broad back, because he had got in front of my visitor and was holding his hands up in a placatory gesture. The visitor was a diminutive mortal gentleman who was glaring around Kalugin at me with an expression of such venom it made my hair curl.

"Where is the Jew Eliphal?" he demanded.

"Uh—Madam Van Drouten, this gentleman was a passenger on my ship, and he seems to have some grievance against one of your tenants—" Kalugin explained hastily, turning around. The mortal used this opportunity to push under Kalugin's arm and slip past me into the hall, and from there into the parlor.

"Where is the diamond cutter?" he shouted, flinging his cloak back over one shoulder and revealing a box he was clutching, also the sword and matching dagger on his hip. Kalugin and I were both beside him at this point, but unfortunately Eliphal had heard all the commotion and come running downstairs.

"What is it? Who wants to see me?" he asked. The mortal singled him out with a deadly look and hurled the box down so that it bounced open at Eliphal's feet, spilling out three or four bricks of something wrapped in oiled paper. A fragrance rose up from the broken box like, well, like paradise. Something tropical and exotic and yet evocative of cozy winter kitchens where you could curl up by the stove with a nice hot cup of . . .

Theobromos. Not the ordinary stuff mortals bought and sold, either, but the high-powered Company cultivar with a kick like a mule. Every immortal in my increasingly crowded parlor leaned forward involuntarily, including me.

"Where the hell are my emeralds?" the mortal snarled, drawing steel.

Eliphal looked up openmouthed from his contemplation of the spilled delight.

"What emeralds?" he replied. "Who are you, sir?"

"Sanpietro del Vaglio," the mortal replied, as though it was terribly obvious. "And I tell you to your face you are a liar and a thief and the son of Barbary apes!"

"How dare you? I've never heard of you in my life," Eliphal shouted, drawing himself up, and I winced because he takes his character very seriously, but before the mortal could lunge forward with his sword there was yet another clatter of feet on the stoop and in came Joost and Latif, all dusted with snow as though they'd just stepped out of a toy globe. They halted and stared at the scene, astonished.

"Do you dare to deny you offered me six Peruvian emeralds of the finest grade, and sent me *this* instead?" screamed del Vaglio. "What do you think I am, a confectioner?"

Joost's eyes went wide with horror, and so did Latif's. They exchanged a glance. Everybody in the room knew right then, except for the mortal, whose back was turned to them.

"Yes, I deny it," Eliphal retorted. "Somebody has been using my name to do business!"

And he turned an accusing stare of terribly righteous wrath on Latif.

Latif met his stare and backed up a pace, unblinking; then he turned and buried his face in my apron, and burst into very, very loud sobs.

Sixteen Turtle and Smythe smirked at each other.

"Mistress, it wasn't his fault," Joost cried. "I must have sent the parcels to the wrong addresses!"

Latif sobbed even more loudly.

"You mean you were supposed to send emeralds to this man and chocolate to somebody else?" I asked Joost. Del Vaglio had turned to stare at us in incomprehension; Eliphal folded his arms in indignant triumph.

Joost looked abashed. "Yes, mistress. But—"

"Where did you get six Peruvian emeralds of the finest grade, Latif?" I inquired, so dazed the minute details were holding my attention. Latif's sobbing went up a decibel.

"You're that little brat who was training with Houbert, aren't you?" remarked Smythe suddenly, leaning forward to stare at him, or at least at the back of his head. "Ha! You put your tour of duty in New World One to good use, I must say."

"You mean—" I began, meaning to ask if the child had spent all his free time making smuggling connections, but at that moment somebody else came slinking up on the stoop and peered in through the door, which was still open and in fact letting in floating snow.

"Er—excuse me," she murmured, or at least that's what I think she said because she was so muffled up in scarves and fur. "I'm looking for Facilitator Van Drouten . . . ?"

"Well, come in and shut the door after you," I said wearily, but she drew back.

"Er . . . no, I—" Her gaze riveted on the broken box and its fragrant contents.

"Oh." Light dawned on me. "You got something you didn't expect in the mail, huh?"

She looked as though she was about to turn and run, but Kalugin stepped close and took her arm firmly. He led her outside and they had a whispered conversation. A moment later he returned, bearing a small wooden box remarkably like the one del Vaglio had brought.

"I believe this is yours, sir," Kalugin said, offering it to him. Del Vaglio sheathed his sword and took it doubtfully, and Kalugin bent down and swept up the broken box and its contents. "Excuse me a moment, won't you?"

Kalugin took the Theobromos outside and a second later we could hear the immortal, whoever she was, running away as if for dear life. Del Vaglio, meanwhile, had opened the new box and carried it over to the window to inspect its contents. He took out a lens in an eyepiece and examined whatever was in there—six Peruvian emeralds of the finest grade?—pretty carefully before closing the box with a snap and tucking it under his arm in a possessive kind of way.

"Acceptable," he said, and swinging his cloak around him he strode to the door. "*Grazie,* Captain Kalugin. Under the circumstances I will seek no further redress for this insult."

"What about the insult to me, you pig?" roared Eliphal, but del Vaglio exited regally, if hurriedly. At least he shut the door after himself. But the room was no less crowded, because here came Lisette down the steps again at a run, crying out: "Joost! You'd better go see Margarite right away."

"Is she all right?" He looked alarmed. Lisette scowled at the rest of us and came and whispered in his ear. The alarm in his face vanished; he lit up like a chandelier.

"Lord God," he whooped. "It worked!" He rushed at Latif to hug him, but Latif was stuck to my apron like a limpet, still sobbing, so he contented himself with kissing the top of his head and yelling: "God bless you, little master, it'll be a son for sure." He turned and ran away upstairs, and we could hear his feet thundering all the way to the fourth floor.

"So . . . you've been slipping Margarite hormones or something, too?" I guessed. Latif was still too wracked with sobs to reply, which was answer enough. Well! Guess who was going to be lighting the fires and sweeping the stoop for the next few months? Not Margarite, huh? "And I'll bet you got Johan transferred, didn't you?"

Sixteen Turtle and Smythe rose to their feet.

"Perhaps we'd best depart," said Sixteen Turtle in a voice like silk. As he was pulling on his furs, his eyes glinted with malevolent humor. *Unless the young gentleman wishes us to take his remaining stock off his hands? Though I'm afraid we couldn't possibly offer more than fifty percent.*

Latif's sobs kept going, but his little fists clenched in the folds of my apron.

"How much . . . merchandise is upstairs, Latif?" I asked him.

"Five hundredweight chests," he paused in his sobbing long enough to say distinctly.

Kalugin and Eliphal reeled. Well, that just about accounted for the hole in my budget. Joost and Latif must have had it brought in by canal barge and lifted it up with the warehouse block and tackle, possibly while I was out shopping. I don't know where I found the presence of mind to look Sixteen Turtle in the eye and transmit to him: *Nothing doing. I'm confiscating his entire stock. You can deal with me now! And you'll either pay me full retail value or—* and I really don't know where I found the nerve to say this—*or maybe I'll go into business for myself. You said you wouldn't mind a little competition. Hmm! This close to Belgium, I'll bet I could cut into your markets with a vengeance.*

I must have expressed myself badly, replied Sixteen Turtle without batting an eyelash. *Naturally we'd pay full retail value for an order that size. Five hundred-weights? Let me think, we could offer . . .*

He conferred briefly and subvocally with Smythe, and then she named a sum. It wasn't quite enough to bring my budget into the black.

What do you think, Latif? I wondered. *Perhaps we could work out a marketing strategy. 'If You're Tired of Waiting for Godiva, Wait No More! Primo Black Magic Is Here!' And we can always claim it's fresher and purer than the competition's because it comes in on the Dutch East Indies ships—*

Smythe winced and named another sum. It was a lot higher than the other sum she'd named. Latif cautiously lifted his perfectly dry face from my apron and mouthed *Take it!* in silence, then buried his face again and gave another wail of misery.

"Done," I said aloud. "Who's your banker?"

Eliphal oversaw the transfer of funds. We had the stuff loaded out of the house by that evening.

"So, you see?" I said, dipping my scrub brush in the soapy water and going after the greasy patch in front of the kitchen hearth. "You weren't ready to be fast-tracked after all."

"You're right, of course," Latif replied gloomily, dipping his scrub brush, too. He put it down a moment to roll up his sleeves again and then attacked a blob of spilled jam. "But it almost worked." *If Joost hadn't mixed those labels and if I'd had a better idea what the black market rate ought to be . . . You know I was only trying to defray operating expenses and make your job easier, I hope?*

"Oh, yeah," I agreed. "And it might have worked at that, sweetie. But the logic's really simple here: you're a child. You don't know everything about this job yet. That's why you're not in Africa. And aren't you glad that if you were going to make a big boomeranging blunder, you did it in front of me and not your hero Suleyman?"

"I guess so," he replied, edging forward to get some tracked-in mud.

"Or Labienus! Though I can't imagine you'd be having a conversation like this one with him," I added, snickering at the idea of Mr. Super-Cyborg Executive Facilitator General on his hands and knees scrubbing a floor. "I guess I must have fallen pretty short of your expectations after you'd studied under Labienus."

"Everybody under his command hates Labienus," Latif told me quietly.

"I'd heard that," I said. "I've heard he treats his mortals like animals."

Latif nodded. He dipped his brush again and went on scrubbing. After a moment he said: "He hates them. He thought I'd hate them, too, because of the slave ship. He told me I could go far with him. But . . . Labienus never breaks the rules where anybody can see. And he always makes sure there's somebody else to take the blame. But I saw. And I thought . . . well, so much for role models." He scowled down at the rust stain he was attacking. "But Suleyman doesn't do stuff like that. I hope?"

I slopped suds on a crusted bit of something I didn't want to think about—how long since the last time Margarite had scrubbed this floor?!—and said:

"No, Suleyman's a nice guy. You'll see, when you finally get yourself assigned to his HQ. And, you know what? Even with a little setback like this, I'll bet you get your wish. I'll bet you'll be assigned to his command in no time at all, a smooth operator like you."

He actually giggled at that.

"Though actually I should probably continue on here a while longer," he said, with elaborate casualness.

"So you can learn the finer points of getting dirt up off of a floor, huh?" I panted, sitting up and dropping my brush in the bucket.

"Or something," he replied, dropping his brush in there, too. He stood up.

"Good, because you wouldn't believe how much of an Executive Facilitator's job is cleaning up messes," I told him, getting to my feet and surveying what we'd done so far. "Okay! Now we mop and then, what do you say? Want to go shopping on the Dam? I could use some marzipan cakes."

"Me too," Latif replied, slipping his little hand into mine.

Labienus shudders, wills the memory away. He puts back the offending file. Settling down with the red project file he opens it, paging through the material with his reports, his annotations.

When he opens it, the first image to greet his eyes is a slightly out-of-focus field photograph of a street in sixteenth-century London. Labienus remembers an overwhelming sense of nausea. Standing in old Egypt, finicky over a little smoke and dung, he'd had no idea of the filth he'd have to endure over the next four thousand years! London had certainly been one of the low points in his long life. He had endured, however. And profited . . .

Turning the page, he sees the face as through a shroud. He removes the protective covering of tissue paper from the drawing. His gesture is almost tender, as though he were lifting a blanket to gaze upon a sleeping child.

It is no more than a study for a portrait never painted, a sketch on paper in red chalk and black ink, by some long-dead Italian master. The subject is a young male mortal. He had posed stiffly, regarding the artist with disapproval, for the artist had been a papist and the subject of the sketch was a heretic.

The artist had therefore not made much effort to flatter his subject. He had presented with blunt realism the boy's long homely face, his broken nose, his small cold eyes, his wide mouth. Even if he had been well disposed toward the boy, however, the artist would have been unable to make him look quite human.

But no mortal living could have known why. The boy himself hadn't known why. Precious few immortals would have known, either, by the year 1543! Labienus looks down at the portrait and mentally calls up Budu's features, superimposes them over the boy's.

There is a resemblance, would be even more of a resemblance if the portrait had been done in color. A certain expression in the eyes. A certain set of the mouth. The same cheekbones. If a god had taken that ancient flatheaded creature in the photograph and sculpted it like clay until it looked human, the result would be the boy in the portrait. One of them is a monster and the other is a man.

The delicious irony, of course, is that it is the boy who is the monster.

Though not in a moral sense, Labienus admits to himself. Regardless of the predilection for violence and the prodigious carnal appetites with which he had been created, Nicholas Harpole had been quite a virtuous boy.

Labienus was never officially posted to London, but there he happened to be, in the dismal year 1527. He chanced to be riding back from Hampstead to his lodgings in the City, one night.

No moon and few stars, under the thin fog. Almost a warm night, if wretched England could be said to have such a thing, for it was high summer. Ahead and to his left were the flickering lights of London, but out here in the fields was unfathomable darkness, unless of course one was a cyborg and could see by infrared. Labienus wasn't bothering to do that, however. He knew the way well and so did his horse.

It paused to crop the long grass at the edge of the ditch and he waited patiently, deciding to cut across the fields toward Gray's Inn Road. As he sat there, however, he heard a faint cryptic signal in the ether.

It was coming from the opposite side of the road, off in the direction of St. Marylebone. Frowning, he turned his head and scanned.

Nothing there in the darkness. He was about to ride on when the signal came again, like a faintly glowing puff of mist in the night. He switched to infrared; no result. Turning his horse's head to the right, he urged it across the ditch and into the fields beyond. The animal trotted forward, then slowed to a walk; then stopped, whickering uneasily.

Labienus saw nothing. In the instant before he realized there was a voice in his head *telling him* he saw nothing, he felt a paralyzing shock, and something black rose up from the ground at tremendous speed.

He found himself caught in darkness, cradled like a child across a lap except for the fact that a massive hand had closed on his windpipe. Another massive hand, on an arm like a tree trunk, had firm hold of his mount's bridle, and though the horse was trembling it stood obediently still. He looked up. A black silhouette rose against the night, a giant crouching in the new-cut hay.

Labienus calmed himself. *Father,* he transmitted.

"Why are you wearing a black armband?" said a voice in the night. It was not the deep, growling voice one would expect to hear coming out of something that looked so much like a bear. It was rather flat and high-pitched.

I'm in deep mourning. Hadn't you heard? Niccolò Machiavelli just died.

The giant shook with silent laughter. Labienus felt his throat released, and he gulped air gratefully.

So the rumors are true. You went rogue!

"Some time ago," said Budu. "The Crusades were the last straw. You can speak out loud. The Company won't hear us."

Remembering the shock, Labienus ran a diagnostic on himself and realized his datafeed to the Company had been shorted out. He felt incredulous delight.

"How long will it last?"

"Long enough." Budu released him and he sat up, brushing hay from his doublet.

"I've been hoping you were out there," Labienus said.

"Have you?"

"They should never have retired you. I had no idea how vile a place the world would become, with the mortals free to spread like pestilence. Our masters are imbeciles, father!"

"You think so?"

"Yes," said Labienus, realizing he'd said too much. He sat back, evening his breath, studying the Enforcer.

"Good," said Budu. He wore layered rags and a leather hood that must have required two cowhides. It was all stained, faded, dull stone colors, superb camouflage. He sheathed an immense hunting knife, making it vanish somewhere in his clothing.

Labienus realized that if he'd said the wrong thing, he might have had his throat cut and Budu would simply have made off with his horse. He had no particular desire to wake, chilled and painful and covered with his own blood, in gray dawn in the middle of nowhere with a long walk ahead of him.

He licked his lips and said: "When the Black Death broke out—I half hoped it was your doing, somehow."

"No," said Budu, "but you were thinking in the right lines. It was impressive."

"It was marvelous! It crippled Justinian's work in Byzantium, and what it did to Europe! Whole towns vanished and went back to clean earth. It swept through their filthy little cities the way you used to, father, and nothing stopped it."

"But it was stupid, son," Budu told him. "Don't waste your admiration on it. It killed indiscriminately. Innocents died with the guilty."

"How many of them are innocent any more?" said Labienus bitterly. "How many of them were ever innocent?"

"You were, once," Budu replied.

Labienus reminded himself never to speak from the heart.

"What have you been doing with yourself, father? Assuming you can tell me."

Budu shrugged. "I've walked in shadows. Continued the work, when I had the chance. One old man with a knife can't do much."

"But the other Enforcers?" asked Labienus. "Haven't any of them followed you into exile?"

"They were betrayed," said Budu. "They've been taken offline, one after another as the years passed, and the Company has hidden them well. I'm the only one left walking free." Idly he took up a long stem of hay and turned it in his fingers, rotating it like the tiniest of quarterstaffs. He pointed it at Labienus. "You see how we were repaid, after we labored for our masters? How do you think they will repay you, when you've served your purpose?"

"Undoubtedly the same," said Labienus. "If they get the chance."

Budu chuckled. "But you won't let them have the chance, eh?"

"No indeed."

"What do you propose to do?"

Labienus looked at him. "What would you do? Wait until they're vulnerable and strike. Their precious Temporal Concordance runs out in 2355; after that they'll have no more foreknowledge of events than we do. Once that playing field's leveled, we'll see who wins the game."

"And who is *we*, son?"

"You and I, presumably. And any of the rest of the Executives who are as disgusted as we are, and I'll bet there are a lot of us."

"There are," said Budu. "Will you join us, son?"

"Oh, yes." Labienus felt a shiver of genuine delight. "Only tell me what you need me to do, father!"

"Work with me," said Budu, staring into his eyes. "We have a lot of preparation to make for 2355. You think this Earth is crowded now, you think it's dirty? You've no idea how much worse it's going to be, in a few more centuries. The mortals will go mad. Cities like termite mounds. Murderers in packs like wolves, roaming unpunished. Not simply one or two tyrants or dictators in a century, not one or two neat world wars, the way you were told. Wars every year, *fuehrers* at the end of every street. No justice. No order. No refuge for the innocent."

"You must have seen the Temporal Concordance." Labienus was awed.

"No," said Budu. "But there are those who have."

"And we can't do anything," said Labienus, "because history cannot be changed."

"We can't prevent it. That doesn't mean we can't do anything." Budu smiled, showing terrifying teeth. "And don't be so certain history is as fixed as they tell you, son."

"You used to say that, but nobody's managed to change it yet," said Labienus. "All the same, time is on our side! Here we are in the past, with centuries to prepare, and there they are in the future, with—what—thirty years?"

"But we face the longest march, to the most necessary victory. Do you have the strength?"

"Yes. Still, we'll have competition, father," Labienus warned. "Some of the Executive line are already making their own plans. You remember Aegeus? He's built what amounts to a private kingdom up there in the Cévennes. It's disgusting. He actually keeps mortal slaves for his own pleasure."

"That is forbidden." Budu's eyes grew small and hard as stones.

"I've already got spies in his organization, gathering evidence."

"Good. He'll suffer the consequences, when that last day comes. The other Executives must be conscripted, or persuaded to stand aside. We need every advantage."

"We can co-opt the Company's resources for our own use." Labienus had an inspiration then. "You should see how I'm presently employed, father—"

"You're a lawyer at Gray's Inn," said Budu. "Twice a year you ride out to Hampstead, to look at a mortal child you placed with foster parents there."

"Yes," said Labienus, feeling a sliver of ice in his heart. "You've observed me closely, I see. Had it occurred to you to look at the boy?"

"Yes. Old blood there. Who is he?"

"Not who; what. The damned thing is a Recombinant! The Company themselves decided to make one. They're experimenting the way they always do, dropping their subject into the past and watching what happens."

"Then they have put the lives of innocents at risk," said Budu, scowling.

"Not in the way you'd think. He's no plague-bearer, father." Labienus looked at Budu slyly. "He's a great deal more dangerous. Old blood indeed! Someone had the bright idea of designing a replacement for *you*, you see. A New Enforcer. Genetically engineered to look more human, and to be less disobedient. The little creature's their prototype. Yes, twice a year I do drag my sorry old bones out to Hampstead to test him. He never fails to impress me."

"How?"

"Utterly different brain. Better reflexes than a human child. He'll never be a beauty, but he'll be bigger and faster than most mortals. Smarter, too." Labienus parodied the syrupy tones of a fond mortal parent. "Why, only today I told our Nicket that a very great man had died, the man I named him for in fact, and do you know what the clever wittle darling said?"

"I don't care what he said," Budu replied. "Are they going to work the immortality process on him?"

"On a prototype? Gods, no! They'll never do that again," said Labienus, with a significant look. "Though I've been sorely tempted, father. Don't you think we could make good use of such a weapon? Especially as it's the blackest of black projects, and I'm the sole handler for the prototype? He'll operate within event shadows, free of recorded history! A man like that could do terrific damage where we aimed him."

"It's been done," said Budu. "More times than you know, these prodigies have walked the Earth. They're never worth the trouble. I'm not interested."

"This one is different," Labienus insisted. "And wouldn't you like another son? An able second-in-command?"

"No; but *you* would," Budu told him. "Someone to laugh at your jokes. Someone to impress with your cleverness. That's vanity. It won't serve my purpose."

"As you wish." Labienus concealed his irritation. "What else did you have in mind?"

"I want a new means of culling the mortal herds, controlled, precise. Something better than war. More selective than plague. You think about it. Use the Company's technology, if you can."

"But I'll need to find the right specialists! Possibly even mortal ones. It will require subtlety, father—"

"And you're a subtle man, yes? Win new recruits to our cause. Take your poor dead Machiavelli as your model." Budu reached out and plucked at the black armband, chuckling again. "You'll find a way."

And then he was gone, and Labienus stared around him in amazement. Nothing to be seen in any direction but the flat floor of mown hay, giving up its sweet scent to the night damps. No sound but night birds crying as they flew toward the river. He climbed to his feet and brushed off his clothes. Mounting his horse once again, he rode on to dark London.

————————

And so nothing useful had been done with Nicholas Harpole.

Labienus sighs. So much potential in a bright child, if trained properly. All that splendid ability, wasted on one martyrdom to prop up some distant causal link to Dr. Zeus Incorporated . . .

Here is a statistic to make his heart bleed over might-have-beens: out of the four hundred seventeen mortals who heard Nicholas preach as he was being burned at the stake, fully twenty-two had heeded his plea to become martyrs to the Protestant cause themselves. Two hundred twelve had gone on to lose their lives in less immediate ways, in the defense of English liberty. Eighty-six more had gone into various levels of what passed for the secret service at that time, working for the downfall of Spain with patient fanaticism under Sir Francis Walsingham. Fifty-one had simply committed suicide, in varying ways, over the three-year period following April 1, 1555.

The point was, of course, that Nicholas Harpole had asked them to die, *and they had.* Or at least given up their lives. A miserable three hundred seventy-one mortals, when he might have laid waste to nations.

Much better success on the second try. Labienus smiles, coming to the pages added later, the reports from other operatives. He hadn't minded when the *Adonai* project had been taken from him. He'd been just settling in here at Mackenzie Base, and had too many irons in the fire to waste time shepherding another hapless youth from one self-destructive crisis to the next. It had helped his ego that the new project head was a close friend, of course.

By 1837, the field wherein Budu had prophesied dystopic madness had long since been enclosed by Regent's Park, as London expanded northward. Noisome as Labienus had found the place in Tudor times, it had been a pastoral idyll compared with the urban sprawl that welcomed the new queen, young Victoria.

So Labienus went nowhere near London when he visited Executive Facilitator Nennius, and was gratified to find that Overton Hall was a dozen miles from the nearest town of any size.

They sat in Nennius's study on an autumn evening, with their feet propped before the cozy fire and a decanter of port on a stand between them.

Behind them, the windows had been firmly locked and curtains had been drawn against the night.

"It could have been worse," said Nennius, who was striving to be philosophical about his dismal posting. "It might have been a national school."

"Not for this boy," Labienus replied, helping himself to the port.

"True. All the same, I wish they'd left the matter in your hands. You'd have enjoyed the role of headmaster a great deal more than I, I suspect. All this piety and *in loco parentis* nonsense one is called upon to display, when one would much rather drown the little bastards!"

They laughed together companionably.

"You've a river here, haven't you?" said Labienus. "Arrange rowing matches and drill holes in the boats beforehand."

"Could do that, yes." Nennius composed his dark features into an expression of suitably shocked regret. "Terribly sorry, Mrs. Peckham-Winsbury, but we've had to drag the marshes for young Cecil and I'm afraid all that's been brought up is his right boot!"

Labienus snickered. "Or lay in some magnesium flares, and arrange the odd case of spontaneous combustion in the dormitories."

"Yes!" Nennius slapped his thigh. "Boys, we are gathered here to pray for the soul of Phipps Minor, who ascended into heaven in quite the brightest blaze of glory on record! Ashes to be forwarded to his careful guardian in a very small paper sack."

"Arrange for an escaped leopard to prowl the grounds."

"I regret to inform you all that the First Form will no longer be permitted on the cricket ground, due to the fact that an unidentified feline has been dragging smaller students into the bushes and eating them!" Nennius rocked in his chair with laughter.

"Secrete a few gelignite charges in their tuckboxes."

"I am quite at a loss to explain this, Mr. Carstairs, but it would appear that just as your son was sinking his teeth into an Eccles cake, he unaccountably exploded!"

Labienus wiped tears from his eyes. "And then there's good old institutional cooking. In *England*! A double whammy if ever there was one."

"Have another helping of blancmange, my dears," growled Nennius. "Oh, just once to be able to add a dash of rat poison to the custard."

"Mm. Or a little live typhus culture."

They fell silent at that, and Nennius couldn't resist scanning the room nervously.

Have you spoken to him about it?

He won't listen. Budu absolutely refuses to sanction the use of biologicals until we come up with something self-limiting. Anything with an incubation period long enough to allow it to be transmitted to what he calls "innocents" is out of the question.

But it could take years before we get a suitable mutation.

I'm aware of that. I had great hopes for this influenza virus. It may well be the one! And he wouldn't even hear me out.

His scruples make no sense. Nennius sighed and shifted in his chair. *Here in their dormitories the wretched monkeys are "innocent." Once they're in army barracks they'll be fair game, by his rules. Yet I'd wager they're twice as savage and bloody-minded at the moment as they will be once they're out in the world.*

That's what I told him, but it's like arguing with a stone wall.

It's just as well you haven't told him about this boy.

Not a word. When the little Corsican was running around, I managed to restrain myself from pointing out that we might have had just as much success with young Harpole. Think of the millions he might have led to the slaughter, with that voice of his.

Can't run an operation like that now, of course.

No, no. All covert, these days.

Shame.

Yes.

He's going to have to see reason some time.

You don't know him as I do.

At that moment there was a timid double knock on the door. Both men jumped.

"What d'you want, blast you?" snapped Nennius, rising to his feet.

"There's been a difficulty, sir," said someone with a slightly panicked voice from the other side of the door. "We've had to call for Dr. Cheke."

"Damn," murmured Nennius, rising. He went to the door and opened it. MacMurdo, the history master, stood there wringing his hands. "What in God's name have the little devils done now?"

"It's Bell-Fairfax, Dr. Nennys. He's nearly killed young Scargill."

"Hmph. Much blood?"

"A great deal, Dr. Nennys, sir. It took Dr. Horsfall and Mr. Petch both to separate them."

"Is Bell-Fairfax hurt?"

"No, sir."

"I'll deal with him. Have him brought."

"Very good, sir. Shall I have his trunk fetched, sir?"

"What for?"

"Well—he'll be sent down for this, sir, I should think."

"Nonsense! Nothing more than a fistfight between a pair of young imbeciles. A sound beating'll teach him."

"You haven't seen Scargill, sir—"

"Have him brought," said Nennius quietly, but in such a voice that the history master fled. Muttering imprecations, Nennius stalked across the room and drained his port at a gulp.

"That's my boy," said Labienus, grinning. "Shall I tactfully withdraw?"

"I'd be obliged if you would," said Nennius. He selected a cane from a basket in the corner. "You can listen from in there, though, if you like. See what you think of the direction I'm taking with him."

"Don't mind if I do," said Labienus, and carrying off the port decanter he retreated to the shadows of the next room. Sitting behind the door he had a fair view of the study, and everything that occurred there within the next half hour.

Nennius positioned himself in front of the fire, cane held before him in both hands. Labienus laughed quietly. *You look like a schoolboy's worst nightmare.*

Shut up. I'm getting into character.

"Sir?"

"Come in, Bell-Fairfax."

The boy entered the room and stepped into the light of the fire. Labienus studied him critically. It might have been young Nicholas, line for line.

Edward Bell-Fairfax at twelve years of age was already close to six feet tall. That he had grown a great deal since the beginning of the term was evident in the way his wrists stuck out beyond the cuffs of his jacket. Though the body was lanky and awkward, his face was still the smooth face of a child.

At this moment, he was white as a ghost. The pupils of his eyes were dilated, wide and black.

"What have you done, Bell-Fairfax?"

Labienus couldn't see Nennius's expression, but was impressed at his performance nonetheless. He sounded somber, regal, and infinitely wise.

"I think I killed Scargill, sir. His head's split open." The boy's voice shook.
"And I broke his jaw."

"Why did you do this, Bell-Fairfax?"

"We were fighting, sir."

"Obviously! The cause, Bell-Fairfax."

The boy blinked. "A private matter, sir."

"You are at school, Bell-Fairfax. There are no private matters here. Fifty
other boys will have seen the fight, and at least three of the masters. I should
prefer to hear your version of events, however."

"It's a private matter, sir. With respect."

"Were you provoked? Scargill's a bully." Nennius lowered his voice. "And
worse. Did he touch you?"

Edward flushed red. His mouth tightened and drew down at the corners.
"I was provoked, sir."

"I see. It means a beating, Bell-Fairfax, and I am sorry for it. You have
grieved me deeply."

"I'm sorry, sir," the boy cried. "I tried to stop. I didn't think I could really
hurt him. He's so big and—and I thought it was a good idea if he was taught
a lesson—and I couldn't stop. And so I thought—"

"That you'd better finish him?" inquired Nennius.

"Yes," said the boy, and then stopped, horrified at what he'd said. In the
gentlest of voices, Nennius said: "It was fun, wasn't it?"

The boy stared at him, unable to speak.

"My dear young man," said Nennius, putting a hand on his shoulder.
"Don't give in to fear, and certainly don't lie to yourself. This is the primal appetite that drives every one of us. It is a natural element in the human character. Without it, we should never have survived in the savage world from
whence we are sprung. Nor, I might add, would we now be able to defend our
national interests abroad. Without this instinct, we should have no heroes."

"But wrath is a deadly sin," said the boy, trembling. "And it says in Scripture, 'Thou shalt not kill.' "

Labienus shook his head, hearing echoes and ghosts.

"No, no; it says, 'Thou shalt do no murder,' " said Nennius. "Good heavens, boy, how would we make sense of God's dictates to His people, if He

really forbade killing? What would you make of the book of Joshua, then? The Lord slaughters lustily, and we are after all made in His image. And aren't they blessed who hunger and thirst after justice? They shall be satisfied. Christ Himself said so. If you enjoyed watching that cowardly knave's blood run, you mustn't blame yourself. Divine Providence put that joy in your heart."

Edward looked bewildered.

"But it was wrong," he said.

"Yes! Allowing yourself to be so carried away by an emotion that you lost control of your hands is certainly wrong. More so for you than for other boys, because you must be above these things."

The boy blinked back tears.

"If Scargill dies, will I be hanged?"

"Are you afraid to die, Bell-Fairfax?"

"No, sir. But if I'm hanged, I will have wasted my life on nothing." He looked at Nennius pleadingly. "I won't have helped anyone! And after all you've told me about what I ought to do in this world—"

"I doubt very much whether Scargill will die. And even were he to do so, there are certain gentlemen of might and influence who would see to it that you live to fulfill your destiny. The question, Bell-Fairfax, is whether you will be fit for it."

"Sir, I will be!"

"There is no question your heart is in the right place, my boy," Nennius said, stroking his chin thoughtfully. "Perhaps the fault lies with me."

"Oh, no, sir."

Nennius held up a hand to silence him. "With me, I say. I have failed to take your growing strength and your natural temper into account. Your manly impulses ought not to be suppressed, because they are—as it were—a gift from God. But they must be guided, or you cannot fulfill the hopes of those to whom you owe everything."

Edward was silent, watching him. Nennius appeared to think deeply.

"We have no arms master here," he said, "but I know of a private tutor who may serve. I will arrange for the extra hours. You must be taught to shoot, to wrestle, to ride. Saber as well, I think. And he will set you to certain exercises that will teach you greater personal restraint. It will be a great deal of hard work, Bell-Fairfax, but it is your duty to excel."

"I will not disappoint you, sir." Edward looked desperately hopeful.

"See to it that you do not." Nennius tapped him on the chest with the cane. "Now. Pain is unavoidable, my boy. If I sent you away with a whole skin, the other boys would whine that you were a favorite, and that is vile. Moreover, you must be punished for your outburst, in order to learn that you are never to lift a hand against another unless your blood is cold as the polar oceans."

"Yes, sir." Reluctantly, Edward moved to unbutton his trousers, but Nennius said scornfully: "We're not in the nursery, Bell-Fairfax. You're not here to be humiliated. You must be a man. The jacket and shirt off, if you please."

"Yes, sir." Hastily the boy pulled them off, standing bare to the waist.

"Face the fire and put your hands on either corner of the mantel. Keep them there until you're ordered to take them down."

"Yes, sir—" Edward obeyed, stretching out his arms. He gasped and squinted, turning his face from the heat.

"Face the fire! You can endure this. You will endure it. You have the strength, boy." Nennius raised the cane and brought it down on Edward's shoulders, with a crack that echoed in the room. Edward grunted and instinctively put his head down, but found he couldn't brace it against the hot mantel. He twisted away, gritting his teeth. The force of the next blow drove him forward again.

"Consider Scargill's pain, and how this balances the scales," said Nennius, delivering another blow. There was nothing in his tone to suggest he was not a sorrowing father administering correction to a well-loved son.

"Yes, sir—"

"Face the fire!" Nennius struck him again, but spoke encouragingly. "You are the steel in the fire, young man, you are the blade being forged. Your pain is necessary."

"Yes, sir—" *Whack!*

"You must be strong, after all, to accomplish your life's work. For nothing matters but the work, after all." *Whack!* "Consider Blake's edifying vow: 'I will not cease from Mental Fight—' " *Whack!*

"Yes, sir—"

Whack! "Complete the line, if you please."

" 'Nor shall my Sword sleep in my hand—' " the boy gasped. *Whack!*

" 'Till we have built Jerusalem,' " prompted Nennius.

" 'In England's green and pleasant land!' " shouted young Edward Alton Bell-Fairfax, gripping the mantel till his knuckles were white. *Whack!*

Thoroughly impressed, Labienus lifted his glass in a silent toast to Nennius. *By God, sir, that's programming.*

He glances now through the later images: the stern young man in the naval uniform, the urbane and smiling gentleman assassin he had become. What a lot Edward had accomplished for his masters! And here are two figures in one image, a kind of secular *Pietà:* an immortal woman howling her grief, cradling Edward's body in her arms, her skirts soaked with his valiantly shed blood.

"Such a waste," murmurs Labienus, considering the woman. She was a Preserver drone, a Botanist. He knew her well; he'd sat in judgment at her hearing and consigned her to official nonexistence, for having had the astonishingly bad luck to encounter both Nicholas Harpole *and,* in his time, Edward. Remarkable coincidence, really. Though such causal Mandelbrots were not unknown in the historical record . . .

Labienus closes the file and wishes, again, that he'd had Botanist Mendoza under his command, and that she'd been someone of more consequence. She'd had all the qualities he looked for in a recruit: inexhaustible rage, loathing for humanity, a proper appreciation of the untainted glories of the natural world. Under the proper conditions, she might have been a truly useful weapon.

But, then again, she'd had that fatal weakness. To have loved a mortal! And *that* mortal, among all men. What a security risk! Still . . .

Labienus despises love, but permits himself sentiment; it lends a certain zest to life, after all. He regards them now, the two lovers, and sighs self-indulgently. How well-paired they had been, Edward and Mendoza! Matched blades. Or flint and steel, with which he might have started an inferno that swept across the world . . .

He is aware that he feels a vague respect for the woman. Mendoza, at least, had never done the reasonable thing, never settled for less, but held to her one insane passion even as it had dragged her into the flames. Such a valuable quality in a pawn. Is it really too late? . . .

But Edward is dead, after all.

Closing the file, Labienus puts it aside. He rises and walks to the window, stretching, thinking that it is a pity one can't have one's cake and sacrifice it, too.

On further reflection, however, he decides that a disposable hero is infinitely to be preferred to the permanent model.

In Egypt, work had just commenced on the Suez Canal. Labienus was grateful he was a world away, in a region of glacier fields no mortal ingenuity could ever turn to profit.

He had walked a long time, following the vaguest hint of directions. After a few days there were no more trees, and the only green he saw was in the aurora borealis when it bannered against the stars. Labienus did not suffer the discomfort a mortal would have felt, but he would certainly have preferred the meeting to take place in a more convenient location. This place had only the advantage that it was in his own sector, and beautiful.

It wasn't until the fifth night, as bright ghosts flared in heaven, that he became aware of a slight alteration in the crunching rhythm of his own footsteps. Two more steps and he was certain, and whirled around to behold Budu following him.

"Damn you! How long were you going to let me keep walking?" Labienus shouted.

The old Enforcer laughed. He stood straight and threw back his fur hood. He was heavily robed in polar bear fur, an immense whiteness on the white field. His breath steamed and froze, settling in icicles on his long beard and mustache. The light of the aurora glittered in his pale eyes.

"I could have taken you out five times by now," he said. "You've grown careless."

Labienus thought of telling him what he could do with his stalking games, but smiled instead. "I trusted you, father."

"Have you brought the codes?"

Labienus glanced around involuntarily, though they were the only living things within miles. "Yes. And my report."

"Good." Budu inclined forward. Labienus set his index finger between Budu's eyes and downloaded. When he had finished, he cleared his throat.

"We've penetrated the Bikkung office at last. Xi Wang-Mu is thoroughly motivated. Moreover, she has a promising second-in-command by the name of Hong Tsieh. They share our grievances."

"Very good. What about Africa?"

"No progress, I regret to say." Labienus shrugged. He preferred to look nonchalant when confessing failure. "Amaunet would be ideal. She has the perfect temperament, but she seems to be one of Aegeus's circle, and she's been posted to Eastern Europe. There's no point in approaching Suleyman at all."

"But you once trained his second-in-command," Budu pointed out.

"Briefly," said Labienus. "We didn't get on. You won't get at Suleyman through Latif, I assure you."

Budu shook his head. "You make so many enemies, you Facilitators," he said. "Such tempers and egos you have. One has to court you. Persuade you. Motivate you. My men knew what was right, and they did it."

"Yes; I suppose even Marco thought he was right, when he disobeyed orders," said Labienus acidly. Budu just looked at him.

"No," he said. "Marco was an idiot. He thought he could frighten our masters into listening. And he did frighten them, and when they retired us because they were afraid of us, he wept like a stupid child. But you aren't stupid."

"Thank you," said Labienus.

"So you will get someone into Aegeus's confidence. I want a link to Amaunet. And we need a cell in Africa."

"It's possible we might be able to turn certain members of Aegeus's cabal," admitted Labienus. "He's not well loved."

"Then do it," said Budu. Labienus nodded. He cleared his throat.

"Father," said Labienus, "I must be honest with you. Gods know you were honest with me, when you told me what things would come to in the future. I've watched the mortals crowding into their stinking cities. Their coal-soot advances on the clean sky. The forests go down before their axes and the whales are pulled in and butchered alongside their ships. But, father, it's not war or crime causing these things. It's peace. Prosperity. Civilization!"

"We will go after the industrialists, too, when we're ready."

"But when will we be ready, father? How badly must it all deteriorate before we move at last?" demanded Labienus, pinning his hopes on sincerity. "You want to exterminate the murderers and generals, but they do the work we should have begun by now. The survival of the world is no longer a moral question, if it ever was. It's a mechanical question. A matter of numbers."

"You think we ought to go after the mortals indiscriminately, to protect the earth," said Budu.

"Yes!"

"You are overruled. There is only the moral question." Budu loomed over him. "Whether the fields are green or black matters nothing. Whether the mortals live or die matters nothing. What they are, while they live, is the only thing with which we are concerned."

Labienus blinked ice crystals from his eyes, looking up at the giant in furs. He made his decision in that moment.

"You're right, of course," he said. "Thank you for putting it in perspective."

He blinked again and Budu was no longer there. The wind was screaming across the snow at ankle-level, obliterating his footprints.

Labienus looks up sharply as the bell rings. Exhaling in annoyance, he reaches for the amplifier.

It is the latest thing in field technology, a crude mechanism which compensates for its crudeness by a wealth of ornamental detail. Gold vines and flowers twine over its surface of gleaming black wax. It looks almost, but not quite, like a Victrola hooked up to a candlestick telephone. There is a headset, of sorts. He slips it on.

Ave! He recognizes the voice at once. It is Nennius, sounding quietly gleeful.

Ave. Executive Section Head for the Northwest—

Yes, yes, I know it's you! Listen to me. How many stones does it take to kill a large fat self-important bird with delusions of grandeur?

If he's immortal, there aren't enough stones in the world, Labienus replies. *But I'd still like to get Aegeus with a good sharp one, right between the eyes. You've had a stroke of luck?*

An unbelievable stroke of luck, transmits Nennius. *How quickly can you come to Bucharest?*

What the hell are you doing in Bucharest?

Attending a street fair. You remember the old green house next door to the Unirii Square HQ? It's a café now. I'll look for you there in twelve hours.

Lesser immortals would be obliged to hike south to the nearest seaport, book passage on a ship as far as Panama, disembark and take a train across the isthmus, travel by ship again across the Atlantic to France, there to travel east, arriving eventually by a series of unreliable stage connections in Romania. Facilitator Generals, however, merely hop a transpolar flight, touching down at a Company transport station in the Carpathians, and enjoy a leisurely ride in a nicely appointed private coach.

Being considerably older and wickeder than any vampires, werewolves, or mysterious blue flames that might dare to cross his path, Labienus arrives unmolested at the Unirii Square HQ, precisely twelve hours after having received Nennius's call.

Nennius is sitting at a street table, looking expectant. A waiter has just set down two glasses of slivovitz.

"Have a seat," says Nennius, reaching into an inner pocket. As Labienus sits, he tosses a field photograph on the table.

Labienus stares. He lifts his glass, with elaborate unconcern, and takes a long slow drink before permitting himself to reach for the photograph.

The image before him is of a small mortal man.

The mortal wears the coarse uniform of some institution, and his big head has been shaved. His slender hands were in the act of rising to his face when the shutter snapped, his weak mouth opening in protest as he turned from the camera. His eyes are wide, dark, wet, blind-looking. Labienus is irresistibly reminded of the little figure in *The Scream.*

Nennius tosses another photograph on the table.

Here is a formal studio portrait: the mortal is wearing a suit now, though it is a badly-fitting one, and he has closed his eyes against the camera flash. He has a curiously inanimate appearance, like a corpse or a waxwork that has been dressed up.

"*Homo umbratilis,*" murmurs Labienus. "Who is he? How did you get him?"

"His name is Emil Bergwurm," says Nennius. "And I haven't got him. We do want him, though, don't we?"

"Yes," says Labienus. "Our own tiny freak of genius? Oh, yes. What do we have to do to get him?"

"Take him away from Amaunet," says Nennius.

Labienus says something so unpleasant that were it written down, in the ancient pictographs of its own language, the little symbols would smoke and snake and spit venom on clay tablet or papyrus.

"It's not as bad as all that," Nennius says hastily. "She's keeping him a secret from Aegeus. You asked me to have her monitored; well, I got word she bribed the director of the lunatic asylum here, three years ago. When I investigated, this is what I found."

"How do you know she hasn't shipped the thing off to the Cévennes?" Labienus demands.

"Perhaps you'd better come and see for yourself," says Nennius

They leave without paying for their drinks. The waiter watches them go, sadly. He is uncertain exactly what variety of *stregoi* they might be, those two sneering gentlemen; but he knows it is as much as his life is worth, to demand payment of something with that particular cold and glaring eye.

Nennius leads and Labienus paces close after him through the narrow streets. Blind cobbled alleys, deepset doors, handsbreadth windows behind which one candle gives faint light, and even the light has a certain quality of gloom, as though it were no more than gold paint on an interior. Night and fog come down.

When they emerge on the open field where the fair has been, any sense of festivity has long departed. Vendors are taking down their booths by lantern light, dropping tent poles. The menagerie has already hauled its wagons into the night, leaving only a reek of exotic manure. But at the far edge of the field, one place is still doing business, still has its banner out on a tall leaning pole. MOTHER AEGYPT, the sign reads. There are two wagons behind the sign, taller and narrower than the vardas of the Romanies. They are painted black.

How frightening, Labienus transmits. *What's next? Bats swooping out of the mist?*

No. The rats haven't finished yet, Nennius responds, nodding at the patient mortals who wait in a line that stretches from darkness into the circle of lamplight before the lead wagon's door. Their impassive faces are turned up to the light. They are hard men, all but the last, who seems to be a peasant woman.

These aren't here to have their fortunes told, guesses Labienus.

Of course not. They're thieves. They bring stolen goods to her; she pays them handsomely, and forwards the loot on to Dr. Zeus. Jewelry, porcelain, plate. It'd be stolen in any case, and this way it won't be melted down or hacked apart. Everyone wins! Except the rightful owners, of course, but that can't be helped.

Ah. The usual story. Shall we take our place in line with the other thieves?

They stroll across the dark field, and step into line behind the woman. As the queue progresses forward, they can hear murmured conversation, the clink of coin. There is surprisingly little talk, no haggling at all. One by one the thieves emerge from the caravan, each face lit for a second by the lantern over the door, and each face bearing the same expression of profound relief to be gone from Mother Aegypt.

The mortal woman is the last to go in. She alone bears no loot. Three minutes later she emerges, and her square heavy face is white as paper.

"Didn't you like your fortune?" inquires Labienus.

"She told me I am dying," the woman whispers.

"Why, so you are," says Nennius. "But don't you believe in eternal life? You must have perfect faith!"

The woman looks at him, and looks at Labienus. With a shudder she makes the sign of the Cross, and hurries away from them.

Dead silence from the wagon.

"So much for surprising her," says Labienus. "Let's pay a call, shall we?"

They step up, and go in.

Stifling warmth and all the perfumes of Arabia, myrrh and frankincense and spices to make the eyes water. Amaunet looks up at them sharply, from the cheap folding table at which she does business.

She gives the impression of great age. Her skin is smooth, but seven millennia of contempt and despair look out of her eyes, and her dark face could cut diamond.

"Hello, Amaunet," says Labienus. "Can you tell our fortunes?"

Her lip curls. "You'll get what's coming to you, in the year 2355," she says. "How about that?"

Labienus chuckles, and closes the door behind him. He lounges there, blocking the exit, and Nennius moves to lounge in turn in front of the one window. This is all largely psychological, of course, because Amaunet could exit straight through a wall if she chose, but a threat is a threat.

"You've been playing a double game, haven't you?" Labienus says. "I don't imagine Aegeus would be happy to learn you've kept a secret from him."

"What do you want?" asks Amaunet.

"Emil Bergwurm."

Amaunet closes her eyes. "Hell," she says. The logic is inescapable: two immortals can overpower one, and even were she to escape them, she'd be unable to take her prize with her.

"You'd better tell us the whole story," Labienus says.

She opens her eyes and looks at him in a way that makes even Nennius flinch, but he just grins at her.

"My slave choked to death on a chicken head. I went to the nearest asylum to buy another. Imagine my surprise when I found Emil," she says.

"Does he cost you much in chicken heads?"

"No. He does other tricks."

"Such as?"

"Magic potions." She smiles now, and it is more frightening than her expression of anger. "That's his little streak of genius, you see. Not machines; chemistry. If the mortals need to abort a child or poison a spouse, little Emil can fix them up with something tasteless, odorless, and untraceable. He's useless at anything else, but now I make double my operating budget from the elixirs I sell."

"And that's why you've kept him from Aegeus?" Labienus takes out a silver case, withdraws a stick of Theobromos. He offers the case to Amaunet. She hesitates a long moment, then takes a stick herself.

"Partly." She peels back the silver paper. "I've had him working on a project of my own, if you must know."

"The Holy Grail, I suppose," says Nennius, and Amaunet nods sadly. She has been trying to die for five thousand years.

"Once a month, he brings me the black cup. You'd be amazed at how close he's come; his last batch stopped my heart for five minutes. The damned thing started up again, alas, since it's as stupid as he is."

"I'll make you a promise," says Labienus. "If we can get him to produce an elixir of death that works on an immortal, we'll send you a bottle."

"How chivalrous of you," she says, leaning back. "Theobromos and promises, my my. You must want something else. And what do you need with my poor little maggot-baby, anyway? *You* don't long for the grave, not an ambitious bastard like you."

"Why, Amaunet, it's elementary! My rival has a fabulous weapon, so of course I want one just like it. That's been the rule of the game since the monkeys discovered fire. And if you betrayed Aegeus once, I'm certainly curious to know whether you'll betray him again," says Labienus.

"Don't count on it," says Amaunet with a snarl. "I haven't forgotten Carthage, Labienus."

He shrugs. "I wouldn't respect you if you had. But we're planning our endgames now, dear Amaunet. I love cleansing fire; you know how well. What will Aegeus do, if he seizes power in 2355? Make the world a vast extension of Eurobase One? Pink carpets and gilded chandeliers! Think of all those immortal gourmands and lechers and esthetes, battening on the monkeys like so many vampires. What will you do in that world, lady?"

Amaunet just looks at him.

"Bring me what I long for, and I'll show you," she says.

He laughs, and rises to his feet. "Why don't you introduce us to little Emil?"

She nods at her narrow bed, which is on a long chest built into the caravan's wall. "Introduce yourselves. He's under there. He likes the dark."

Nennius thrusts the mattress back and opens the side of the chest. There is a shrill scream. Emil Bergwurm curls away from the light, hiding his face. Labienus leans down to smile at him.

"Come out, little man! I've work for you to do." He begins to chortle. "Nothing matters except our work, you know."

Even Amaunet laughs at that.

In the end they have to haul him out bodily, and he squeals and fights until they shut him in a fake mummy case Amaunet has had propped in the corner. They take their leave of Amaunet. Labienus walks with the case tucked under his arm, like a devil carrying off a soul.

"That went rather well, really," says Nennius.

"Didn't it, though?" says Labienus cheerfully. He has already thought of a use for Emil Bergwurm.

TWO

1906

SON OBSERVE THE TIME

On the eve of destruction we had oysters and Champagne.

Don't suppose for a moment that we had any desire to lord it over the poor mortals of San Francisco, in that month of April in that year of 1906; but things weren't going to be so gracious there again for a long while, and we felt an urge to fortify ourselves against the work we were to do.

London before the Great Fire, Delhi before the Mutiny, even Chicago—I was there and I can tell you, it requires a great deal of mental and emotional self-discipline to live side by side with mortals in a Salvage Zone. You must look, daily, into the smiling faces of those who are to lose all, and walk beside them in the knowledge that nothing you can do will affect their fates. Even the most prosaic of places has a sort of haunted glory at such times; judge then how it looked to us, that gilded fantastical butterfly of a city, quite unprepared for its approaching holocaust.

The place was made even queerer by the fact that there were so many Company operatives there at the time. The very ether hummed with our transmissions. In any street you might have seen us dismounting from carriages or the occasional automobile, we immortal gentlemen tipping our derbies to the ladies, our immortal ladies responding with a graceful inclination of their picture hats, smiling as we met each others' terrified eyes. We dined at the Palace and as guests at Nob Hill mansions; promenaded in Golden Gate Park, drove out to Ocean Beach, attended the theater and everywhere saw the pale, set faces of our own kind, busy with their own particular preparations against what was to come.

Some of us had less pleasant places to go. I was grateful that I was not required to brave the Chinese labyrinth by Waverly Place, but my associate Pan had certain business there amongst the Celestials. I myself was obliged to venture, too many times, into the boardinghouses south of Market Street. Beneath the Fly Trap was a Company safe house and HQ; we'd meet there sometimes, Pan and I, at the end of a long day in our respective ghettoes, and we'd sit shaking together over a brace of stiff whiskeys. Thus heartened, it was time for a costume change: dock laborer into gentleman for me, coolie into cook for him, and so home by cable car.

I lodged in two rooms on Bush Street. I will not say I slept there; one does not rest well on the edge of the maelstrom. But it was a place to keep one's trunk, and to operate the Company credenza necessary for facilitating the missions of those operatives whose case officer I was. Salvaging is a terribly complicated affair, requiring as it does that one hide in history's shadow until the last possible moment before snatching one's quarry from its preordained doom. One must be organized and thoroughly coordinated; and timing is everything.

On the morning of the tenth of April I was working there, sending a progress report, when there came a brisk knock at my door. Such was my concentration that I was momentarily unmindful of the fact that I had no mortal servants to answer it. When I heard the impatient tapping of a small foot on the step, I hastened to the door.

I admitted Nan D'Arraignee, one of our Art Preservation specialists. She is an operative of West African origin with exquisite features, slender and slight as a doll carved of ebony. I had worked with her briefly near the end of the previous century. She is quite the most beautiful woman I have ever known, and happily married to another immortal, a century before I ever laid eyes on her. Timing, alas, is everything.

"Victor." She nodded. "Charming to see you again."

"Do come in." I bowed her into my parlor, acutely conscious of its disarray. Her bright gaze took in the wrinkled laundry cast aside on the divan, the clutter of unwashed teacups, the half-eaten oyster loaf on the credenza console, six empty sauterne bottles, and one smudgily thumb-printed wineglass. She was far too courteous to say anything, naturally, and occupied herself with the task of removing her gloves.

"I must apologize for the condition of the place," I stammered. "My duties have kept me out a good deal." I swept a copy of the *Examiner* from a chair. "Won't you sit down?"

"Thank you." She took the seat and perched there, hands folded neatly over her gloves and handbag. I pulled over another chair, intensely irritated at my clumsiness.

"I trust your work goes well?" I inquired, for there is of course no point in asking one of us if *we* are well. "And, er, Kalugin's? Or has he been assigned elsewhere?"

"He's been assigned to Marine Transport, as a matter of fact," she told me, smiling involuntarily. "We are to meet on the *Thunderer* afterward. I am so pleased! He's been in the Bering Sea for two years, and I've missed him dreadfully."

"Ah," I said. "How pleasant, then, to have something to look forward to in the midst of all this . . ."

She nodded quickly, understanding. I cleared my throat and continued: "What may I do for you, Nan?"

She averted her gaze from dismayed contemplation of the stale oyster loaf and smiled. "I was told you might be able to assist me in requisitioning additional transport for my mission."

"I shall certainly attempt it." I stroked my beard. "Your present arrangements are unsuitable?"

"Inadequate, rather. You may recall that I'm in charge of presalvage at the Hopkins Gallery. It seems our original estimates of what we can rescue there were too modest. At present, I have five vans arranged for to evacuate the gallery contents, but really, we need more. Would it be possible to requisition a sixth? My own case officer was unable to assist me, but felt you might have greater success."

This was a challenge. Company resources were strained to the utmost on this operation, which was one of the largest on record. Every operative in the United States had been pressed into service, and many of the European and Asian personnel. A handsome allotment had been made for transport units, but needs were swiftly exceeding expectations.

"Of course I should like to help you," I replied cautiously, "if at all possible. You are aware, however, that horsedrawn transport utilization is impossible, due to the subsonic disturbances preceding the earthquake—and motor transports are, unfortunately, in great demand—"

A brewer's wagon rumbled down the street outside, rattling my windows. We both leaped to our feet, casting involuntary glances at the ceiling; then sat down in silent embarrassment. Madame D'Arraignee gave a little cough. "I'm so sorry—my nerves are simply—"

"Not at all, not at all, I assure you—one can't help flinching—"

"Quite. In any case, Victor, I understand the logistical difficulties involved; but even a handcart would greatly ease our difficulties. So many lovely and unexpected things have been discovered in this collection, that it really would be too awful to lose them to the fire."

"Oh, certainly." I got up and strode to the windows, giving in to the urge to look out and assure myself that the buildings hadn't begun to sway yet. Solid and seemingly as eternal as the pyramids they stood there, for the moment. I turned back to Madame D'Arraignee as a thought occurred to me. "Tell me, do you know how to operate an automobile?"

"But of course!" Her face lit up.

"It may be possible to obtain something in that line. Depend upon it, madame, you will have your sixth transport. I shall see to it personally."

"I knew I could rely on you." She rose, all smiles. We took our leave of one another with a courtesy that belied our disquiet. I saw her out and returned to my credenza keyboard.

QUERY, I input, *RE: REQUISITION ADDTNL TRANSPORT MOTOR VAN OR AUTO? PRIORITY RE: HOPKINS INST.*

HOPKINS PROJECT NOT YOUR CASE, came the green and flashing reply.

NECESSARY, I input. *NEW DISCV OVRRIDE SECTION AUTH. PLEASE FORWARD REQUEST PRIORITY.*

WILL FORWARD.

That was all. So much for my chivalrous impulse, I thought, and watched as the transmission screen winked out and returned me to my status report on the Nob Hill presalvage work. I resumed my entry of the Gilded Age loot tagged for preservation.

When I had transmitted it, I stood and paced the room uneasily. How long had I been hiding in here? What I wanted was a meal and a good stretch of the legs, I told myself sternly. Fresh air, in so far as that was available in any city at the beginning of this twentieth century. I scanned the oyster loaf and found it already pulsing with bacteria. Pity. After disposing of it in the dustbin

I put on my coat and hat, took my stick and went out to tread the length of Bush Street with as bold a step as I could muster.

It was nonsense, really, to be frightened. I'd be out of the city well before the first shock. I'd be safe on air transport bound for London before the first flames rose. London, the other City. I could settle into a chair at my club and read a copy of *Punch* that wasn't a month old, secure in the knowledge that the oak beams above my head were fixed and immovable as they had been since the days when I'd worn a powdered wig, as they would be until German shells came raining down decades from now . . .

Shivering, I dismissed thoughts of the Blitz. Plenty of *life* to think about, surely! Here were bills posted to catch my eye: I might go out to the Pavilion to watch the boxing exhibition—Jack Joyce and Bob Ward featured. There was delectable vaudeville at the Orpheum, I was assured, and gaiety girls out at the Chutes, to say nothing of a spectacular sideshow recreation of the Johnstown flood . . . perhaps not in the best of taste, under the present circumstances.

I might imbibe Gold Seal Champagne to lighten my spirits, though I didn't think I would; Veuve Cliquot was good enough for me. Ah, but what about a bottle of Chianti, I thought, arrested by the bill of fare posted in the window of a corner restaurant. Splendid culinary fragrances wafted from within. Would I have grilled veal chops here? Would I go along Bush to the Poodle Dog for chicken *chaud-froid blanc*? Would I venture to Grant in search of yellow silk banners for duck roasted in some tiny Celestial kitchen? Then again, I knew of a Swiss place where the cook was a Hungarian, and prepared a light and crisply fried Wiener schnitzel to compare with any I'd had . . . or I might just step into a saloon and order another oyster loaf to take home . . .

No, I decided, veal chops would suit me nicely. I cast a worried eye up at the building—pity this structure wasn't steel-framed—and proceeded inside.

It was one of those dark, robust places within, floor thickly strewn with fresh sawdust not yet kicked into little heaps. I took my table as any good operative does, back to the wall and a clear path to the nearest exit. Service was poor, as apparently their principal waiter was late today, but the wine was excellent. I found it bright on the palate, just what I'd wanted, and the chops when they came were redolent of herbs and fresh olive oil. What a consolation appetite can be.

Yes, life, that was the thing to distract one from unwise thoughts. Savor the wine, I told myself, observe the parade of colorful humanity, breathe in the fragrance of the joss sticks and the seafood and the gardens of the wealthy, listen to the smart modern city with its whirring steel parts at the service of its diverse inhabitants. The moment is all, surely.

I dined in some isolation, for the luncheon crowd had not yet emerged from the nearby offices and my host remained in the kitchen, arguing with the cook over the missing waiter's character and probable ancestry. Even as I amused myself by listening, however, I felt a disturbance approaching the door. No temblor yet, thank heaven, but a tempest of emotions. I caught the horrifying mental images before ever I heard the stifled weeping. In another moment he had burst through the door, a young male mortal with a prodigious black mustache, quite nattily dressed but with his thick hair in wild disarray. As soon as he was past the threshold his sobs burst out unrestrained, at a volume that would have done credit to Caruso.

This brought his employer out of the back at once, blurting out the first phrases of furious denunciation. The missing waiter (for so he was) staggered forward and thrust out that day's *Chronicle*. The headlines, fully an inch tall, checked the torrent of abuse: MANY LOSE THEIR LIVES IN GREAT ERUPTION OF VESUVIUS.

The proprietor of the restaurant, struck dumb, went an ugly sallow color. He put the fingertips of one hand in his mouth and bit down hard. In a broken voice, the waiter described the horrors: roof collapsed in church in his own village. His own family might even now lie dead, buried in ash. The proprietor snatched the paper and cast a frantic eye over the columns of print. He sank to his knees in the sawdust, sobbing. Evidently he had family in Naples, too.

I stared at my plate. I saw gray and rubbery meat, congealing grease, seared bone with the marrow turned black. In the midst of life we are in death, but it doesn't do to reflect upon it while dining.

"You must, please, excuse us, sir," the proprietor said to me, struggling to his feet. "There has been a terrible tragedy." He set the *Chronicle* beside my plate so I could see the blurred rotogravure picture of King Victor Emmanuel. REPORT THAT TOTAL NUMBER OF DEAD MAY REACH SEVEN HUNDRED, I read. TOWNS BURIED UNDER ASHES AND MANY CAUGHT IN RUINED BUILDINGS. MANY BUILDINGS CRUSHED BY ASHES. Of course, I had known about the coming tragedy; but it was on the other side of the world, the business of other Company operatives, and I envied them that their work was completed now.

"I am so very sorry, sir," I managed to say, looking up at my host. He thought my pallor was occasioned by sympathy: he could not know I was seeing his mortal face like an apparition of the days to come, and it was livid and charring, for he lay dead in the burning ruins of a boardinghouse in the Mission district. Horror, yes, impossible not to feel horror, but one cannot empathize with them. One must not.

They went into the kitchen to tell the cook and I heard weeping break out afresh. Carefully I took up the newspaper and perused it. Perhaps there was something here that might divert me from the unpleasantness of the moment? Embezzlement. A crazed admirer stalking an actress. Charlatan evangelists. Grisly murder committed by two boys. Deadly explosion. Crazed derelict stalking a bank president. Los Angeles school principals demanding academic standards lowered.

I dropped the paper, and, leaving five dollars on the table, I fled that place.

I walked briskly, not looking into the faces of the mortals I passed. I rode the cable car, edging away from the mortal passengers. I nearly ran through the green expanse of Golden Gate Park, dodging around the mortal idlers, the lovers, the nurses wheeling infants in perambulators, until at last I stood on the shore of the sea. Tempting to turn to look at the fairy castles perched on its cliffs; tempting to turn to look at the carnival of fun along its gray sand margin, but the human comedy was the last thing I wanted just then. I needed, rather, the chill and level grace of the steel-colored horizon, sun-glistering, wide-expanding. The cold salt wind buffeted me, filled my grateful lungs. Ah, the immortal ocean.

Consider the instructive metaphor: every conceivable terror dwells in her depths; she receives all wreckage, refuse, corruption of every kind, she pulls down into her depths human calamity indescribable; but none of this is any consideration to the sea. Let the screaming mortal passengers fight for room in the lifeboats, as the wreck belches flame and settles below the extinguishing wave; next morning she'll still be beautiful and serene, her combers no less white, her distances as blue, her seabirds no less graceful as they wheel in the pure air. What perfection, to be so heartless. An inspiration to any lesser immortal.

As I stood so communing with the elements, a mortal man came wading out of the surf. I judged him two hundred pounds of athletic stockbroker, muscles bulging under sagging wet wool, braving the icy water as an act of self-disciplinary sport. He stood for a moment on one leg, examining the sole of his other foot. There was something gladiatorial in his pose. He looked up and saw me.

"A bracing day, sir," he shouted.

"Quite bracing." I nodded and smiled. I could feel the frost patterns of my returning composure.

And so I boarded another streetcar and rode back into the mortal warren, and found my way by certain streets to the Barbary Coast. Not a place a gentleman cares to admit to visiting, especially when he's known the gilded beauties of old Byzantium or Regency-era wenches; the raddled pleasures available on Pacific Street suffered by comparison. But appetite is appetite, after all, and there is nothing like it to take one's mind off unpleasant thoughts.

"Your costume." The attendant pushed a pasteboard carton across the counter to me. "Personal effects and field equipment. Linen, trousers, suspenders, boots, shirt, vest, coat, and hat." He frowned. "Phew! These should have been laundered. Would you care to be fitted with an alternate set?"

"That's all right." I took the offending rags. "The sweat goes with the role, I'm afraid. Irish laborer."

"Ah." He took a step backward. "Well, break a leg."

Fifteen minutes later I emerged from a dressing room the very picture of an immigrant yahoo, uncomfortably conscious of my clammy and odiferous clothing. I sidled into the canteen, hoping there wouldn't be a crowd in the line for coffee. There wasn't, at that: most of the diners were clustered around one operative over in a corner, so I stood alone watching the food service technician fill my thick china mug from a dented steel coffee urn. The fragrant steam was a welcome distraction from my own fragrancy. I found a solitary table and warmed my hands on my dark brew there in peace, until an operative broke loose from the group and approached me.

"Say, Victor!"

I knew him slightly, an American operative so young one could scan him and still discern the scar tissue from his augmentations. He was one of my Presalvagers.

"Good morning, Averill."

"Say, you really ought to listen to that fellow over there. He's got some swell stories." He paused only long enough to have his cup refilled, then came and pulled out a chair across from me. "Know who he is? He's the guy who follows Caruso around!"

"Is he?"

"Sure is. Music Specialist Grade One! That boy's wired for sound. He's caught every performance Caruso's ever given, even the church stuff when he was a kid. Going to get him in *Carmen* the night before you-know-what, going to record the whole performance. He's just come back from planting receivers in the footlights! Say, have you gotten tickets yet?"

"No, I haven't. I'm not interested, actually."

"Not interested?" he exclaimed. "Why aren't you—how *can't* you be interested? It's *Caruso*, for God's sake!"

"I'm perfectly aware of that, Averill, but I've got a prior engagement. And, personally, I've always thought de Reszke was much the better tenor."

"De Reszke?" He scanned his records to place the name and, while doing so, absently took a great gulp of coffee. A second later he clutched his ear and gasped. "Christ almighty!"

"Steady, man." I suppressed a smile. "You don't want to gulp beverages over sixty degrees Celsius, you know. There's some very complex circuitry placed near the Eustachian tube that gets unpleasantly hot if you do."

"Ow, ow, ow!" He sucked in air, staring at me with the astonishment of the very new operative. It always takes them a while to discover that immortality and intense pain are not strangers, indeed can reside in the same eternal house for quite lengthy periods of time. "Should I drink some ice water?"

"By no means, unless you want some real discomfort. You'll be all right in a minute or so. As I was about to say, I have some recordings of Jean de Reszke I'll transmit to you, if you're interested in comparing artists."

"Thanks, I'd like that." Averill ran a hasty self-diagnostic.

"And how is your team faring over at the New Brunswick, by the way? No cases of nerves, no blue devils?"

"Hell no." Averill started to lift his coffee again and then set it down respectfully.

"Doesn't bother you that the whole place will be ashes in a few days' time, and most of your neighbors dead?"

"No. We're all O.K. over there. We figure it's just a metaphor for the whole business, isn't it? I mean, sooner or later this whole world"—he made a sweeping gesture, palm outward—"as we know it, is going the same way, right? So what's it matter if it's the earthquake that finishes it now, or a wrecking ball someplace further on in time, right? Same thing with the people. There's no reason to get personally upset about it, is there? No, sir. Specially since *we'll* all still be alive."

"A commendable attitude." I had a sip of my coffee. "And your work goes well?"

"Yes, *sir*." He grinned. "You will be so proud of us burglary squad fellows when you get our next list. You wouldn't believe the stuff we're finding! All kinds of objets d'art, looks like. One-of-a-kind items, by God. Wait'll you see."

"I look forward to it." I glanced at my chronometer and drank down the rest of my coffee, having waited for it to descend to a comfortable fifty-nine degrees Celsius. "But, you know, Averill, it really won't do to think of yourselves as burglars."

"Well—that is—it's only a figure of speech, anyhow!" Averill protested, flushing. "A joke!"

"I'm aware of that, but I cannot emphasize enough that we are not stealing anything." I set my coffee cup down, aware that I sounded priggish, and looked sternly at him. "We're preserving priceless examples of late Victorian craftsmanship for the edification of future generations."

"I know." Averill looked at me sheepishly, "But—aw, hell, do you mean to say not one of those crystal chandeliers will wind up in some Facilitator General's private HQ somewhere?"

"That's an absurd idea," I told him, though I knew only too well it wasn't. Still, it doesn't do to disillusion one's subordinates too young. "And now, will you excuse me? I mustn't be late for work."

"All right. Be seeing you!"

As I left he rejoined the admiring throng around the fellow who was telling Caruso stories. My way lay along the bright tiled hall, steamy and echoing with the clatter of food preparation and busy operatives; then through the dark security vestibule, with its luminous screens displaying the world without; then through the concealed door that shut behind me and left no trace of itself to any eyes but my own. I drew a deep breath. Chill and silent morning air; no glimmer of light, yet, at least not down here in the alley. Half past five. This time three days hence—

I shivered and found my way out in the direction of the waterfront.

Not long afterward I arrived at the loading area where I had been desultorily employed for the last month. I made my entrance staggering slightly, doing my best to murder "You Can't Guess Who Flirted with Me" in a gravelly baritone.

The mortal laborers assembled there turned to stare at me. My best friend, an acquaintance I'd cultivated painstakingly these last three weeks, came forward and took me by the arm.

"Jesus, Kelly, you'd better stow that. Where've you been?"

I stopped singing and gave him a belligerent stare. "Marching in the Easter parade, O'Neil."

"O, like enough." He ran his eyes over me in dismay. Francis O'Neil was thirty years old. He looked enough like me to have been taken for my somewhat bulkier, clean-shaven brother. "What're you doing this for, man? You know Herlihy doesn't like you as it is. You look like you've not been home to sleep nor bathe since Friday night!"

"So I have not." I dropped my gaze in hungover remorse.

"Come on, you poor stupid bastard, I've got some coffee in my dinner pail. Sober up. Was it a letter you got from your girl again?"

"It was." I let him steer me to a secluded area behind a mountain of crates and accepted the tin cup he filled for me with lukewarm coffee. "She doesn't love me, O'Neil. She never did. I can tell."

"You're taking it all the wrong way, I'm sure. I can't believe she's stopped caring, not after all the things you've told me about her. Just drink that down, now. Mary made it fresh not an hour ago."

"You're a lucky man, Francis." I leaned on him and began to weep, slopping the coffee. He forbore with the patience of a saint and replied: "Sure I am, Jimmy, and shall I tell you why? Because I know when to take my drink, don't I? I don't swill it down every payday and forget to go home, do I? No indeed. I'd lose Mary and the kids and all the rest of it, wouldn't I? It's self-control you need, Jimmy, and the sorrows in your heart be damned. Come on now. With any luck Herlihy won't notice the state you're in."

But he did, and a litany of scorn was pronounced on my penitent head. I

took it with eyes downcast, turning my battered hat in my hands, and a dirt-
ier nor more maudlin drunk could scarce have been seen in that city. I would
be summarily fired, I was assured, but they needed men today so bad they'd
employ even the likes of me, though by God next time—

When the boss had done excoriating me I was dismissed to help unload a
cargo of copra from the *Nevadan*, in from the islands yesterday. I sniveled and
tottered and managed not to drop anything much. O'Neil stayed close to me
the whole day, watchful lest I pass out or wander off. He was a good friend to
the abject caricature I presented; God knows why he cared. Well, I should repay his kindness, at least, though in a manner he would never have the opportunity to appreciate.

We sweated until four in the afternoon, when there was nothing left to
take off the *Nevadan*; let go then with directions to the next day's job, and
threats against slackers.

"Now, Kelly." O'Neil took my arm and steered me with him back toward
Market Street. "I'll tell you what I think you ought to do. Go home and have
a bit of a wash in the basin, right? Have you clean clothes? So, put on a clean
shirt and trousers and see can you scrape some of that off your boots. Then,
come over to supper at our place. Mary's bought some sausages, we thought
we'd treat ourselves to a dish of coddle now that Lent's over. We've plenty."

"I will, then." I grasped his hand. "O'Neil, you're a lord for courtesy."

"I am not. Only go home and wash, man!"

We parted in front of the Terminal Hotel and I hurried back to the HQ to
follow his instructions. This was just the sort of chance I'd been angling for
since I'd sought out the man on the basis of the Genetic Survey Team report.

An hour later, as cleanly as the character I played was likely to be able to
make himself, I ventured along Market Street, heading down in the direction
of the tenement where O'Neil and his family lived, the boardinghouses in the
shadow of the Palace Hotel. I knew their exact location, though O'Neil was of
course unaware of that; accordingly he had sent a pair of his children down to
the corner to watch for me.

They failed to observe my approach, however, and I really couldn't blame
them; for proceeding down Market Street before me, moving slowly between
the gloom of twilight and the electric illumination of the shop signs, was an
apparition in a scarlet tunic and black shako.

It walked with the stiff and measured tread of the automaton it was pretending to be. The little ragged girl and her littler brother stared open-mouthed, watching its progress along the sidewalk. It performed a brief business of marching mindlessly into a lamppost and walking inexorably in place there a moment before righting itself and going on, but now on an oblique course toward the children.

I too continued on my course, smiling a little. This was delightful: a mortal pretending to be a mechanical toy being followed by a cyborg pretending to be a mortal.

There was a wild reverberation of mirth in the ether around me. One other of our kind was observing the scene, apparently; but there was a gigantic quality to the amusement that made me falter in my step. Who was that? That was someone I knew, surely. *Quo vadis?* I transmitted. The laughter shut off like an electric light being switched out, but not before I got a sense of direction from it. I looked across the street and just caught a glimpse of a massive figure disappearing down an alley. My visual impression was of an old miner, one of the mythic founders of this city. Old gods walking? What a ridiculous idea, and yet . . . what a moment of panic it evoked, of mortal dread, quite irrational.

But the figure in the scarlet tunic had reached the children. Little Ella clutched her brother's hand, stock-still on the pavement: little Donal shrank behind his sister, but watched with one eye as the thing loomed over them.

It bent forward, slowly, in increments, as though a gear ratcheted in its spine to lower it down to them. Its face was painted white, with red circles on the cheeks and a red cupid's bow mouth under the stiff black mustaches. Blank glassy eyes did not fix on them, did not seem to see anything, but one white-gloved hand came up jerkily to offer the little girl a printed handbill.

After a frozen motionless moment she took it from him. "Thank you, Mister Soldier," she said in a high clear voice. The figure gave no sign that it had heard, but unbent slowly, until it stood ramrod-straight again; pivoted sharply on its heel and resumed its slow march down Market Street.

"Soldier go." Donal pointed. Ella peered thoughtfully at the handbill.

" 'CH—IL—DREN'," she read aloud. What an impossibly sweet voice she had. "And that's an exclamation point, there. '*Babe—Babies, in, To—Toy—*' "

" '*Toyland*,' " I finished for her. She looked up with a glad cry.

"There you are, Mr. Kelly. Donal, this is Mr. Kelly. He is Daddy's good friend. Supper will be on the table presently. Won't you please come with us, Mr. Kelly?"

"I should be delighted to." I touched the brim of my hat. They pattered away down an alley, making for the dark warren of their tenement, and I followed closely.

They were different physical types, the brother and sister. Pretty children, certainly, particularly Ella with her glossy black braids, with her eyes the color of the twilight framed by black lashes. But it is not beauty we look for in a child.

It was the boy I watched closely as we walked, a sturdy three-year-old trudging along holding tight to the girl's hand. I couldn't have told you the quality nor shade of his skin, nor his hair nor his eyes; I cared only that his head appeared to be a certain shape, that his little body appeared to fit a certain profile, that his limbs appeared to be a certain length in relation to one another. I couldn't be certain yet, of course: that was why I had maneuvered his father into the generous impulse of inviting me into his home.

They lived down a long dark corridor toward the back of the building, its walls damp with sweat, its air heavy with the odors of cooking, of washing, of mortal life. The door opened a crack as we neared it and then, slowly, opened wide to reveal O'Neil standing there in a blaze of light. The blaze was purely by contrast to our darkness, however; once we'd crossed the threshold, I saw that two kerosene lamps were all the illumination they had.

"There now, didn't I tell you she'd spot him?" O'Neil cried triumphantly. "Welcome to this house, Jimmy Kelly."

"God save all here." I removed my hat. "Good evening, Mrs. O'Neil."

"Good evening to you, Mr. Kelly." Mary O'Neil turned from the stove, bouncing a fretful infant against one shoulder. "Would you care for a cup of tea, now?" She was like Ella, if years could be granted Ella to grow tall and slender and wear her hair up like a soft thundercloud. But there was no welcoming smile for me in the gray eyes, for on the previous occasion we'd met I'd been disgracefully intoxicated—at least, doing my best to appear so. I looked down as if abashed.

"I'd bless you for a cup of tea, my dear, I would," I replied. "And won't you allow me to apologize for the condition I was in last Tuesday week? I'd no excuse at all."

"Least said, soonest mended." She softened somewhat at my obvious sobriety. Setting the baby down to whimper in its apple-box cradle, she poured and served my tea. "Pray seat yourself."

"Here." Ella pulled out a chair for me. I thanked her and sat down to scan the room they lived in. Only one room, with one window that probably looked out on an alley wall but was presently frosted opaque from the steam of the saucepan wherein their supper cooked. Indeed, there was a fine layer of condensation on everything: it trickled down the walls, it lay in a damp film on the oilcloth cover of the table and the blankets on the bed against the far wall. The unhappy infant's hair was moist and curling with it.

Had there been any ventilation it had been a pleasant enough room. The table was set with good china, someone's treasured inheritance, no doubt. The tiny potbellied stove must have been awkward to cook upon, but O'Neil had built a cabinet of slatwood and sheet tin next to it to serve as the rest of a kitchen. The children's trundle was stored tidily under the parents' bed. Next to the painted washbasin on the trunk, a decorous screen gave privacy to one corner. Slatwood shelves displayed the family's few valuables: a sewing basket, a music box with a painted scene on its lid, a cheap mirror whose frame was decorated with glued-on seashells, a china dog. On the wall was a painted crucifix with a palm frond stuck behind it.

O'Neil came and sat down across from me.

"You look grand, Jimmy." He thumped his fist on the table approvingly. "Combed your hair, too, didn't you? That's the boy. You'll make a gentleman yet."

"Daddy?" Ella climbed into his lap. "There was a soldier came and gave us this in the street. Will you ever read me what it says? There's more words than I know, see." She thrust the handbill at him. He took it and held it out before him, blinking at it through the steamy air.

Here I present the printed text he read aloud, without his many pauses as he attempted to decipher it (for he was an intelligent man, but of little education):

CHILDREN!

Come see the Grand Fairy Extravaganza BABES IN TOYLAND
Music by Victor Herbert—Book by Glen MacDonough—
Staged by Julian Mitchell Ignacio Martinetti and 100 Others!
Coming by Special Train of Eight Cars!
Biggest Musical Production San Francisco Has Seen in Years!

*   *   *

AN INVITATION FROM MOTHER GOOSE HERSELF:

MY dear little Boys and Girls,

I DO hope you will behave nicely so that your Mammas and Papas will treat you to a performance of Mr. Herbert's lovely play Babes in Toyland at the Columbia Theater, opening Monday, the 16th of April. Why, my dears, it's one of the biggest successes of the season and has already played for ever so many nights in such far-away cities as New York, Chicago, and Boston. Yes, you really must be good little children, and then your dear parents will see that you deserve an outing to visit me. For, make no mistake, I myself, the only true and original MOTHER GOOSE, shall be there upon the stage of the Columbia Theater. And so shall so many of your other friends from my delightful rhymes such as Tom, Tom the Piper's Son, Bo Peep, Contrary Mary, and Red Riding Hood. The curtain will rise upon Mr. Mitchell's splendid production, with its many novel effects, at eight o'clock sharp.

OF course, if you are very little folks you are apt to be sleepyheads if kept up so late, but that need not concern your careful parents, for there will be a matinee on Saturday at two o'clock in the afternoon.

WON'T you please come to see me?

Your affectionate friend, Mother Goose.

"O, dear," sighed Mary.

"Daddy, can we go?" Ella's eyes were alight with anticipation. Donal chimed in: "See Mother Goose, Daddy!"

"We can't afford it, children," Mary said firmly. She took the saucepan off the stove and began to ladle a savory dish of sausage, onions, potatoes, and bacon onto the plates. "We've got a roof over our heads and food for the table. Let's be thankful for that."

Ella closed her little mouth tight like her mother's, but Donal burst into tears. "I wanna go see Mother Goose!" he howled.

O'Neil groaned. "Your mother is right, Donal. Daddy and Mummy don't have the money for the tickets, can you understand that?"

"You oughtn't to have read out that bill," said Mary in a quiet voice.

"I want go see the soldier!"

"Donal, hush now!"

"Donal's the boy for me," I said, leaning forward and reaching out to him. "Look, Donal Og, what's this you've got in your ear?"

I pretended to pull forth a bar of Ghirardelli's. Ella clapped her hands to her mouth. Donal stopped crying and stared at me with perfectly round eyes.

"Look at that! Would you ever have thought such a little fellow'd have such big things in his ears? Come sit with your uncle Jimmy, Donal." I drew him onto my lap. "And if you hush your noise, perhaps Mummy and Daddy'll let you have sweeties, eh?" I set the candy in the midst of the oilcloth, well out of his reach.

"Bless you, Jimmy," said O'Neil.

"Well, and isn't it the least I can do? Didn't know I could work magic, did you, Ella?"

"Settle down, now." Mary set out the dishes. "Frank, it's time to say grace."

O'Neil made the sign of the Cross and intoned, with the little ones mumbling along, "Bless-us-O-Lord-and-these-Thy-gifts-which-we-are-about-to-receive-from-Thy-bounty-through-Christ-Our-Lord-Amen."

Mary sat down with us, unfolding her threadbare napkin. "Donal, come sit with Mummy."

"Be easy, Mrs. O'Neil, I don't mind him." I smiled at her. "I've a little brother at home he's the very image of. Where's his spoon? Here, Donal Og, you eat with me."

"I don't doubt they look alike." O'Neil held out his tumbler as Mary poured from a pitcher of milk. "Look at you and me. Do you know, Mary, that was the first acquaintance we had—? Got our hats mixed up when the wind blew 'em both off. We wear just the same size."

"Fancy that."

So we dined, and an affable mortal man helped little Donal make a mess of his potatoes whilst chatting with Mr. and Mrs. O'Neil about such subjects as the dreadful expense of living in San Francisco and their plans to remove to a cheaper, less crowded place as soon as they'd saved enough money. The immortal machine that sat at their table was making a thorough examination of Donal, most subtly: an idle caress of his close-cropped little head measured his skull size, concealed devices gauged bone length and density and measured his weight to the pound; data was analyzed and preliminary judgment made: optimal morphology. Augmentation process possible. Classification pending blood analysis and spektral diagnosis.

"That's the best meal I've had in this country, Mrs. O'Neil," I told her as we rose from the table.

"How kind of you to say so, Mr. Kelly," she replied, collecting the dishes.

"Chocolate, Daddy?" Donal stretched out his arm for it. O'Neil tore open the waxed paper and broke off a square. He divided it into two and gave one to Donal and one to Ella.

"Now, you must thank your uncle Jimmy, for this is good chocolate and cost him dear."

"Thank you, Uncle Jimmy," they chorused, and Ella added, "But he got it by magic. It came out of Donal's ear. I saw it."

O'Neil rubbed his face wearily. "No, Ella, it was only a conjuring trick. Remember the talk we had about such things? It was just a trick. Wasn't it, Jimmy?"

"That's all it was, sure," I agreed. She looked from her father to me and back.

"Frank, dear, will you help me with these?" Mary had stacked the dishes in a washpan and sprinkled soap flakes in.

"Right. Jimmy, will you mind the kids? We're just taking these down to the tap."

"I will indeed," I said, and thought: *Thank you very much, mortal man, for this opportunity.* The moment the door closed behind them I had the device out of my pocket. It looked rather like a big old-fashioned watch. I held it out to the boy.

"Here you go, Donal, here's a grand timepiece for you to play with."

He took it gladly. "There's a train on it!" he cried. I turned to Ella.

"And what can I do for you, darling?"

She looked at me with considering eyes. "You can read me the funny papers." She pointed to a neatly stacked bundle by the stove.

"With pleasure." I seized them up and we settled back in my chair, pulling a lamp close. The baby slept fitfully, I read to Ella about Sambo and Tommy Pip and Herr Spiegleburger, and all the while Donal pressed buttons and thumbed levers on the diagnostic toy. It flashed pretty lights for him, it played little tunes his sister was incapable of hearing; and then, as I had known it would, it bit him.

"Ow!" He dropped it and began to cry, holding out his tiny bleeding finger.

"O, dear, now, what's that? Did it stick you?" I put his sister down and got up to take the device back. "Tsk! Look at that, the stem's broken." It vanished

into my pocket. "What a shame. O, I'm sorry, Donal Og, here's the old han-
kie. Let's bandage it up, shall we? There. There. Doesn't hurt now, does it?"

"No," he sniffled. "I want another chocolate."

"And so you'll have one, for being a brave boy." I snapped off another
square and gave it to him. "Ella, let's give you another as well, shall we? What
have you found there?"

"It's a picture about Mother Goose." She had spread out the Children's
Page on the oilcloth. "Isn't it? That says Mother Goose right there."

I looked over her shoulder. " 'Pictures from Mother Goose,' " I read out,
" 'Hot Cross Buns. Paint the Seller of Hot Cross Buns.' Looks like it's a contest, darling. They're asking the kiddies to paint in the picture and send it off
to the paper, to judge who's done the best one."

"Is there prize money?" She had an idea.

"Two dollars for the best one," I read, pulling at my lower lip uneasily.
"And paintboxes for everyone else who enters."

She thought that over. Dismay came into her face. "But I haven't got a
paintbox to color it with at all! O, that's stupid! Giving paintboxes out to kids
that's got them already. O, that's not fair!" She shook with stifled anger.

"What's not fair?" Her mother backed through the door, holding it open
for O'Neil with the washpan.

"Only this Mother Goose thing here," I said.

"You're never on about going to that show again, are you?" said Mary
sharply, coming and taking her daughter by the shoulders. "Are you? Have
you been wheedling at Mr. Kelly?"

"I have not!" the little girl said in a trembling voice.

"She hasn't, Mrs. O'Neil, only it's this contest in the kids' paper," I hastened to explain. "You have to have a set of paints to enter it, see."

Mary looked down at the paper. Ella began to cry quietly. Her mother
gathered her up and sat with her on the edge of the bed, rocking her back and
forth.

"O, I'm so sorry, Ella dear, Mummy's so sorry. But you see, now, don't you,
the harm in wanting such things? You see how unhappy it's made you? Look
how hard Mummy and Daddy work to feed you and clothe you. Do you know
how unhappy it makes us when you want shows and paintboxes and who
knows what, and we can't give them to you? It makes us despair. That's a
Mortal Sin, despair is."

"I want to see the fairies," wept the little girl.

"Dearest dear, there aren't any fairies! But surely it was the devil himself you met out in the street, that gave you that wicked piece of paper and made you long after vain things. Do you understand me? Do you see why it's wicked, wanting things? It kills the soul, Ella."

After a long, gasping moment the child responded, "I see, Mummy." She kept her face hidden in her mother's shoulder. Donal watched them uncertainly, twisting the big knot of handkerchief on his finger. O'Neil sat at the table and put his head in his hands. After a moment he swept up the newspaper and put it in the stove. He reached into the slatwood cabinet and pulled a bottle of Wilson's Whiskey up on the table, and got a couple of clean tumblers out of the washpan.

"Will you have a dram, Kelly?" he offered.

"Just the one." I sat down beside him.

"Just the one," he agreed.

You must not empathize with them.

When I let myself into my rooms on Bush Street, I checked my messages. A long green column of them pulsed on the credenza screen. Most of it was the promised list from Averill and his fellows; I'd have to pass that on to our masters as soon as I'd reviewed it. I didn't feel much like reviewing it just now, however.

There was also a response to my request for another transport for Madame D'Arraignee: *DENIED. NO ADDITIONAL VEHICLES AVAILABLE. FIND ALTERNATIVE.*

I sighed and sank into my chair. My honor was at stake. From a drawer at the side of the credenza I took another Ghirardelli bar and, scarcely taking the time to tear off the paper, consumed it in a few greedy bites. Waiting for its soothing properties to act, I paged through a copy of the *Examiner*. There were automobile agencies along Golden Gate Avenue. Perhaps I could afford to purchase one out of my personal operation's expense account?

But they were shockingly expensive in this city. I couldn't find one for sale, new or used, for less than a thousand dollars. Why couldn't *her* case officer delve into his own pocket to deliver the goods? I verified the balance of my

account. No, there certainly wasn't enough for an automobile in there. However, there was enough to purchase four tickets to *Babes in Toyland*.

I accessed the proper party and typed in my transaction request.

TIX UNAVAILABLE FOR 041606 EVENT, came the reply. *041706 AVAIL-
ABLE OK?*

OK, I typed. *PLS DEBIT & DELIVER.*

DEBITED. TIX IN YR BOX AT S MKT ST HQ 600 HRS 041606.

TIBI GRATIAS! I replied, with all sincerity.

DIE DULCE FRUERE. OUT.

Having solved one problem, an easy solution to the other suggested itself
to me. It involved a slight inconvenience, it was true: but any gentleman
would readily endure worse for a lady's sake.

My two rooms on Bush Street did not include the luxury of a bath, but the late
Mr. Adolph Sutro had provided an alternative pleasure for his fellow citizens.

Just north of Cliff House Mr. Sutro had purchased a rocky little purgatory
of a cove, cleaned the shipwrecks out of it and proceeded to shore it up
against the more treacherous waves with several thousand barrels of cement.
Having constructed not one but six saltwater pools of a magnificence to rival
old Rome, he had proceeded to enclose it in a crystal palace affair of no less
than four acres of glass.

Ah, but this wasn't enough for San Francisco! The entrance, on the hill
above, was as near a Greek temple as modern artisans could produce;
through the shrine one wandered along the museum gallery lined with ex-
hibits both educational and macabre and descended a vast staircase lined
with palm trees to the main level, where one might bathe, exercise in the
gymnasium, or attend a theater performance. Having done all this, one might
then dine in the restaurant.

However, my schedule today called for nothing more strenuous than
bathing. Ten minutes after descending the grand staircase I was emerging
from my changing room (one of five hundred), having soaped, showered, and
togged myself out in my rented bathing suit, making my way toward the
nearest warm-water pool under the bemused eyes of several hundred mortal
idlers sitting in the bleachers above.

I was not surprised to see another of my own kind backstroking manfully across the green water; nothing draws the attention of an immortal like sanitary conveniences. I must confess my heart sank when I recognized Lewis. I hadn't seen him since that period at New World One, when I'd been obliged to monitor him again. His career was in ruins, of course. Rather a shame, really. A drone, but a gentleman for all that.

He felt my regard and glanced up, seeing me at once. He smiled and waved.

Victor! he broadcast. *How nice to see you again.*

It's Lewis, isn't it? I responded, though I knew his name perfectly well, and far more of his history than he knew himself. Still, it had been centuries, and he had never shown any sign of recovering certain memories. I hoped, for his sake, that such was the case. Memory effacement is not a pleasant experience.

He pulled himself up on the coping of the pool and swept his wet hair out of his eyes. I stepped to the edge, took the correct diver's stance and leapt in, transmitting through bubbles: *So you're here as well? Presalvaging books, I suppose?*

The Mercantile Library, he affirmed, and there was nothing in his pleasant tone to indicate he'd remembered what I'd done to him at Eurobase One.

God! That must be a Herculean effort, I responded, surfacing.

He transmitted rueful amusement. *You've heard of it, I suppose?*

Rather, I replied, practicing my breaststroke. *All those Comstock Lode silver barons went looting the old family libraries of Europe, didn't they? Snatched up medieval manuscripts at a tenth their value from impoverished Venetian princes, I believe? Fabulously rare first editions from London antiquarians?*

Something like that, he replied. *And brought them back home to the States for safekeeping.*

Ha!

Well, how were they to know? Lewis made an expressive gesture taking in the vast edifice around us. *Mr. Sutro himself had a Shakespeare first folio. What a panic it's been tracking* that *down! And you?*

I'm negotiating for a promising-looking young recruit. Moreover, I drew Nob Hill detail, I replied casually. *I've coordinated a team of quite talented youngsters set to liberate the premises of Messrs. Towne, Crocker, Huntington et al. as soon as the lights are out. All manner of costly bric-a-brac has been tagged for rescue— Chippendales, Louis Quatorzes—to say nothing of jewels and cash.*

My, that sounds satisfying. You'll never guess what I found, only last night!
Lewis transmitted, looking immensely pleased with himself.

Something unexpected? I responded.

He edged forward on the coping. *Yes, you might say so. Just some old papers that had been mislaid by an idiot named Pompeo Leoni and bound into the wrong book. Just something jotted down by an elderly left-handed Italian gentleman!*

Not da Vinci? I turned in the water to stare at him, genuinely impressed.

Who else? Lewis nearly hugged himself in triumph. *Not just any doodlings or speculation from the pen of Leonardo, either. Something of decided interest to the Company! It seems he devoted some serious thought to the construction of articulated human limbs—a clockwork arm, for example, that could be made to perform various tasks!*

I've heard something of the sort, I replied, swimming back toward him.

Yes, well, he seems to have taken the idea further than robotics. Lewis leaned down in a conspiratorial manner. *From a human arm he leapt to the idea of an entire articulated human skeleton of bronze, and wondered whether the human frame might not be merely imitated but improved in function.*

By Jove! Was the man anticipating androids? I reached the coping and leaned on it, slicking back my hair.

No! No, he was chasing another idea entirely, Lewis insisted. *Shall I quote? I rather think I ought to let him express his thoughts.* He leaned back and, with a dreamy expression, transmitted in flawless fifteenth-century Tuscan: *'It has been observed that the presence of metal is not in all cases inimical to the body of man, as we may see in earrings, or in crossbow bolts, spearpoints, pistol balls, and other detritus of war that have been known to enter the flesh and remain for some years without doing the bearer any appreciable harm, or indeed in that practice of physicians wherein a small pellet of gold is inserted into an incision made near an aching joint, and the sufferer gains relief and ease of movement thereby.*

'Take this idea further and think that a shattered bone might be replaced with a model of the same bone cast in bronze, identical with or even superior to its original.

'Go further and say that where one bone might be replaced, so might the skeleton entire, and if the articulation is improved upon the man might attain a greater degree of physical perfection than he was born with.

'The flaw in this would be the man's pain and the high likelihood he would die before surgery of such magnitude could be carried out.

'Unless we are to regard the theory of alchemists who hold that the Philosopher's

Stone, once attained, would transmute the imperfect flesh to perfection, a kind of supple gold that lives and breathes, and by this means the end might be obtained without cutting, the end being immortality.' Lewis opened his eyes and looked at me expectantly. I smacked my hand on the coping in amusement.

By Jove, I repeated. *How typical of the Maestro. So he was all set to invent us, was he?*

To say nothing of hip replacements.

But what a find for the Company, Lewis!

Of course, to give you a real idea of the text I ought to have presented it like this: Lewis began to rattle it out backwards. I shook my head, laughing and holding up my hands in sign that he should stop. After a moment or two he trailed off, adding: *I don't think it loses much in translation, though.*

I shook my head. *You know, old man, I believe we're treading rather too closely to a temporal paradox here. Just as well the Company will take possession of that volume, and not some inquisitive mortal! What if it had inspired someone to experiment with biomechanicals a century or so too early?*

Ah! No, we're safe enough, Lewis pointed out. *As far as history records those da Vinci pages at all, it records them as being lost in the Mercantile Library fire. The circle is closed. All the same, I imagine it was a temptation for any operatives stationed near Amboise in da Vinci's time. Wouldn't you have wanted to seek the old man out as he lay dying, and tell him that something would be done with this particular idea, at least? Immortality and human perfection!*

Of course I'd have been tempted; but I shook my head. *Not unless I cared to face a court-martial for a security breach.*

Lewis shivered in his wet wool and slid back into the water. I turned on my back and floated, considering him.

The temperature doesn't suit you? I inquired.

Oh . . . They've got the frigidarium all right, but the calidaria here aren't really hot enough, Lewis explained. *And of course there's no sudatorium at all.*

Nor any slaves for a good massage, either, I added, glancing up at the mortal onlookers. *Sic transit luxuria, alas.* Lewis smiled faintly; he had never been comfortable with mortal servants, I remembered. Odd, for someone who began mortal life as a Roman, or at least a Romano-Briton.

Weren't you recruited at Bath . . . ? I inquired, leaning on the coping.

Aquae Sulis, it was then, Lewis informed me. *The public baths there.*

Of course. I remember now! You were rescued from the temple. Intercepted child sacrifice, I imagine?

Oh, good heavens, no! The Romans never did that sort of thing. No, I was just left in a blanket by the statue of Apollo. Lewis shrugged, and then began to grin. *I hadn't thought about it before, but this puts a distinctly Freudian slant on my visits here! Returning to the womb in time of stress? I was only a few hours old when the Company took me, or so I've always been told.*

I laughed and set off on a lap across the pool. *At least you were spared any memories of mortal life.*

That's true, he responded, and then his smile faded. *And yet, you know, I think I'm the poorer for that. The rest of you may have some harrowing memories, but at least you know what it was to be mortal.*

I assure you it's nothing to be envied, I informed him. He set out across the pool himself, resuming his backstroke.

I think I would have preferred the experience, all the same, he insisted. *I'd have liked a father—or mother—figure in my life. At the very least, those of you rescued at an age to remember it have a sort of filial relationship with the immortal who saved you. Haven't you?*

I regret to disillusion you, sir, but that is absolutely not true, I replied firmly.

Really? He dove and came up for air, gasping. *What a shame. Bang goes another romantic fantasy. I suppose we're all just orphans of one storm or another.*

At that moment a pair of mortals chose to roughhouse, snorting and chuckling as they pummeled each other in their seats in the wooden bleachers; one of them broke free and ran, scrambling apelike over the seats, until he lost his footing and fell with a horrendous crash that rolled and thundered in the air, echoing under the glassed dome, off the water and wet coping.

I saw Lewis go pale; I imagine my own countenance showed reflexive panic. After a frozen moment Lewis drew a deep breath.

"One storm or another," he murmured aloud. "Nothing to be afraid of here, after all. Is there? This structure will survive the quake. History says it will. Nothing but minor damage, really."

I nodded. Then, struck in one moment by the same thought, we lifted our horrified eyes to the ceiling, with its one hundred thousand panes of glass.

"I believe I've got a rail car to catch," I apologized, vaulting to the coping with what I hoped was not undignified haste.

"I've a luncheon engagement myself," Lewis said, gasping as he sprinted ahead of me to the grand staircase.

On the sixteenth of April I entertained friends, or at least my landlady received that impression; and what quiet and well-behaved fellows the gentlemen were, and how plain and respectable the ladies! No cigars, no raucous laughter, no drunkenness at all. Indeed, Mrs. McCarty assured me she would welcome them as lodgers at any time in the future, should they require desirable Bush Street rooms. I assured her they would be gratified at the news. Perhaps they might have been, if her boardinghouse were still standing in a week's time. History would decree otherwise, regrettably.

My parlor resembled a war room, with its central table on which was spread a copy of the Sanborn map of the Nob Hill area, up-to-date from the previous year. My subordinates stood or leaned over the table, listening intently as I bent with red chalk to delineate the placement of salvage apparatus.

"The Hush Field generators will arrive in a baker's van at the corner of Clay and Taylor Streets at midnight precisely," I informed them. "Delacort, your team will approach from your station at the end of Pleasant Street and take possession of them. There will be five generators. I want them placed at the following intersections: Bush and Jones, Clay and Jones, Clay and Powell, Bush and Powell, and on California midway between Taylor and Mason." I put a firm letter x at each site. "The generators should be in place and switched on by no later than five minutes after midnight. Your people will remain in place to remove the generators at half past three exactly, returning them to the baker's van, which will depart promptly. At that moment a private car will pull up to the same location to transport your team to the central collection point on Ocean Beach. Is that clear?"

"Perfectly, sir." Delacort saluted. Averill looked at her slightly askance and turned a worried face to me.

"What're they going to do if some cop comes along and wants to know what they're doing there at that time of night?"

"Any cop coming in range of the Hush Field will pass out, dummy," Philemon informed him. I frowned and cleared my throat. Cinema Standard (the language of the schoolroom) is not my preferred mode of expression.

"If you please, Philemon!"

"Yeah, sorry—"

"Your team will depart from their station at Joice Street at five minutes after midnight and proceed to the intersection of Mason and Sacramento, where a motorized drayer's wagon will be arriving. You will be responsible for the contents of the Flood mansion." I outlined it in red. "Your driver will provide you with a sterile containment receptacle for item number thirty-nine on your acquisitions list. Kindly see to it that this particular item is salvaged first and delivered to the driver separately."

"What's item thirty-nine?" Averill inquired. There followed an awkward silence. Philemon raised his eyebrows at me. Company policy discourages field operatives from being told more than they strictly need to know regarding any given posting. Upon consideration, however, it seemed wisest to answer Averill's question; there was enough stress associated with this detail as it was without adding mysteries. I cleared my throat.

"The Flood mansion contains a 'Moorish' smoking room," I informed him. "Among its features is a lump of black stone carefully displayed in a glass case. Mr. Flood purchased it under the impression that it is an actual piece of the Qaaba from Mecca, chipped loose by an enterprising Yankee adventurer. He was, of course, defrauded; the stone is in fact a meteorite, and preliminary spectrographic analysis indicates it originated on Mars."

"Oh," said Averill, nodding sagely. I did not choose to add that plainly visible on the rock's surface is a fossilized crustacean of an unknown kind, or that the rock's rediscovery (in a museum owned by Dr. Zeus, incidentally) in the year 2210 will galvanize the Mars colonization effort into making real progress at last.

I bent over the map again and continued: "All the items on your list are to be loaded into the wagon by twenty minutes after three. At that time, the wagon will depart for Ocean Beach and your team will follow in the private car provided. Understood?"

"Understood."

"Rodrigo, your team will depart from their Taylor Street station at five minutes after midnight as well. Your wagon will arrive at the corner of California and Taylor; you will proceed to salvage the Huntington mansion." I marked it on the map. "Due to the nature of your quarry you will be allotted ten additional minutes, but all listed items must be loaded and ready for removal by half past three, at which time your private transport will arrive. Upon arrival at Ocean Beach you will be assisted by Philemon's team, who will already (I should hope) have loaded most of their salvage into the waiting boats."

"Yes, sir." Rodrigo made a slight bow.

"Freytag, your team will be stationed on Jones Street. You depart at five after midnight, like the rest, and your objective is the Crocker mansion, here." Freytag bent close to see as I shaded in her area. "Your wagon will pull up to Jones and California; you ought to be able to fill it in the allotted time of two hours and fifteen minutes precisely, and be ready to depart for Ocean Beach without incident. Loong? Averill?"

"Sir!" Both immortals stood to attention.

"Your teams will disperse from their stations along Clay and Pine Streets and salvage the lesser targets shown here, here, here, and here—" I chalked circles around them. "I leave to your best judgment individual personnel assignments. Two wagons will arrive on Clay Street at one o'clock precisely and two more will arrive on Pine five minutes later. You ought to find them more than adequate for your purposes. You will need to do a certain amount of running to and fro to coordinate the efforts of your ladies and gentlemen, but it can't be helped."

"I don't anticipate difficulties, sir," Loong assured me.

"No indeed; but remember the immensity of this event shadow." I set down the chalk and wiped my hands on a handkerchief. "Your private transports will be waiting at the corner of Bush and Jones by half past three. Please arrive promptly."

"Yes, sir." Averill looked earnest.

"In the entirely likely event that any particular team completes its task ahead of schedule, and has free space in its wagon after all the listed salvage has been accounted for, I will expect that team to lend its assistance to Madame D'Arraignee and her teams at the Mark Hopkins Institute." I swept them with a meaningful stare. "Gentlemen doing so can expect my personal thanks and commendation in their personnel files."

That impressed them, I could see. The favorable notice of one's superiors is invariably one's ticket to the better sort of assignment. Clearing my throat, I continued: "I anticipate arriving at no later than half past two to oversee the final stages of removal. Kindly remain at your transports until I transmit your signal to depart for the central collection point. Have you any further questions, ladies and gentlemen?"

"None, sir," Averill said, and the others nodded agreement.

"Then it's settled," I told them, and carefully folded shut the map book. "A word of warning to you all: you may become aware of precursors to the shock in the course of the evening. History will record a particularly nasty seismic disturbance at two A.M. in particular, and another at five. Control your natural panic, please. Upsetting as you may find these incidents, they will present no danger whatsoever, will in fact go unnoticed by such mortals as happen to be awake at that hour."

Averill put up his hand. "I read the horses will be able to feel it," he said, a little nervously. "I read they'll go mad."

I shrugged. "Undoubtedly why we have been obliged to confine ourselves to motor transport. Of course, *we* are no brute beasts. I have every confidence that we will all resist any irrational impulses toward flight before the job is finished.

"Now then! You may attend to the removal of your personal effects and prepare for the evening's festivities. I shouldn't lunch tomorrow; you'll want to save your appetites for the banquet at Cliff House. I understand it's going to be rather a Roman experience!"

The tension broken, they laughed; and if Averill laughed a bit too loudly, it must be remembered that he was still young. As immortals go, that is.

Astute mortals might have detected something slightly out of the ordinary on that Tuesday, the seventeenth of April; certainly the hired-van drivers must have noticed an increase in business, as they were dispatched to house after house in every district of the city to pick up nearly identical loads, these being two or three ordinary-looking trunks and one crate precisely fifty centimeters long, twenty centimeters wide, and twenty centimeters high, in which a credenza might fit snugly. And it would be extraordinary if none of them remarked upon the fact that all these same consignments were directed to the same location on the waterfront, the berth of the steamer *Mayfair*.

Certainly in some cases mortal landladies noticed trunks being taken down flights of stairs, and put anxious questions to certain of their tenants regarding hasty removal; but their fears were laid to rest by smiling lies and ready cash.

And did anyone notice, as twilight fell, when persons in immaculate evening dress were suddenly to be seen in nearly every street? Doubtful; for it was, after all, the second night of the opera season, and with the Metropolitan company in town all of Society had turned out to do them honor. If a certain number of them converged on a certain warehouse in an obscure district, and departed therefrom shortly afterward in gleaming automobiles, that was unlikely to excite much interest in observers, either.

I myself guided a brisk little four-cylinder Franklin through the streets, bracing myself as it bumped over the cable car tracks, and steered down Gough with the intention of turning at Fulton and following it out to the beach. At the corner of Geary I glimpsed for a moment a tall figure in a red coat, and wondered what it was doing so far from the theater district; but a glance over my shoulder made it plain that I was mistaken. The red-clad figure shambling along was no more than a bum, albeit one of considerable stature. I dismissed him easily from my thoughts as I contemplated the O'Neil family's outing to the theater.

Had I a warm, sentimental sensation thinking of them, remembering Ella's face aglow when she saw me present her father with the tickets? Certainly not. One magical evening out was scarcely going to make up for their ghastly deaths, in whatever cosmic scale might be supposed to balance such things. Best not to dwell on that aspect of it at all. No, it was the convenience of their absence from home that occupied my musings, and the best way to take advantage of it with regard to my mission.

At the end of Fulton I turned right, in the purple glow of evening over the vast Pacific. Far out to sea—well beyond the sight of mortal eyes—the Company transport ships lay at anchor, waiting only for the cover of full darkness to approach the shore. In a few hours I'd be on board one of them, steaming off in the direction of the Farallones to catch my air transport, with no thought for the smoking ruin of the place I'd lived in so many harrowing weeks.

Cliff House loomed above me, its turreted mass a blaze of light. I saw with some irritation that the long uphill approach was crowded with carriages and automobiles, drawn in on a diagonal; I was obliged to go up as far as the rail depot before I could find a place to leave my motor, and walk back downhill past the baths.

I dare say the waiters at Cliff House could not recall an evening when so large a party, of such unusual persons, had dined with such hysterical gaiety as on this seventeenth of April, 1906.

If I recall correctly, the reservation had been made in the name of an international convention of seismologists. San Francisco was ever the most cosmopolitan of cities, so the restaurant staff expressed no surprise when elegantly attired persons of every known color began arriving in carriages and automobiles. If anyone remarked upon a certain indefinable similarity in appearance among the conventioneers that transcended race, why, that might be explained by their common avocation—whatever seismology might be; no one on the staff had any clear idea. Only the queer nervousness of the guests was impossible to account for, the tendency toward uneasy giggling, the sudden frozen silences and dilated pupils.

I think I can speak for my fellow operatives when I say that we were determined to enjoy ourselves, terror notwithstanding. We deserved the treat, every one of us; we faced a long night of hard work, the culmination of months of labor, under circumstances of mental strain that would test the resolution of the most hardened mercenaries. The least we were owed was an evening of silk hats and tiaras.

There was a positive chatter of communication on the ether as I approached. We were all here, or in the act of arriving; not since leaving school had I been in such a crowd of my own kind. I thought how we were to feast here, a company of immortals in an airy castle perched on the edge of the Uttermost West, and flit away well before sunrise. It is occasionally pleasant to embody a myth.

I saw Madame D'Arraignee stepping down from a carriage, evidently arriving with other members of the Hopkins operation team. No bulky Russian sea captain in sight, of course, yet; I hastened to her side and tipped my hat.

"Madame, will you do me the honor of allowing me to escort you within?"

"M'sieur Victor." She gave me a dazzling smile. She wore a gown of pale blue-green silk, a shade much in fashion that season, which brought out beautifully certain copper hues in her intensely black skin. Diamonds winked from the breathing shadow of her bosom. Oh, fortunate Kalugin! She took my arm and we proceeded inside, where we had the remarkable experience of having to shout our transmissions to one another, so crowded was the ether: *I am very pleased to inform you I have arranged for an automobile for your use this evening,* I told her as we paused at the cloakroom for checks.

Oh, I am so glad! I do hope you weren't put to unnecessary trouble.

Through the door to the dining room we caught glimpses of napery like snow, folded in a wilderness of sharp little peaks, with here and there a gilt epergne rising above them.

Not what I'd call unnecessary trouble, no, though it proved impossible to requisition anything at this late date. However, I did have a vehicle allocated for my own personal use and that fine runabout is entirely at your disposal.

Merci, merci mille fois! But will this not impede your own mission?

Not at all, dear lady. I shall be obliged to you for transportation as far as the Palace, I think, after we've dined; but since my mission involves nothing more strenuous than carrying off a child, I anticipate strolling back across the city with ease.

You are too kind, my friend.

A gentleman could do no less. I pulled out a chair for her.

We chatted pleasantly of trifling matters as the rest of the guests arrived. We studied the porcelain menu in some astonishment—the Company had spent a fortune here tonight, certainly enough to have allotted me one extra automobile. I was rather nettled, but my irritation was mollified somewhat by the anticipation of our *carte du jour:*

Green Turtle Soup   Consommé Divinesse
Salmon in Sauce Veloute   Trout Almandine   Crab Cocktail
Braised Sweetbreads   Roast Quail Andaluz
Le Faux Mousse Faison Lucullus
Early Green Peas   White Asparagus   Risotto Milanese
Roast Saddle of Venison with Port Wine Jelly
Curried Tomatoes   Watercress Salad
Chicken Marengo   Plovers' Eggs   Virginia Ham Croquettes

Lobster Salad   Oysters in Variety
Gateau d'Or et Argent   Assorted Fruits in Season
Rose Snow   Tulip Jellies   Water Ices
Surprise Yerba Buena

All accompanied, of course, by the appropriate vintages, and service *à la russe*. We *were* being rewarded.

A shift in the black rock, miles down, needle-thin fissures screaming through stone, perdurable clay bulging like the head of a monstrous child engaging for birth, straining, straining, STRAINING!

The smiling chatter stopped dead. The waiters looked around, confused, at that elegant assembly frozen like mannequins. Not a scrape of chair moving, not a chime of crystal against china. Only the sound that we alone listened to: the cello-string far below us, tuning for the dance of the wrath of God. I found myself staring across the room directly into Lewis's eyes, where he had halted at the doorway in midstep. The immortal lady on his arm was still as a painted image, a perfect profile by da Vinci.

The orchestra conductor mistook our silence for a cue of some kind. He turned hurriedly to his musicians and they struck up a little waltz tune, light, gracious accompaniment to our festivities. With a boom and a rush of vacuum the service doors parted, as the first of the waiters burst through with tureens and silver buckets of ice. Champagne corks popped like artillery. As the noises roared into our silence, an immortal in white lace and spangles shrieked; she turned it into a high trilling laugh, placing her slender hand upon her throat.

So conversation resumed, and a server appeared at my elbow with a nap-kined bottle. I held up my glass for Champagne. Madame D'Arraignee and I clinked an unspoken toast and drank fervently.

Twice more while we dined on those good things, the awful warning came. As the venison roast was served forth, its dish of port jelly began to shimmer and vibrate—too subtly for the mortal waiters to notice more than a pretty play of light, but we saw. On the second occasion the oysters had just come to table, and what subaudible pandemonium of clattering there was: half-shell against half-shell with the sound of basalt cliffs grinding together, and the staccato rattle of all the little sauceboats with their scarlet and yellow and pink and green contents; though of course the mortal waiters couldn't hear it. Not even the patient horses waiting in their carriage-traces heard it yet. But the sparkling bubbles ascended more swiftly through the glasses of Champagne.

The waiters began to move along the tables bearing trays: little cut-crystal goblets of pink ices, or red and amber jellies, or fresh strawberries drenched in liqueur, or cakes. We heard the ringing note of a dessert spoon against a wineglass, signaling us all to attention.

The Chief Project Facilitator rose to address us. Labienus stood poised and smiling in faultless white tie and tuxedo. As he waited for the babble of voices to fade he took out his gold chronometer on its chain, studied its tiny screen, then snapped its case shut and returned it to the pocket of his white silk waistcoat.

"My fellow seismologists." His voice was quiet, yet without raising it he reached all corners of the room. Commanding legions confers a certain ease in public speaking. "Ladies." He bowed. "I trust you've enjoyed the bill of fare. I know that, as I dined, I was reminded of the fact that perhaps in no other city in the world could such a feast be so gathered, so prepared, so served to such a remarkable gathering. Where but here by the Golden Gate can one banquet in a splendor that beggars the Old World, on delicacies pre-sented by masters of culinary sophistication hired from all civilized nations— all the while in sight of forested hills where savages roamed *within living memory*, across a bay that *within living memory* was innocent of any sail?

"So swiftly has she risen, this great city, as though magically conjured by djinni out of thin air. Justifiably her citizens might expect to wake tomorrow in a wilderness, and find that this gorgeous citadel had been as insubstantial as their dreams."

Archly exchanged glances between some of our operatives as his irony was appreciated.

"But if that were to come to pass—if they were to wake alone, unhoused and shivering upon a stony promontory, facing into a cold northern ocean and a hostile gale—why, you know as well as I do that within a few short years the citizens of San Francisco would create their city anew, with spires soaring ever closer to heaven, and mansions yet more gracious."

Of course we knew it, but the poor mortal waiters didn't. I am afraid some of our younger operatives were base enough to smirk.

"Let us marvel, ladies and gentlemen, at this phoenix of a city, at once ephemeral and abiding. Let us drink to the imperishable spirit of her citizens. I give you the city of San Francisco."

"The city of San Francisco," we chorused, raising our glasses high.

"And I *give* you"—smiling, he extended his hand—"the city of San Francisco!"

Beaming, the waiters wheeled it in, on a vast silver cart: an ornate confection of pastry, of spun-sugar and marzipan and candies, a perfect model of the City. It was possible to discern a tiny Ferry Building rising above chocolate wharves, and a tiny Palace, and Nob Hill reproduced in sugared peel and nonpareils. Across the familiar grid of streets Golden Gate Park was done in green fondant, and beyond it was the hill where Sutro Park rose in nougat and candied violets, and beyond that Cliff House itself, in astonishing detail.

We applauded.

Then she was destroyed, that beautiful city, with a silver cake knife and serving wedge, and parceled out to us in neat slices. One had to commend Labienus's sense of humor, to say nothing of his sense of ritual.

It was expected that we would wish to dance after dining; the ballroom had been reserved for our use, and at some point during dessert the orchestra had discreetly risen and carried their instruments up to the dais.

I thought the idea of dancing in rather poor taste, under the circumstances, and apparently many of my fellow operatives agreed with me; but Averill and some of the other young ones got out on the floor eagerly enough, and soon the stately polonaise gave way to ragtime tunes and two-stepping.

Under the pretense of going for a smoke I went out to the terrace, to breathe the clean night air and metabolize my portion of magnificent excess in peace. By ones and twos several of the older immortals followed me. Soon there was quite an assemblage of us out there between two worlds, between the dark water surging around Seal Rock and the brilliant magic lantern of Cliff House.

"Victor?" Madame D'Arraignee was making her way to me through the crowd. Her slippers, together with her diamonds, had gone into the leather case she was carrying, and she had donned sensible walking shoes; she had also buttoned a long motorist's duster over her evening gown. The radiant Queen of the Night stood now before me as the Efficient Modern Woman.

"You didn't care to dance either, I see," she remarked.

"Not I, no," I replied. Within the giddy whirl, Averill pranced by in the arms of an immortal sylph in pink satin; their faces were flushed and merry. Don't think them heartless, reader. They did not understand yet. Horror, for Averill, was still a lonely prairie and a burning wagon; for the girl, still a soldier with a bayonet in a deserted orchard. *Those* nightmares weren't here in this bright room with its bouncing music, and so all must be right with the world.

But we were old ones, Madame D'Arraignee and I, and we stood outside in the dark as they danced.

Down, miles down, the slick water on the clay face and the widening fissure in darkness, dead shale trembling like an exhausted limb, granite crumbling, rock cracking with the strain and crying out in a voice that rose up, and up at last through the red brick, through the tile and parquet, into the warm air and the music!

The mortal musicians played on, but the dancers faltered. Some of them stopped, looking around in confusion; some of them only missed a step or two and then plunged back into the dance with greater abandon, determined to celebrate something.

Madame D'Arraignee shivered. I threw my unlit cigar over the parapet into the sea.

"Shall we go, Nan?" I offered her my arm. She took it readily and we left Cliff House.

Outside on the carriage drive, and all the way up the steep hill to where my motor was parked, the waiting horses were tossing their heads and whickering uneasily.

Madame D'Arraignee took the wheel, easily guiding us back down into the City through the spangled night.

Even now, at the Grand Opera House, Enrico Caruso was striking a pose before a vast Spanish mountain range rendered on canvas and raising his carbine to threaten poor Bessie Abott. Even now, at the Mechanic's Pavilion, the Grand Prize Masked Carnival was in full swing, with throngs of costumed roller skaters whirling around the rink that would be a triage hospital in twelve hours and a pile of smoking ashes in twenty-four. Even now, the clock on the face of Old St. Mary's Church—bearing its warning legend SON OB-SERVE THE TIME AND FLY FROM EVIL—was counting out the minutes left for heedless passersby. Even now, the O'Neil children were sitting forward in their seats, scarcely able to breathe as the cruel Toymaker recited the incantation that would bring his creations to life.

And we rounded the corner at Devisadero and sped down Market, with Prospero's *après*-pageant speech ringing in our ears. At the corner of Third I pointed and Madame D'Arraignee worked the clutch, steered over to the curb and trod on the brake pedal.

"You're quite sure you won't need a ride back?" she inquired over the chatter of the cylinders. I put my legs out and leapt down to the pavement.

"Perfectly sure, Nan." I shot my cuffs and adjusted the drape of my coat. Reaching into the seat, I took my stick and silk hat. "Give my seat to the Muse of Painting. I'm off to lurk in shadows like a gentleman."

"*Bonne chance,* then, Victor." She eased up on the brake, clutched, and cranked the wheel over so the Franklin swung around in a wide arc to retrace its course up Market Street. I tipped my hat and bowed; with a cheery wave and a double honk on the Franklin's horn, she steered away into the night.

So far, so good. The night was yet young and there were plenty of debonair socialites in evening dress on the street, arriving and departing from the restaurants, the hotels, the theaters. For a block I was one of their number; then accomplished my disappearance down a black alleyway into another world, to thread my way through the boardinghouse warren.

Rats were out and scuttling everywhere, sensing the coming disaster infallibly. In some buildings they were cascading down the stairs like trickling water, and cats ignored them and drunkards stood watching in stupefied amazement, but there was nobody else there to remark upon it; these streets did not invite promenaders.

I found the O'Neils' building and made my way up through the unlit stairwell, here and there kicking vermin out of my way. I left the landing and proceeded down their corridor, past doors tight shut showing only feeble lines of light at floor level to mark where the occupants were at home. I heard snores; I heard weeping; I heard a drunken quarrel; I heard a voice raised in wistful melody.

No light at the O'Neils' door, naturally; none at the door immediately opposite theirs. I scanned the room beyond but could discern no occupant. Drawing out a skeleton key from my waistcoat pocket, I gained entrance and shut the door after me.

No tenant at all; good. It was death-cold in there and black as pitch, for a roller shade had been drawn down on the one window. A slight tug sent it wobbling upward but failed to let much more light into the room. Not that I needed light to see my chronometer as I checked it; half past eleven, and even now my teams were assembling at their stations on Nob Hill. I leaned against a wall, folded my arms and composed myself to wait.

Time passed slowly for me, but in Toyland it sped by. Songs and dances, glittering processions came to their inevitable close; fairies took wing. Innocence was rewarded and wickedness resoundingly punished. The last of the ingenious special effects guttered out, the curtain descended, the orchestra fell silent, the house lights came up. A little while the magic lingered, as the O'Neil family made their way out through the lobby, a little while it hung around them like a perfume in the atmosphere of red velvet and gilt and fashionably attired strangers, until they were borne out through the doors by the receding tide of the crowd. Then the magic left them, evaporating upward into the night and the fog, and they got their bearings and made their way home along the dark streets.

I heard them, coming heavily up the stairs, O'Neil and Mary each carrying a child. Down the corridor their footsteps came, and stopped outside.

"Slide down now, Ella, Daddy's got to open the door."

I heard the sound of a key fumbling in darkness for its lock, and a drowsy little voice singing about Toyland, the paradise of childhood to which you can never return.

"Hush, Ella, you'll wake the neighbors."

"Donal's asleep. He missed the ending." Ella's voice was sad. "And it was such a beautiful, beautiful ending. Don't you think it was a beautiful ending, Daddy?"

"Sure it was, darling." Their voices receded a bit as they crossed the threshold. I heard a clink and the sputtering hiss of a match; there was the faintest glimmer of illumination down by the floor.

"Sssh, sh, sh. Home again. Help Mummy get his boots off, Ella, there's a dear."

"I'll just step across to Mrs. Varian's and collect the baby."

"Mind you remember his blanket."

"I will that."

Footsteps in the corridor again, discreet rapping on a panel, a whispered conversation in darkness and a sleepy wail; then returning footsteps and a pair of doors closing. Then, more muffled but still distinct to me, the sound of the O'Neils going to bed.

Their lamps were blown out. Their whispers ceased. Still I waited, listening as the minutes ticked away for their mortal souls to rest.

Half past one on the morning of Wednesday, the eighteenth of April in the year 1906, in the city of San Francisco. Francis O'Neil and his wife and their children asleep finally and forever, and the world had finished with them. In the gray morning, at precisely twelve minutes after the hour of five, this boardinghouse would lurch forward into the street, bricks tumbling as mortar blew out like talcum powder, rotten timbers snapping. That would be the end of Frank's strength and Mary's care and Ella's dreams, the end of the brief un-happy baby, and no one would remember them but me.

And, perhaps, Donal. I stepped across the hall and let myself into their room, perfectly silent.

The children lay in their trundle on the floor, next to their parents' bed. Donal slept on the outer edge, curled on his side, both hands tucked under his chin. I stood for a moment observing, analyzing their alpha patterns. When I was satisfied that no casual noise would awaken them, I bent and lifted Donal from his bed. He sighed but slept on. After a moment's hesitation I drew the blanket up around Ella's shoulders.

I stood back. The boy wore a nightshirt and long black stockings, but the night was cold. Frank's coat hung over the back of a chair: I appropriated it to wrap his son. Shifting Donal to one arm, I backed out of the room and shut the door.

Finished.

No sleeper in that building woke to hear our rapid descent of the stairs. On the first landing a drunk sat upright, leaning his head on the railings, sound asleep with his lower jaw dropped open like a corpse's. We fled lightly past him, Donal and I, and he never moved.

Away through the maze, then, away forever from the dirt and stench and poverty of that place. In twelve hours it would have ceased to exist, and the wind would scatter white ashes so the dead could never be named nor numbered.

Even Market Street was dark now, its theaters shut down. Over at the

Grand Opera House on Mission, Enrico Caruso's costumes hung neatly in his dark dressing room, ready for a performance of *La Bohème* that would never take place. Up at the Mechanic's Pavilion, the weary janitor surveyed the confetti and other festive debris littering the skating rink and decided to sweep it up in the morning. Toyland, at the Columbia, was shut away in its properties room: fairy tinsel, butterfly wings, bear heads peering down from dusty shelves into the darkness.

Even now my resolute gentlemen and ladies were despoiling Nob Hill, flitting through its darkened drawing rooms at hyperspeed like so many whirring ghosts, bearing with them winking gilt and crystal, calfskin and morocco, canvas and brass, all the very best that money could buy but couldn't hope to preserve against the hour to come. Without the Franklin I'd have a tedious walk uphill to join them, but at a brisk pace I might arrive with time to spare.

Donal stretched and muttered in his sleep. I shifted him to my other shoulder, changed hands on my walking stick, and was about to hurry on when I caught a whiff of some familiar scent on the air. I halted.

It was not a pleasant scent. It was harsh, musky, like blood or sweat but neither; like an animal smell, but other; it summoned in me a sudden terror and confusion. When I tried to identify it, however, I had only a mental image of a bear costume hanging on a hook, the head looking down from a shelf. When had I seen that? *I* hadn't seen that! *Whose memories were these?*

I controlled myself with an effort. Some psychic disturbance was responsible for this, my own nerves were contributing to this, there was no real danger. Why, of course: it must be nearly two o'clock, when the first of the major subsonic disruptions would occur.

Yes, here it came now. I could hear nearby horses begin to scream and stamp frantically, I could feel the paving bricks grind against one another under the soles of my boots, and the air groaned as though buried giants were praying to God for release.

Yes, I thought, this must be it. I balanced my stick against my knee and drew out my chronometer, trying to verify the event. As I peered at it, the door of a stable directly across the street burst open, and a white mare came charging out, hooves thundering. Donal jerked and cried.

Timing is everything. My assailant chose that perfect moment of distraction to strike. I was enveloped in a choking wave of *that smell* as a hand closed on my face and pulled my head back. Instantly I clawed at it, twisted my head to bite; but a vast arm was wrapping around me from the other side and cold steel entered my throat, opened the artery, wrenched as it was pulled out again.

So swiftly had this occurred that my stick was still falling through midair, had not yet struck the pavement. Donal was pulled upward and backward, torn from me, and I heard his terrified cry mingle with the clatter of the stick as it landed, the rumbling earth, the running horse, a howling laughter I knew but could not place. I was sinking to my knees, clutching at my cut throat as my blood fountained out over the starched front of my dress shirt and stained the diamond stud so it winked like Mars. Ares, God of War. *Thor.* I was conscious of a terrible anger as I descended to the shadows and curled into fugue.

"Will you get on to this, now? Throat cut and he's not been robbed! Here's his watch, for Christ's sake!"

"Stroke of luck for us, anyhow."

I sat up and glared at them. The two mortal thieves backed away from me, horrified; then one mustered enough nerve to dart in again, aiming a kick at me while he made a grab for my chronometer. I caught his wrist and broke it. He jumped back, stifling an agonized yell; his companion took to his heels and after only a second's hesitation he followed.

I remained where I was, huddled on the pavement, running a self-diagnostic. The edges of my windpipe and jugular artery had closed and were healing nicely at hyperspeed; if the thieves hadn't roused me from fugue I'd be whole now. Blood production had sped up to replace that now dyeing the front of my previously immaculate shirt. The exterior skin of my throat was even now self-suturing, but I was still too weak to rise.

My hat and stick remained where they had fallen, but of Donal or my assailant there was no sign. I licked my dry lips. There was a vile taste in my mouth. My chronometer told me it was a quarter past two. I dragged myself to the base of a wall and leaned there, half swooning, drowning in unwelcome remembrance.

That smell. Sweat, blood, the animal, and smoke. Yes, they'd called it the Summer of Smoke, that year the world ended. What world had that been?

The world where I was a little prince, or nearly so; better if my mother hadn't been a Danish slave, but my father had no sons by his lady wife, and so I had fine clothes and a gold pin for my cloak.

When I went to climb on the beached longship and play with the gear, a warrior threatened me with his fist; then another man told him he'd better not, for I was Baldulf's brat. That made him back down in a hurry. And once, my father set me on the table and put his gold cup in my hand, but I nearly dropped it, it was so heavy. He held it for me and I tasted the mead and his companions laughed, beating on the table. The ash-white lady, though, looked down at the floor and wrung her hands.

She told me sometimes that if I wasn't good the Bear would come for me. She was the only one who would ever dare to talk to me that way. And then he *had* come, the Bear and his slaughtering knights. All in one day I saw our tent burned and my father's head staring from a pike. Screaming, smoke and fire, and a banner bearing a red dragon that snaked like a living flame, I remember.

My mother had caught me up and was running for the forest, but she was a plump girl and could not get up the speed. Two knights chased after us on horseback, whooping like madmen. Just under the shadow of the oaks, they caught us. My mother fell and rolled, loosing her hold on me, and screamed for me to run; then one of the knights was off his horse and on her. The other knight got down too and stood watching them, laughing merrily. One of her slippers had come off and her bare toes kicked at the air until she died.

I had been sobbing threats, I had been hurling stones and handfuls of oak-mast at the knights, and now I ran at the one on my mother and attacked him with my teeth and nails. He reared up on his elbows to shake me off; but the other knight reached down and plucked me up as easily as if I'd been a kitten. He held me at his eye level while I shrieked and spat at him. His shrill laughter dropped to a chuckle, but never stopped.

A big shaven face, dun-drab hair cropped. Head of a strange helm shape, tremendous projecting nose and brows, and his wide gleeful eyes so pale a blue as to be colorless, like the eyes of my father's hounds. He had enormous broad cheekbones and strange teeth. That smell, that almost-animal smell, was coming from him. That had been where I'd first encountered it, hanging there in the grip of that knight.

The other knight had got up and came forward with his knife drawn and ready for me, but my captor held out his huge gauntleted hand.

"Sine eum!" he told him pleasantly. *"Noli irritare leones."*

"Faciam quicquid placet, o ingens simi tu!" the other knight growled, and brandished his knife. My captor's eyes sparkled; he batted playfully at my assailant, who flew backward into a tree and lay there twitching, blood running from his ears. Left in peace, my knight held me up and sniffed at me. He sat down and ran his hands all over me, taking his gauntlets off to squeeze my skull until I feared it would break like an egg. I had stopped fighting, but I whimpered and tried to wriggle away.

"Do you want to live, little boy?" he asked me in perfectly accented Saxon. He had a high-pitched voice, nasally resonant.

"Yes," I replied, shocked motionless.

"Then be good, and do not try to run away from me. I will preserve you from death. Do you understand?"

"Yes."

"Good." He forced my mouth open and examined my teeth. Apparently satisfied, he got up, thrusting me under one arm. Taking the two horses' bridles, he walked back to the war camp of the Bear with long rolling strides.

It was growing dark, and new fires had been lit. We passed pickets who challenged my captor, and he answered them with smiles and bantering remarks. At last he stopped before a tent and gave a barking order, whereupon a groom hurried out to take the horses and led them away for him. Two other knights sat nearby, leaning back wearily as their squires took off their armor for them. One pointed at me and asked a question.

My captor grinned and said something in fluting reply, hugging me to his chest. One knight smiled a little, but the other scowled and spat into the fire. As my captor bore me into his tent I heard someone mutter *"Amator puer!"* in a disgusted tone.

It was dark in the tent, and there was no one there to see as he stripped off my clothes and continued his examinations. I attempted to fight again but he held me still and asked, very quietly, "Are you a stupid child? Have you forgot what I said?"

"No." I was so frightened and furious I was trembling, and I hated the smell of him, so close in there.

"Then listen to me again, Saxon child. I will not hurt you, neither will I outrage you. But if you want to die, keep struggling."

I held still then and stood silent, hating him. He seemed quite uncon-

cerned about that; he gave me a cup of wine and a hard cake, and ignored me
while I ate and drank. All his attention was on the two knights outside. When
he heard them depart into their respective tents, he wrapped me in a cloak
and bore me out into the night again.

At the other end of the camp there was a very fine tent, pitched a little distance from the others. Two men stood before it, deep in conversation. After a
moment one went away. The other remained outside the tent a moment,
breathing the night air, looking up at the stars. When he lifted the flap and
made to go inside, my captor stepped forward.

"Salve, Emres."

"Invenistine novum tironem, Budu?" replied the other. He was a tall man
and elderly—I thought: his hair and eyebrows were white. His face, however,
was smooth and unlined, and there was an easy suppleness to his move-
ments. He was very well dressed, as Britons went. They had a brief conversation and then the one called Emres raised the flap of the tent again, gesturing
us inside.

It was so brilliantly lit in there it dazzled my eyes. I was again unrobed, in
that white glare, but I dared do no more than clench my fists as the old one
examined me. His hands were remarkably soft and clean, and *he* did not smell
bad. He stuck me with a pin and dabbed the blood onto the tongue of a little
god he had, sitting on a chest; it clicked for a moment and then chattered to
him in a tinny voice. He in his turn had a brief conversation with my captor.
At its conclusion, Emres pointed at me and asked a question. My captor
shrugged. He turned his big head to look at me.

"What is your name, little boy?" he asked in Saxon.

"Bricta, son of Baldulf," I told him. He looked back at Emres.

"Nomen ei Victor est," he said.

The taste in my mouth was unbearable. I hadn't wanted this recollection, this
squalid history! I much preferred time to begin with that first memory of the
silver ship that rose skyward from the circle of stones, taking me away to the
gleaming hospital and the sweet-faced nurses.

I got unsteadily to my feet, groping after my hat and stick. As I did so I
heard the unmistakable sound of an automobile approaching. In another sec-

ond a light runabout rattled around the corner and pulled up before me. Labienus sat behind the wheel, no longer the jovial master of ceremonies. He
was all hard-eyed centurion now.

"We received your distress signal. Report, please, Victor."

"I was attacked," I said dully.

"Tsk! Rather obviously."

"I . . . I know it sounds improbable, sir, but I believe my assailant was another operative," I explained. To my surprise he merely nodded.

"We know his identity. You'll notice he's sending quite a distinct signal."

"Yes." I looked down the street in wonderment. The signal lay on the air
like a trail of green smoke. Why would he signal? "He's . . . somewhere in
Chinatown."

"Exactly," agreed Labienus. "Well, Victor, what do you intend to do about
this?"

"Sir?" I looked back at him, confused. Something was wrong here. Some
business I hadn't been briefed about, perhaps? But why—?

"Come, come, man, you've a mission to complete! He took the mortal boy!
Surely you've formed a plan to rescue him?" he prompted.

The hideous taste welled in my mouth. I suppressed an urge to expectorate.

"My team on Nob Hill is more than competent to complete the salvage
there without my supervision," I said, attempting to sound coolly rational.
"That being the case, I believe, sir, that I shall seek out the scoundrel who did
this to me and jolly well kill him. Figuratively speaking, of course."

"Very good. And?"

"And, of course, recapture my mortal recruit and deliver him to the collection point as planned and according to schedule," I said. "Sir."

"See that you do." Labienus worked both clutch and brake expertly and
edged his motor forward, cylinders idling. "Report to my cabin on the *Thunderer* at seven hundred hours for a private debriefing. Is that clear?"

"Perfectly clear, sir." So there was some mystery to be explained. Very well.

"You are dismissed."

"Sir." I doffed my hat and watched as he drove smoothly away up Market
Street.

I replaced my hat and turned in the direction of the signal, probing. My
dizziness was fading, burned away by my growing sense of outrage. The filthy

old devil, how dare he do this to me? What was he playing at? I began to walk briskly again, my speed increasing with my strength.

Of course, the vow to kill him hadn't been meant literally. We do not die. But I'd find some way of paying him out in full measure, I hadn't the slightest doubt about that. He had the edge on me in strength, but I was swifter and in full possession of my faculties, whereas he was probably drooling mad, the old troll.

Yes, mad, that was the only explanation. There had always been rumors that some of the oldest operatives were flawed somehow, those created earliest, before the augmentation process had been perfected. Budu had been one of the oldest I'd ever met. He had been created more than forty thousand years ago, before the human races had produced their present assortment of representatives.

Now that I thought of it, I hadn't seen an operative of his racial type *in the field* in years. They held desk jobs at Company bases, or were air transport pilots. I'd assumed this was simply because the modern mortal race was now too homogenous for Budu's type to pass unnoticed. What if the true reason was that the Company had decided not to take chances with the earlier models? What if there was some risk that all of that particular class were inherently unstable?

Good God! No wonder I was expected to handle this matter without assistance. Undoubtedly our masters wanted the whole affair resolved as quietly as possible. They could count on my discretion; I only hoped my ability met their expectations.

Following the signal, I turned left at the corner of Market and Grant. The green trail led straight up Grant as far as Sacramento. What was his game? He was drawing me straight into the depths of the Celestial quarter, a place where I'd be conspicuous were it daylight, but at no particular disadvantage otherwise.

He must intend some kind of dialogue with me. The fact that he had taken a hostage indicated that he wanted our meeting on his terms, under his control. That he felt he needed a hostage could be taken as a sign of weakness on his part. Had his strength begun to fail somehow? Not if his attack on me had been any indication. Though it had been largely a matter of speed and leverage . . .

I came to the corner of Grant and Sacramento. The signal turned to the left again. It traveled up a block, where it could be observed emanating from a darkened doorway. I stood considering it for a moment, tapping my stick impatiently against my boot. I spat into the gutter, but it did not take the taste from my mouth.

I walked slowly uphill, past the shops that sold black and scarlet lacquerware and green jade. Here was the Baptist mission, smelling of starch and good intentions. From this lodging-house doorway a heavy perfume of joss sticks; from this doorway a reek of preserved fish. And from this doorway . . .

It stood ajar. A narrow corridor went straight back into darkness, with a narrower stair ascending to the left. The bottommost stair tread had been thrown open like the lid of a piano bench, revealing a black void below.

I scanned. He was down there, and making no attempt to hide himself. Donal was there with him, still alive. There were no other signs of mortal life, however.

I paced forward into the darkness and stood looking down. Chill air was coming up from below. It stank like a crypt. Rungs leading down into a passageway were just visible, by a wavering pool of green light. So was a staring dead face, contorted into a grimace of rage.

After a moment's consideration, I removed my hat and set it on the second step. My stick I resolved to take with me, although its sword would be useless against my opponent. No point in any further delay; it was time to descend into yet another hell.

At the bottom of the ladder the light was a little stronger. It revealed more bodies, lying in a subterranean passage of brick plastered over and painted a dull green. The dead had been Celestials, and seemed to have died fighting, within the last few hours. They were smashed like so many insects. The light that made this plain was emanating from a wide doorway that opened off the passage, some ten feet farther on. The smell of death was strongest in there.

"Come in, Victor," said a voice.

I went as far as the doorway and looked.

In that low-ceilinged chamber of bare plaster, in the fitful glow of one oil lamp, more dead men were scattered. These were all elderly Chinese, skeletally emaciated, and they had been dead some hours and they had not died quietly. One leaned in a chair beside the little table with the flickering lamp; one was hung up on a hook that protruded from a wall; one lay half in, half out of a cupboard passage, his arm flung out as though beckoning. Three were sprawled on the floor beside slatwood bunks, in postures suggesting they had been slain whilst in the lethargy of their drug and tossed from the couches like rags. The apparatus of the opium den lay here and there; a gold-wrapped brick of the poisonous substance, broken pipes, burnt dishes, long matches, bits of wire.

And there, beyond them, sat the monster of my long nightmares.

"You don't like my horrible parlor," chuckled Budu. "Your little white nose has squeezed nearly shut, your nostrils look like a fish's gills."

"It's just the sort of nest you'd make for yourself, you murdering old fool," I told him. He frowned at me.

"I have never murdered," he told me seriously. "But these were murderers, and thieves. Who else would keep such a fine secret cellar, eh? A good place for a private meeting." He leaned back against the wall, lounging at his ease across the top tier of a bunk, waving enormous mud-caked boots. His dress consisted of stained blue-jean trousers, a vast shapeless red coat made from a blanket, and a battered black felt hat. He had let his hair and beard grow long; they trailed down like pale moss over his bare hairy chest. He looked rather like St. Nicholas turned monster.

Donal sat stiffly beside him. Budu had placed his great hand about the boy's neck, as easily as I might take hold of an axe handle.

"Uncle Jimmy," moaned Donal.

"Explain yourself, sir," I addressed Budu, keeping my voice level and cold. He responded with gales of delighted laughter.

"I was the Briton, and you were the little barbarian," he said. "Look at us now!"

I stepped into the room, having scanned for traps. "I followed your signal," I told him. "You certainly made it plain enough. May I ask why you thought it was necessary to cut my throat?"

He shrugged, regarding me with hooded eyes. "How else to get your attention but to take your quarry from you? And how to do that but by disabling you? What harm did it do? Spoiled your nice white shirt, yes, and made you angry."

I tapped my stick in impatience. "What was your purpose in calling me here, old man?"

"To tell you a few truths, and see what you do when you've heard them. You were wondering about us, we oldest Old Ones, wondering what became of us all. You were thinking we're like badly made clockwork toys, and our Great Toymakers decided to pull us off the shelves of the toyshop." He stretched luxuriously. Donal tried to turn his head to stare at him, but was held fast as the old creature continued: "No, no. We're not badly made. I was better made than you, little man. It's a question of purpose." He thrust his prognathous face forward at me through the gloom. "I was made a war axe. They made you a shovel. Is the metaphor plain enough for you?"

"I take your meaning." I moved a step closer.

"You've been told all your life that our masters wish only to save things, books and pretty pictures and children, and for this purpose we were made, to creep into houses like mice and steal away loot before time can eat it."

"That's an oversimplification, but essentially true."

"Is it?" He stroked his beard in amusement. I could see the red lines across the back of his hand where I'd clawed him. He hadn't bothered to heal them yet. "You pompous creature, in your nice clothes. You were made to save things, Victor. I wasn't. Now, hear the truth: I, and all my kind, were made because our perfect and benign masters wanted *killers* once. Can you guess why?"

"Well, let me see." I swallowed back bile. "You say you're not flawed. Yet it's fairly common knowledge that flawed immortals were produced, during the first experiments with the process. What did the Company do about them? Perhaps you were created as a means of eliminating them."

"Good guess." He nodded his head. "But wrong. They were never killed, those poor failed things. I've seen them, screaming in little steel boxes. No. Guess again."

"Then . . . perhaps at one time it was necessary to have agents whose specialty was defense." I tried. "Prior to the dawn of civilization."

"An easy guess. You fool, of course it was. You think our masters waited, so gentle and pure, for sweet reason to persuade men to evolve? Oh, no. Too many wolves were preying on the sheep. They needed operatives who could kill, who could happily kill fierce primitives so the peaceful ones could weave baskets and paint bison on walls." He grinned at me with those enormous teeth, and went on: "We made civilization dawn, I and my kind. We pushed that bright ball over the horizon at last, and we did it by killing! If a man raised his hand against his neighbor, we cut it off. If a tribe painted themselves for war, we washed their faces with their own blood. Shall I tell you of the races of men you'll never see? They wouldn't learn peace, and so we were sent in to slay them, man, woman, and child."

"You mean," I exhaled, "the Company decided to accelerate mankind's progress by selectively weeding out its sociopathic members. And if it did? We've all heard rumors of something like that. It may be necessary, from time to time, even now. Not a pretty thought, but one can see the reasons. If you hadn't done it, mankind might have remained in a state of savagery forever." I took another step forward.

"We did good work," he said plaintively. "And we weren't hypocrites. It was fun." His pale gaze wandered past me to the doorway. There was a momentary flicker of something like uneasiness in his eyes, some ripple across the surface of his vast calm.

"What is the point of telling me this, may I ask?" I pressed.

"To show you that you serve lying and ungrateful masters, child," he replied, his attention returning to me. "Stupid masters. They've no understanding of this world they rule. Once we cleared the field so they could plant, how did they reward us? We had been heroes. We became looters.

"And you should see how they punished the ones who argued! No more pruning the vine, they told us, let it grow how it will. You're only to gather the fruit now, they told us. Was that fair? Was it, when we'd been created to gather heads?"

"No, I dare say it wasn't. But you adapted, didn't you?" To my dismay I was shaking with emotion. "You found ways to satisfy your urges in the Company's service. You'd taken your share of heads the day you caught me!"

"Rescued you," he corrected me. "You were only a little animal, and if I hadn't taken you away, you'd have grown into a big animal like your father. There were lice crawling in his hair, when I stuck his head on the pike. There was food in his beard."

I spat in his face. I couldn't stop myself. The next second I was sick with mortification, to be provoked into such operatic behavior, and dabbed hurriedly at my chin with a handkerchief. Budu merely wiped his face with the back of his hand and smiled, content to have reduced my stature.

"Your anger changes nothing. Your father was a dirty beast. He was an oathbreaker and an invader, too, as were all his people. You've been taught your history, you know all this! So don't judge me for enjoying what I did to exterminate his race. And see what happened when I was ordered to stop killing Saxons! When Arthur died, Roman order died with him. All that we'd won at Badon Hill was lost and the Saxon hordes returned, never to leave. What sense did it make, to have given our aid for a while to one civilized tribe, and then leave it to be destroyed?"

His gaze traveled past me to the doorway again. Who was he expecting? They weren't coming to join him, that much was clear.

"We do not involve ourselves in the petty territorial squabbles of mortals," I recited. "We do not embrace their causes. We move amongst them, saving what we can, but we are never such fools as to be drawn into their disputes."

"Yes, you're quoting Company policy to me. But don't you see that your fine impartiality has no purpose? It accomplishes nothing! It's wasteful! You know the house will burn, so you creep in like thieves and steal the furniture beforehand, and then watch the flames. Wouldn't it be more efficient use of your time to prevent the fire in the first place?" He paused a moment and looked at the back of his hand with a slight frown. I saw the red lines there fade to pink as he set them to healing over.

"It would be more efficient, yes," I said, "but for one slight difficulty. You couldn't prevent the fire happening. It isn't possible to change history."

"*Recorded* history." He bared his big teeth in amusement once more. "It isn't possible to change recorded history. And do you think even that sacred rule's as unbreakable as you've been told? I have made the history that was written and read. It disappoints me. I will make something new now."

"Shall you really?" I folded my arms. Doubtless he was going to start bragging about being a god. It went with the profile of this sort of lunatic.

"Yes, and you'll help me, if you're wise. Listen to me. In the time before history was written down, in those days, our masters were bold. All mortals have inherited the legend that there was once a golden age when men lived simply in meadows, and the Earth was uncrowded and clean, and there was no war, but only arts of peace.

"But when recorded history began—when we were forbidden to exterminate the undesirables—that paradise was lost. And our masters let it be lost, and that is the condemnation I fling in their teeth." He drew a deep breath.

"Your point, sir?"

"I'll make an end of recorded history. I can so decimate the races of men that their golden age will come again, and never again will there be enough of them to ravage one another or the garden they inhabit. And we immortals will be their keepers. Victor, little Victor, how long have you lived? Aren't you tired of watching them fight and starve? You creep among them like a scavenger, but you could walk among them like—"

"Like a god?" I sneered.

"I had been about to say, an angel," Budu sneered back. "I remember the service I was created for. Do you, little man? Or have you ever even known? Such luxuries you've had, among the poor mortals! Have you never felt the urge to *really* help them? But the time's soon approaching when you can."

"Ridiculous," I stated. "You know as well as I do that history won't stop. There'll be just as much warfare and mortal misery in this new century as in the centuries before, and nothing anyone can do will alter one event." I gauged the pressure of his fingers on Donal's neck. How quickly could I move to get them loose?

"Not one event? You think so? Maybe." He looked sly. "But our masters will turn what can't be changed to their own advantage, and why can't I? Think of the great slaughters to come, Victor. How do you know I won't be working there? How do you know I haven't been at work already? How do you know I haven't got disciples among our people, weary as I am of our masters' blundering, ready as I am to mutiny?"

"Because history states otherwise," I told him flatly. "There will be no mutiny, no war in heaven if you like. Civilization will prevail. It is recorded that it will."

"Is it?" He grinned. "And can you tell me who recorded it? Maybe I did. Maybe I will, after I win. Victor, such a simple trick, but it's never occurred to you. History is only writing, and *one can write lies!*"

I stared at him. No, in fact, it never had occurred to me. He rocked to and fro in his merriment, dragging Donal with him. Silent tears streamed down the child's face.

Budu lurched forward, fixing me with his gaze. "Listen now. I have my followers, but we need more. You'll join me because you're clever, and you're weary of this horror, too, and you owe me the duty of a son, for I saved you from death. You're a Facilitator and know the Company codes. You'll work in secret, you'll obtain certain things for me, and we'll take mortal children and work the augmentation process on them, and raise them as our own operatives, for our own purposes, loyal to us. Then we'll pull the weeds from the Garden. Then we'll geld the bull and make him pull the plough. Then we'll slaughter the wolf that preys on the herd. Just as we used to do! There will be order.

"For this reason I came as a beggar to this city and followed you, watching. Now I've made you listen to me." He looked at the doorway again. "Tell me I'm not a fool, little Victor, tell me I haven't walked into this trap with you to no purpose."

"What will you do if I refuse?" I demanded. "Break the child's neck?"

This was too much for the boy, who whimpered like a rabbit and started forward convulsively. Budu looked down, scowling as though he had forgotten about him. "Are you a stupid child?" he asked Donal. "Do you want to die?"

I cannot excuse my next act, though he drove me to it; he, and the horror of the place, and the time that was slipping away and bringing this doomed city down about our ears if we tarried. I charged him, howling like the animal he was.

He reared back. Instead of closing about Donal's throat, his fingers twitched harmlessly. As his weight shifted, his right arm dropped to his side, heavy as lead. My charge threw him backward so that his head struck the wall with a resounding thud.

All the laughter died in his eyes, and they focused inward as he ran his self-diagnostic. I caught up Donal in my arms and backed away with him, panting.

Budu looked out at me.

"A virus," he informed me. "It was in your saliva. It's producing inert matter even now, at remarkable speed. Blocking my neuroreceptors. I don't think it will kill me, but I doubt if even your masters could tell. I'm sure they hope so. You're surprised. You had no knowledge, of this weapon inside yourself?"

"None," I said.

Budu was nodding thoughtfully, or perhaps he was beginning to be unable to hold his head up. "They didn't tell you about this talent of yours, because if you'd known about it I would have seen it in your thoughts, and then I'd never have let you spit on me. At the very least I wouldn't have wiped it away with my wounded hand."

"A civilized man would have used a handkerchief," I could not resist observing.

He giggled, but his voice was weaker when he spoke.

"Well. I guess we'll see now if our masters have at long last found a way to unmake their creations. Or I will see; you can't stay in this dangerous place to watch the outcome, I know. But you'll wish you had, in the years to come, you'll wish you knew whether or not I was still watching you, following you. For I know your defense against me now, think of that! And I know who betrayed me, with his clever virus." Budu's pale eyes widened. "I was wrong. The rest of them may be shovels, but you, little Victor—you are a poisoned knife. *Victor veneficus!*" he added, and laughed thickly at his joke. "Oh, tell him— never sleep. If I live—"

"We're going now, Donal Og, Uncle Jimmy'll get you safe out of here," I said to the child, turning from Budu to thread my way between the stinking corpses on the floor.

I heard Budu cough once as his vocal centers went, and then the ether was filled with a cascade of images: a naked child squatting on a clay floor, staring through darkness at a looming figure in a bearskin. Flames devouring brush huts, goatskin tents, cottages, halls, palaces, shops, restaurants, hotels. Soldiers in every conceivable kind of uniform, with every known weapon, in every posture of attack or defense the human form could assume.

If these were his memories, if this was the end of his life, there was no emotion of sorrow accompanying the images; no fear, no weariness, no relief either. Instead, a loud yammering laughter grew ever louder, and deafened the inner ear at the last image: a hulking brute in a bearskin, squatting beside a fire, turning and turning in his thick fingers a gleaming golden axe; and on the blade of the axe was written the word VIRUS.

Halfway up the ladder, the trap opening was occluded by a face that looked down at me and then drew back. I came up with all speed; I faced a small mob of Chinese, grim men with bronze hatchets. They had not expected to see a man in evening dress carrying a child.

I addressed them in Cantonese, for I could see they were natives of that province.

"The devil who killed your grandfathers is still down there. He is asleep and will not wake up. You can safely cut him to pieces now."

I took up my hat and left the mortals standing there, looking uncertainly from my departing form to the dark hole in the stair.

The air was beginning to freshen with the scent of dawn. I had little more than an hour to get across the city. In something close to panic I began to run up Sacramento, broadcasting a general assistance signal. Had my salvage teams waited for me? Donal clung to me and did not make a sound.

Before I had gone three blocks, I heard the noise of an automobile, echoing loud between the buildings. It was climbing up Sacramento toward me. I turned to meet it. Over the glare of its brass headlamps I saw Pan Wen-Shi. His tuxedo and shirtfront, unlike mine, were still as spotless as when he'd left the Company banquet. On the seat beside him was a tiny almond-eyed girl. He braked and shifted, putting out a hand to prevent her from tumbling off and rolling away downhill.

"Climb in," he shouted. I vaulted the running board and toppled into the backseat with Donal. Pan stepped on the gas and we cranked forward again.

"Much obliged to you for the ride," I said, settling myself securely and attempting to pry Donal's arms loose from my neck. "Had a bit of difficulty."

"So had I. We must tell one another our stories someday," Pan acknowledged, rounding the corner at Powell and taking us down toward Geary. The baby had turned in her seat and was staring at us. Donal was quivering and hiding his eyes.

"Now then, Donal Og, now then," I crooned to him. "You've been a brave boy and you're all safe again. And isn't this grand fun? We're going for a ride in a real motorcar!"

"Bad Toymaker gone?" asked the little muffled voice.

"Sure he is, Donal, and we've escaped entirely."

He consented to lower his hands, but shrank back at the sight of the others. "Who's that?"

"Why, that's a China doll that's escaped the old Toymaker, same as you, and that's the kind Chinaman who helped her. They're taking us to the sea, where we'll escape on a big ship."

He stared at them doubtfully. "I want Mummy," he said, tears forming in his eyes.

The little girl, who till this moment had been solemn in fascination, suddenly dimpled into a lovely smile and laughed like a silver bell. She pointed a finger at him and made a long babbling pronouncement, neither in Cantonese nor Mandarin. For emphasis, she reached down beside her and flung something at him over the back of the seat, with a triumphant cry of *"Dah!"* It was a wrapped bar of Ghirardelli's, only slightly gummy at one corner where she'd been teething on it. I caught it in midair.

"See now, Donal, the nice little girl is giving us chocolates." I tore off the wrapper hastily and gave him a piece. She reached out a demanding hand and I gave her some as well. "Chocolates and an automobile ride and a big ship! Aren't you the lucky boy, then?"

He sat quiet, watching the gregarious baby and nibbling at his treat. His memories were fading. As we rattled up Geary, he looked at me with wondering eyes.

"Where Ella?" he asked me.

When I had caught my breath, I replied: "She couldn't come to Toyland, Donal Og. But you're a lucky, lucky boy, for you shall. You'll have splendid adventures and never grow old. Won't that be fun, now?"

He looked into my face, not knowing what he saw there. "Yes," he answered in a tiny voice.

Lucky boy, yes, borne away in a mechanical chariot, away from the perishable mortal world, and all the pretty nurses will smile over you and perhaps sing you to sleep before they take you off to surgery. And when you wake, you'll have been improved; you'll be ever so much cleverer, Donal, than poor mortal monkeys like your father. A biomechanical marvel, fit to stride through this new century in company with the internal combustion engine and the flying machine.

And you'll be so happy, boy, and at peace, knowing about the wonderful work you'll have to do for the Company. Much happier than poor Ella would ever have been, with her wild heart, her restlessness and anger. Surely no kindness to give her eternal life, when life's stupidities and injustice could never be escaped?

. . . But you'll enjoy your immortality, Donal Og. You will, if you don't become a thing like me.

The words came into my mind unbidden, and I shuddered in my seat. Mustn't think of this just now: too much to do. Perhaps the whole incident had been some sort of hallucination? There was no foul taste in my mouth, no viral poison sizzling under my glib tongue. The experience might have been some fantastic nightmare brought on by stress, but for the blood staining my elegant evening attire.

I was a gentleman, after all. No gentleman did such things.

Pan bore left at Mason, rode the brakes all the way down to Fulton, turned right and accelerated. We sped on, desperate to leave the past.

There were still whaleboats drawn up on the sand, still wagons waiting there, and shirtsleeved immortals hurriedly loading boxes from wagon to boat. We'd nearly left it too late: those were my people, that was my Nob Hill salvage arrayed in splendor amid the driftwood and broken shells. There were still a pair of steamers riding at anchor beyond Seal Rock, though most of the fleet had already put out to sea and could be glimpsed as tiny lights on the gray horizon, making for the Farallones. As we came within range of the Hush Field both of the children slumped into abrupt and welcome unconsciousness.

We jittered to a stop just short of the tavern, where an impatient operative from the Company's motor agency took charge of the automobile. Pan and I jumped out, caught up our respective children, and ran down the beach.

Past the wagons loaded with rich jetsam of the Gilded Age, we ran: lined up in the morning gloom and salt wind were the grand pianos, the crystal chandeliers, the paintings in gilt frames, the antique furniture. Statuary classical and modern; gold plate and tapestries. Cases of rare wines, crates of phonograph cylinders, of books and papers, waited like refugees to escape the coming morning.

I glimpsed Averill, struggling through the sand with his arms full of priceless things. He was sobbing loudly as he worked; tears coursed down his cheeks, his eyes were wide with terror, but his body served him like the clockwork toy, like the *fine machine* it was, and bore him ceaselessly back and forth between the wagon and the boat until his appointed task should be done.

"Sir! Where did you get to?" he said, gasping. "We waited and waited— and now it's going to cut loose any second, and we're still not done!"

"Couldn't be helped, old man," I told him as we scuttled past. "Carry on! I have every faith in you."

I shut my ears to his cry of dismay and ran on. A boat reserved for passengers still waited in the surf. Pan and I made for the boarding officer and gave our identification.

"You've cut it damned close, gentlemen," he grumbled.

"Unavoidable," I told him. His gaze fell on my gore-drenched shirt and he blinked, but waved us to our places. Seconds later we were seated securely, and the oarsmen pulled and sent us bounding out on the receding tide to the *Thunderer* where she lay at anchor.

We'd done it, we were away from that fated city, where even now bronze hatchets were completing the final betrayal—

No. A gentleman does not betray others. Nor does he leave his subordinates to deal with the consequences of his misfortune.

Donal shivered in the stiff breeze, waking slowly. Frank's coat had been lost somewhere in Chinatown; I shrugged out of my dinner jacket and put it around Donal's shoulders. He drew closer to me, but his attention was caught by the operatives working on the shore. As he watched, something disturbed the earth, and the sand began to flurry and shift. Another warning was sounding up from below. It hit the bottom of our boat as though we'd struck a rock, and I feared we'd capsize.

The rumbling carried to us over the roar of the sea, as did the shouts of the operatives trying to finish the loading. One wagon settled forward a few inches, causing the unfortunate precipitation of a massive antique clock into the arms of the immortals who had been gingerly easing it down. They arrested its flight, but the shock or perhaps merely the striking hour set in motion its parade of tiny golden automata. Out came its revolving platforms, its trumpeting angels, its pirouetting lovers, its minute Death with raised scythe and hourglass. Crazily it chimed five.

Pan and I exchanged glances. He checked his chronometer. Our boatmen increased the vigor of their strokes.

Moment by moment the east was growing brighter, disclosing operatives massed on the deck of the *Thunderer*. Their faces were turned to regard the sleeping city. Pan and I were helped on deck and our mortal charges handed up after us. A pair of white-coifed nurses stepped forward.

"Agent Pan? Agent Victor?" inquired one, as the other checked a list.

"Here, now, Donal, we're on our ship at last, and here's a lovely fairy to look after you." I thrust him into her waiting arms. The other received the baby from Pan, and the little girl went without complaint; but as his nurse turned to carry him below decks, Donal twisted in her arms and reached out a desperate hand for me.

"Uncle Jimmy," he screamed. I turned away quickly as she bore him off. Really, it was for the best.

I made my way along the rail and emerged on the aft deck, where I nearly ran into Nan D'Arraignee. She did not see me, however; she was fervently kissing a great bearded fellow in a brass-buttoned blue coat, which he had opened to wrap about them both, making a warm protected place for her in his arms. He looked up and saw me. His eyes, timid and kindly, widened, and he nodded in recognition.

"Kalugin," I acknowledged with brittle courtesy, tipping my hat. I edged on past them quickly, but not so quickly as to suggest I was fleeing. What had I to flee from? Not guilt, certainly. No gentleman dishonorably covets another gentleman's lady.

As I reached the aft saloon we felt it beginning, in the rising surge that lifted the *Thunderer* with a crash and threatened to swamp the fleeing whale-boats. We heard the roar coming up from the earth, and in the City some mortals sat up in their beds and frowned at what they could sense but not quite hear yet.

I clung to the rail of the *Thunderer*. My fellow operatives were hurrying to the stern of the ship to be witness to history, and nearly every face bore an expression compounded of mingled horror and eagerness. There were one or two who turned away, averting their eyes. There were those like me, sick and exhausted, who merely stared.

And really, from where we lay offshore, there was not much to see; no De-Mille spectacle. No more at first than a puff of dust rising into the air. But very clear across the water we heard the rumbling, and then the roar of bricks coming down, and steel snapping, and timbers groaning, and the high sweet shattering of glass, and the tolling in all discordance of bronze-throated bells. Loud as the Last Trumpet, but not loud enough to drown out the screams of the dying. No, the roar of the earthquake even paused for a space, as if to let us hear mortal agony more clearly; then the second shock came, and I saw a distant tower topple and fall slowly, and then the little we had been able to see of the City was concealed in a roiling fog the color of a bloodstain.

I turned away, and chanced to look up at the open doorway of a stateroom on the deck above. There stood Labienus, watching the death of three thousand mortals with an avid stare. That was when I knew, and knew beyond question whose weapon I was.

I hadn't escaped. My splendid mansion, with all its gilded conceits, had collapsed in a rain of bricks and broken plaster.

A hand settled on my shoulder and I dropped my gaze to behold Lewis, of all people, looking into my face with compassion.

"I know," he murmured, "I know, old fellow. At least it's finished now, for those poor mortals and for us. Brace up! Can I get you a drink?"

What did he recognize in my sick white face? Not the features of a man who had emptied a phial into an innocent-looking cup of wine. Why, I'd always been a poisoner, hadn't I? But it had happened long ago, and he had no memory of it anyway. I'd seen to that. And Lewis would never suspect me of such behavior in any case. We were both gentlemen, after all.

"No, thank you," I replied, "I believe I'll just take the air for a little while out here. It's a fine restorative to the nerves, you know. Sea air."

"So it is," he agreed, stepping back. "That's the spirit! It's not as though you could have done anything more. You know what they say: history cannot be changed." He gave me a final helpful thump on the arm and moved away, clinging to the rail as the deck pitched.

Alone, I fixed my eyes on the wide horizon of the cold and perfect sea. I drew in a deep breath of chill air.

One can write lies. And live them.

Two operatives in uniform were making their way toward me through the press of the crowd. "Executive Facilitator Victor?"

I nodded. They shouldered into place, one on either side of me.

"Sir, your presence is urgently requested. Mr. Labienus sends his apologies for unavoidably revising your schedule," one of them recited.

"Certainly." I exhaled. "By all means, gentlemen, let us go."

We made our way across deck to the forward compartments, avoiding the hatches where the crew were busily loading down the art, the music, the literature, the fine flowering of the humanity that we had, after all, been created to save.

THE ANGEL OF
THE BOTTOMLESS DEEP

Getting Budu out of the way had been the first step.

"It was Aegeus's idea," Labienus said, holding out his hands in an apologetic gesture. "He recommended you for the job in the highest terms, Victor. And, really, what were we to do? We needed someone for swift, discreet, and effective work. You were the man."

"You might have warned me," said Victor, ignoring the aftershock that struck the hull of the *Thunderer* with an unnerving thump. He had gone ghastly pale. There was an expression in his eyes reminding Labienus of one of Van Gogh's more disturbed self-portraits.

"Come now, man, how could we have done that? You needed the advantage of surprise. The old creature had uncanny faculties of perception, as madmen frequently do. It should be obvious why the Company didn't want a lunatic immortal wandering about loose, especially one his size!"

"And the others of which he spoke? His cabal?"

"We've already investigated that," Labienus assured him. "He was delusional, of course. There are no others."

But Victor had not relaxed.

"What about the virus?" he demanded. "Why was that necessary?"

"Could you have defeated him without it?"

"I doubt it very much," Victor admitted, and dropped his staring eyes at last. Labienus cleared his throat.

"Not a gentleman's weapon, I know. If Aegeus hadn't insisted you were experienced in this sort of job—well. No use dwelling on what can't be helped. But you have my personal apology, for what it's worth."

"Am I still producing the virus?"

"Ye gods, no! It was designed to run its course quite quickly, once activated. In any case, it was harmless to anyone but an operative of that particular racial type," Labienus explained. "You're perfectly immune to it yourself, and anyone else you're likely to encounter would be as well."

"But how was it done? When was I infected?"

Time for the grandstand play. Labienus looked pained. He deepened the pain to anguish; rose from his seat and paced the cabin a moment before turning to Victor in a decisive manner.

"Victor, it's a classified matter, but—by God, sir, you're entitled to the truth." He drew from a sheaf of papers on his desk a photograph of Emil Bergwurm. "This was a protégé of Aegeus's. I don't know where he found the man, but evidently he was some sort of spectacular polymath—"

Victor rose from his chair and seized the picture. He stared at it for a long moment before handing it back.

"I know where he found him," he said quietly.

"Interesting," remarked Labienus. He pretended to study Victor in shrewd speculation. "There have been rumors for years—but, of course, I won't pry. One does feel a certain loyalty to one's old case officer. I have nothing but respect for Aegeus. If he did experiment with something, in defiance of Company regulations, I am certain it was in the Company's best interests . . . and perhaps you know more than I do in this matter."

Victor said nothing. Labienus cleared his throat and continued.

"There you have it. The mortal was brilliant with disease cultures, it seems. He was asked to come up with a, to coin a phrase, 'designed virus.' I assume you were armed with it at some point in the recent past. Have you been at Eurobase One recently?"

"I'm not at liberty to say, sir."

"Quite. Perhaps it's best we say no more on the matter, then, eh? You've earned a rest now. My private suite is through there—" Labienus pointed. "You'll find a change of clothes laid out for you. I'll have hot coffee and a breakfast sent in. Your personal effects are already waiting for you on the air transport, of course."

"Thank you, sir," Victor said mechanically, getting to his feet.

"And, Victor—" Labienus paused, as if reluctant to be too effusive. He shrugged, smiled wryly and said: "You're an excellent operative, sir. If you haven't always been appreciated, you should know that I, at least, have found it an honor working with you."

"Thank you, sir," Victor repeated. Was he even listening? Labienus clapped him on the shoulder and sent him off to the suite with a gentle push.

Not a bad beginning. He would improve on it.

April 29, 2100. If a place can hold the memory of death, surely the badlands of Montana retained it. Labienus peered from the window of the Silverbolt as it bounced over bare rusty earth and rock, trying to imagine what it had been like on that hellacious Cretaceous day when the end had come for them all: the maiasaur with its touching maternal concern, the vicious tyrannosaur no less a good mother, the little sneaking egg thieves with no shred of moral respectability whatsoever, all the rumbling honking thundering life that had held sway since forever. Even if they'd had the brains to see it coming, how could any of them have understood the End? What, for *us*? Rulers of the earth for the last hundred and sixty million years?

But the earth had understood, and remembered still, and offered up white bones still bedded in clay red as fresh meat for the edification of its present rulers, who utterly failed to take the hint. It was almost a duty to explain the lesson, thought Labienus.

He crested the last hill and braked a moment, gazing out at the spectacle in the valley below. There, the glittering expanse of domed backs in dust-dulled jewel colors: parked vehicles by the hundreds, for all the world like a massed herd grazing. The real herd was streaming up from the parking lot toward the immense white tent, only pausing and milling at the gate, where two parked ticket trailers blocked the way under the hanging sign: JURASSIC RANCH. Above the sign a banner had been poked up on poles: WELCOME CHILDREN OF MARIEL PROPHET!

Labienus grinned and fingered the little laminated tag he wore on a loose chain about his neck, that bore the single word MEDIA.

The tag got him preferred parking, and got him past the two trailers without paying for a ticket, and got him through the maze of hay bales and tent anchors to the trailer behind the big tent. He didn't even have to raise his voice, as he surely must have done if he'd wanted to be heard above the air conditioner's drone; he merely flapped the tag at the two husky mortals standing guard there. They looked him over, decided he fit the description they'd been given, and stood aside to let him climb the steps to their mistress's Abode of Repose, as the flowing script on the trailer's side declared it to be.

The refrigerated atmosphere inside was like a blessing from God, if one's idea of God fit the Mediterranean model and not the Nordic one whose hell was a region of eternal ice. Flies dotted the screen, motionless, chilled practically into hibernation. Labienus made no move to swat them. They were innocents, after all.

He picked his way through the power cables for the various communications hookups, edged through the bath and dressing room, where the high wig and outrageous false eyelashes were set out like armor to be donned for battle. There were five pots of eye shadow alone, in five different shades, each to be applied in its turn in the elaborate face paint patterns five generations of white trash had come to expect from evangelists, no matter what belief system they were peddling.

She was sprawled on the bed in the room beyond, naked, holding a frosted bottle of Perrier to her face.

Labienus bowed and waved his MEDIA tag.

"Ms. Mariel Prophet, ma'am?" he whined. "I'm from the Flathead Lake *Tribune,* and we just wondered if you had anything to say about those rumors that you ain't actually one of the High Holy Ascended Ones but in reality is Mary Ellen Kew from Provo, and ain't been any nearer them monasteries in Tibet than Taiwan, which you had to leave on account of a morals charge?"

"All lies," said Facilitator General Kiu, not even bothering to move the bottle so she could look at him directly. "Really."

"What, even that story that you slept with that little rich boy in New York and got him so crazy in love with you he went and willed his daddy's pharmaceuticals empire to your ministry before he blew his own brains out?" persisted Labienus, perching on the edge of the bed.

"Especially that story," drawled Kiu. "Doonie had no brains to blow out."

"But we got a private source says the FBI and them Tobacco and Firearms people are, quote, very concerned unquote about reports you been meeting with survivalist supremacist sociopaths and planning a old-fashioned Doomsday suicide party," said Labienus, stretching out beside her. She groaned and shifted.

"Your clothes are hot," she complained.

"Get used to it, sugar," Labienus told her, moving closer. "It'll be even hotter out there, once you've got your prophet costume on."

"I go naked under the robe," she informed him.

"Angel Mariel! What would your faithful followers say if they knew?" he chuckled, pulling her against him.

"They know," she murmured, kissing him. "The idea inflames them. All those big boys with guns and half those big girls with knives dream about seeing their Holy Ascended Mother's merciful bosom up close and personal."

Labienus shuddered. "I don't see how you can stand the idea of one of them lusting after you. Let alone hordes of the things."

Kiu laughed and drew back from him, rising on her elbow and resting her head on her hand. "You men," she said sadly. "Though you're more finicky than most, Labienus. If I gave a damn what happened to my body that way, I'd have curled up and gone into fugue the first time I was raped. We can't afford that kind of fastidiousness. Flesh is too useful! If you'd bent over and offered that darling ass to the monkeys a few times, you'd have gotten things you wanted with much less trouble."

"Thank you, but I'll abstain," said Labienus. "And you can't tell me all you ladies are so free with your immortal charms. Why, I knew a little Botanist drone who so loved one man, she refused ever to take another lover after he died."

"Never heard of her," said Kiu. "And she loved a mortal, didn't she? That just proves my point."

"Maybe," replied Labienus, realizing with a start that he'd never thought of Nicholas/Edward as mortal. "Oh, well. Getting back to business: how is that Doomsday party shaping up? Plenty of odorless flavorless stuff to put in the Tasty-Ade?"

"It's not *that* old-fashioned," she said reprovingly. "I've got my inner circle of initiates convinced that the federal government is about to release a plague among all true believers."

"Because they're being controlled by Satan?"

"Ahriman, darling. I like to mix and match my bad guys. Anyway, I'm about to reveal that the latest divine avatar has given me the secret formula for an antidote." Kiu yawned and stretched. "A little chanting, a little light show with holographic chakras, and then I'll implore them all to come join me and the Apostles of Liberty at the meditation center on the night of the full moon, for an announcement of major importance. That ought to give the Feds time to hear about it."

"So that history can pursue its tragically inalterable course with another mass suicide," said Labienus, taking the Perrier from her and setting it aside.

"You got it, honey," Kiu agreed. "I'm making sure push will come to shove. With all those SWAT teams on the horizon, my faithful ones will clamor for the antidote. I'll administer the injections myself, assisted by the Apostles. They won't start dying for five hours, by which time I'll have departed to ask the Ascended Masters for guidance, but the Apostles will stay at their posts to record everything significant. Et voilà! We'll have field-tested a new poison on abundant volunteers."

"Five hours!" Labienus smiled, loosening his tie. "That must be one of Pryleak's toxins. He's a genius at timed-release poison."

"I don't know where you find these awful little moron scientists, but they certainly know their jobs," said Kiu. "If nothing else."

"You might say I've got a guaranteed supplier," said Labienus. He leaned over her and spoke seriously: "Easy enough to coax them into doing what they're good at; you might as well ask a rabbit to run. Far harder to persuade ordinary mortals to glorious idiocy. What a job you've done with those Apostles of yours!"

"Oh, but darling, that's just show business," Kiu replied, smiling as she unbuttoned his shirt. "Listen!"

They paused and focused on the hymn welling from the speakers in the big tent, the soul-stirring anthem so cunningly recorded it incorporated a host of subliminal subsonic hypnotic suggestions. They could hear the Apostles on the smaller stages outside working the crowd, and the first of the warm-up acts starting within the tent itself.

"Everything but the sign saying THIS WAY TO THE EGRESS," said Labienus, removing more of his clothing.

"Well, there is no egress," admitted Kiu. "As they'll discover."

"Much too late," said Labienus, and bit her. He thought of the scene as history would record it: the hundreds of corpses lying side by side in the desert, like sea lions on an infinite beach, bloating and blackening in the sun, all fallen in attitudes of prayer . . . the image intoxicated him.

Later he lay side by side with her in the chill, listening to the rising frenzy. The Apostles had moved into the big tent now and were building anticipation for Holy Mariel Prophet's eventual appearance.

"Sex," Kiu said thoughtfully. "And Fear. Get that big old devil behind them with a stick, and my radiant beauty in front of them, and they'll run right off a cliff, if I ask."

"I'm a firm believer in Guilt, personally," said Labienus.

"Works well on individuals," Kiu conceded.

"Nothing like it for subtle motivation. Plant it deeply enough into a mortal's psyche and it twists them endlessly." Labienus sighed. "Get it in there young enough and it'll do all your work for you. You'll have only to prod the mortal along with a suggestion now and then."

"You realize, of course, that we learned this from the Company?" said Kiu. "Deep programming to keep us running? I was supposed to feel guilty about surviving when everyone else in my village was slaughtered. 'Kiu-Ba, you bad girl, why didn't you die with us?' Conditioning nightmares for centuries, every time I had a disobedient thought, until I learned to work around them."

"Well, of course," said Labienus. "I did, too. What a lot you can do with a child, if you handle them properly!"

A metallic voice spoke from the communications console, echoing through the trailer. *"Beloved of the Avatar, this is your one-hour call."*

Kiu reached out to a bedside unit and thumbed its button. "I copy, Sergei. How's the preshow going?"

"As you divinely ordained it, Beloved."

"You will be blessed. Out." Kiu slid from the bed and hurried to her dressing table. Giggling, Labienus rose and began to dress himself.

"Do you have many Russians working for you?"

"Just Sergei." Kiu spread a coat of primer onto her face, working quickly. She had, after all, had millennia of practice.

"There was a Russian Preserver drone in my sector, and talk about conditioning! You'll never guess how the Company put his survivor's guilt to good use."

"They sent him down in shipwrecks to salvage valuables?" Kiu fanned the first coat dry and considered her pots of rouge.

"You've heard about Kalugin, then?"

"Ashoreth's worked with him. What an emotional mess!" Kiu loaded a canister of flesh tone into her airbrush and, closing her eyes, applied the base coat of foundation.

"But the most obliging fool it was ever my privilege to manipulate," said Labienus, slipping on his MEDIA tag again. "I could make that fellow believe anything."

Kiu set the airbrush aside and turned her masklike face to Labienus. Just at this stage of her toilette she looked queenly, cold, wise as a serpent.

"Give me a broken man every time. Putty can be every bit as useful as tempered steel, you know," she said. "Whatever happened to Kalugin, anyway?"

Labienus smiles, remembering.

The transmission had been picked up on the *Soter*'s receiver in 2083, as Kalugin had rambled, had shouted, had mumbled and at last fallen into the nearest thing to eternal silence an immortal could preserve . . .

I suppose I can just keep talking until the oxygen runs out.

Yes, that would probably be a good idea, wouldn't it? Because then it'll be an anaerobic environment in here and no bacteria will grow. I'll be in better shape when they find me, and I'll have left an audio record. Less effort for the one who has to piece together what happened . . . and less upsetting for Nan, I mustn't forget that.

For of course I'll be rescued. They'll find me. Even though the *Alyosha*'s disappearance is masked by an event shadow, even though the portholes are beginning to be obscured by a film of what I am terribly afraid is mineral deposit that will set like concrete and entomb me in here, to say nothing of making the little sub impossible to spot way down here in the Aleutian Basin . . .

I do wish those appalling ticking noises would stop. Anyone less cheerfully determined than I am would suspect they were hairline cracks forming in the hull. I could survive the hull collapsing, of course, but then I'd be . . .

But the Company will find me. I'll be repaired, someday. I believe in that, yes, I do, with my whole heart and soul, don't I? Certainly I do. Keep talking, Vasilii Vasilievich. That way you won't start screaming, and after all why should you scream? Everything's going to be perfectly all right. The Company will find you. You've been broadcasting your distress signal loud enough to reach every cyborg operative in the eastern hemisphere and possibly one or two Kabalist rabbis in Poland.

Hm, hm, hm, life flashing before one's eyes. Very large red worm dragging itself across the glass and leaving a clear trail, oh, dear, there really is quite a lot of dark debris drifting down from the volcanic vent, isn't there? But that's why they call them *black smokers,* isn't it?

Is it? Would you like me to tell you my life story, large red worm? If I do, will you stay? Perhaps if you keep clearing the debris from that one porthole there'll be some clue for the rescue team, one tiny circle of light in the darkness with my frightened face pressed to it, mouth moving endlessly in pointless conversation. Yes, perhaps.

All right. What's my earliest memory? Being a mortal child. I was the big boy of the family. I was four. I think. Two sisters, Dunya and Sima. I remember them very well. Dunya was eight and Sima was three. Dunya had long braids and Sima had little short ones. We lived in a big house. I was frightened of Papa. He beat the servants, even the girls. But we had a lot of servants. We had fine clothes and toys, too, and our house had a wooden floor. So you can see we were somebody, my family.

Maybe the money and estates belonged to Mama? She never seemed bothered that Papa beat the servants and shouted at her, she just pretended he didn't exist. I don't know how trustworthy my memory is, of course, since I'd run and hide whenever Papa would rage. Dunya called me a coward. Hardly fair. She'd run and hide, too. But she never cried. I cried all the time. How squalid it all is, this memory, and how brief.

It ends, you see, the day it was warm enough to go outside and take bread to old Auntie Irinka. She can't have been my aunt really. I have the impression she lived in a little dark house in the fir woods, like Baba Yaga, and we were taking bread to her for charity. An old retainer put out to honorable pasture, perhaps? Sadly, she never got her bread.

Was it Dunya's fault? She was old enough to know better. I was the big boy of the family, though, I ought to have done something.

You see, the footpath ran along the bank of the river. Quickest route. Our nurse should have taken us some other way, I suppose, but Masha (that was our nurse, Masha) was impatient. We weren't going quickly enough for her, either, at least Dunya was but it took Sima ages to get anywhere on her little fat legs and I was slow, too, carrying the big bread loaf because I was the big boy, and so bundled up in my stiff coat I must have looked like a penguin walking. I should have fallen in, too . . .

Well, Masha decided she couldn't wait, and told us to stop there on the path and not to move until she came back, and then she ducked away into the trees to attend to a private matter. We stood and waited. There was such sunlight! Such a raw powerful smell of new life beginning! The wild smell of the trackless forest. Dark wet earth where the snow was melting, buds swelling on the branches, little green shoots sprouting everywhere. And the yellow-white surface of the river, still frozen solid. And Dunya said, "Let's go skating," and I said, "We haven't got skates with us."

Dunya tossed her braids at this and told me we could make skates out of sticks, and I said we couldn't, and she said she'd show me, and she scrambled down the embankment and broke a couple of forked sticks from a dead branch and stepped into them, and she actually did manage to sort of limp around on the ice. Sima wanted to skate, too, and staggered down the embankment. There weren't any other good sticks, but Dunya hobbled over and took her hands and towed her out after her, slipping and complaining, and they went way out across the river, and had just started back. None of us paid attention to the noises like thunder, far off, or noticed that they were coming nearer. We didn't even know what they meant.

But Masha knew, and her anger was almost greater than her fear, I think, when she came running back through the forest. She called us all sorts of names as she jumped down to the edge of the ice and demanded that the girls return immediately. Both the little faces turned up to her in surprise, and then, *boom* . . .

I think I closed my eyes. I'm sure I did. I always used to close my eyes when I was frightened. There was some shouting, I think, but I can't recall much about that; and when I finally opened my eyes, I recall how astonished I was. Everything had changed! The glaring bright surface of the river had broken up, all that stillness was now a surging living current of brown water, and great islands and bobbing floes of ice, and the *boom-boom-boom* like thunder was still going on all around.

But of Masha or my sisters there was no sign. They had vanished. I stood there staring, hugging the big loaf of bread. I had no idea what had happened. Minutes passed and nothing changed. I was still alone there on the footpath with the bread.

No, no, big worm, come back! The sad part is over. Now the story takes a most unexpected turn. You'll like this.

I heard a big deep voice saying, "What are you going to do, Vasilii Vasilievich?" I thought it might be the devil or Saint Mikhail, and I almost closed my eyes again, but something made me turn and look. And there, standing on the edge of the forest, was a man I recognized: one of our serfs, Grigori. He was leaning on his axe, just looking at me with his big pale eyes.

I said, if I recall correctly, "What?" and he said: "You've lost your sisters! What are you going to do now? Your father will beat you, no mistake about it. Didn't he tell you to be the big boy of the family?"

I started to cry. "Oh," I sobbed. "What am I going to do? I'm scared to go home!"

He came at once and crouched in front of me, looking me in the eye. He said, "Hey, Master, don't worry! I'll tell you what. You and I have always been friends, right?"

Now, I don't think that was quite true, I think he'd been brought from another village not long before, but he'd done a lot of work around the house lately and gone out of his way to be friendly to me, even binding up my knee once when I'd fallen and scraped it. I just sniffled now and said "Yes."

And he said: "Well! I'd hate to see your mother and father kill you, Master, so I'll take you to a safe place I know of. The people are nice there. It's warm. There's plenty of food. They'll let you live with them, and nobody will ever know what you've done. How about that, eh?"

I think I might have argued, but in the end I went with him. He took my hand and we walked away into the fairy-tale forest, and I never saw the mortal world, as a mortal child, again. I have never been able to remember what happened to the bread.

Where did you go, worm? The porthole's silting up again. No matter. I'll just go on talking as though you were still there. Wouldn't you like to know what happened to me? It's really an extraordinary story. After all, I started out in medieval Russia and here I am in a submarine in the year 2083, still alive. How did I become immortal? Did Grigori bite me in the neck? Certainly not. He wasn't that kind of a monster.

No, it seems my serf was in reality a cyborg posing as human, just as I am now, and once he had been a mortal child, just as I was then. What were all these cyborgs doing, running around Mother Russia? You might well ask!

Stealing icons out of lovely old cathedrals that are going to be blown up by Bolsheviks, amongst other things, or making off with a czar's ransom in amber wall panels before the Nazis can take them. Snatching orphans out of snowbanks, or from under the very hooves of Tatars' horses, and whisking them away to hidden Company bases to be converted to cyborgs. It's a little painful, the immortality process, but I can't deny there are advantages. Super intelligence, phenomenal abilities, and of course immortality.

Personally I've always thought Grigori was a bit sloppy. I don't think I was quite fit to become an immortal; but I was made into one anyway, so there you are.

Nan loves me as I am, at least. I've never understood why . . .

I was programmed to be a Marine Operations Specialist, and, as soon as I was out of school, began my long and illustrious career of going down with ships. Yes! That's what I do, worm, I sink for a living. Ha ha. When history records that a ship will go down with a particularly valuable item on board, it's my job to be aboard somehow, as captain or able-bodied seaman, and arrange to get the desired loot well sealed in a protective casing before the fatal storm or reef or whatever Fate has in store.

And then down we go, the poor mortals and I, to the bottom. I never like that part. I'm so sorry, you know, so sorry for them and there's nothing I can do at all, I can't save them . . . And then, to blunder around in the dark like a bloated corpse in the hold, waiting with the loot until the recovery ships are dispatched from the Company, that's not the pleasantest job in the world either, but somehow that's what my career aptitude tests recommended.

But I can't complain, and do you know why? Why I'm a lucky man, worm? I'll tell you: I found love.

Is that rare for a cyborg? Very rare, I assure you. You understand of course we're not emotionless creatures at all, not machines, heavens no! But the danger in loving mortals is that one faces inevitable tragedy: they must age and die, however much one cares for them. Yet somehow we immortals never

seem to form more than the warmest of platonic friendships amongst ourselves . . . I thought, until I learned otherwise.

I met and fell in love with an Art Preservation Specialist. Met her quite by
accident, too, it wasn't the work brought us together at all. And oh, worm,
she's beautiful, she's kind, she's strong, much stronger character than mine.
Fearless. And, do you know, we actually got married, my little darling and I?
Sleek black lioness and clumsy polar bear, what a match.

We weren't supposed to wed, of course. The Company doesn't generally
approve of marriages amongst its operatives. And of course it can't be mar-
riage as mortals have it; we're parted for long periods of time. That's never
mattered, though. We always meet again. And what exquisite bliss, that re-
union, always . . .

I wonder how long it will be this time? . . .

But you want to hear an action story, don't you, big red worm? Yes, here
you come, pushing your sucker-mouth across my tiny window, wiping clear
an inch-wide view of hell itself, the dark-glowing fumarole. Thanks so awfully much. I'm afraid I don't see much in the way of heroic action because
I'm not much of a hero, am I? But I tried to be. Failed miserably, too. Here's
what happened:

They call it the Sattes virus, after the prison where it first broke out.
Some form of hemorrhagic fever, symptoms vomiting and voiding of blood,
attacking the intestines and spleen, killing the host within hours. It killed
every single inmate and guard at Sattes Men's Colony in Montana, United
States of America. Then it spread to the families of the guards. Then it
stopped.

Before anyone could draw breath in relief, it had broken out in two other
prisons, one in Utah and one in California. It followed the same pattern there,
exactly. Within twenty-four hours it had broken out in prisons in Arizona,
New Mexico, British Columbia. Within a week it was in prisons all over the
world. How is it transmitted? Plenty of theories, but no real evidence. This
was just a month ago, worm.

And do you know what the mortals did? They smirked. Just imagine, the
criminal element wiped out in a week! Why, it was like a judgment of God.
Never mind that men and women serving a week's time for traffic violations
died, too, and there were a great many more of those than serial killers sitting
in cells. It *must* be a judgment of God.

But even as it ran its course in the prisons, it started in the armed forces of the world. Broke out at military bases, on battleships, in civil defense training camps. That wiped the smiles off their faces. Millions of young men and women dying the world over. Perhaps it isn't a judgment of God after all? The death toll is amazing, surpassed the Black Death in its first week. It kills so quickly, you see! And nobody knows what to do.

Though certain things are obvious. Groups of people living crowded together catch it, men catch it more easily than women. Age is no barrier, neither is race or location. There are theories: testosterone somehow linked? Schools have been closed, public assemblies forbidden, all the usual stuff governments do during a plague, depressingly familiar to us immortals but quite shocking to the poor little mortals who had somehow assumed that living in the twenty-first century exempted them from disasters of this kind. There has even been a resurgence of millennial paranoia: perhaps the count was off by eighty-three years, somehow?

And of course everyone working for the Company knows that's not the case at all. We all know Sattes won't bring on the end of the world, that it will disappear as quickly as it began, that no cure nor any cause will ever be found. Business as usual will continue for the human race. Well, not quite as usual . . . the human gene pool will be gravely diminished.

Now, when all this started, where was I? In the navy, of course. Posted to the Gorbachev Science Base on Avacha Bay. Heroic Lieutenant Kalugin waiting like an actor to play his part, with a worse than usual case of performance nerves.

You see, worm, here's what history says happened: that even with its armies and navies devastated, even as the whole world waited terrified and scarcely able to hope the dread epidemic had run its course, Russia bravely went ahead with its test voyage of a revolutionary new miniature submersible, the prototype *Alyosha*, powered by an experimental fusion drive. Future histories—when they mention it at all, tiny footnote to history as it is—will characterize this as a supremely gallant gesture of hope for the future in a very uncertain time.

A doomed gesture, too; for the *Alyosha* has been lost and will never be recovered, taking that experimental fusion drive with her (we could only afford to build one, you see; in fact we could only afford to build a little one, which is why it went in a submersible) and by the way her one-man-crew was lost as well, fearless Lieutenant Kalugin. Perhaps I'll get a statue, worm, every bit as grand as Peter the Great's, me in bronze towering among the kiosks that sell vodka and shoe polish in Petropavlovsk-Kamchatsky. Ah, but I won't be lost, really. I won't, worm, and you know why? Listen closely.

Almost the first thing the Company discovered, when it went into this time travel business so many ages ago, was that *history cannot be changed*. Recorded history anyway. But if you work within the parameters of recorded history, you actually have quite a bit of leeway, because recorded history is frequently wrong, and there are always event shadows—places and times for which there *is* no recorded history. See how it works?

So the Company decided that what would appear to be a tragedy could in fact be subtly erased. We could conform to the historical facts: I would volunteer for the mission, take out the *Alyosha* on its test run into the Aleutian Basin, transmit a distress signal and maintain silence thereafter, presumably lost in the abyssal darkness beyond recovery, for the navy will never find even a trace of the *Alyosha* . . . because I'll have taken the *Alyosha* straight to a Company recovery ship waiting off Karaginskiy Island.

No death after all for valiant Lieutenant Kalugin, and the fusion technology won't be lost, but co-opted by Dr. Zeus Incorporated, which will be regrettably unable to give it back to its inventors because history cannot be changed. Still, humanity will benefit in the long run. We—

Mother of God and all the holy angels, what was that?

It can't have been a probe camera from the *Soter*. They can't have noticed yet I'm in trouble, and even if they had they couldn't get here so quickly! Could they? I don't think so, but then I'm in an event shadow, aren't I, worm?

It can't be pressure on the hull. It can't. This hull is made out of a new super-composite. We tested it. It ought to withstand much worse than this. I'm only a thousand meters down. Or, or, well, maybe it will give just a little and then no more? Flexing, not breaking? It won't collapse. Not with me in it. That won't happen, worm. Really.

I know what it was! The black smoker must have thrown out a chunk of rock or something. Yes, of course, just a bit of larger-than-ordinary debris raining down on the hull. The rest of it is falling so softly, so silently, it might have been only a little pebble, and perhaps only sounded loud by contrast. Yes. We're all right, worm. No cause for concern.

Let's get back to our story, shall we?

The reason I'm sitting here, talking so desperately to you, worm, is, as you must have guessed, that *something went wrong*. All began according to plan, I bubbled away through the deep, reached the *Alyosha*'s last known position, transmitted my last tragic message and then took off for Karaginskiy Island.

But three hours out, I lost forward propulsion. I began to drop. Tried to jettison ballast: no use. And down I went, down through water that grew ever darker but not colder, into this previously undiscovered field of volcanic chimneys smoking out mineral-rich filth. Bump, down I came.

I've tried everything. It's not the fusion drive. That's still working beautifully, if pointlessly, not actually driving me anywhere. No, it seems to be a series of little malfunctions that have all compounded to make one very big malfunction, and as near as I can tell it's because a two-ruble bolt cracked and gave a valve more play than it should have had, so that it stuck in an open position . . . so much loving care was lavished on the wonderful new fusion drive that the rest of the *Alyosha*'s construction was just a bit shoddy, or so it seems.

Ironic, isn't it? Especially as I might have detected the problem if I'd done a routine scan before climbing in. I didn't, though. I was tired this morning. Sleepy. Hung over. See why mortals really needn't fear being conquered by a super-race of cyborgs? We can be just as stupid as they are.

Though you'd have been hung over, too, red worm, if you'd been drinking what I'd been drinking for three days. A cocktail of my own devising: I call it a Moscow Bobsled. Chocolate milk and vodka. Goes down fast and then you crash! Yes, I know, it sounds horrible, but the Theobromine in the chocolate interacts wonderfully with the vodka. What was my excuse for getting into such a state? Well, you'd have been drinking, too.

You see, my friends had died. You wouldn't know about that, of course. Red worms don't have friends, I suppose. Cyborgs really shouldn't, either.

When the plague spread to Russia, it came from the west. Hit St. Petersburg first. All those training ships, all those mortal boys and girls . . . Well, panicking, and drawing the obvious conclusion that it wasn't safe to crowd its armed forces together, the government hit on a desperate plan to salvage its remaining navy.

The orders went out to Okhotsk, to Magadan, to Petropavlovsk-Kamchatsky, to the island bases: empty the ships! Empty the barracks! Disperse and quarter the enlisted forces amongst the civilian population, or in remote areas spread out, and perhaps by the time the Sattes virus had worked its way across Siberia it wouldn't be able to find new victims.

You can imagine the alacrity with which this order was obeyed, worm. The old ships emptied and sat silent at anchor, and truckloads of sailors were taken up into the mountains. Some of them went to old mining camps, old logging camps, hunting lodges; all kinds of places were pressed into service as emergency quarters. Some just took off into the woods with camping gear, happy to get a vacation and save their lives into the bargain, promising to stay in contact electronically. The officers were quartered at hot spring resorts all through Paratunka. Holidays for everybody! If only the Grim Reaper hadn't been expected to show up as well. Moving into his little dacha amongst the stone birches, checking his black robe and scythe at the changing-room door and slipping into the hot pool . . .

The mortals didn't know what else to do. I didn't either, really; here we were two weeks from the date of my historic mission and everything was falling to pieces. I knew that most of the people at Gorbachev would survive the plague, because history recorded their names, and of course there was no danger to me. But what do you do socially when the Dies Irae is playing everywhere? How do you pass the time? Watch news on the Wire? Far too depressing. Go out for a drink at a cozy club? Not in a naval uniform, which in this dark hour marks you for one of the damned. Sit in your flat and play solitaire?

I did that, actually, until I got a call from the mortal Litvinov. He and I'd served together on the *Timoshenko,* before I'd been transferred; and guess where he was now! Ten kilometers out of Paratunka, sprawling at his ease in the private tub that came with his dacha. True, the dacha was a little ruinous, because the resort had been closed for years; but the hot water just kept bubbling, that was the great thing about these places, and Larisa was there, and Antyuhin was there, and there was plenty to drink, and wouldn't I like to come up for a visit?

I probably shouldn't have gone, worm. But my coworkers at Gorbachev were glad enough to see the back of me for a few days—they were all civilians, after all, and seemed to think that would protect them—so I spruced up and caught the tram out to Paratunka, and walked from there. I'd had some idea of renting a bicycle, but the road was impossible, steep switchbacks rutted and boulder-strewn, straight back into the mountains.

But at last, as the first cold stars were peeping through the trees, I heard the whine of a generator and saw yellow lights; and a minute or so later I was walking in under a leaning arch that had once proclaimed the name of this little resort. I couldn't tell what it had been, because a new sign had been made from a piece of cardboard and tacked up across the arch. It read:

SATTES SPA—YOUR HOST, BOCCACCIO

I walked in and stood in the central clearing, looking around uncertainly. There were perhaps a dozen little tumbledown dachas visible, all at the edges of the forest. Half a dozen had lights behind the windows, and in some cases light streamed up into the trees through holes in the sagging roofs. There was a strong smell of dry rot and mildew, and all the damage that a mountain winter can inflict on a place like that, to say nothing of a vague sulphurous aroma. Still, the wind from the stars was cold and fresh. I could hear mortal voices in conversation, and music, and laughter. A fire had been lit in half an oil drum before one of the dachas: someone was grilling slabs of some sort of meat product.

As I watched, the door opened and a mortal man appeared, silhouetted black against the yellow light. Warm air steamed out around him. He wore only fatigue trousers, slippers, and a bathrobe, and he carried a drink. As he stepped out he was directing a remark over his shoulder to someone within the dacha: "But that's exactly my point. How do we know museums aren't full of evidence that's been mislabeled—"

He noticed me and started.

"Hell! Christ Almighty, Kalugin, I thought you were a bear after our Spam."

"Is that what it is?" I came close to the fire and peered in at the coals. Grilled Spam, all right. "Hello, Rostya Anfimovich."

"Good to see you!" Litvinov jumped down the steps and embraced me. "Did you walk all the way from the tram stop? Everyone, Vasilii Vasilievich got here!"

There was a chorus of happy shouts from the interior of the dacha, and in a matter of minutes I was soaking in the bath, mug of vodka in one hand and sandwich—grilled Spam between two Finnish crackers—in the other.

"Pretty nice, huh?" said Antyuhin gleefully. "And it's all ours! All we had to do was clean the dead leaves out. And, well, a couple of other things. We won't tell you about them."

"Thank you," I said, looking around. I wouldn't have been surprised to learn they'd had to clean a mastodon skeleton out of there. The little house was a wreck, and can't have been made of more than plywood and screens anyway. You could see stars through the roof, and birds had nested in the corners. The floor was spongy and gave alarmingly under Litvinov as he stripped down prior to rejoining us in the tub.

"And it's the junior officer's mess of the *Timoshenko* together again!" said Larisa Katerinovna, raising her tin cup. "For however long we have."

"No," Antyuhin pointed a finger at her admonishingly. "No references to you-know. Back to our symposium. We've got a Frivolity Symposium going, Kalugin, see? We're diverting ourselves with discussion on matters of no social or philosophical significance whatsoever."

"Current topic under discussion is whether or not Almas really exist," said Litvinov, splashing in beside me.

"The Mongolian bigfoot?" I stared.

"I don't see how you can deny it, with the Podgorni footage," challenged Verochka Sofianovna.

"The point, you see, Kalugin, is: if any supernatural creature who shall remain nameless comes to judge whether or not we're ready to be taken to the next world, he'll think we're a pack of hopeless twits and leave in disgust," said Antyuhin.

"And for that matter I don't think the possible existence of an unclassified hominid is a frivolous subject," Verochka said.

"What if they've been sighted in UFOs?" said Larisa.

"Good . . ." Antyuhin nodded, frowning thoughtfully.

"Pilots or abductees, though?" said Litvinov. "That would make a difference, don't you think?"

"Only in degrees of absurdity," said Verochka.

I had another bite of my sandwich and listened, so happy. I love mortals. I love their bravery and their craziness, their ability to tell jokes under fire. I suppose it's something they have to develop, since they know their deaths are inevitable; but it's magnificent all the same, don't you think, worm?

We sat there talking for hours, every now and then getting up to run out, all steaming and pink, to the cold pool, where we'd plunge into black water to keep ourselves from heart failure, or at least that was the idea. It was full of floating leaves but Litvinov assured me it was clean water, in fact he promised to show me just how pure it was later. When we were sufficiently revived we'd race back to the dacha for more vodka and more tales of the paranormal. We covered ghosts, UFOs, persons with the ability to teleport, talking animals, visions of the Mother of God, and anything else we could think of in our attempt to repel the angel of death.

Now and again other crew members in varying states of hilarious undress would stop in for a visit, making the rounds from their dachas across the clearing, usually bringing another bottle. Only once was there sadness, when the engineer Serebryannikov insisted on singing "The Last Night of the World"; other than that the stars shown down undimmed. It was long after midnight when we began to climb out and towel our wrinkled selves, and then to crawl into sleeping bags.

There was a slight social awkwardness then, because everyone was pairing off. Another gesture of defiance at death, I suppose, or perhaps just mutual comforting. I, by myself, was looking for a clean place to unroll my sleeping bag when Larisa approached me shyly.

"Vasilii Vasilievich, you came alone . . . if you'd like—?" She made an including gesture at herself and Antyuhin. He looked across at me, waiting to see what I'd say as he unrolled their bedding.

"You're very kind," I said, bending to kiss her between the eyes. "But I'm a married man, remember?"

"Oh! That's right. Well, anyway—" She kissed me back, quickly, and hurried off to help Antyuhin. "Dream about your wife, then."

And I did, worm. I did.

Next day we went climbing, Litvinov and I, and he directed my attention to the considerable beauty of the place with proprietary pleasure. Such trees! Such mountains! Such a beautiful land of fire and ice in high summer, worm. Such a wide sky. I wonder when I'll see the sky again? No point dwelling on that. No, I'll tell you how Litvinov and I climbed the trail above the ruined resort and came out above the most perfect little lake, green as malachite. It was artificial, quite round within its stone coping, and fed by a wide pipe that emerged from the hillside above. Clear as glass, that water cascaded out.

"Here," said Litvinov, "this is what I was telling you about last night. This is the reservoir they built to supply the dachas and the cold pool. See the snow on those mountains? This is snow-melt, can you imagine? Absolutely pure. It tastes wonderful."

"This is the stuff that feeds into the taps?" I bent and scooped a little into my palm, doing a content analysis. He was right: quite pure melted snow and nothing else.

"Yes. Dozhdalev and I traced the pipes." Litvinov crouched down and cupped his hands to drink. "Aah! Good stuff. You know what I'd like to do, after all this is over? I'd like to come back here. Maybe trace title and see if the owners would like to sell. Of course, I haven't got any money . . . but, I'll tell you what I could do! I could offer to be caretaker for them, free of charge. And I'd quietly fix up the best of the dachas to withstand the winter. Scrounge lumber from somewhere or even learn carpentry and plane logs I cut myself, eh? And live by foraging and hunting, and selling pelts for ammo and propane. Wouldn't that be a great life?"

"You'd have everything you needed," I said in admiration.

"I would, wouldn't I? If Verochka wanted to live here too I'd really have it all." Litvinov looked out over his prospective homestead dreamily. "I'm a city boy, but I could live like this in a minute. If only the world wasn't being turned upside down . . ."

"Well, you never know," I said. Even I didn't know, then. We immortals are told in a general way what the future holds, but the Company very rarely gives us specifics, you see, worm? For all I knew at that moment Litvinov might well survive to be living on salmon and bear meat in five years' time, a real pioneer of the post-atomic age.

For all I know . . . oh, worm, it's all very well to be hopeful, but we immortals fall so easily into the habit of lying to ourselves. It's hard to resist. You tell yourself that the years aren't bearable otherwise and then the lies become a habit, more and more necessary, and eventually there comes a point where you run on the truth like a rock at low tide and it splits you wide open. Shipwrecked. Good-bye.

We walked back down the trail and, to our surprise, encountered a hiker coming up, a pleasant-looking little woman in bright outdoor gear. She smiled and nodded at us as we passed her, and I started involuntarily: she was an immortal, too! She winked at me and kept going, striding along uphill on tireless legs. I couldn't very well turn to stare after her, with Litvinov there; and after all it's not so unusual to meet another operative now and then.

I thought she might have even been on a vacation. The Company has promised they'll begin granting us such perquisites, you see, as we get further into the future and more and more of our work for them is accomplished. It's been intimated that one day we'll even have lives of our own. Wouldn't that be charming, worm? Nan and I never parted any more, far from this sea that divides us . . .

I left next day, after hugs and kisses all around from my shipmates. I would have preferred to stay, but I had that crawling sensation we operatives get when we're off the job for too long; all those programmed urges to get back to work, I suppose.

So I walked back down to Paratunka and waited for the tram, and as I waited, who should come to wait too but the little immortal woman in her bright orange jacket. She smiled and nodded at me again. I looked around to be certain there were no mortals in earshot and said to her, in Cinema Standard: "I, er, noticed you up at the old resort."

Well, so I'm not a brilliant conversationalist, worm. But neither was she. She just smiled her unfading smile and said: "Yes. I was doing my work. It's very important, you know."

"You're a Botanist?" I said.

"Oh, no," she said. "Nothing like that. I have to be sure all the mortals are all right, you know."

Well, now I really had a crawling sensation, worm, because that was rather a strange answer to have given.

"Ah," I said carefully, "you mean you're an Anthropologist?"

Her smile never dimmed. "Uh uh," she said. "I just take care of the mortals."

I suppose at a moment like this mortals feel their hearts pounding, find their breath constricted, feel icy chills. Heaven knows I did! All I could think was, *Not again.*

But, oh, yes, again. What had happened, you see, was that I had stumbled on another Defective.

What's a Defective, worm? Well, officially they don't exist, of course; but the truth is, when the Company was learning how to transform human be-ings into immortal creatures with prodigious strength and intelligence, it didn't learn how to do it all at once. No indeed. It took a few tries to get the immortality process right. Unfortunately, the immortality part was the first thing that worked, so the first few deeply flawed individuals produced were permanent problems. What do you do with an idiot who's been given eternal life? Or a psychopath?

Dirty little secret, eh? I'd only learned about their existence because I'd had an unlucky encounter with one back in 1831, a pleasant-seeming fellow the Company was using as a courier. He was just intelligent enough to deliver packages, and, as long as he was kept continually on the move doing that, his other personality problems weren't apparent. But, surprise! On a routine mis-sion to bring me some botanical access codes I'd requested, his clerk had ne-glected to program his next posting. I was treated to a harrowing two days with a very unpleasant fellow indeed.

So I knew all too well what a Defective looked like, sounded like, worm; and here was one seated next to me, on the tram bench in Paratunka.

Oh! Oh, holy saints. That was another rock, wasn't it? You can see out there, worm, tell me it was another rock, just a little harmless one plunking down on the *Alyosha*'s hull. Yes, thank you, you've taken a lot off my mind. You're doing a splendid job clearing the porthole, too, by the way. I can see so much farther now.

Where was I? This Defective I had met. She looked like some sweet little babushka with a preternaturally young face, gave an impression of being slightly hunchbacked, though I think this was because of the way she carried herself, bent slightly at the waist and rocking to and fro. Her smile was com-placent, all-wise, all-knowing, tolerant. You might think, looking at her, that she had achieved great wisdom. I need hardly add, worm, that we correctly functioning immortals never smile in that way. We're too exhausted.

At least I am. Frightened, too. My instinct was to grab my luggage and run all the way back to Petropavlovsk-Kamchatsky, and the tram could follow any time it liked. But I smiled back, to avoid offending the creature, and I said: "You take care of them? That's very kind of you."

"Yes," she said, nodding again. "You know what happens if they don't get their vitamins, after all."

"That's bad, is it?"

"Oh, terrible!" Her face wrinkled up comically. "There'll be too many of them and they'll starve! Poor little things."

"We certainly don't want that to happen, do we?" I said.

"No," she said, and then her face changed. I tensed and clutched my bags, ready to bolt; but she lifted her head with a regal expression and regarded me coolly. And I tell you, worm, she was somebody else entirely then.

"I don't believe we've been introduced," she said.

"M-marine Operations Specialist Vasilii Vasilievich Kalugin, at your service," I said, trying to get the words out without my teeth chattering.

"What an awful lot of names you have," she said. "I'm Nicoletta."

Just Nicoletta.

"Pretty name," I said, like an idiot. "You weren't Russian, then?"

"No," she said. "There weren't countries when I was made. I'm very old, you know. I've traveled a long, long way. Traveling all the time. Oh, look; here comes a tram."

Yes, thank God and all His angels, it was the tram at last, and we boarded, and I ran to the back in childish terror that she'd follow me. She didn't. She rode only a short way and got out at the next stop, another little resort town. As the tram rolled away, though, she looked up and caught my eye. She smiled for me again, that serene and knowing smile.

I congratulated myself all the way home that I'd escaped another nightmarish confrontation with a Defective. I went up to my flat, put away my things, took out a frozen *kulebyaka* and heated it through, and relaxed in front of the Wire screen to catch up on the news.

It wasn't good news by any means, worm.

The plague had jumped clear across Siberia in the time I'd been gone, and had already broken out in Okhotsk. No sign of it in Vladivostok or Japan yet, but that was anticipated. Depressing. I mailed the personnel coordinator at Gorbachev to let her know I was home again, I fixed a drink, and put on a disc to watch Pitoev's remake of *The Loves of Surya*.

I woke late, roused by the commotion at my door. Nobody was knocking on it or anything like that; it was being sealed. I could hear the hiss of the extrusion foam being jetted into place.

"Er—excuse me!" I came staggering out in my pajamas and gaped at the blank door lined in pink foam. A note had been pushed through at the bottom. I picked it up off the mat and read a hastily printed note informing me that I was under quarantine by order of the City Council.

"Miron Demyanovich," I shouted, hoping the superintendent was still within earshot. "Why am I being quarantined?"

There was silence for a moment and then he shouted: "You just came back from Paratunka!"

"Yes, well?"

"The news just came through! It's started there!"

"Oh," I said. Well, I had known it would happen, hadn't I? History records that the Sattes virus wiped out the armed forces of the world.

"I'm sorry, Lieutenant Kalugin! God have mercy on you!"

"That's all right," I said numbly, and went in to fix myself breakfast. I think I must have sat there staring into my coffee for an hour, worm, before I got the courage to get up and check my mail.

Three messages, and they had all come in in the last half hour. One was an electronic version of the note that had been slipped under my door, simply the official notification that I was under quarantine until one week from the present date. If I were still alive and well at the end of that time, I was to notify the proper department and they would process my petition for release.

The second note was from Gorbachev Science Center acknowledging my return and telling me that the *Alyosha*'s test launch was being postponed four days due to the outbreak, and requesting that I please inform them immediately in the event of any problems I might have with this schedule. Ha ha! I composed a brief reply informing them of my present scheduling conflict and assuring them that if I were still alive in a week's time I would report for duty at the appointed hour.

The third note was from Litvinov. It was very simple, worm, it told me what was happening. Serebryannikov and Verochka were gone already. Many of the others had begun to manifest symptoms and were expected to go soon. Litvinov was sorry and hoped I had better luck. If anyone survived he, or they, would write again in a couple of days.

But I never heard from any of them after that, worm, though I sent messages every day all that week.

Oh, worm, I'm afraid their Frivolity Symposium must have backfired;

Death must have come to inspect them, and decided he'd be unlikely to find a more gallant crew anywhere, and conscripted them immediately to join the hosts of Heaven. Don't you think?

But so much for Litvinov's dream of homesteading that tumbledown resort, so much for dear Larisa with her bright smile, so much for crazy Antyuhin.

I cried, like the miserable weak creature I am, cried for hours. Only with terrible effort did I refrain from mailing Nan. Why sadden her with my help-less misery? The less she knew about this posting of mine, the better. I watched through swollen eyelids as the Wire broadcasts got more grim. Paratunka was devastated. The rest of Kamchatka got off fairly easily, but then as expected the plague traveled down to Vladivostok and so through Japan. There was some desperate hope that Korea and China might escape, that it might move on south, but no; after it had finished with Japan it turned, as though purposefully, and started in on Korea.

As though purposefully.

I'm not sure now exactly when I began to form my theory, worm, but there was a point where I set aside my drink and made a conscious effort to sober myself up by the dull blue light of the Wire. When I had converted enough of the mess in my bloodstream into sugars and water, I looked at my idea again. Nicoletta?

What had she said? That she was looking after the mortals, giving them their vitamins so . . . so there wouldn't be too many of them? What could she have meant?

She had been hiking up toward the reservoir when I'd first seen her. She'd been working her way through the Paratunka Valley, giving the mortals their—vitamins.

What was she doing, worm?

She was a Defective! And it occurred to me then that Nicoletta might have got some horrible idea in her head that the Sattes virus was a good thing—after all, a lot of mortals had thought just the same, when it was only attacking prisons—and decided to help it on its way, lest the world overpopulation problem continue. How easily one person with immortal abilities might slip over borders and do such a thing, I knew all too well. Traveling all the time . . . and the pattern of deliberate infection would be detected even by the mortals. There would be countless theories afterward that the Sattes virus had been part of a plot to reduce the world population, by taking draconian measures.

Most historians would decide that the prime suspect was the extremist Church of God-A, who preached drastic population reduction, though nothing would ever be proven. But what if it was one Defective with a big idea in her faulty little head? Dear God, I thought, I've got to warn somebody! She's got to be stopped!

Ah, but, you see, worm, there was a slight problem here. Officially, there are no Defectives. The Company won't admit to them. When that business with Courier had to be cleaned up, the Company sent in a covert operations squad; and I was informed, as clearly as they could tell me in oblique phrases, that nothing had really happened, and I was never to tell anyone that anything had. The Company has never made any Defective operatives. So whom might I contact with my warning?

Obviously the only safe thing to do would be to contact Labienus, the Northwest American Section Head at Mackenzie Base. He, after all, was the very one who'd been sent to deal with Courier's little accident, he was the one who'd delivered that so delicately veiled threat to me as he'd departed. Surely if discretion were called for, I ought to contact Labienus and none other. Don't you think, worm?

So I sat down at my keyboard and, after agonizing deliberation, composed the following communication: "Dear Executive Facilitator General Labienus, you may recall me from the year 1831 at the Fort Ross Colony, when we had occasion to speak. I understand you are doubtless a very busy man, but I should like very much to discuss a matter of mutual interest at your convenience. Respectfully yours, Marine Operations Specialist Kalugin."

Beautifully circumspect and tactful, yes, worm? I thought so. And it must have worked, because within the hour my terminal beeped on a shrill frequency inaudible to mortals, had any been there with me, announcing that a message was coming in on a secured channel.

I interfaced hurriedly with the terminal. *Kalugin receiving,* I transmitted. And there came his signal, quite clear and even slightly cordial in tone:

Marine Operations Specialist Kalugin? Labienus here. What is this matter you wish to discuss?

So I explained, worm, as quickly as I could. I told him all about Nicoletta and my suspicions. He heard me out patiently and his signal, when he replied, was grave and thoughtful.

Yes, Kalugin, there's no question you did the right thing by contacting me pri-

vately. I appreciate your discretion. Very well; we'll have her picked up immediately for interrogation. You understand, of course, that you'll need to distance yourself from this unfortunate situation?

I answered that I understood perfectly. My only concern was whether or not it would impact on my mission. Labienus assured me there was no need to be concerned on that account and—

HEY! HEY, I'M HERE! THANK GOD, THANK GOD, THANK GOD! You see, worm? I told you! Well, you've been wonderful company and I truly appreciate all your efforts on my behalf, but I'm afraid I won't be able to finish my fascinating story. I'll be on the *Soter* in an hour or two, or possibly three, I've rather lost track of the time, and I think I'll take a hot shower first—silly, isn't it? With all the hot water I've been in lately, you'd think I'd have had enough to last me for a while, but actually sitting here under this black smoker has given me the most awful creeps, watching the sooty stuff rain down endlessly, I feel as though it's all over me somehow and not just the hull of the *Alyosha*.

I'll request a weekend leave after this, I've got one due me, I'm quite certain, and I'll go to Nan. Perhaps we'll go somewhere together. Marseilles, perhaps, or Casablanca! Somewhere full of sunlight. I want sunlight, I want it by the bucketful, I want to walk in the warmth and the clean dry air and lie down in the yellow sand with her. She'll make the nightmares go away. She can always make them go away. I'm never frightened when I'm with her, worm, I—

What are they doing back there?

What—?

They're removing the fusion drive. They're cutting it out with welding torches. They're not answering my transmissions, worm.

Well, don't be silly, of course they've got to be Company operatives! Mortal divers couldn't work at this depth. It's a pair of security techs in pressure suits, I'm certain. And they're taciturn fellows, everyone knows that, so perhaps they're just too busy to respond.

Oh . . .

And now they've gone.

They've left me here.

Why would they do that, worm?

Well, it seems I'm to impose on your hospitality a bit longer, worm. I'm really terribly sorry; I can't think what's happened. Unless the *Alyosha* with its fusion drive was too heavy for the winch on the *Soter*, and it was decided to bring it up in two dives? Yes, undoubtedly. And I'm sure the reason they weren't hearing my transmissions was the mess that's all over the hull from the black smoker, it must be full of metals in solution and that's somehow blocking my signal. So. I suppose while I'm waiting for them to come back I'll finish my story, shall I?

Labienus told me to go ahead with my mission, you'll remember. And that's exactly what I did: waited in my sealed room a whole week, while the Sattes virus spread into China and Indochina. I stopped tracking its progress after the first few days. Too depressing. History records that the plague hit China and India particularly hard. I didn't need to see the Wire footage to know what was happening. No, I lived off my cupboard shelf and out of my freezer, I watched film after film after film, I drank like a fish and occasionally sobered myself up long enough to send hopeful little communications to my colleagues at Gorbachev, letting them know I was still alive.

They let me know they were still alive, too. The decision had been made to go ahead with the launch, as I had known perfectly well it would be. The director intervened on my behalf with the City Council and the result was, I was spared a lot of bureaucratic delay. At the end of that week Miron Demyanovich was duly authorized to break the seal on my room. I was sitting there, shaved and combed and in uniform, when I heard the seal being cracked away and then the timid knock; and I opened the door to behold Miron Demyanovich with a biohazard mask over his pinched face, and two frightened-looking council members behind him.

I was manifestly alive and well, so they let me go. I reported to Gorbachev Science Center and underwent a series of tests, from which it was deduced that, yes, I was still alive and well, or at least alive and hung over. Then they stuffed me into the *Alyosha* rather hurriedly, and I kept my appointment with history.

And this is where you came in, worm.

Well, that was tidy, I must say. The oxygen is almost gone. How nice that you got to hear the whole story.

If it is the whole story.

I can't help feeling a certain nagging discomfort, worm, about one thing.

If I was right about Nicoletta—and Labienus seemed to think I was—where did she get the Sattes virus culture to put in unsuspecting people's water supplies? How did a poor simpleminded Defective manage the steamroller logistics of that sweeping outbreak?

So many people died, worm, were killed *discriminately*. It's going to drastically affect the course of history. There won't be any full-scale wars for decades (except in Northern Ireland, of course) and it will be a century before the crime rate even approaches its previous figures.

It'll be a much more peaceful, law-abiding, uncrowded world after this, worm. That's going to be good, yes? The poor stupid mortals will think so at first. But, you see, their gene pool will have shrunk so drastically. All those young men, young women gone. Most of a generation. Never so many of them after this. Less and less every year. And then, the next time a plague hits . . .

Won't affect us, of course. We're immortal. We'll go right on working for the Company. Company will still be around. Plenty of us immortals still around.

Company wouldn't do a thing like this, worm. I'm positive. We're ethical creatures, for heaven's sake! Programmed to look after them. Take care of the poor mortals.

Though some of us have a rather low opinion of them. It's a job hazard, worm. Despair.

I don't feel like that, of course. It's not their fault. Capable of such wonderful things, too. But I know some immortals who think . . .

Oh, God and Saint Mikhail, what if one of *us* . . . what if Labienus . . .

Hello, Dunya. Hello, Sima. You want me to come out there to you? Isn't this enough for you, that I'm down here under the water with you at last? And I'm with you to stay, I think. I don't believe I'm ever coming up again, not now. I stumbled on something I shouldn't have seen.

But I won't go out to you. The black smoker's so dirty. Dark and wet and dirty. It's burying me under dirty little secrets and soon not even you will be able to get to me, with your reproachful faces, not even my friend the worm will be able to help me.

Oh, but that makes you angry, how Papa's eyes flash, and he's lifting his giant hand and it's coming down now with the bloodstone ring on his knuckle and it will do more than black my eye this time, I'm sure . . . but it's not the bloodstone after all, it's become an aquamarine. How strange, and what a beautiful color the stone is!

I can't take my eyes off its pure light and in fact I'm floating up toward it now, I've been accidentally netted. They're dragging me through the shallows, because the wreck wasn't deep. Now I've left the rotting hulk down there below me but I shouldn't be here, should I? Here where I first met my beloved? What's gone wrong with time?

Yet I bob up into the bright air. I behold a lovely picture, the water and the sky so blue and the lateen sails like old parchment, and golden cliffs in the distance, and very surprised black faces regarding me from the deck of the fishing boat.

I struggle free of the net but it's a mistake, because the water's claiming me again, I'm plummeting back down into depths of sea the color of Spanish glass. No! I'll swim, I'll make my way to the shore because I know she's coming to meet me, she's heard my distress signal. I must meet her, up there in the sunlight.

I blunder up out of the surf, soaked and sick and exhausted, but it's all right because I see her now. Nan! On a long curve of golden sand, under swaying palms, seated in majesty on the tallest camel I've ever seen, the tiny goddess carved of blackest jet. My Queen of the Night with her eyes like desert stars, veiled in a blue that puts the sky to shame. She extends her little hand to me. I reach, and reach, but I can't seem to pull free of the water, my legs are like lead, and in my ears ever louder is the roar of breakers on the Moroccan coast.

FOUR
2225

FATHER OF PESTILENCE

The office has changed.

The credenza on the desk has a sleek post-postmodern look. The furniture matches it in style, everything ergonomically correct, in the bright primary colors of the first half of the twenty-third century. Labienus likes to move with the times. As far as it is possible to dress elegantly in that particular era, he is elegantly dressed.

He is frowning as he gazes out the window at his wilderness.

It has not quite the pristine splendor that it had. There is not that lucent quality to the air that there was; particulate matter from air pollution has found its way farther north than even the Yukon. There are a great many more skeletal silver trees in his line of sight than there used to be, and many trees nominally alive but tipped with brown needles. Contrails stripe the sky. Satellites cross it at night. No more than a century ago, he had looked up from his work one morning just as a grinning snowboarder waved at him from the other side of his window. A small and well-aimed missile disposed of the mortal; but, really, the annoyance!

It is not this that causes Labienus to frown, however.

The air pollution has been worse than at present, and is diminishing yearly. Likewise the aircraft; and as for the mortals, their birth rate has been steadily dropping for a century now. This is particularly unfortunate (for them) in light of the pandemics that have been sweeping the world population with increasing frequency since the beginning of the twentieth century. Influenza, AIDS, Ebola 3, the Sattes virus . . .

Labienus is pondering the Sattes experiment.

"No good deed goes unpunished," he murmurs to himself. Kalugin had been handily disposed of, but the Sattes virus had not been what he would call an unqualified triumph. So much for a gesture of filial piety! They'd tried Budu's preferred method of a quick directed kill at last, and what had happened? They'd drawn attention to the operation. Much too obvious.

True, the body count had been impressive. All the same, conspiracy theorists everywhere had pointed fingers at the blatant pattern in the disease's progress, its unsubtle choice of victims. Thank the gods most of the suspicion had been shifted onto the Church of God-A, but the fact that even a lump like Kalugin had been able to figure out what was really going on was clear evidence that selective culls would never have worked as a long-term strategy.

What a pity Budu hadn't been there to witness it! Would he have been baffled? Angry? Apologetic?

It was fun to imagine, yet Labienus knew the truth: the old monster would have refused to change his methods. He simply hadn't a human mind. He'd have pushed straight on winnowing the unrighteous from the righteous by degrees of wickedness, playing Ten Little Indians on a global scale, and sooner than later it would have all come out. Not that Labienus feared anything the mortal masters could do in retaliation; but Aegeus and his people would have objected to the complete extinction of the mortals (too *useful!*), and they had real weapons in reserve.

So it was just as well Budu remained where Victor had left him, buried under tons of rubble in San Francisco. More than likely in two or three pieces, too. Labienus smiles.

That was pure Victor, that touch, sending in the tong members with hatchets. Spiteful, but coldly effective, too.

He wonders again why Victor has delayed stepping in and consoling Kalugin's wife, with whom he is so comically smitten. Another generous gesture on Labienus's part, getting the husband out of the way, and what good has it done?

But perhaps he's drawing out the luxury of conquest. Victor is methodical in his pleasures. Exquisite taste and iron resolve coupled with that venomous temperament . . . really a pity he wasn't brought all the way in sooner. Everything ripens in its own time, however.

Labienus turns his attention to a minor problem that has been niggling for his attention. His sources have been reporting excruciatingly detailed and fre-quent attempts, by a low-level Preserver drone, to access classified data.

The data concerns Project *Adonai.* The drone in question is, of all people, Literature Preservation Specialist Grade Three Lewis.

Labienus knits his brows. Project *Adonai* has been defunct for centuries, more's the pity. Nennius has promised to advise him if it is ever reactivated.

So what the deuce is a Literature Preservation drone doing, poking his silly nose into the matter of an obscure British spy who died in 1863? Not once has he attempted to find out anything about *Homo umbratilis,* as might be ex-pected from his unfortunate history. Why Bell-Fairfax, instead?

Standard procedure is to draw the operative in by dangling more informa-tion before him, luring him into a trap, and Labienus duly composes a memo giving the order to follow procedure. He fires it off to Nennius. As he waits for confirmation, the thought drifts into Labienus's mind: for a comparative nonentity, Lewis has been associated with far too many classified matters . . .

Is it possible that Nennius's favorite assassin can be employed, from be-yond the grave, to claim another victim?

Something about the idea warms Labienus's heart. He glances up at the locked cabinet where the red file still sits, though its contents have long since been transferred to disk. He has been reluctant to consign the hard copy to a fusion hopper; Nicholas's portrait is an original work of art, after all. And how could he part with those meticulous mission reports in Edward's elegant cop-perplate script, such a painstaking list of horrifying deeds committed with the noblest possible intentions? Labienus chuckles, imagining a tall spectral fig-ure rising from the dust, advancing implacably on Lewis . . .

"*Vae victis,*" he says cheerily. Sacrifices, always sacrifices to keep the world rolling in its profitable orbit . . .

A call comes in on the secured channel. Labienus lifts the amplifier—no more than a twist of silver wire now, like a piece of modern art—from its cra-dle, and slips it on.

Labienus, he transmits.

Nennius. Ave. Just got your memo about the Literature drone. How the bloody hell did you hear the news before I did?

Labienus is startled, but covers his wave of confusion.

I have my ways. Still, I'd like a fuller report from you.

Well, did you hear why *Lewis had to run?*

My sources were a bit sketchy on that, Labienus admits blandly, wondering what has happened. *Details, please.*

Apparently some nests of Homo sapiens umbratilis *evaded us. They've been out there all this while, hiding. They found Lewis again!*

I knew that, Labienus prevaricates. *But—*

You'll never believe this. The damned kobolds have been hunting for him since he ran into them in Ireland.

But it's been nearly two millennia! Labienus remembers the illuminated pages, the uncials switching from Gaelic to Latin and back again. What had the *umbratilis* Prince threatened? That if it took them years, they'd still get Lewis back?

They're incompetent but they have long memories, it seems. And they hold a grudge. Blew his cover and chased him from London to Dieppe, before he got away last night. Aegeus's people have had their hands full dealing with the mortal witnesses.

Labienus begins to grin incredulously. *The things want him that badly, do they? I wonder if they're more talented than our in-house idiots?*

There is a silence on the ether. He can almost feel the shock waves as his meaning gets across to Nennius. Then there is wild laughter.

Do you suppose they'd be willing to cut a deal?

What do you suppose they'd give us for him?

Beyond the glass of his window, something momentarily distracts Labienus. A lost hiker, emaciated, bearded, filthy, his parka in rags, has climbed to the window ledge and is staring inward in disbelief. He presses his palms to the glass, uncertain whether or not he is hallucinating but desperately sincere in his silent plea for help.

Labienus exhales in annoyance and reaches over to flip a switch. With the release of a powerful spring under the ledge, the mortal is launched, screaming, into midair. He tumbles end over end into the rocky chasm beyond, and drops from sight.

Focusing again, Labienus transmits: *I wonder if by any chance they could be persuaded to do us a favor in return?*

You never mean . . .

Wouldn't it be nice to have a permanent way to get rid of our rivals, when 2355 comes at last? We can smash the masters like insects, but Aegeus won't go down without a fight. To say nothing of mortal-loving idiots like Suleyman.

You brilliant bastard.

Thank you.

If the little cretins haven't yet found a silver bullet, perhaps they can experiment on Lewis to make one.

We can suggest it.

And then it's only a matter of delivering the merchandise to them . . .

All the more reason to bait a trap for him. What did you think of my suggestion about luring him in with a false lead on Adonai?

Could be useful. Why on earth is the idiot snooping around a black project?

That's for you to find out.

Very well. You know, Adonai's *still running.*

Are you sure?

I still get the updates once a month, reminding me to search for a host mother. They don't seem to realize that a stunt like that's a good deal harder to pull off in this day and age than it was in 1825.

Or 1525. But a third boy . . . Think of the uses we could find for him, in these modern times! Perhaps something truly worthy of his talents.

I suppose I could arrange for some hapless girl to dream she's been abducted by aliens and implanted with a space hybrid . . .

They both roar with laughter, booming through the ether like static. Labienus dances without getting out of his chair, an elbows-out buck and wing.

Do let me know if anything is ever done. Vale.

Vale, Labienus.

Labienus puts down the amplifier and lounges back in his chair, still smiling broadly. His thoughts return to Victor . . .

MESSIS VERO CONSUMMATIO SAECULI EST

I first saw the boy through the wavering light of a flame; rather ironic, as things turned out.

It was in a pleasant suburban villa out beyond the Vondelpark. We'd had to leave the car a good distance off and walk, Labienus and I, because so many people had already arrived for the party. The night was clear for early December, with a black sky full of stars, and the red windows of the house looked warm and inviting. As we drew near we could smell the fragrances of a mid-winter celebration: evergreens, spices, mulled wine.

"How festive," remarked Labienus, smiling. "If only they knew, eh?"

I found his remark in the worst of taste under the circumstances, but I smiled back. Labienus is very much my superior in rank, however much I dislike him.

And he had told me, after all, to play this lightly, for my own emotional health; stress levels would be reduced if I resolutely put gory details out of my mind. I wasn't even being told everything about the job. Better that way.

The door was already open as we came to the bottom of the steps, for our hostess was welcoming in a young couple and their child. Anna Karremans was a plain smiling woman in her mid-forties. Her guests edged past her into the hall, and she stood gazing down at us expectantly as we started up the steps.

Yes, that was the first unnerving moment, for me: the mortal woman seemed to be standing in the open mouth of an oven, smiling as an inferno blazed behind her. But it was only the scarlet light of the holiday decorations, after all, and it was a gentle heat that flowed down on our cold faces.

"Michel Labeck," Anna exclaimed, recognizing Labienus. "Oh, we were beginning to be afraid you'd had an accident!"

"Not at all, Dr. Karremans," Labienus greeted her, and his smile widened as he stepped up to the door and took her hand. "I wouldn't let an accident derail a media event like this one! And the party does seem to be proceeding success-fully," he added, looking in through the hall at something I was unable to see.

"They're all here," she leaned forward to tell him in an undertone. "All the journalists. Everyone on the list you gave me. You're a miracle worker, Michel."

"Not at all," he told her, still smiling, and beckoned me forward. "But I've kept another promise: here's the assistant Doss and Waters has sent you. Nils Victor. Nils, this is Dr. Anna Karremans."

"Delighted, madam." I bowed slightly and attempted to smile.

"How nice to meet you," she exclaimed. "Oh, but you look so serious! Not to say half frozen. Please, come in, let me take your coats—"

So I entered the mortal woman's house, and stood in her bright hall look-ing in at the party.

Yes, there were plenty of journalists in evidence. I recognized several from the Amsterdam Wire and the global Wires, too. There were a number of kam-eramen, but they were all unplugged; so far as they knew, yet, there was noth-ing to See. No, they stood in small groups chatting, like the other mortals, helping themselves from the buffet or admiring the Yule tree, or gathering about the piano to argue over the lyrics to the new Yule songs. Ranks of real candles were burning on the buffet table, long red tapers in bright-painted wooden candlesticks, quite old-fashioned and charming in a rural sort of way. It might have been a room from the twentieth century, or the nineteenth.

And here were children running to and fro, in and out of the rooms, cir-cling the furniture and yelling happily. Really, one expected Herr Drossel-meyer to make a swooping entrance with a nutcracker. But there was no Clara for him to woo here. All these children seemed to be little boys, six of them, all between the ages of five and eight. Not much to tell them apart: tousled hair, cheeks pink with exertion, bulky-knitted sweaters with patterns of reindeer or fir trees or snowflakes. A fair-haired boy, an ash-blond boy, a boy with hair red as mine, two brunettes who seemed to be twins . . . well, he wouldn't be one of them. A boy with sable hair . . . ? Yes. I spotted him stand-ing still for a moment on the other side of the buffet table, beyond the bright candles, and his image shimmered through their flames.

I found I didn't care to look at his face.

I concentrated on the buffet instead. What a feast: smoked salmon, goose, turkey, baked goods in profusion, spiced apples, chocolates. Theobromos would help . . .

"Nils?"

I managed to avoid starting guiltily as I turned from sampling a truffle. Labienus saw, of course, and his eyes glinted as he touched the shoulder of a mortal man with a stupid gentle face.

"Nils, may I present Dr. Geert Karremans?"

"Sir!" I ate the last of the truffle hastily, smiled and reached to shake his hand. "It's an honor to meet you."

"Very, very kind of you," the man replied with enthusiasm. He, like Anna, was just entering middle age but dressed boyishly. *His* bulky-knit sweater was patterned with little figures of skiers. "So—what do you think? Will it go over well?"

"I can't imagine a more wholesome scene," I told him, fairly truthfully.

"It'll go over well," decided Labienus, surveying the room. "Look at everyone! Happy, well-fed, full of sentimental memories of childhood. This was exactly the approach to take."

"And all your idea, too," Geert congratulated him.

"Not mine alone, Dr. Karremans. This is why Doss and Waters has retained its premiere position in public relations counseling for more than fifty years," Labienus replied. "I think you'll find you made the right choice in retaining our services."

"Oh, I'm sure we did," agreed Geert, stepping aside whilst two of the boys thundered past the table, shrieking as they chased each other with toy dinosaurs. One jostled a corner in his passing, and a candlestick toppled over; I caught it rather more quickly than I ought to have, but Geert didn't notice. He was frowning after the boys.

"The children are getting restless. Do you suppose it's time to make the—?" He looked at Labienus with a combination of nerves and eagerness.

"Showtime," Labienus told him, smiling again. "Leave it to me."

He strode to the fireplace and stood with his back to the flames, calling for attention with his mere presence. He had dressed for the part, certainly: black trousers and a red shirt cut to give the impression of informal power. Labienus was an imposing-looking fellow in any case, tall, with elegant Roman features. As one after another of the guests stopped speaking and turned to stare at him, he put his hands up and said, in a pleasing voice that penetrated without effort to the far corners of the house: "Friends? Everybody! May I have your attention, please?"

He had it at once, naturally. Beside me a kameraman murmured appreciatively, "Check it out! He's not even miked."

"Thank you. Now, I'm going to tell you all a story, so I'd suggest you make yourselves comfortable. Yes, here—let's bring the children up to the front, this is their time of year, after all. Are you having a good time, boys? Wonderful. And the rest of you, you're all relaxed, you've all helped yourselves to the fine feast our hostess has set out? I haven't seen a holiday table like that since I was a child, have you? All settled now. Good!

"My name is Michel Labeck, of Doss and Waters Public Relations, and I've been retained by the Drs. Karremans for my professional expertise; but I'd like to add that I'm also a personal friend, as are most of you here." This wasn't quite true, as the party was fairly exclusively a press event, but he was unlikely to be contradicted.

"Now, you ladies and gentlemen of the press amongst us may have been suspecting that an announcement of some kind was going to be made—and, of course, you're correct. There will be an official press conference tomorrow, you see, but tonight we'll make the unofficial announcement to you favored ones we regard as personal friends. We wanted you to know first, to have a unique opportunity for an intimate look at what we're unveiling."

The little boys were bored by this, lined up as they were in a row at Labienus's feet. A velociraptor screamed silently and leapt at a stegosaur, which bashed it back.

"Oh-oh! Looks as though we've got a dinosaur conflict, ladies and gentlemen. I think I'd better cut to the chase, here. Are you ready for the story, boys?"

"Ye-es," chorused half a dozen little voices. There was of appreciative laughter from the adults.

"Good." Labienus looked out into the room, making eye contact, drawing them all in. "Once upon a time, children, there was a man and there was a woman. They loved each other very much, and they were very happy together. In another age, long ago, he might have been a toymaker, she might have been a milkmaid; but they happened to be born into an age of science, and so scientists they were. They were good people. The woman worked to keep the children of the world safe from diseases. The man worked to make certain the children of the world would never go hungry. They did this with their research into DNA."

Murmurs from the crowd as heads turned to Geert and Anna, smiling self-consciously by the buffet table with their arms about each other, flushed with the warmth of the candles.

Labienus cleared his throat. "Now, as I said, this couple were very happy together. There was only one sorrow in their lives: they had always longed to have a child of their own. But the years went by, and no little child came to them. Perhaps, they thought to themselves, it was for the best. After all, there were histories of certain kinds of illness in both their families, and maybe they oughtn't pass on their genetic inheritance. They tried to adopt, but so few babies were available in this country they'd have been awfully old by the time their names came to the top of the list to get one. It was very sad.

"And then, one day, the woman had a daring idea: they might combine their knowledge of DNA to make themselves a child."

A stunned silence in the room. The mortals looked at one another, wondering if Labienus was really going to say what they imagined he might say.

He nodded, acknowledging their excitement. "Yes! Now, this was a very unconventional idea, I need hardly tell you. After all, ignorant people find the thought of creating anything from recombinant DNA quite scary. They think of white-coated mad scientists from the movies creating terrible things, creating, oh, I don't know, tomatoes with claws and teeth. A ketchup monster! Or some strange hybrid like this—" He leaned down and took a toy dinosaur from one of the boys, and, grabbing an apple from the mantelpiece decorations, stuck it on the dinosaur's head and held it up for everyone to see. "Look! Applesauce monster."

The children squealed with laughter, and the adults laughed, too. Smiling, Labienus returned the dinosaur to its owner and continued: "Of course, that's not really what happens when you work with recombinant DNA at all, and scientists are not mad characters from the movies. But people in other countries made their governments forbid research into recombinant DNA, even though it might hold the key to eliminating disease and hunger throughout the whole world forever. It's sad when people are stupid.

"Ah, but this is Amsterdam! We have a tradition of tolerance and enlightenment going back to our very beginnings. We have never fallen into step with the bigots and the short-sighted. We have gone our own way, triumphantly and successfully, for centuries now. We have never passed laws to forbid the pursuit of human knowledge, and as a result our scientific and technological discoveries have brightened the world, and made it a better place for children everywhere to be born into. We're not afraid"—he pulled an absurd face—"of applesauce monster, eh?"

Laughter throughout the room, and a pleasant sense of smug superiority. Labienus regarded us all, smiling. He put his hands in his pockets and went on: "Now, our friends, the two scientists, knew perfectly well how to make a child from recombinant DNA. We've known how for decades. But, probably because of worries over applesauce monsters, nobody had ever made one. Well, the man and the lady sat down and came up with a simple design. All they wanted, after all, was an ordinary, healthy little child.

"And then the lady remembered her poor brother, who had been in the Civil Guard before his life was cut short by the Sattes virus." Labienus's face grew very somber, and there were sighs as people remembered the death toll from that terrible interlude, when the virus had spread through the armies of the world.

"And the man remembered his own childhood, how clumsy he'd been, how hopeless at sports, and how mercilessly other children had teased him for it.

"This was why they decided to improve their simple design. What if it were possible to make a child with an immune system engineered to resist viral infections? What if it were possible to make a child with a brain engineered to better process information, to send signals more quickly and clearly to the body? What would they have then? Why, they'd have an ordinary little child who could catch a ball with ease, and more: a child who would be able to survive any plagues that might evolve. You see?

"No superman. No atomic genius. No applesauce monster. Only a healthy, well-coordinated child you wouldn't notice if you passed in the street. This was all they wanted, ladies and gentlemen."

He paused to let them think about that.

"And the purpose of this party is to tell you, ladies and gentlemen, that—with the help of dear friends, doctors, and other scientists—a healthy, average child is exactly what they got."

Quite a reaction at that, all manner of mortal emotions in that crowded room, and a chorus of clicks and curses as all the kameramen realized they ought to have been recording this. Kameramen aren't ordinarily caught flat-footed, but they tend to pay more attention in moments of horror and tragedy than at pleasant parties. Now the kameramen belatedly plugged themselves in and Saw Labienus. He nodded just perceptibly, and for their benefit he re-iterated: "Yes. This man and this woman have produced the first human child using recombinant DNA, ladies and gentlemen. Will you be permitted to see the embryo? I'm afraid that's not possible, because, you see, this child was produced *six years ago.* He has already been with us for quite some time."

Now they really gasped, the mortals, and Geert and Anna clung together more tightly. Labienus took his hands out of his pockets and held them out to the children sitting at his feet.

"Now, boys, I'd like to ask you to stand up and turn around for the cam-eras. You're all going to be on the Wire!"

Shyly, awkwardly they clambered to their feet and turned, six little boys in bright sweaters, clutching their toy dinosaurs, blinking at the kameramen. Labienus's voice rose on a note of command.

"Look at them, ladies and gentlemen! Our own children. Could you possi-bly tell that one of them was made from recombinant DNA? You couldn't, could you? Which boy do you think it is?"

A few people (though not his parents) pointed uncertainly at the blue-eyed blond child. Labienus grinned.

"No indeed. No, as it happens"—he put his hand on the shoulder of the black-haired boy—"it's little Hendrick. The rest of you children may sit down now."

Little Hendrick's eyes widened. He turned and stared up at Labienus in horror, turned back and stared at the kameramen recording his image avidly. He started forward through the seated crowd, desperate to get to Anna and Geert.

"Wait!" called Labienus, laughing. "Hendrick, people would like to speak with you!"

"I want to go to see my mommy now," Hendrick wailed, and reaching her at last he wrapped his arms around her legs and hid his face.

Well! Could anything have been more disarming? Anna lifted Hendrick in her arms and what a heartwarming picture they made, all three, the two proud parents and their shy little son. Technically I suppose he was no more their son than anyone else's, of course. A host mother had gestated him (she later sold her story to a journalist) and nobody was ever able to determine afterward just where Anna had obtained the source DNA they'd used.

The boy didn't look enough like Anna and Geert, or unlike them either, to be able to tell. I had to look at his face now and, I must admit, I'd never have known he was a Recombinant. After all, what was a Recombinant supposed to look like? Nobody had any idea, then. This one was slender and dark, with wide dark eyes and very ordinary features. He clung with his arms around Anna's neck as she and Geert fielded questions from the press. Labienus had coached them carefully for this, knowing when to fade back and let them tell it in (very nearly) their own words.

Yes, it was all true; Hendrick Karremans was five years old. No, they hadn't raised him here in Amsterdam City. They'd been living out in the country until a couple of weeks ago. No, he hadn't attended preschool. Yes, he was going to enter an ordinary kindergarten when the 2093 session started, in two weeks. This was why they had felt they ought to go public with his story at last.

What was his IQ? They declined to state, but added that he was a reasonably bright boy. He liked to paint and listen to music. His favorite food was Apple Puffs. His favorite game was Super Soccer-Man. What did he want to be when he grew up? A fireman! Why hadn't they revealed his existence to the world before now? Because they had wanted him to have a normal childhood.

Until today, I thought to myself, watching the child's face as he peered at the kameramen. If he'd known the truth about himself, he certainly hadn't had any idea what the truth meant. He was beginning to know now; and how frightened he looked, little Hendrick Karremans.

Though he grew calmer as the room became less crowded. The parents of the human children took them home to bed, the journalists rushed home to their keyboards to get the story out. The kameramen lingered, intent on catching visuals of the child wandering around the emptying room, waving disconsolately at the other boys as they left, going to the buffet and helping himself to chocolates before Anna caught him at it, picking up his dinosaur and making it walk along the wall.

I had found an uncrowded corner and seated myself there. Eventually Geert came and settled beside me, as Labienus escorted the last of the kameramen out with some concluding remarks for print.

"Well! I don't see how it could have gone any more smoothly, can you?" Geert said happily. "I think we made quite a good impression."

"I think so, yes," I replied.

"You'll be staying over? I see you didn't bring a bag, but—"

"In the car," I assured him. "I'll get it before Michel leaves."

"Good. We have the guest bedroom ready for you. Michel gave you some idea of your duties?" Geert looked just slightly uneasy. He'd never been a celebrity before.

"Handling the press and your correspondence on a day-to-day basis," I recited. "Making any arrangements, security or otherwise, that become necessary." This included acting as the child's bodyguard, though I felt it tactless to say so in so many words.

Geert nodded. "We're very grateful to you, really. I didn't realize there were people who did this sort of thing! Of course, it'll be very important to make sure that our lives go on just the same as before, as far as that's possible. That's just the point of it all, you see? Hendrick is really no different from any other child. Nothing is going to change."

Fool, I thought. Even the child knew better.

He sidled up to us now, looking troubled.

"Daddy?" He wrung his hands. "I'm afraid we have rather a problem."

"And what's that, Hendrick?" Geert turned to him, smiling at his big words.

"Well—there's one of those bugs in here, it came out of the coat closet and now it's flying around—I don't know what they're called—"

"A fly?"

"No, Daddy, the ones that eat clothes, you know?" How anguished his dark eyes were.

"Moths," I said.

"Yes, thank you. And they like to get near candles—and we've got all these candles in here—and one of them could fly too close and catch fire and then fly all around the room and set it on fire, too."

Geert roared with laughter at that. Hendrick just looked at him, on the point of tears, I think.

"No, no," I assured him. "Because the wings would burn up instantly, so the moth wouldn't be able to fly. You see? It'd just fall harmlessly to the table."

"But then the table might burn," Hendrick pointed out.

"True," I acknowledged. "Let's see what we can do about preventing that, shall we?" I looked up into the room and acquired the moth. On its next pass through the air above our heads I lunged up and got it.

"Bravo!" Geert applauded. "What speed! But you missed, didn't you? It was way up there by the ceiling."

"Do you see it, sir?" I inquired.

"No, but—"

I opened my hand to reveal the moth's crushed body. Geert went off into gales of laughter again. I think he'd had more wine than perhaps had been quite wise. Hendrick smiled at me.

"And now the moth won't burn your house down," I told him.

"Thank you," he replied gravely. He considered me a long moment. "What's your name?"

"Nils Victor," I told him. "I'm here to help your mother and father."

"Oh. Are you going to live with us?"

"Yes, I am."

"That'll be nice," he said. Anna came in then.

"Hendrick, it's past your bedtime," she said severely. She was quite sober. "And we've still got the food to clear away, Geert."

"Allow me, please," I told her, and got to my feet. She started to protest, and then realized she had a *servant* now. How her face lit up.

"If you don't mind—it's too kind of you, really. Hendrick, say good night to dear Mr. Victor and we'll go upstairs." She held out her hand to him and he went dutifully, but not before pausing to say: "Good night, Mr. Victor." He knit his brows, and remarked: "You're different, too."

Interesting. I smiled and inclined from the waist in a bow. Neither of his parents seemed to notice the remark. Anna took the child's hand and led him upstairs, as Geert yawned hugely and got up to help me put away the remnants of the buffet. He had just proposed that we open another bottle of wine when there came a polite double knock at the door: Labienus, returning from the car with my bag. I excused myself and went to let him in.

"Good thing I didn't drive away with this," he said in a jolly voice, presenting me with the bag. He scanned briefly, to assure himself there were no mortals within earshot, and said in a lower voice: "You'll be all right here, of course."

"Certainly, sir," I replied. But what expression was this on his face? Sympathy?

"Look here . . . this will be hard for you, I know. Regrettable that he's a delightful child. This is strictly against regulations, of course, but, to fortify you in your hour of need—you'll find a few bars of Theobromos in with your things." He took my hand in his and clenched it briefly.

I was speechless with shock. Labienus was the last man I should have thought capable of gestures of affection. I know from bitter experience how little compassion he feels for the mortals we purportedly serve. I still had a vivid memory of old San Francisco, when I'd seen him straining eagerly to hear the death screams of mortals trapped in the ruins of the earthquake.

"Thank you very much, sir," I said, finding my voice at last. He smiled again and stepped back out into the night.

"You're welcome. There are times, Victor, when one needs additional strength to endure what is necessary in order to obtain Company goals. But I'm sure you're far too experienced a field operative to need to be told that! I'll be in touch in the morning."

And he ran lightly down the steps and away, under the cold stars.

The official press conference the next day was much more difficult. Word had got out, as we'd intended, and the press knew what to expect, what pointed questions to ask. Fortunately Labienus had prepared answers to all of them, but Geert and Anna were still flustered. They really had not expected any negative reaction to what they'd done.

I was tempted to blame them, but it was easy to understand their ingenuousness. They'd lived cloistered with Hendrick night and day for five years. He seemed the most lovable and ordinary of children to them. How could anyone object to his existence?

The religious leaders of the world had various condemnatory answers for them, of course, including the Ephesian Church, which formally demanded to know why Anna had not created a daughter instead of a son. Fortunately Anna was a practicing Ephesian, and her pious answer—that she'd left the choice of the baby's gender up to the Goddess—mollified them somewhat. We put out a certain amount of Ephesian-slanted publicity, too, depicting Anna as bravely defying the paternalist laws of the world to exercise her reproductive rights, which helped.

More difficult to deal with were all the tedious little laws Anna and

Geert had so blithely disregarded. No, they hadn't registered Hendrick's birth with the proper civil authorities: how could they, when they'd meant to keep his existence a secret until the press conference? So of course he had no papers and no legal identity, and that meant dealing with a hostile bureaucracy.

And, no, he'd never had vaccinations of any kind. He didn't need them. He was engineered to be disease-free, with an antibody system much more aggressive and powerful than ordinary mortals had. He'd never been ill a day in his life! So why should there be any need to give the child inoculations now, especially as he was afraid of such things, like any little boy?

The answer, of course, was that he would not be permitted to attend kindergarten until he'd had the inoculations. They were required by law. Moreover, the kindergarten Anna and Geert had chosen for Hendrick now refused to take him, and in fact filed suit against the Karremans family for lying on the application form about his legal status. No use to explain that they hadn't thought they were lying; as far as they were concerned, Hendrick was really their son, and wasn't that what mattered?

Naive idiots. We did our best, Labienus and I, at defusing the problems caused by superstition and ignorance, but really the mounting lawsuits—filed seemingly by everyone, anyone who felt they might have reason to suspect that Hendrick's creation infringed on their civil liberties—and bureaucratic stalemates were another matter entirely. I don't know what we'd have done if the situation had continued.

We took the most outrageous of the lawsuits, the one demanding Hendrick be euthanized, and had a field day with it: posters of Hendrick's sad little face with the words CONDEMNED TO DIE!! screaming below, and—even more effective—posters of Hendrick's picture side by side with that of Anne Frank, and the same caption. I think it might have done the trick, actually, for within a few days of that second poster the Anne Frank Kindergarten publicly announced that it would be happy to accept Hendrick Karremans as a pupil.

This occurred on New Year's Eve, so Labienus dropped by the house with Champagne to celebrate; though by this time Anna and Geert were in such emotional states they didn't particularly feel like celebrating.

Labienus took them upstairs for a firm talk about future strategies, and I was left to amuse Hendrick.

We stood looking at one another uncertainly, and I cleared my throat and said: "Well, Hendrick. Would you like to play Super Soccer-Man?"

He made a slight face.

"No," he said. "I don't really like it so much. Daddy does, though. Could we go for a walk?"

"Probably not the best idea," I said apologetically. We'd only had one or two incidences of vandalism outside the house, but it had been decided to keep Hendrick out of sight until he started school, by which time the more violent protest would have died down somewhat.

"I don't like living here," Hendrick told me, sighing. "I wish we could move back to our other house. But we're not going to now, are we?"

"I'm afraid not," I told him. He looked resigned. Then a furtive brightness came into his eyes.

"I know what we can do," he said, glancing guiltily in the direction of the second floor.

"What, Hendrick?" I couldn't suppress a smile. "You know I can't permit anything your parents forbid."

"Oh, it isn't anything bad," he said, taking my hand and leading me to the dining nook. "You'll like this, it'll be lots of fun! Really. Now, you sit down there—" He pushed me into the nook and I sat awkwardly on the little bench seat. He lifted the lid of the other seat and drew out an ancient imitation leather case. Stamped on it in gold letters were the words TOURNAMENT CHESS SET.

"You know how to play this game?" he inquired, setting up the board and pieces with remarkable speed, and correctly, I might add.

"Yes," I replied, stroking my mustaches. Poor little fellow, I thought, inviting a cyborg to play chess! "Do your parents object to chess, Hendrick?"

"Not—exactly," said Hendrick, avoiding my eyes. "It's just Daddy says I can't look like a brainiac or something." He smiled slyly. "And anyway Daddy isn't so good at it. I think that's why really." He turned the board on the diagonal and pushed it toward me. "Would you like to play black or white?"

I took white, and moved king's knight to F-three. He promptly advanced a queen's pawn to D-five and sat looking at me expectantly. I moved a king's pawn to G-three; his queen's bishop went to G-four. I moved my king's bishop to G-two. He countered with moving his queen's knight to D-seven. I sent a king's pawn to H-three. Hendrick sidled his queen's bishop over to capture my king's knight. I responded in kind, taking his queen's bishop with my king's bishop.

Anyone watching us would have thought we were only pretending to play, simply jumping the pieces around without purpose, so quickly were our moves made. I leaned back, setting his queen's bishop to one side, and considered him. His face was alight as he studied the pieces and quickly advanced a queen's pawn to C-six.

"You're actually enjoying this," I observed. I advanced a queen's pawn to D-three.

"Uh-huh," he replied, advancing a king's pawn to E-six. "This is the time I like the most, though. Before everything locks up."

I moved a king's pawn to E-four. "Locks up?"

"You know," he replied absently, moving his queen's knight to E-five. "It all locks up. So much has happened you can see how it's going to end."

"Can you indeed?" I slid my king's bishop back to G-two.

"Uh-huh." He captured my king's pawn at E-four. I took his capturing pawn with my king's bishop. "Then it just gets bor-ing."

"Because you know who's going to win?" I inquired, watching him move his king's knight to F-six.

"Uh-huh." He rubbed his nose thoughtfully as I returned my king's bishop to G-two once more. "Usually it's me. You're kind of good, though." He reached out and sent his king's bishop to B-four. "Check."

I blocked it with my king's knight. To my astonishment, he responded by moving his king's pawn to H-five.

"Did you mean to do that?" I asked him. He looked up at me in surprise.

"Can't you see the way it's going to go?"

"No, I'm afraid I can't." What an admission to make to a mortal child, of all people! He looked disappointed.

"I thought maybe you could. You play almost as good as me," he added tactfully.

I advanced my queen to E-two. He edged his queen over to C-seven.

"You said I was different, Hendrick," I said carefully, setting my queen's pawn on C-three. "Is that why you thought I could see the moves in advance, as you can?"

He nodded, moving his king's bishop back to E-seven.

"How am I different?"

He looked up at me, knitting his brows again. "Well, you just are. You move different. You smell different. You talk like one of those people on the Wire. You and Michel, too. You know what I mean! Don't you know?"

I knew; but it was impossible he should know, or rather it would have been impossible were he a human child. I scanned him. Yes; not quite a human brain. *Engineered to better process information.* So the child would be able to catch a ball, as clumsy schoolboy Geert had never been. Able, moreover, to distinguish a cyborg from a mortal human. Able to see the outcome of a chess game after a certain number of moves.

What else might Hendrick Karremans have been able to do?

He took my prolonged silence for embarrassment and said quickly: "Don't worry! I won't tell anybody. I don't like being different, either."

Not knowing how to reply, I simply nodded and moved my queen's pawn to D-four. His knight retreated but he stepped up his attack after that, until the thirtieth move, when I took his queen and he took mine. Then he yawned and waved his hands over his head.

"*Now* it's boring," he told me. "It's going to be a draw."

"Really?" I looked at the board. I analyzed the positions. He was quite correct.

"Uh-huh. In eighteen—" Hendrick cocked his head and studied the board. "No! Nineteen moves. You play good, Mr. Victor. It took a long time to know what you'd do."

We had been playing for all of six minutes.

"Thank you," I said. "That was a remarkable experience." I meant it, too.

"Want to play again?" he said hopefully.

"Some other time," I said, though I knew it was unlikely there would ever be another time.

"Okay. Can I have a Fruit Pop?" he inquired, carefully putting the board and its pieces away. From what I had observed I knew Anna didn't allow him sweets between meals, but I went to the kitchen and got the child his Fruit Pop.

He took it gleefully and we went out to the parlor, where he sat at the piano kicking his legs. He seemed completely uninterested in the keyboard, however.

"Do you play the piano?" I asked him.

"Uh-uh." He looked at me as though I were mad. "I'm only a little kid."

"Ah," I said, nodding. He nibbled away at the Fruit Pop a moment later and then his face grew suddenly apprehensive.

"What's the matter?"

"If those people said I can go to their school—then I'll have to get those shots, won't I?"

"I suppose you will," I said.

"I don't want to have shots," he cried, tears welling in his eyes.

"Well, perhaps you won't, then."

"But it's locked up now! They're the only school I can go to so Mommy and Daddy will have to send me there, but Michel will tell them I have to get shots to make the law people happy and make things easier," Hendrick wailed, forgetting his Fruit Pop, which dripped on the shining black finish of the piano. I got up hastily and mopped it with a tissue.

He was right, of course. One of the things Labienus was even now explaining to Anna and Geert was that they would have to make this particular concession, to have Hendrick vaccinated to comply with Civil Ordinance Number 435.

"You'll simply have to be brave, Hendrick," I told him. "After all, it's not as though they stick children with needles any more."

"But it still hurts," he wept. "I know it does. It went *hiss* and the medicine jumped into Mommy when she got *her* shots and she said *ow!* I'm scared to be hurt."

Why on earth had Anna let him watch her being inoculated?

"It's perfectly reasonable to be afraid of pain," I told him. "But you mustn't be a baby about it, after all. All the other children in that school had to have shots, you know."

"But I don't need the shots. They did," he said angrily. "And it's not fair. They're not going to die."

Was he precognitive as well? But he showed no sign of being a Crome generator, one of those mortals who produces a freak bioelectric field that carries over into the temporal wave. They occasionally seem to pick up information from the pattern of the future. "Well, neither are you," I lied. "You surely don't suppose a few little shots are going to kill you?"

"No," he said, irritably wiping his nose on his sleeve. "Not that kind of shots. I mean people are going to kill me. That's all locked up, too."

"Why would you think that, Hendrick?" I asked him, crouching to offer him a tissue. He looked at me with an expression of weary patience.

"Be-*cause*," he told me. "Don't you know what's been going on? All those people who are mad at Mommy and Daddy? They're scared of me. They threw things at our windows. Mommy and Daddy want me to be alive but a lot more people want me to not be alive. It would be real easy to kill me. All somebody has to do is shoot through those windows with a gun. When I go to that school it would be even more easy. They could just shoot me in the street. They could shoot me in the car. Even if I wore a soldier helmet they could get me. So it's all locked up. See?"

I stared at him, aghast at the matter-of-fact way he spoke.

"You don't seem frightened," I said at last. "Why are you afraid of shots, but not afraid to die?"

He had turned his attention to his melting Fruit Pop and was attempting to eat it before it fell off the stick. After a moment he said: "Well, when you die, it hurts but then it's over. My cat had to die and it didn't hurt him. He just went to sleep. But when you get a shot, it hurts and you're still alive, so it keeps hurting."

At that moment we heard their voices echoing down the stairs as they came, Anna and Geert sounding tired, Labienus sounding placatory.

"I thought we lived in a reasonable world," Anna was saying. "I really thought the human race had evolved beyond this sort of thing."

"Ah, but evolution is an ongoing process, isn't it?" Labienus said. "Think of yourselves as part of the change. You're fighting prejudice and irrational fear. When you've proved that what you did was right, you will have advanced civilization that much farther. But you won't manage it without a few sacrifices."

"That's true, of course," Geert said dispiritedly. They stepped down into the parlor and looked at Hendrick with identical expressions of shame. Anna cleared her throat.

"Hendrick, I'm afraid we're going to have to take you to the doctor after all—"

That was as far as she got before he began to howl, and threw himself down on the floor crying hopelessly.

"You promised," he shrieked. "I knew! I *knew* you'd do it—" They bent over him, murmuring reproaches. I backed away from them and turned to Labienus.

"I must get away," I murmured.

"Of course," he said immediately. "I quite understand. Take the night off. I'll stay with them." Once again he reached out and clasped my hand, startling me.

I shrugged into my coat and slipped out, scarcely taking time to wonder at the change in Labienus's administrative style. Perhaps he wasn't entirely the smiling manipulator I had known him to be.

I caught a bus into Old Amsterdam. There was a fine old restaurant on the Dam, soothing to the soul, unfashionably fitted out in red leather and crystal, with an excellent wine cellar. The food was of the sort generally described as "hearty fare" but prepared well; what should be fresh was fresh, and what should be high was just delicately so. I dined in comparative solitude and lingered over my meal, watching from my table as the Dam began to fill up with merrymakers for the countdown to midnight.

Dusk fell. I watched the lights begin to glow, sipping my coffee, savoring my dessert. New Year's Eve, and the year 2092 was about to slip into history. What was the first New Year's Eve I could remember? The Eurobase One celebration in 503 A.D. Very clearly I remembered lying in the ward recovering from my latest augmentation, furious at the pain I felt, as the nurses hung pink and purple and yellow streamers in the hall. There were cut-out decorations, too: a smiling baby wreathed in a banner, and a terrible old man with a scythe and hourglass. The nurse told us a story about the old man. She explained how we needn't be afraid of him, ever, for we lucky little children were becoming immortal.

She didn't tell us about the other things we had to fear. But that would have been cruel, really, wouldn't it? We'd learn the rest of the truth soon enough.

I ordered another dessert, a torte rich in Theobromos. Pleasure is at its best when one proceeds at a deliberate pace, I find. I ate slowly, and emptied my mind of any considerations save what I was doing and what I was about to do. Presently I walked out into the night.

It was cold, damp under the stars, with a thin sea-fog lying at ground level that made haloes around the streetlights. Over the crowd assembling around the Nationaal Monument, there hung a steamy cloud of exhaled vapor. People festooned with little electronic lights were dancing. I walked away into darkness, having no interest in that particular aspect of the mortal carnival, but I hadn't far to go. Amsterdam is quite a conveniently arranged city.

I found what I wanted near the Oz Achterburgwal.

A long quiet street along a still canal, pleasantly shadowed, no lamps to cast unwanted glare on the faces of passersby. Quite unnecessary, when all the windows afforded such illumination. Just visible, along the street, pacing slowly and staring, were the dark figures in overcoats like mine; but who could spare a glance or a thought for anything but the windows?

Uncurtained and wide, each displayed its occupant in her own particular pose or ambiance. Some were straightforward and traditional, with scarlet lighting, with black lace and classically provocative poses. There were the fantasies: a window that glowed with blue flickering light, La Sirene in green sequins reclining in a languid pose on her undersea couch. A girl with mime's training in a bare window under harsh white lights, made up in dead flesh tones, the perfect motionless image of a smiling display mannequin. A girl in the habit of a nun, her face innocent of paint, kneeling rapt before a photographer's backdrop of a rose window.

Some windows were dark, with a small apologetic electronic crawl at eye level: *Presently engaged. Will reopen shortly. All currencies accepted. Free certification available on premises. Presently engaged . . .*

Some places clearly catered to a sense of sin; there one looked into a garishly lit hell where the occupant was doing her best to convey the idea of pleasures cheap and degrading. In others there were promises of delights for the most eclectic, not to say criminal, tastes.

No. No. And no again, not for me . . . I generally preferred more Nature and less Art.

I found her at last in a window that glowed with amber light, radiated heat like summer.

So little artifice, and such charm. Quite without clothing save for a loincloth of white linen. She sat perched on a metal folding chair, in an ordinary sitting room. The only hint of a theme was a poster on one wall depicting some North African city. A music system on a shelf was playing a dance song with a quick beat, Reggae Nouveau perhaps. I could hear the music, but to most passersby she rocked silently in her chair as she regarded the evening, supremely unconcerned.

Her hair was superb, heavy as an Egyptian wig in its complex corn-row beading, and the bright beads—blue faience, copper, and brass—swung as she rocked, and tapped out a rhythm on the back of her chair. As I watched she parted her full lips and began to whistle out a counterpoint to the music. She had the slightest of gaps between her front teeth. Skin like midnight.

She noticed me at last and arched an eyebrow in cheerful inquiry. I nodded and climbed the steps to her door.

"Good evening, dear, may I see your credit ID please?" she greeted me, extending a pink-palmed hand. "Thank you."

She led me into the house, pausing only to key in the light control that dimmed her window and set its crawl message going. She named a price. I agreed to it.

"Coffee while I run your check? Little glass of gin?" she inquired, waving me to a comfortable chair. I declined. She patted my cheek and went off to her terminal to verify that I was healthy, sane, law-abiding, and could pay.

It was a Company-issued credit ID and of course pronounced me a worthy client, whether or not I was in fact healthy, sane, or law-abiding. But I could certainly pay. She came back smiling, led me deeper into the house, waved me into a small lavatory.

"Pre-prophylaxis, eh? You're a big boy, you know what to do. When you come out, turn to the right. I'll be waiting in there." She indicated a beaded doorway, all darkness beyond it.

I went in. It was furnished as most chambers for that purpose are. Concealed within a smoke detector was a tiny closed-circuit camera lens. I scanned: no gentlemen accomplices lurking anywhere in the house. She herself watched me, from a curtained booth on the other side of the wall where she was preparing for the encounter.

Having mutually assured ourselves that no murder was intended, we proceeded to the business at hand.

"What a charming conceit," I remarked, stepping through the curtain. Each bead was a touch of ice on my skin. The contrast with the warm air was a shivering pleasure. "I haven't seen a beaded curtain in ages. Was it your idea?"

Her voice came out of the darkness, amused. "Yes, thank you. But no personal details, eh? Less effort for you and they'll only spoil your fun, dear. For the sake of your pleasant and guilt-free experience, I will be only your desire personified. Not a person."

"I'm not a person either," I replied, and walked forward into the mystery.

As I left, something small and bright blue caught my eye by the door; I bent to pick it up. It was a toy rabbit, a tiny figure from a block set. I turned to offer it to my hostess.

"You have a child?"

"I might," she replied, accepting it. "Another personal detail you don't want to think about, you see? Not sexy at all. Thank you for your patronage, sir. Good night and happy New Year!"

I walked back past the crowd of mortals on the Dam. There were more of them now, still whooping and celebrating. Vendors sold hot drinks, sausages, parade horns, gnome hats, dance-lights. Wire screens, vast as city blocks, were mounted on the sides of buildings and displayed New Year's jollity from other cities as though they were occurring simultaneously, creating a sense of worldwide party.

I found an all-night coffeehouse some blocks away and edged into a booth at the back. It was dark and quiet there. I ordered coffee and pastry, and watched from the darkness as the New Year came upon us, the bright child in his banner emblazoned HAPPY 2093!

Celebrate while you can.

Hendrick got his shots on January 2. On the fifth of January he started kindergarten.

I took him to school. Anna and Geert were dismayed by the crowd of kameramen in the street, didn't know what to do, what to say. But what were Doss and Waters paying me for, after all? I shrugged into my overcoat, took Hendrick by the hand, and escorted him down the steps.

He looked pale and frightened, but he went without question. Children endure so much, so steadfastly, once they learn to abandon hope. He stared unsmiling into the blank avid eyes of the kameramen and let them See him for a moment before following me as I pushed through the mortals.

And there the gunman was, as I'd known he'd be, the heavy-set young man in the green shirt, holding up the bag with the Amsterdam Wire logo, stepping suddenly too close. As I reached out to break his wrist, before the shouting started, I heard Hendrick saying quietly: "That one's not a kameraman. See his eyes? Here it comes. Good-bye—"

But the gun went off, in accordance with recorded history, pointed up and away from Hendrick. It broke a window in a villa across the street, and I knew without bothering to look up the unnerving pattern the shattered glass had formed, like a six-pointed star, for this too was in accordance with recorded history. I heard the scream, as much in frustration as pain, of the would-be assassin. I heard the whirring of the kameramen as they ran close to frame our struggle (no attempt to help me!) except for the one who turned his devouring face up to the broken window, catching that unforgettable image. And, at last, here were a few police.

And Labienus, to manage statements, so that I was permitted to walk on at last towing Hendrick after me, down the quiet street toward the waiting car. I bowed my head, striding along, feeling Hendrick's hand twist in mine as he looked back.

So I too entered recorded history, of course with my face well hidden: that dark overcoat flowing back from those striding legs, the stiff arm extended to the boy who turned to peer over his shoulder so somberly into the cameras. By that evening a billion mortals had seen the image.

They were waiting for us at the school with tremulous applause, for of course Labienus made certain that word of what had happened preceded our arrival. That was where the reaction set in. I was trembling, sweating, and really in no mood to shake all the tiny hands extended to me; but I had saved Hendrick's life, and the more enlightened citizens of Amsterdam wanted to thank me. I was given flowers. Toddlers were put into my arms and told to kiss me. The teachers kissed me. I disengaged as politely as I could and retreated to an empty office, to mop my perspiring face and endure, until it should be time to take Hendrick home, being the hero of the hour.

And what a brief hour it was.

Oh, we had waves of positive publicity from the murder attempt. The gunman had been acting alone, but was associated with the Church of God-A, a cult calling for more than zero population growth. They resolutely denied they had any intention of bringing this about by violence, though they admitted they were opposed to Hendrick's existence on principle.

There was a great deal of self-congratulation within Amsterdam. Once again its good citizens had shown themselves tolerant, humane, and enlightened! Hendrick got on well with his playmates. Anne Frank was invoked again, wan smiling ghost to give her blessing on another little outsider.

On his third day at school Hendrick developed a slight fever, a mild headache. I escorted him home. Anna was furious, positive his illness was a reaction to the unnecessary vaccinations. Geert wrung his hands. Before nightfall, however, the boy's splendid superior engineered antibodies had clearly done their trick. His fever fell, his headache went away, he was fine.

Not so his classmates.

Three children showed up at the school on the fourth day. The rest were at home, violently ill. By nightfall most of them had died.

Most of the teachers were dead by the following morning, and all the children had died. The illness spread through their families. Their families died. Drastically enforced quarantine measures seemed to contain the outbreak, though it was also possible that the plague killed its hosts so quickly that it was unable to spread effectively after a certain point.

The Wire coverage was heartbreaking: images, from happier days, of the smiling little faces. There were around-the-clock broadcasts as people cowered in their homes. Ratings soared. Rumors spread quickly as only the electronic media could spread them, especially with a captive audience.

Once it had started, it didn't take long.

The Amsterdam Center for Disease Control assaulted the question immediately. The obvious conclusion to be drawn was that the outbreak was somehow associated with Hendrick, since he had survived it and none of the other children had. From the moment that theory was widely known, the public had decided.

Useless for Anna and Geert to protest via voicelink that Hendrick had come into contact with plenty of people from the day of his birth, without harming anyone; we couldn't get any of the other doctors who'd worked with them to come forward and make a statement in their support. Useless to point out that Hendrick had been ill, too, and that undoubtedly only his unique antibody system had enabled him to recover. Anna and Geert were not professional entertainers, they spoke poorly, without stage presence or vocal training. Though Labienus repeated their statements an hour later, the first stammering denials were the ones that had the most impact.

Moreover a biologist, who spoke well and who *did* have stage presence, was interviewed immediately afterward. He put forward his opinion that Hendrick's much-touted immune system might be responsible. Perhaps, somehow, it had perceived his little classmates with their ordinary coughs and colds as dangers to his survival, and manufactured a toxin to eliminate them.

This was immediately accepted as a glaringly obvious fact.

The truth came far too late, as we were being evacuated; and no one listened, I think, but Hendrick and I.

Labienus was hurrying Anna and Geert through their packing. Hendrick was already packed. I was buttoning him into his coat in the flickering light of the Wire images, for it had been deemed unsafe to turn on any of the other household lights, and in truth we only dared keep the Wire on because we needed the constant flow of information.

Abruptly a grim-faced commentator broke in over the latest "news" (endless recapitulation of everything that had already been shown) to announce that investigators had uncovered a possibly significant fact that might prove Hendrick wasn't responsible for the plague after all. The first instance of illness had occurred at the school *before* he had ever arrived. He had got there late the first morning, due to the attempt on his life. During the time we were making statements to the police, as his future classmates waited for Hendrick's appearance, one of the children had been taken ill and sent home, escorted by a teacher because her mother was too ill to come for her. She had never returned. The teacher who had escorted her home was the first to die.

I had never heard this. These details had never become part of recorded history. I stared, astonished, at the images, forgetting to hand Hendrick his mittens. He took them from me, patiently, and pulled them on.

Then I was Seeing, through the eyes of a kameraman, the Disease Control investigators in their protective suits, emerging from the house where they'd just found the mother and child dead.

I knew that house. I'd been inside it. It was in the red light district. The kameraman was running close to get a shot through the window, before being pushed back by police. The only image he was able to frame that was clearly recognizable was a travel poster on one wall, its subject a city in North Africa.

The commentator was unable to interview any of the investigators, but the suited figures rushing to and fro in the background lent weight to his expressed opinion that this might explain at last the origin of the plague: for the child's mother was a licensed prostitute of African descent, and she may have contracted the disease from an African customer, likely enough in view of the plagues that had decimated so much of Africa's population in recent years . . .

I had kissed her. Children, teachers, had kissed me.

It really is remarkable how our immortal senses take control at such times. I rose like the perfect machine I should have been and shut off the Wire. I took Hendrick's hand and led him through the dark house to wait by the back door. We could hear Labienus helping Anna and Geert carry their bags downstairs. They were stumbling, dropping things. There were already barricades at the end of the street and crowds assembling there, shouting at the police.

How sad, how sad, the poor girl had been exposed to a virus and unwittingly passed it on to me, and I'd—

But I'd have known if there had been anything wrong with her.

We heard the first shots fired in the front street, not what you'd expect at all, an insignificant-sounding popping.

"There it goes," said Hendrick, almost calmly. He was in shock, his dark eyes enormous. "All locked up now. I told you so."

I had scanned the mortal woman before our encounter. She hadn't been carrying any virus.

"Here, here!" whispered Labienus, shepherding Anna and Geert before him. "Out to the car. Now! Nils will drive you to a safe location." He looked into my eyes and transmitted: *You've got the blood effects ready?*

The woman hadn't been carrying any virus. I, however, had.

It didn't feel like rage. It felt like a white flare, so intense it was, so unlike a human emotion. I stared back at him.

Was it in the Theobromos you gave me? I transmitted.

His face told the truth, though he hastily transmitted back: *What? Don't be ridiculous! Get them out of here, now, we can't waste time on this.*

How true. We couldn't waste time, not when history was dictating that Anna and Geert and the child escaped from their house at nineteen hundred hours precisely, exiting through the back and making their departure in a rented car driven by Hendrick's bodyguard.

The perfect automaton went briskly down the back steps, opened the doors of the waiting Volta, took bags and loaded them into the boot while the Karremans family scrambled into their seats. He shut them in, and climbed behind the wheel to take them to their appointment with history.

As we drove away, a faint transmission came from the dark house: *I'll explain when we rendezvous.*

How pleasant to have an explanation offered.

How heavily I'd been perspiring in the school. And with the woman.

The last act played out quickly.

I drove the mortals to their previous home in the country, the loft apartment above the laboratory where they'd done their work. The apartment was closed up now, though the laboratory was still in use; it was within commuting distance and the Karremans had planned to go back to work after Hendrick was in school full-time.

We let ourselves in and they took shelter upstairs, in the rooms where Hendrick had played as a baby. The place can't have afforded him any comfort of familiarity now, dark and empty as it was. I remained below in the laboratory, ostensibly to stand guard but in reality following through on what I had been told was the point of this entire operation: locating and securing all the files, all the project notes for the Karremans' work with recombinant DNA. History would record it as lost in the course of the evening's events.

The Company knew otherwise, naturally. The Company knew that a man placed in the event shadow—for history did not record what happened in the laboratory during the hour the Karremans family cowered upstairs—might remove the data on Hendrick's creation to a safe location for later retrieval. Anna's and Geert's work would be saved, would pass into the possession of Dr. Zeus Incorporated, presumably to be of some benefit to mortal humanity at some unspecified time in the twenty-fourth century.

Though I had no real idea of what would be done with the knowledge. We're told so little, we operatives struggling through the past. Our masters assure us it's better that way. Easier on our nerves.

I seemed to have no nerves left in the forty-five minutes I searched through the laboratory. Eventually I found the files, or at least their backups, neatly labeled in—what else?—a file box. I carried it out into the night, ran with it to the nearest drainage ditch, dug a hole in the snow and buried it. Then I returned to the laboratory to keep my own appointment with history.

Not long to wait. Glancing at my chronometer, I saw that the mobs would by now have stormed the house and found it deserted, but set it afire anyway and gone looking for the monster and his wicked creators, pausing only to raid the Civil Guard arsenal. Thanks to the splendid media coverage Labienus had masterminded, a good many people knew exactly where the Karremans' laboratory was. Yes: here came the line of headlights through the night.

Car doors slamming. Shouted consultation. Upstairs, inaudible to mortal ears, Hendrick's whimpering, Anna's stifled sobs. Heartbeats pounding, both within and without, for the attackers were frightened, too.

So it was a brave man who climbed back into his utility vehicle, after pounding had failed to force the door, and simply drove it through the wall.

He died almost at once. Pointless to shoot him, I suppose, but I had no choice: history stated that he was shot by Hendrick's bodyguard before he had time to jump from the cab of his vehicle. It stated further that other members of the mob, pouring in through the breach he'd made in the wall, promptly gunned down the bodyguard.

So I took my pose there in the dark, as their shots went wide, and I thumbed the electronic device that set off the little detonations in my heavily padded clothing. The blood bags exploded. I toppled forward, as dead as I would ever be.

The mob advanced cautiously, fearful. There came an echoing clatter of feet down the stairs. Who was running down the stairs? This hadn't been mentioned in any of the accounts, and of course I couldn't turn over to see.

"*Make it be over,*" I heard Hendrick crying in desperation. "Make it be over now!"

Geert and Anna were close behind him, frantic to pull him back out of danger.

Deafening barrage of shots. They died there, on the stairs.

I hope it was over quickly.

Certainly I could hear no failing heartbeats, no last gasps in the moment of profound silence that came when the shooting stopped. The mortals seemed stunned at what they'd done. At last somebody had presence of mind to say:

"We'll have to burn this place. It's the only way to keep the plague from spreading!"

Yes! That was a plan all of them understood. It was done quickly, because some of them had thoughtfully brought along accelerant as well as guns. They dumped it around, ran back out through the breach, and somebody lit a firecracker—perhaps left over from New Year's Eve—and tossed it in. Very effective: a roar and a fireball at once.

I winked out to the lavatory at the back of the building. Forcing the window over the basin, I crawled out and dropped into the snow that had drifted behind the wall. No need to worry about the telltale print of my body in the drift. It would have melted away within the hour, as the laboratory became an inferno.

I fled, secure in the knowledge that my escape wouldn't be spotted. History recorded otherwise, after all. Pausing only long enough to retrieve the file box from the ditch where I'd hidden it, I ran away, back toward Amsterdam.

One oughtn't to think at such times. Undeniably a foolish thing to do.

I thought and thought as I ran, you see, with the result that by the time I reached the outskirts of the city all my questions had resolved into just two: Could I do it? How was I to do it?

Hard to find a fire hot enough, intense enough. Probably even the fire at the laboratory wouldn't have been of sufficient heat. No bonfires permitted nowadays, in safety-conscious 2093, and most homes were heated with electricity.

As I marched along, I came to a shop licensed to sell liquor. It was gated and locked against the night, but the lock could be forced; and the shop contained everything I'd need, which was to say rows of bottles of alcohol and little packets of hotpoints to start the fire. Yes. Would the fire cleanse away my filth?

Undoubtedly, if it burned away all but the indestructible skeleton within me and the augmented brain protected within my ferroceramic skull. I wouldn't die—I was immortal, after all—but I might be so badly damaged the Company would be unable to repair me. I might spend the rest of eternity in a bioregeneration vat, only marginally alive. Better than I deserved, to be sure, but I hadn't many alternatives. I wasn't even certain I could force myself to remain there in the fire. They made us such cowards, when they made us deathless.

I had set down the file box and was wrestling with the lock when Labienus stepped from the shadows behind me.

"Let it go, Victor. It was a wretched business, but it's over now."

I turned to stare at him. He scooped up the file box and tucked it securely under one arm. He met my stare.

"Why?" I demanded.

"Why were you used as the carrier or why weren't you told?" he inquired. No attempt to brazen out the lie. I hadn't expected that. He smiled slightly at my confusion.

"What's the first rule we learn, Victor? That *history cannot be changed.* History recorded that the Karremans plague would kill a certain number of people. History recorded that the Recombinant would be killed, along with his creators, and their research lost. How was the Company to alter any of those historical facts? We couldn't, of course.

"All we could do was work within the historical record, to place ourselves in the position of greatest advantage and thereby control the situation. You see? But it was decided to do more than simply take the research files. Wouldn't it be better to ensure that there was no Karremans plague after all? No unknown and uncontrollable virus evolving from a Recombinant's body? There'd be no way to change the historical facts as known, those little victims must die—but wouldn't it be much less dangerous for humanity if they actually died of something controllable? Something we could deactivate once the historical facts had been *apparently* matched? We were minimizing the potential for a greater disaster, Victor, you see?

"Terrible that the tragedy had to occur, certainly. Terrible that it will galvanize all the nations of the world to forbid any further research into work of this kind. Impossible to change these things. But at least this way we've been able to derive something positive from it! The research has been saved. And the 'plague' will never spread further, because we know it never existed in the first place."

So, once again, Dr. Zeus Incorporated had become the beneficiary of mortal suffering. I leaned on the grate, longing for those bottles of vodka and aquavit behind the glass. I wondered what Labienus would do if I grappled him close, if I forced his mouth open with my own and spat my misery down his throat.

He narrowed his eyes, perhaps picking up the image from my thoughts, and continued: "As to why you were chosen for the job—well, really, Victor, it must have occurred to you by now that you're unique among our operatives."

"I'm an ordinary Executive Facilitator," I stated.

"Oh, Victor, so much more than that! You have a talent none of the rest of them have. You were augmented to do in fact what that poor child was assumed to be doing: your body can produce customized toxins in response to specific stimulus. Surely that affair in San Francisco gave you a clue, beyond what we were permitted to tell you at the time? Budu attacked you, and you immediately manufactured a virus to disable him."

"And the woman, here?" I demanded. "The children? What threat did they present?"

He cleared his throat.

"Well—none, of course, but their deaths were a regrettable necessity. There was nothing in the Theobromos. You'd have detected any adulteration, you know that. Your ability is programmed to activate when certain signals are transmitted. Do you recall when I shook your hand, New Year's Eve? You felt, perhaps, a slight shock? No? But your body responded to the order I gave it by producing what history will call the Karremans Recombinant Defensive. As we had intended it to do, I might add. Nothing was ever out of our control."

"You're saying, then"—I fought to keep my voice steady—"that the Company is able to make my body generate poisons without my knowledge. At any time."

"Exactly so."

"Why was this thing done to me?" I asked.

"Now, now, you're taking entirely the wrong attitude! Though you can be excused, in view of what you've just been through." Labienus smiled indulgently. "The Company was considering a special-threat design, and Aegeus felt you were the nearest match to the desired psychological profile."

"Did he really?"

"Oh, yes. Of course, you still underwent years of tests to see if you'd be emotionally up to the work. Placed in certain situations to see how you responded. Why, when you were still at Eurobase One, hardly more than a neophyte, there was a drone named Lewis—"

"I remember." I closed my eyes. "Please. Enough."

Labienus seemed to feel it was safe to step close and place a comradely hand on my shoulder. He was correct; however extraordinary my revulsion might be, I hadn't the will, just now, to attack him. If only he'd go away, I could get on with my immolation. Myself I hated most of all.

"Now then," he continued, "you'll be relieved to know, I'm sure, that you're no longer manufacturing the virus. It's served its purpose. You can go on to your next assignment without endangering any other mortals." He drew a small case from an inner pocket and put it into my nerveless hand. "That contains your new credit ID. You're to report to the Herengracht HQ before daylight, for a change of clothes and a shave. The Section Head there will brief you on your next posting. I'd discard that coat before you go much farther, however. You're a little conspicuous."

I looked down at the bullet holes, the imitation blood.

When I looked up he was gone.

A little nonsensical voice sang in my ear: *Victor. Vector. Virus. Victor Veneficus . . .*

Like the good machine I was, I slogged away through the night and found my way at last, sick and chilled, to the Herengracht HQ. Van Drouten, red-eyed with weeping, let me in and was very kind to me. She stuffed me full of a hot breakfast, and I managed to keep it down until I was alone in the lavatory.

I showered. I shaved. I put on clean pajamas and slept, in a quaint little room at the top of the house where Van Drouten had once hidden Jewish children, and woke to find Facilitator General Aegeus sitting on a chair beside my bed, regarding me with cold eyes. I'd so admired him, once.

There were recorded voices speaking in the room. It was the conversation Labienus and I had had outside the liquor shop.

When the voices stopped at last, Aegeus spoke briefly and to the point. He informed me that Labienus was a liar, the leader of a genocidal cabal within the Company. *He* had augmented me to produce viruses, intending me as a weapon for his group. My own loyalty to our masters was now suspect, by association.

It was expected that Labienus would shortly offer me a chance to join his inner circle. I would accept his offer. I would monitor the cabal's activities. I would keep Aegeus informed on what they planned to do next . . .

And perhaps one day I might be trusted again.

———

How to trust either one of them? I suspect there is no solution to my particular dilemma. Not at the present time, at least.

I proceed with extreme care, as indeed one ought when one may become a source of disease at any moment, quite unawares. It has necessitated some changes in my personal habits. Obviously, I can never engage in intimacies of any kind again.

It is not a pleasant life. And it continues, for I am unable to die; and so the pain never goes away.

History took its course, and recorded that the plague had been generated by Hendrick's overpowerful immune system. Horrified by the tragedy, all the nations of the world signed the treaty that would outlaw forever any further experimentation with recombinant human DNA.

The Karremans became infamous, their story dramatized to its full potential to shock, horrify, and entertain. After the manner of storytellers, the filmmakers altered the facts for greater mythic appeal: in the American version of the story, Hendrick (or the Recombinant) was depicted as a perfect Aryan type, blond and blue-eyed, coldly adult in his manner. Anna was a lesbian, Geert an alcoholic. I was played by a hulking actor (bodyguards must be huge, mustn't they?) as a simpleminded muscleman, faithful to his doglike death.

But all that came later.

Amsterdam mourned, and it had so much to mourn. So much was buried with all those white coffins.

All the same, the city had justly earned its reputation for tolerance and common sense, and in time those virtues reasserted themselves. Anna and Geert were never to be vindicated, but Hendrick was recognized for the innocent victim he had been.

A statue was erected on the site of the house where they'd tried to live. The sculptor utilized the famous image taken that first day of school, after the murder attempt, and there it stands to this hour in black metal: Hendrick being pulled along by the hand, turning to look back, his little face sad and enigmatic. Dynamic, the grim striding figure that drags him relentlessly forward, the folds of its long black coat flowing out behind.

The sculptor has chosen not to give the figure a face.

EPILOGUE

Labienus opens another file case.

He regards a field photograph taken by an operative, of a street in what can only be San Francisco. Before a hotel, a young mortal woman is being helped down from a carriage. She is heavily pregnant. From her clothing and the rest of the setting, the photograph would appear to have been taken in the early 1860s. And here is a second picture, a portrait of a man, taken much later: perhaps the first quarter of the twentieth century?

Another face inhuman, but much more subtly so. Smiling, but the deep-set eyes are as cold as Budu's. There is something suggestive of a shark in the too-boyish grin. Labienus's frown deepens.

A loose cannon. A compromise. An unacceptable exception to the rules.

What had Aegeus been planning? Some kind of parity with the old project *Adonai*? Take an extraordinary child, gift him with extraordinary resources, and put him in a position to affect world events to the Company's advantage?

If so, Aegeus had been successful. The really awful part was that it had been a public success.

"Spoiled millionaire's brat," Labienus mutters. He looks down at the face of William Randolph Hearst. Crass, naïve, arrogant, *American*. Given unlim-ited attention from the moment of his birth, an only child who had but to point at something and, if money could buy it, it was his. Where was the shaping discipline? Where was the inner pain to spur him on to great deeds? He should have been profitless to the Company, a crashing failure for

Aegeus. At the very least, he should have become an empty-souled Charles Foster Kane.

Instead he's been a rampant success, a monster with a heart solid as a diamond, voraciously alive, motivated, powerful, breaking even Company rules with comparative impunity because of his usefulness. Posing as his own descendant, he has rebuilt his empire. Hearst News Services is an invaluable tool for the Company, and the Hearst museums throughout Europe continue to accrue as much priceless art for Dr. Zeus as the most dedicated team of Preservers.

The idea that the child had been wanted and loved by his parents might figure in the equation, somehow, never even occurs to Labienus.

He flips on through the dossier. Here are the later pictures, with the big American in modern dress, still strangely old-fashioned looking. Smiling at museum openings, scholarship awards banquets, *orphanage dedications* for God's sake. Immortal, and immature enough to believe he could improve the world. Labienus shakes his head.

There's the fool smiling on the steps of the National Museum of Tunisia, on the occasion of its grand rededication. Here is an insert of the priceless Carthaginian artifacts he (or rather, his paid experts) had tracked down and restored to the museum. Did he imagine for a moment he would win their love? The American really has no grasp of history, has he?

Carthage hadn't changed much since the third Punic War. Labienus had gone there on a whim, celebrating the two-thousand-three-hundredth anniversary of its destruction, and even in 2154 there weren't many amenities for tourists. No trams at all to the infamous Tophet; he'd had to walk more than a mile through an ankle-turning wilderness of spiny weeds and broken stone before he'd come to the site.

Labienus stood surveying what had been Baal-Hammon's shrine. Vague rectangles in the pale rock, broken stele, long-eroded pits from bygone archaeological digs. And, underneath his feet to an unknown depth, the crumbled bones and ashes of thousands upon thousands of mortal children.

Closing his eyes, Labienus could still hear the voices:

"They're a morally inferior race as well," Cato had told him, glaring over his wine cup. In the villa's atrium, a fountain babbled quietly and slaves played soothing music.

"What, because Dido lay down for Aeneas?" Caecilianus shouted impatiently. He was a young member of the *populares*. "That's no reason to trounce somebody we've already defeated! The Carthaginians have changed. Hannibal's so much history. They're peaceful merchants now, and they'll stay that way—"

"If you please," Labienus had said. "Let the honorable Cato speak his mind." He said it in such a way as to imply a broad wink to the younger guests sprawled around his table, but the truth was that Labienus rather liked Cato. The old mortal might be a warmonger, but he was ruthlessly pragmatic. "Why would you say our ancient enemy is morally inferior, dear Cato?"

"Their religious practices are an offense to the holy gods," said Cato, staring down Caecilianus. "As is well known. They worship Cronus. The old baby-eater, you see? Over there he's got some damned Eastern name, Baal or Moloch if I remember rightly. Your 'peaceful merchants' have a huge bronze image made of him, a bull-headed figure with a gaping mouth and cleverly articulated arms, and do you know what they do?

"They build a pyre inside Moloch so intense he glows red-hot, and then they place their firstborns in the thing's hands and some priest pulls a lever. Up go the arms and the children fall screaming through Moloch's mouth, into the fire."

Caecilianus winced. Cato pressed his advantage: "And then, the Carthaginians clash cymbals and skirl pipes as loudly as they can, to drown out the cries of their little victims!" The other guests grimaced. They weren't soldiers; only politicians.

"Oh, that's too horrible," cried Caecilianus. "Nobody would do that."

Labienus looked at him and smiled, thinking of the infants his legions had put to the sword: little Gauls, little Nubians, little Greeks, all in the name of the Pax Romana.

"Believe it, young man," insisted Cato. "And that is only one of the reasons I say, as I have said and will say again—"

"*Carthago delenda est!*" they all shouted, including Labienus, who could remember a time when Cato's ancestors had not only sacrificed children but eaten them.

In the end, Cato had finally had his way.

———

It had been a long siege, and it had cost a lot of money. Caecilianus and his fellow *populares* had complained about that; they had complained, too, about the underhanded means and ridiculous pretext Rome had used to justify the war. Further justification was needed.

So Labienus strode through the ruin of Carthage, pausing now and again to cheer on the legions in their good work, sometimes even setting his own torch to purple hangings, or directing the crews that toppled walls. He was there to see that Dr. Zeus got its share of the loot, of course, but he was also there in his official capacity as the nearest thing Rome had to a journalist, gathering reports for the Senate.

This was why he made his way now to the temple of Baal-Hammon, stepping over the sprawled bodies, the pooled blood that reflected bright fire climbing, and smiled as he came.

Marcus Gracchus was waiting for him on the steps of the temple. Blood ran down the steps, a thick stream flowing. Two legionaries stood alongside, supporting between them a man in chains.

"Ave, Labienus." Gracchus saluted. He took his helmet off, wiped his face with a bit of torn curtain: fine stuff, sea-green and cloth of gold.

"Ave, Gracchus!" Labienus bounded up the steps and surveyed the prisoner. "So this is my interviewee? He doesn't look much like a high priest."

Gracchus squinted at his men. "He was a lot more impressive before the boys had a bit of fun with him. Well, where do you want the bastard?"

"Are all the temple buildings secured? Find us an administrative office," said Labienus, and five minutes later he was comfortably ensconced in the high priest's own chair, pouring himself a glass of the high priest's own wine. The high priest knelt before him, blinking through blood from a scalp wound. The legionaries stood just outside the door, sullen because they were missing out on the temple loot. Labienus tasted the wine.

"Mmm. Falernian, isn't it?" he asked the priest, in the priest's own language. The priest raised weary eyes. He was past shock.

"Yes," he replied. "Roman wine."

"You ought to have bought more of our wine. You ought to have bought our olive oil, too. It might have prevented all this," Labienus said, gesturing widely with the cup. "Trade imbalance is worse than a few elephants over the

Alps, you see. Takes bread from the mouth of the Roman olive grower. We can't have that."

"What will you do with me?" the priest asked.

"Ultimately? Parade you in a triumph, I imagine. We'll want to clean you up, first; you're certainly not very imposing as you are." Labienus looked the priest over critically. "What you've got on, is that your ceremonial regalia?"

"Some of it," said the priest. "The legionaries took the rest."

"Tsk! Not splendid enough at all. We'll have to make you up something in cloth of gold for the triumph. Rome likes a good show. It wants its villains larger than life." Labienus set the wine aside and leaned back, surveying the priest. "Now, why don't you tell me all about the worship of Baal-Hammon?"

"He is our lord of the fertile fields," said the priest, his voice trembling. "He is the Good Father, the consort of Tanit. To him we offer our first fruits, and the young of the beasts."

"How many babies do you burn in a month?"

The priest blinked. "It depends," he said. "In the fever season, sometimes one every day. Other times, we can go a month without a child-offering, if it pleases the Lord."

"Do you kill them before they go into the fire, or drop them in alive?"

"What?" the priest cried. "What are you saying? They're dead! We offer them to the Lord because they're dead! Holy gods, is this why you hate us? You think we kill children?"

"No, no; we hate you because you sell olive oil at lower prices than we do," Labienus explained. "But if everyone believes you kill children, we can run you out of business and even the *populares* can't complain."

"You must understand, these are babies who have *already* died!" the priest insisted, horrified. "Miscarriages. Stillbirths. All who die of sickness or mischance. How could we let their little souls go into the darkness? We give them back to the Lord, he takes them through the fire, and they become his angels."

"He takes them through the fire. That would be in the great bronze idol, the one with the head of a bull?"

"A bull?" The priest frowned. "Baal-Hammon hasn't got the head of a bull. You're thinking of the Egyptians."

Labienus withdrew a pair of gauntlets from a pouch at his belt. He put them on and half rose in the chair, just far enough to reach out and slap the priest.

"Baal-Hammon has the head of a bull, and you feed him children," he said. "You place them in his hands, and they're dropped into a fire in his belly."

"No! Come into the temple and see for yourself!" said the priest. "He has a beard, and a high crown—eating children, what kind of minds do you Romans have? We put the babies in the Lord's hands. He lowers them into the holy fire and gives them life again! I have seen them smile, before they pass through to Paradise! This is all a misunderstanding—"

Labienus hit him this time, hard enough to break a tooth.

"Listen to me, very carefully," he said in a quiet voice. "You feed your first-born children to Baal-Hammon. That's what you'll tell everyone in Rome. You deck the poor little things with flowers, and then you drop them screaming down his gullet, to be roasted alive in the bronze furnace. Your own people hate you for it. They were happy to be conquered by Rome."

"No," said the priest, clutching his jaw. There were tears in his eyes from the pain. "I think—long ago, people used to offer human sacrifices. I have heard of it being done. But we never did. And never children. Why do you—"

Labienus hit him again.

"You're not listening," he said patiently. "I want you to tell me the truth. The truth is that you burn your own children alive. You see? It's very simple. Tell me that truth."

"But I don't—"

Labienus raised his hand. "Tell me the truth," he repeated. "I can call the legionaries in here with a word, and you know what they'd do. If you tell me what I want to hear, things will be much more pleasant. Your tooth's giving you agony, isn't it? I can have a dentist see to it. Rome has excellent dentists, you know. We're a civilized nation."

"We have dentists, too, you son of an ape," wept the priest.

"Not any more," Labienus pointed out. "Now, tell me the truth. You offer up sacrifices of living children to your bestial god, don't you? Trust me, the hour will come when you'll say it, and you'll believe it, too. The only thing you can control, my friend, is how much pain you go through before that hour comes. Think carefully."

In despair, the priest shouted: "The Lord will punish Rome, Roman! He'll send plague, and brimstone, and armies for her destruction!"

Labienus grinned. "Yes. Rome will fall, in her turn. Does that make you feel better? Now . . . tell me the truth."

Who says history cannot be changed? thought Labienus smugly, opening his eyes to regard the bleached wasteland. There was no salt covering the ruin to the thickness of a common soldier's toe—that would have *really* cost money, beyond any spin doctor's ability to shut the complainers up. But the landscape was just as white, and Carthage had been poisoned just as effectively, as though it were true.

And Baal-Hammon, in his persona as bull-headed monster, had served Labienus's purposes wonderfully well. How far his horned shadow had been thrown! Out beyond the classical world, into the feverish minds of medieval scholars and princes of the church, yea, even unto the televangelists.

The Company had profited, too, of course; its coffers filled with plunder from the sack, and its investments in Roman olive oil futures yielded heavy dividends.

Labienus felt a mortal approaching him, now, and turned to see a shabby little man in modern Tunisian dress peering at him speculatively.

"Monsieur, may I offer the services of a tour guide?" he inquired, and without waiting for a reply scurried closer. "You know where you are? Famous sacrificial altar of Baal-Hammon! Look!"

He drew a holo device from his pocket and switched it on. Hazy and transparent in the midday glare, computer-generated figures knelt to offer a swaddled bundle to their awful horned god.

"Then, Romans invaded and began their genocidal persecution of my countrymen," said the man, changing the scene to a blurry diorama of Roman armies sacking a town.

"You consider yourself a Carthaginian?" Labienus regarded him scornfully, scanning the mortal's genetic makeup. Some Euro-mongrel, Almerian and Balearic; he hadn't a drop of the ancient blood in him. "Are you proud of being descended from people who sacrificed children?"

"Ancient times," the man explained, looking a little uncomfortable. "Carthaginians had not yet heard the word of God. But Romans were *much* worse, killed millions of children. Carthaginians at least believed they were giving them as servants to their gods. And all nations have given children to their gods, in all times everywhere!"

"That's certainly true," said Labienus, deciding he was amused by the mortal. "And sacrifice is relative, isn't it? What do mortals bear them for, anyway, but to be of use?"

"It is every son's duty to do his father's will," agreed the mortal solemnly.

Unseen all around them the little ghosts were standing, not merely the lost children of Carthage but of Rome and Britain, of every nation on earth, watching, an army of specters gray as ashes, silent. No need to play the cymbals or the pipes now to drown them out, no need to tell them *Hush, don't cry! Don't shame us!*

An image flashed into Labienus's mind, memory of an illustration by Edward Gorey: Death, in the formal costume of a governess, skull-faced, grinning pleasantly at the viewer as she holds her umbrella aloft. Gathered around her feet are her tiny listless charges, a flock of children in old-fashioned clothes. Their eyes are vacant. They stand together like so many stuffed penguins.

The mortal children had done the job their parents asked of them, gone wide-eyed into Hell in exchange for victory, good harvests, gold, status, love. *Pro patria mori.* And they were fortunate, after all, compared to the children taken by Zeus.

"What if one of those children stood before you now?" said Labienus. "What do you suppose he'd have to tell you, about eternal life in the service of the gods?"

The mortal blinked at him.

"Would you like to purchase a holocard, monsieur?" he asked.

Labienus laughed. He bought a holocard and the mortal went away.

Nothing matters but the work. Yet the work is meaningless.

History cannot be changed. Yet history is a tissue of lies.

And if one can't leave the world, and if there is no better place, then the world will have to do for Paradise. No reason, then, not to shape the world to one's own desires, is there? But it will take scouring fire to purify it, and seas of blood to wash out its imperfections . . .

So. What about this third boy, old *Adonai* revived at last?

Yet is there really a place for him now, at this end of the long corridor of time? It's hardly an age for heroes. No sweeping religious upheavals in which he might immolate himself, like Nicholas Harpole; no British Empire whose burden he might shoulder, as Edward Bell-Fairfax had done. Only a dwindling and pusillanimous global village, bickering feebly with its colonies on Luna and Mars . . .

Though there will be *real* nastiness erupting on Mars . . .

The rotten tree must fall; what wedge might be placed, to cause the profitable trunk to topple in just the right direction? What lord with a golden voice, and absolute confidence in his ideals?

What if the woman were brought in again, in her fatal role of catalyst? *The Botanist Mendoza* . . .

Labienus glances up at his wilderness, distracted by something at the edge of his field of vision. He frowns.

"Damn!" He goes to inspect the window where the frantic mortal had stood. Smudged on the outer surface of the glass are a pair of handprints and . . . yes . . . that blob can only be the print of the mortal's nose. Disgusting monkeys!

He puts his head on one side, considering. Which of his subordinates has displeased him lately?

Spoyka! he transmits.

Yes, sir! The reply comes hastily.

Report to room 218 with a rag, a bottle of Windex, eighty feet of rope, and a rappelling harness. Further orders to follow.

Immediately, sir!

Labienus folds his arms and gazes out at the view. His smile has returned. Room 218 is two floors above his office. To reach his window, the man will actually need ninety feet of rope. Can he be creative, or will he suffer a painful accident?

Either way, it ought to be fun to watch.

Southborough Library
Southborough, MA
01772

DISCARDED